DIARY OF A HIJACKER

DIARY OF A HIJACKER

The D. B. Cooper Story

by

Richard Kavanaugh

authorHOUSE®

AuthorHouse™
1663 Liberty Drive
Bloomington, IN 47403
www.authorhouse.com
Phone: 1-800-839-8640

Published by AuthorHouse 06/06/2012

ISBN: 978-1-4685-6327-6 (sc)
ISBN: 978-1-4685-6326-9 (hc)
ISBN: 978-1-4685-6325-2 (e)

Library of Congress Control Number: 2012904850

Contents

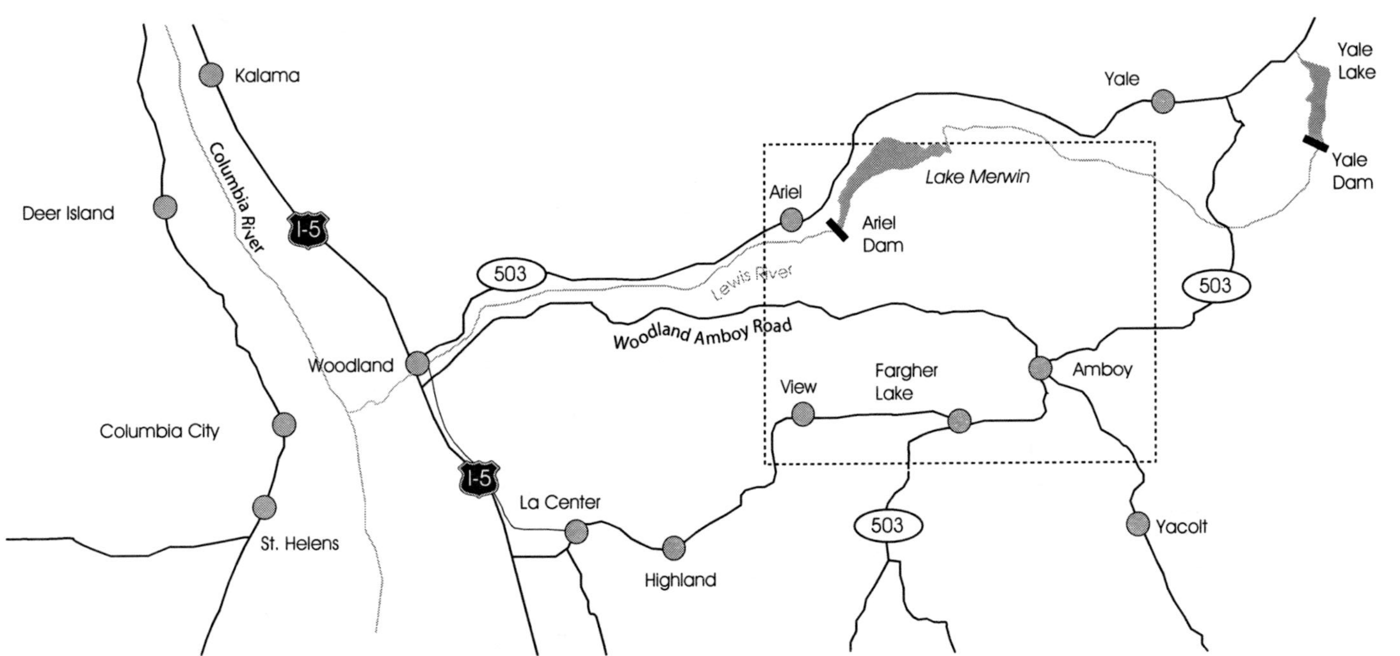

AREA OF SOUTHWEST WASHINGTON WHERE COOPER BAILED OUT

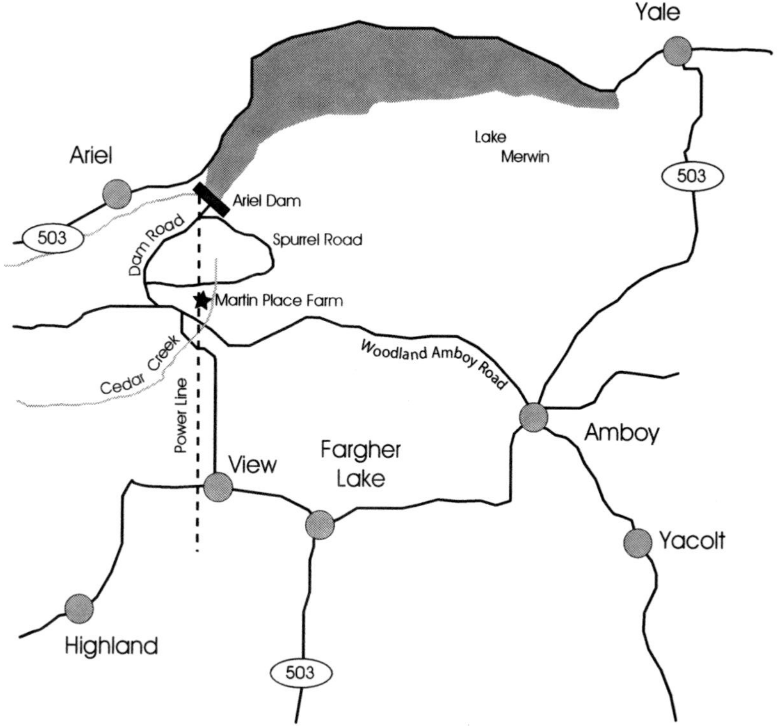

DETAIL MAP OF AREA WHERE COOPER BAILED OUT

Foreword

During the early eighties the United States witnessed a renewed flurry of domestic aircraft hijackings, but nothing to compare with the epidemic this country and the world experienced between 1968 and 1972. Then, many of the hijackers were homesick Cubans wishing to return to their native land, but in those dark days of civil aviation, many others were political terrorists, psychotic thrill seekers or avaricious criminals.

According to the U. S. Department of Transportation, the only person to hijack a domestic airliner during that turbulent period that was not killed or brought to justice was the man who came to be known as D. B. Cooper. Now, more than forty-one years after he parachuted from a Northwest Airlines' jet with $200,000 in ransom money, he still remains a mystery and a folk hero.

In this book I have taken what few facts are known about Cooper and the hijacking, embellished them with details, and produced a novel about a man who could have been D. B. Cooper. All of the characters, with the exception of the hijacker and the crew of Northwest 305 on November 24, 1971, are fictional and any resemblance to persons, living or dead is purely coincidental. The actions, reactions and thoughts attributed to Captain Scott, Stewardess Schaffner, and other persons who were involved in the actual hijacking are also fiction and may or may not reflect what actually took place during the event.

While press accounts disagree on some of the details of the hijacking, it is accepted that the man who gave his name as Cooper bought a one-way ticket to Seattle at Portland on the afternoon of November 24, 1971. Once in the air he handed a stewardess a note saying he had a bomb. At his direction she sat beside him and wrote down instructions to the pilot. He demanded $200,000 and four parachutes—otherwise he would blow up the plane. Airline officials and FBI agents complied with his requests and Cooper allowed the passengers and two stewardesses to disembark at Seattle. He then ordered the plane to fly south at 200 miles an hour at 10,000 feet.

Not long after takeoff a red light flashed in the cockpit indicating the plane's rear boarding ramp had been unlatched. Around 8:10 PM as they were approaching the Lewis River in southwestern Washington, Captain Scott, concerned that the hijacker was having trouble with the ramp, called back over the plane's interphone: "Anything we can do for you?"

There was no immediate answer but after another light flashed indicating the ramp was fully extended, Cooper came on the interphone for the last time. When the plane landed in Reno some three hours later the hijacker, the twenty-one pound sack of money and one set of parachutes were gone. He had carefully reclaimed his note to the stewardess and left no fingerprints.

Believing Cooper had jumped from the plane somewhere near Woodland, Washington, authorities transformed this small logging town into a bustling command post for a small army of newsmen and dozens of FBI agents, police, and soldiers from Fort Lewis, Washington. With planes, helicopters, jeeps and tracking dogs, they combed the vast, densely wooded region for a week. Much of it was rugged terrain, thick with freshly fallen snow, and virtually impassable. Believing the hijacker had left the plane clad only in a light business suit and street shoes, they reasoned he could not have survived. They said they were simply looking for a body and a bag of money. Eventually the army of searchers was disbanded.

In the ensuing months Cooper became a legend in the Northwest—pictured as a lone Robin Hood who stole from a giant corporation, hurt no one and got away. The media had erroneously identified him as D. B. Cooper, rather than Dan Cooper, the name he had used to purchase his ticket, and now "D. B. Cooper Where Are You" T-shirts sold by the thousands. A song extolling his feat became a hit.

Then in late March 1972, three hundred soldiers from Fort Lewis searched the thawing terrain for eighteen days without finding a trace of the skyjacker or the money. The FBI investigated hundreds of men who might have been Cooper without success and circulated a 34-page booklet with the serial numbers of the ten thousand, $20 bills he was given. None turned up until 1980 when some of the bills were found buried in a beach on the Columbia River.

At this point in time the man who called himself Dan Cooper remains a mystery despite claims the FBI had new leads in 2011. The story you are about to read is a tale of what might have been.

PART I

"A Little Trouble in the Cockpit"

LATE NOVEMBER, AND an iron sky pressed down on Portland, Oregon. A biting wind hooted faintly outside the big plate windows of the control tower at Portland International Airport, an acrid drizzle slanted from choked clouds, greasy fog swirled off the Columbia River and drifted across the airport in spidery tendrils. It was a dreary and depressing day.

At 2 PM the weather observer reported a ceiling of eight hundred feet, visibility one mile in light rain, occasionally dropping to one-half mile in patchy ground fog. It wasn't exactly perfect flying weather, but well above minimums for Captain William Scott and the capable crew of Northwest 305. Turning final on their ILS approach to Runway 10 Right at Portland that Wednesday afternoon, the Captain was flying the big Boeing 727-200, N327E. First Officer Bob Ratacazak handled communications. Behind them in the jump seat Flight Officer H. E. Anderson looked on. As they rolled out on their final approach heading of 099 degrees, he could see the left-right needle of the ILS slide slowly to the center of the indicator and stop there. They were level at twenty-five hundred feet and steady on 160 knots, a speed they would hold until intercepting the glide path. The landing gear was down and locked, the flaps extended to the fifteen degree position. With all this drag it required ninety percent power to hold the big aircraft level. But that was the way it was suppose to be. If, for any reason, they had to abort the approach, the drag could be immediately reduced by raising the landing gear and the plane would begin to accelerate.

When the ILS needle began to drift a hair to the left, the Captain changed his heading slightly to bring it back. At that moment the voice of the approach controller crackled through the cockpit speaker, "Northwest 305 you are now ten miles from touchdown. Contact Portland Tower on one-eighteen-point-seven over the outer marker."

"Three-oh-five, roger", Ratacazak barked tersely into his microphone. Hanging it up, he quickly called off the remaining items on the landing checklist before reaching over to flick the switch which would change his mike to transmitter number one. It was already set on 118.7 megacycles, the frequency for Portland Tower.

The glide slope needle of the ILS, which had been pegged at the top of the instrument, began to move slowly downward. This was the signal that the aircraft was about to intercept the glide path and begin its final descent to the runway. "Thirty degrees flaps," the Captain called out, and without waiting the First Officer complied by moving the flap lever down until the indicator showed thirty degrees, then returned it to the neutral position. As the flaps descended they could feel the big aircraft hunch forward, changing its attitude in the air, then gradually losing speed. The airspeed dropped to 150, then 140, and was approaching 130 when the glide path needle reached the center of the dial. It made a plus-mark with the left-right needle which was stubbornly holding just left of center. With a movement so small it wasn't visible, Captain Scott released back pressure on the yoke, and the plane began a slow descent. The airspeed held steady now at 130, but the glide path needle settled a little lower, indicating they were rolling out slightly high on the glide path.

"Forty degrees flaps," said the Captain, and the First Officer lowered another ten degrees. For an instant the aircraft seemed to hang suspended just above the glide path, then as the rate of descent increased, the needle began to rise very, very slowly toward the center of the dial.

"Ninety-two percent," the Captain growled without looking up. This time Ratacazak loosened the friction knob that held the three throttle levers and eased them forward ever so slightly. The needles on the power gauges crept forward to ninety-two percent. It all happened so quickly and routinely that Scott might have been asking the First Officer to hand him a cup of coffee.

Anderson, staring out the window, caught occasional glimpses of the ground. Checking the altimeter, he noted they were passing through 900 feet MSL (900 feet above Mean Sea Level), 880 feet above the surface of the runway. As they descended through 800 feet a blue light on the instrument panel began flashing and a steady signal, dit-dah, dit-dah, dit-dah, came through the cockpit speaker. Immediately Ratacazak depressed his transmitter button and declared, "Portland Tower, Northwest 305 is outer marker inbound."

"Roger 305, you are cleared to land on Runway ten Right. The winds are seventy degrees at eight knots."

They could now look down and see the ground, but ahead, mist and rain hid the runway. Suddenly two bright lights flashed at them through the gloom directly ahead—then another—and another.

"Approach lights, Captain," said Ratacazak sharply as the line of yellow approach lights blazed up through the fog and the white lights of the rabbit pulsed sequentially like an electrical traffic cop directing them to their runway.

The Captain mumbled an acknowledgement but continued to concentrate on his instruments, cross checking the ILS indicator with his airspeed. Only when the First Officer said "Runway in sight," did he glance up to look through the rain-streaked wind screen at the big white "10R" painted on the black asphalt. The yellow light indicating the middle marker flashed, but now they paid it no attention, smoothly they crossed the airport boundary and touched down five hundred feet along the eight thousand foot runway.

Suddenly Ratacazak was busy: cutting power, reversing thrust, increasing power, retracting flaps. They slowed and taxied clear of the runway, turning back toward the terminal building which lay north of the landing runway. A half-mile away, it looked like it had shrunk in the rain.

At about that moment a man dressed in a non-descript brown business suit and carrying a large black attaché case and plaid bowling-ball bag was checking in at Gate 46. He presented his ticket to the gate agent and waited patiently while the one-way ticket to Seattle was pulled and deposited in the appropriate slot.

"We'll be boarding in about ten minutes," the gate agent said, smiling patently as he returned the folder. "Have a pleasant trip Mr. Cooper."

Outwardly Cooper appeared little different from numerous others who were crowding the terminal in Portland that Wednesday afternoon, the twenty-fourth of November, 1971. Of average height and weight, he looked older than his 37 years. His boot black hair was made to appear thin and receding by the way it was cut and combed straight, away from a narrow handsome face. He displayed an olive complexion and washed-blue eyes which looked out dissolutely from under arched brows. He wore a bland, almost bored expression.

Several passengers deplaned and a line of those waiting to board formed behind Cooper. The waiting area was less than half full. It appeared the flight would not be crowded.

At 2:40 PM Northwest 305 was called for boarding. They loaded through the front door and, after showing his boarding pass to the stewardess, the man known as Cooper continued through the aircraft to the last row of seats on his right (the left hand side of the aircraft looking from back to front). He placed his attaché case in the center seat and pushed the bowling ball bag under the center seat in the row ahead. Taking the seat next to the aisle, he fastened his seat belt loosely and carefully studied the other passengers taking their places in the cabin ahead. The intercom which the stewardess in the rear cabin would use for announcements and for talking with the cockpit was mounted on a bulkhead directly behind him. The galley and the lavatory were also located back of him. The space opposite on the right side of the plane contained a few empty seats including the jump seats the stewardesses would occupy during takeoffs and landings. At the very back of the cabin was the rear stairway, a set of steps that folded out and down to allow passengers to enter or leave the cabin from this end. It was now closed.

With everyone on board, the front door was closed and locked and the crew fired up the engines. The three stewardesses were busy getting the passengers settled. There were a total of 36, 10 in the first class section up front, and 26 in coach. There were lots of empty seats. No one had bothered to go back as far as Cooper.

As the plane was pushed back from the gate the stewardesses began their routine of explaining the emergency procedures. Cooper took the case from the seat beside him and placed it gently on the floor. As they taxied out and took off, he kept his feet on it so it wouldn't slide away.

In the cockpit First Officer Ratacazak was copying the ATC clearance for the 25 minute flight to Seattle. The weather there was about the same as Portland—nine hundred feet overcast, two miles visibility in light drizzle and fog. He read back the clearance as the big plane was pushed back, then switched to ground control and asked for taxi instructions as the tug was snapped loose and backed away.

Stewardess Florence Schaffner, responsible for the rear half of the coach section, noticed Cooper as she worked her way back to him demonstrating the use of the oxygen mask. She noted he had donned a pair of yellowish tinted glasses and moved his attaché case from the seat.

Schaffner, a two year veteran with Northwest, was a poised self-confident young woman who was good at her job and knew it. She enjoyed helping people—making passengers feel at home in her cabin—and as she came abreast of Cooper she gave him a wide, reassuring smile which he returned in a friendly fashion. Passing him, she put away the demonstration mask and sat down on one of the jump seats to wait for Alice Hancock, the other stewardess working coach.

There was no aircraft in front of them as Northwest 305 taxied out. As they neared the approach end of Runway 10 Left, the tower cleared them for immediate takeoff. Without stopping, they taxied into position and rolled.

As the airspeed increased, passengers and crew alike were pressed back into their seats by the force of the acceleration. When the airspeed indicator read 120 Captain Scott said, "Rotation", and First Officer Ratacazak pulled back smoothly on the yoke until the nose of the aircraft reached the proper pitch attitude. The landing gear bumped once or twice as the shock struts extended themselves fully, and then they were airborne, climbing rapidly up into the dirty gray overcast.

The landing gear was retracted and the 727 climbed straight ahead. At 500 feet MSL the first officer requested a power reduction and a partial retraction of the flaps for climb. Captain Scott switched the radio to departure control and spoke briskly into his mike. "Portland Departure Control, Northwest 305 over."

"Roger 305, we have you just off runway ten left. Turn left now to heading three-five-zero degrees and climb to flight level two-zero-zero. Report out of ten."

"Three-oh-five, understand left to 350, climb to 20, report out of 10."

"Roger 305."

In the rear cabin the two stewardesses deftly unbuckled their seat belts and began their routine. Since they would only be in the air 25 minutes on the short flight to Seattle, they wouldn't attempt to serve any refreshments in the rear cabin. Alice Hancock went forward immediately to assist Tina Mucklow, the stewardess in the first class cabin, in serving drinks to the passengers there, while Florence Schaffner remained behind to perform any chores required by those in coach. She had taken only a few leisurely steps up the aisle when she heard a husky, low-pitched voice behind her.

"Stewardess!"

She turned and realized it was the thin-faced man in the dark suit sitting by himself in the last row who had spoken. His attaché case was in his lap and he was beckoning to her furtively, a sly smile on his lean, feral face.

"Yes sir, what is it?" she asked solicitously in her best "coffee, tea or milk" voice as she moved back to him.

"Here, this is for you," he replied conspiratorially in tight, tense tones, thrusting a folded sheet of paper at her.

She was momentarily nonplused. The thought that he might be trying to hustle her for a date crossed her mind and she quickly stuffed the note into the pocket of her jacket without looking at it.

"No, read it now!" he expostulated as she started to move away again.

Irritated, but still not apprehensive, Florence took the note back out, unfolded it and read:

> PLEASE DO NOT BECOME EXCITED AND DO ANYTHING RASH. I HAVE A BOMB IN THIS BRIEFCASE AND IF YOU DO NOT DO AS I SAY I WILL DETONATE IT IMMEDIATELY AND WE WILL ALL DIE. DO AS I SAY AND EVERYTHING WILL BE ALL RIGHT.

For just an instant she did not comprehend. Then, as she suddenly realized what was happening, the incredulity was chased from her pleasant, picture-book face by a welter of stronger emotions: dismay, disgust, and unreasoning fear. She felt the world tilt irrationally and had to grasp a seat back to steady herself as the implications hit her one by one—slowly, then in a rush.

As she stared in horror at the grim visage of the hijacker her mind momentarily became a black and seething dungeon where too many thoughts fought for air. Could this be real? Was this man, this ordinary looking passenger really threatening her and forty others with sudden violent death? She knew she mustn't panic, but terror tore at her self-control and she had to clench her teeth to keep from crying out as the choking realization rose up in her that she might be about to die.

He saw her recoil in terror and spoke quickly in an effort to forestall an abortive outcry. "Don't panic," he intoned reassuringly.

This solicitous exclamation broke the spell and her momentary feeling of faintness passed—she did not fall or cry out. As her self-control ebbed slowly back she remembered a class in stewardess school about the handling of hijackers. The instructor had said to keep calm and to comply with their requests. Do nothing to excite them, to cause them to do anything rash.

Although she still felt staggered by this abject burden so rudely thrust upon her, Florence realized that at least she hadn't blown it—not yet. He had the ominous black attaché case in his lap with the top open enough to allow his left hand inside. She couldn't see what that hand was doing, could only assume it was holding some kind of trigger that he might release at any moment, sending them all to kingdom-come. His right hand steadied the lethal case in his lap.

"Please sit down here," he continued in grave measured tones. He had a resonant baritone voice, almost musical, his words clearly enunciated—a commanding voice. As he spoke he slid deftly into the window seat without changing the position of his deadly case. Schaffner, emerging from her catatonic state, stepped forward and sat down in the aisle seat. Before she could open her mouth to disgorge the myriad questions ravaging her mind, he indicated the seat back in front of her and spoke again in that hypnotic voice. "There is a pen and paper in the seat pocket. Please take it out. I want you to write a note to the Captain for me. Place the note I gave you in the pocket."

He was very composed. Or so it seemed to Schaffner. She had always pictured hijackers as wild-eyed fanatics, and it was the benign efficacy he projected that made the whole thing so unbelievable. He could have been asking for a drink or about the landing time.

She took the paper and pen from the seat pocket and put the note inside. Lowering the tray table, she laid the paper on it, and then looked sideways at him with trepidation. Outwardly she now appeared calm, but inside her head the wheels were still turning a-mile-a-minute.

"You will write what I tell you," he ordered dourly. "Say, I have a bomb that I can detonate immediately by flipping a switch. If you do not do as I say I will blow this aircraft and all it occupants into the next world." As he paused to give her time to catch up, he studied her intently. She glanced boldly over at the case in his lap and he raised the lid so she could glimpse the bomb inside. It appeared to be a small black box with two ordinary wall switches mounted flush into the top of it. Several red cylinders which she assumed were dynamite were lashed to the bottom with black electrical tape, and yellow wires ran from them into the box. It was padded on all sides with some type of gray woolen-looking material.

Although she inwardly quaked at the sight of the device, she gave no outward sign of her distress and he continued. "Please radio your headquarters in Seattle. I want two hundred thousand dollars in used twenty-dollar bills in a good stout laundry sack. I also want four sport-type parachutes, two chest packs and two back packs. We will circle Seattle until they have these things ready. I will give you further instructions at that time. In the meantime you and your officers are to stay in the cockpit."

Schaffner wrote rapidly, glancing up only when he mentioned the money and the parachutes. She continued to feel a certain abhorrence of this man but her natural self-confidence gradually returned as she recognized he had a plan, that he was not hell-bent to kill them all no matter what she did.

When she had finished writing and looked up he spoke again, accentuating his words with a harsher tone as he inclined his head slightly in the direction of the cockpit. "Take that note to the Captain," he said with an edge on his voice. "Tell him not to disturb the passengers. He can make up some excuse for the delay at Seattle. When you know something definite you can come back and tell me. I'll deal only with you. In the meantime I'll be waiting here with my hand on the trigger. Now get going!"

Responding to his exhortation, she quickly fastened the tray table back in place, took the note, and started forward. In her travail she didn't dare look back. She could feel his eyes fastened malevolently on her back as she hurried up the aisle. Passing into the first class section she met Alice and Tina distributing cocktails. Before they could ask what she was doing up front she blurted, "Captain wants me, I'll be right back," and rushed on by.

She knocked stridently as the cockpit door and Anderson let her in. The aircraft had just leveled off at their cruising altitude of 20,000 feet and the crew was completing the level-off checklist. Glancing outside she noted they were flying in the clear, well above the dingy gray clouds below. The weak winter sun shone palely through another layer of cirrus higher up.

They finished the checklist and the Captain turned in his seat. "What is it Schaffner?" he asked pleasantly.

"Captain, there's a man back there with a bomb," she babbled in a voice that was wild and forced. "He made me sit down and write out a note to you. Here" she cried, presenting the portentous paper with a trembling hand.

In his years of flying Scott had been through his share of emergencies. He's had landing gear that didn't want to come down, engine failures, and the usual assortment of minor problems. But this was a new one for him. Still it was nothing to panic over, not yet anyway. Stoically he took the note and read it.

Looking up he fixed the stewardess with a baleful eye. "Is he serious?" he asked sternly.

I'm afraid he is Captain," Schaffner ruminated abjectly, relieved to have someone share the burden of her knowledge. "He has it in a big black briefcase. I couldn't tell much about it but it was a box with a couple of switches mounted on it and several red cylinders connected by wires. He had his hand on the switches. He said to tell you not to alarm the passengers. He wants me to come back when you have some word from Seattle and then he will tell me what we are to do then. He said he'd be waiting with his hand on the trigger!"

Although Florence controlled herself well during this recitation, the profound shock she had undergone and the consummate dread she felt for herself and everyone aboard came through loud and clear. There was no doubt she thought this larcenous ghoul was serious.

Scott studied her for a few seconds. In his tribulation he felt a strong compulsion to go back and have a look at the man himself, to use his own judgment as to just how serious this hijacker was, and to see if there was any way to talk him out of it. But the note had said they were to stay in the cockpit. And Schaffner certainly believed the man was serious. He could not take the chance. Not just now anyway. Besides, if he went back there the other passengers might realize what was happening and do something to cause the hijacker to set off the bomb. No, he couldn't take any chances; he'd do just as the note said.

"Where is he sitting?" he asked quietly.

"In 24A, the last seat on the right side next to the window. The other seats back there are vacant."

"Well, go back and tell him we are doing as he asked. I'll radio headquarters and call you on the interphone as soon as I know something. Try to keep him calm and happy. Are you all right?"

"Yes sir," she said bravely, trying to smile but not quite making it. "I'll be okay. I'll tell him. Call me as soon as you can."

She turned and left, closing the cockpit door behind her. The other girls were still serving. She scurried past them headed toward the rear. As she came into the coach section she could see him, now sitting back in the aisle seat. She had thought she was becoming inured to the terrible tension, but the sight of him sitting there calmly eyeing her prompted new feelings of rage and frustration in her breast. As she moved toward him a man in the fifth row stopped her and asked for aspirin and a cup of water.

"Yes, I'll get it for you in just a minute," she equivocated as she paused momentarily. She didn't really want to go back there. But she knew she had better do so right now. He had seen her and she had better move at once to assure him everything was all right, to placate him so he wouldn't set off the dreadful thing he had in his case.

As she came up to his seat she could see it still resting on his lap, his left hand still inside. Bending forward in a conspiratorial way, she spoke quietly with as much earnestness as she could muster. "The Captain is doing as you asked. He will call me on the interphone as soon as he knows anything."

"All right," he replied firmly. "Please use the cabin speaker to inform the passengers that the rest rooms back here are out of order."

She did as he requested, then got the aspirin and water for the man in the fifth row. "Don't say anything to the passengers," he warned her menacingly as she started forward. "I'll be here watching you with my hand on the trigger." His vitriolic speech frightened her but she hid her dread as she went about her job. She had never felt so hollow in her life, never felt such a presentment of being in over her head. Surely this wasn't happening. Surely she'd wake up in a minute and find she was at home, in her cozy apartment in Alexandria, Virginia, and this was all a bad dream.

Up front, in the cockpit, Captain Scott too was wishing it was all a bad dream. But he had no time for wool gathering. Company policy dictated that in a situation where the safety of the passengers and crew was threatened by a hijacker, he was to appease the man as best he could; requests were to be complied with. This guy seemed to have a couple of new angles. Apparently he didn't have a gun or if he did he wasn't threatening to shoot anybody. But worse, he was threatening to kill them all by setting off a bomb. Several sticks of dynamite would certainly blow them out of the air. And he wasn't asking them to change course for Cuba or anywhere else just now. Instead he wanted money—$200,000—and parachutes. As soon as Schaffner left, Scott hit his transmitter button and passed along the word.

"Seattle Center, this is Northwest 305. I'm afraid we have a little trouble in the cockpit."

"Roger 305, what is the nature of your trouble?"

"Center, 305, we have a hijacker on board. He has a bomb which he is threatening to detonate if we do not comply with his demands. We request permission to continue to Seattle and hold there for the present. He wants $200,000 in used twenty-dollar bills put into a laundry sack and brought to the airport. He also wants four sport-type parachutes, two chest packs and two back packs. We are to circle Seattle until these things are ready. Then he will give us further instructions. Over."

"Roger 305. You are cleared to proceed direct to the Seattle Vortac, maintain flight level two-zero-zero. At Seattle, hold southeast, squawk code seven-seven-zero and stand by."

"Understand cleared to Seattle, flight level two-zero-zero, hold southeast and squawk seventy-seven hundred, Three-oh-five standing by"

Although he couldn't see it, Scott could imagine the excitement his message was causing. In the radar control room at Seattle Center the controller would be signaling his boss, the supervisor. Then it would be up to him to set in motion a prearrange notification to the FBI, all segments of the FAA, and others concerned with hijacking.

The radio came to life again almost immediately, a different voice, "Northwest 305, this is Seattle. Let me get this straight. The hijacker wants ten thousand twenty-dollar bills, that's two hundred thousand dollars, put in a laundry bag and brought to the airport. Then he wants two sets of parachutes. Is that it?"

"Roger Seattle, sport-type parachutes, two back packs and two chest packs. He may have an accomplice who is planning on bailing out with him although we haven't identified anyone else yet. We are to circle Seattle until the money and the chutes are at the airport. Then he will tell us what to do. Do you want us to remain on this frequency or should we contact our operations on company frequency and notify them of his demands? Over."

"Standby on this frequency 305. We are clearing all other aircraft to other frequencies and out of your way. We will notify your operations and if they want to talk with you directly we will let you know. Is the hijacker in the cockpit with you? Over."

"Negative, he is in the rear of the second cabin."

"Roger 305. Standby."

On the intercom Florence spoke up, "Captain, the hijacker wants to know what's going on. Do you have any estimate on time?"

"Not yet," he replied with some asperity. "We have given the information to Seattle Center and they are relaying it to the proper people."

He heard her repeating this message to the hijacker and an answering murmur before she came back on the line. "Captain he wants to know what your intentions are. He says he wants you to hold over Seattle until things are ready on the ground."

"Tell him that's exactly what we are doing. We're cleared to the Seattle Vortac and we will hold there at 20,000 feet until he tells us to do otherwise." Apparently that satisfied the man. After another short exchange with him, Schaffner acknowledged and hung up. As the minutes ticked by, message after message flew back and forth between the plane and the center. For a short time they switched to Northwest Operation's frequency and retold their saturnine story to the astonished company officials who had hurried to the radio room. Then back to center frequency to answer questions for FAA officials and the FBI who had been summoned. In the meantime they arrived over the Seattle Vortac and began their holding pattern. The Captain decided it was time to say something to the passengers.

"Ladies and gentlemen, this is Captain Scott. We are over Seattle now but there are problems on the ground and we are having to hold until they can be cleared up. We are sorry for the delay and will keep you informed. Thank you."

After what seemed like hours—but was in reality only forty minutes—word came back that the company was rounding up the money and the parachutes. They were to relay this message to the hijacker and keep him pacified. While this was going on could the Captain get any more information for them on the hijacker? Scott had been thinking about that himself. He didn't want to do anything to upset the guy, but he needed to know a little more about him—what he might do, might respond to. These thoughts were passing through his mind as he switched to interphone and buzzed Florence Schaffner in the rear cabin.

"Schaffner, this is the Captain" he said briefly when she came on the line. "How are things back there?"

"Everything is the same Captain," she replied with antipathy. "He strikes me as being just a little bit crazy, but seems calm now. He hasn't taken his hand out of that case the whole time. Do you have anything I can tell him?"

"Yes, you can tell him the company is getting the money and parachutes. They will call me when they get to the airport with everything, probably in an hour or so. Tell him I would like to send the First Officer back to talk with him. Tell him that while I standby."

Florence was standing in the aisle just behind where Cooper was sitting. Holding the phone in her left hand she leaned forward and repeated the Captain's message.

The hijacker nodded grimly without comment when she told him about the money and the parachutes. But when she mentioned the First Officer coming back he spoke up belligerently. "NO! He thundered in a flash of anger, his rage washing over her like hot air escaping from an open oven door. "I don't want anyone back here but you. You can relay any message the Captain has for me. Tell him that if he trys any tricks or does anything other than what I tell him to do, it'll be curtains for all of us. Now tell him that!"

Scott heard Cooper's sear fulmination over the wire and sat transfixed while Florence meekly repeated it. With more aplomb than he felt, he assured her he would not send anyone back and urged her to remain calm in the face of the man's diatribe. He knew now he certainly wouldn't try any tricks. He would do just what the bastard said.

Despite her own fears, Florence retained her composure and calmly repeated the Captain's apologies and assurances. It seemed to appease the hijacker and they settled down to wait in minatory silence.

More minutes, that seemed like hours, dragged by as they circled in the gloomy skies over Washington. Again the Captain switched on the cabin speaker and laconically apologized to the restless passengers. He knew they were getting impatient but he didn't want to upset them further by telling them their true plight.

It was after five o'clock when word finally came that the money and parachutes were ready below. Scott called Florence and relayed the message. She repeated it to Cooper.

"Very well," he replied in an arrogant way. "Tell him to take us down. When we land I want him to taxi back to the takeoff end of Runway 34 Left. Have them meet us there and first fuel the plane to maximum capacity. When this is done the other two stewardesses can use the front entrance to bring the money and chutes on board. If everything is in order, the passengers and then two stewardesses can deplane. As soon as they are off we will depart for Mexico City. Tell him not to let anyone pull any tricks. You are to stand by here to relay any further instructions."

Pulling tricks was the last thing on Scott's mind as he listened solemnly to Cooper's instructions relayed by Florence. He was glad the hijacker was willing to let the passengers off at Seattle. It looked like it might just end up as another unscheduled charter to Mexico or wherever. He'd been up fifteen hours now. He'd flown nearly twelve. And he' been under this strain for the last two. But if that man back there would just sit still he wouldn't mind another ten or twelve. No, he wouldn't mind at all.

There was a low overcast at Seattle and they had to make another ILS approach. They broke out below the clouds at 900 feet and made a smooth, uneventful landing on Runway 34 Right. Veering off at the high speed turnoff six thousand feet down, they taxied slowly to the takeoff end of the parallel runway, 34 Left. En route the cabin speaker came alive again, Scott's voice clear and incisive.

"Ladies and gentlemen, this is the Captain. Due to congestion at the terminal it will be necessary to deplane you in a remote area of the field. They are sending buses out. There will be only a slight delay. Please remain in your seats until you are instructed to deplane. Thank you."

Up ahead he saw the fuel trucks and numerous other vehicles. A Follow Me truck directed them to an unused section of ramp on the west side of 34 Left, and there he shut the engines down. The external power was plugged in and refueling began. The moment they were parked Cooper suddenly announced, "I'm moving to the rest room, please stay by the door so you can relay any messages between myself and the Captain."

Almost before the words were out of his mouth he had scuttled into the rearmost lavatory on the left side of the plane and closed the door. "Can you hear me all right?" he asked Florence who now stood in the aisle, staring at the closed door.

"Yes I can." she replied hesitantly.

"Now get this straight," he said adamantly, opening the door a crack. "I do not want anyone else to come back here. If I even suspect you are trying to trick me I will detonate this bomb and that will be the end of it. Be certain you understand that and that the Captain and those on the ground get that message!"

She assured him that she understood and would pass the message on but did so with misgivings. She was really afraid the situation might get out of hand. The exasperated passengers were grumbling louder now. They were three hours late already and here they were still waiting. Some could see the buses parked down the taxiway and they couldn't understand the delay. One drunk kept demanding another drink and it was all Tina and Alice could do to keep things under control, to preempt any rash actions which might aggravate the Captain's delicate dealings with the hijacker and jeopardize everyone's safety.

During the refueling the Captain came on the speaker once more, promising that it would be only a few minutes. He told them they would unload by the front entrance as soon as a portable ramp arrived.

"I have some further instructions for the Captain now," Cooper said, opening the rest room door and glancing out. "As soon as the fuel trucks depart the second officer can come out of the cockpit and open the front door. The passengers must remain in their seats. Then the ramp can be moved in placed and the airline people outside can bring the chutes and the money to the top of the stairs, just outside the door. The other two stews can bring them back here. The second officer is to stay by the door and be certain the passengers neither leave nor anyone from outside come on board. I don't want anyone from the outside coming into the cabin. No one! Is that clear?"

She nodded a yes and he continued. "When I have checked the money and the chutes I will tell you and the passengers can begin deplaning. While they are getting off the Captain is to start the engines and prepare for immediate takeoff. Tell him to depart to the north and climb to 10,000 feet. Have you got all of that?"

She assured him she did, then speaking clearly and cautiously, relayed these latest instructions to the cockpit. With the rest room door partially open Cooper listened carefully, twice interrupting to asseverate his instructions and accentuate the importance of following them exactly.

Outside the scene was surreal. A half-circle of motley vehicles crouched around the airplane like a pride of lions waiting to pounce, their lights splashing unevenly over the tarmac, creating pools of harsh light between the puddles of black darkness. A steady drizzle choked the sky and misted the windshields of the watchers. As the fuel trucks trundled noisily off in the direction of the terminal, a portable ramp was positioned at the front door of the aircraft. The door was opened and a shiny black sedan crept forward stealthily and stopped at the foot of the ramp. Two men in dark raincoats got out, opened the rear doors, and quickly began transferring its contents to the waiting plane.

Although the hijacker remained in the rear rest room, he continually stuck his head out to check what was going on. Despite the fact that he made her stay a couple of steps up the aisle, Schaffner could see the bomb case, open on top of the lavatory where he could easily get to it.

Tina and Alice brought the money bag, then the first chutes to the rear. A man in a black raincoat followed them with the last chute. When Cooper saw him he went berserk.

"Get him back! Tell him to put down that chute and go back immediately or I will set off this bomb," he cried, grabbing up the case and stepping out into the aisle.

Tina Mucklow, who was the chief stewardess, saw the problem and quickly took action. "You there," she said to the man in the raincoat. "Put that down and get out of here. This minute!"

"Listen," the man replied, pausing paces up the isle, "I'm just from the FAA. I'm not FBI. And I just want to talk to your man. Ask him if I can come on back for just a second."

"No!" screamed Cooper, panicky now. "Get the hell off of this plane this minute or I will blow it to hell and back!"

"You had better get out of here now," Mucklow said, taking the last parachute from the man and pushing him back up the aisle. "Alice, you see this gentleman off and start the passengers on down the ramp now."

"He's leaving," Florence told the nervous Cooper. "It's all right to start deplaning now isn't it?"

"Yes," he replied. "But you'd better do it fast. I can't take much more of this tension and no more fuckups like that guy coming back here."

Tina had placed the money in the aisle just outside the rest room, and Cooper had checked it and Florence had placed it in a seat just before the confrontation over the FAA man erupted. Now he had her arrange the parachutes in other seats. Alice was up front assisting the deplaning passengers while Tina hovered near the rear, ready to help Florence with the nervous hijacker. There was a lot of grumbling from the passengers but most were so glad to be getting off they paid little attention to what was going on in the back of the cabin. It was only after they stepped to the ground and were hustled across the runway to the waiting buses that they learned they had spent the last five hours on an airplane with a live bomb.

Cooper remained in the rest room but continued to peer around the bulkhead, being careful not to expose himself needlessly. He kept the case with the bomb on the lavatory and steadied it with his left hand. He was prepared to carry out his grisly threat should a trigger-happy hero try to sabotage his avaricious plan.

But none did and as the last passengers were leaving the coach section he spoke up. "You there—the blond stew. Why don't you come go to Mexico with us and let this little girl get off? She's had a pretty hard day."

Caught by surprise, Florence turned a grateful face to him? "You don't mind if I go and she stays?" she questioned.

"No, that's what I said," he replied evenly, most of the tension now gone from his strong bass voice.

"Go ahead then Florence," Tina said. "I'll stay."

The brown-haired stewardess flashed a look of relief, and then hurried up the aisle to follow the last passengers and Alice Hancock out the door. Anderson closed it after them and Cooper, now standing in the aisle outside the rest room, picked up the intercom and for the first time spoke directly to Scott. "Captain, let's get this show on the road," he said with some elation.

Scott had done as he had been instructed and the engines were running. As soon as the ramp was moved back, he taxied forward onto the runway and started his takeoff roll. Cooper, still holding the bomb, settled in a seat and checked his watch for the time. Seven thirty-nine the Rolex announced in iridescent hands.

Once they were airborne he told Mucklow to join the crew in the cockpit and lock the door. When she had done this he put down the bomb and picked up the interphone again.

"Good evening Captain, this is the hijacker speaking" he declared forcefully, a note of triumph in his voice. I want you to level off at 10,000 feet and set up cruise at exactly 200 knots indicated. Please file a flight plan to Mexico City via Victor 23 East to Portland, Victor 21 to Bakersfield and so on. You and your crew are to remain in the cockpit at all times. Please turn out the overhead cabin lights, unlock the rear stairs, and dump the cabin pressure now. If you want to ask me a question, just come on the speaker. Is that clear?"

"Yes, it's clear," Scott replied evenly. "But at 10,000 feet we can't make it to Mexico City without a refueling stop."

"Well, how about stopping in Yuma?" the hijacker replied.

"At 200 knots we can't even make it that far," said Scott. "Standby just a minute while I check my maps." After a brief pause he continued. "We can fly down Victor 23 to Yuba intersection just south of Red Bluff, then cut across the mountains and land at Reno for our first refueling stop. From there we can probably make it to Yuma, then Mexico City. Is that all right?"

"That will be all right as long as we go via Victor 23 East to Portland then on down Victor 23. Will you give me a time check now and call me when you are over the Seattle Vortac southbound with a Portland estimate."

"Roger, we show the time to be exactly forty-three minutes past seven. I'm dumping cabin pressure now."

"Thank you," the hijacker said and hung up. In the cockpit a feeling of thick tension hung in the air. Then conversion was all business, coming and going in short bursts. They felt their ears pop as the cabin pressure equalized with that outside the aircraft.

The First Officer was at the controls, the Captain handling communications. Switching his mike to departure frequency, he betrayed no emotion.

"Seattle Departure Control, Northwest 305. We are leveling off now at 10,000 feet. We would like to request this altitude and continue our Tacoma One departure. After the Seattle Vortac we request Victor 23 East Portland, Victor 23 to the Yuba intersection, Victor 97 Reno with landing there. The hijacker has requested we fly at an indicated airspeed of 200 knots, over."

"Roger 305, you are cleared as requested. Say again on that airspeed, over."

"Roger 305, that's 200, two-zero-zero knots indicated, over."

"Roger, understand 200 knots indicated. Switch to Seattle Center on one-twenty-three-point-five over the Vortac. Good night and good luck!"

"Roger departure, good night and thanks!"

At seven fifty-three they crossed the Seattle Vortac southbound and took up a heading of 195 degrees for Portland. The Captain did a quick calculation, then switched to cabin speaker and spoke to the hijacker.

"We just passed the Seattle Vortac at five-three," he stated. "Our estimated time over Portland is twenty-three minutes after the next hour."

Immediately the hijacker came on the interphone. "That's fine Captain," he replied. "Now do a good job of staying on course and maintaining the proper altitude and airspeed. And don't deviate from my instructions. Is that understood?"

"Yes, understood," Scott answered. Glancing out he could see nothing but solid cloud. Rain streaked the windscreen. He figured the man was planning to jump and he wondered when and where. The weather here was certainly not favorable and neither was the terrain below. What kind of demons must be driving him to put his life on the line for $200,000? To Scott it didn't even seem like a lot of money. The man must be mad.

At seven-fifty-nine a red light came on in the cockpit when the rear ramp was unlocked. The crew, who had just begun to relax a little, was suddenly confounded by new anxieties.

"Looks like he must be getting ready to jump," commented Anderson.

"Yes, we'd better tell Center," Scott replied. Squeezing his mike button, he transmitted. "Seattle Center, Northwest 305 here. It looks like our man is getting ready to jump. He has unlatched the rear ramp, over."

"Roger 305. We are vectoring three ADC interceptors to your position. What are your flight conditions?"

"We are in solid cloud at the moment encountering moderate turbulence. We are level at 10,000 feet maintaining an indicated airspeed of 200 knots."

"Roger, the closest interceptor is 20 miles behind you. He will lock on using his radar. However he advises he may not be able to establish visual contact at that speed in present weather conditions."

The Captain checked the time—eight minutes past eight. Ratacazak was still flying the plane and he felt a slight change in the control pressures indicating the ramp was being lowered further. He told Scott and the Captain switched to cabin speaker to ask, "Anything we can do for you?"

The light came on in the cockpit showing the rear ramp to be fully extended. A moment later the hijacker answered over the interphone. "Yes Captain," he said, "Please give me the DME to the Portland Vortac."

Glancing at the DME readout, the Captain answered automatically. "Forty-point-two. Anything else?"

"No"

That was the last they heard from the mysterious hijacker. When they arrived in Reno he was gone. Obviously he had plunged out somewhere north of Portland into the blackness, solid cloud and malevolent emptiness below.

PART II

"There's A Place for Us, Somewhere A Place for Us"

Friday, December 20, 1968

DURING THE NIGHT a cold front had passed, its heavy rains washing the city and now, at dawn, the air was crisp and cold. A brisk wind stripped the last of the autumn leaves from the fine old trees of Ansley Park and flung them across the windshields of commuters thundering southward along Piedmont Avenue in the morning rush toward the dazzling skyline of Atlanta etched sharply against the deep blue December sky. It was December 20th, 1968, and the city rushed toward Christmas and the New Year.

In a small high-rise apartment on Piedmont Avenue, just off the expressway downtown, the man who would later become infamous as D. B. Cooper (we shall continue to call him that) was languishing over an elaborate breakfast while his beautiful young wife ministered lovingly to him, bringing hot biscuits, pouring coffee without being asked, picking up his napkin when it fell. Her movements, assured and feminine, gave no impression of haste. Yet each movement was sure, and flowed into the next without hesitation. Occasionally she would reach out and put her hand lightly on his arm in an affectionate gesture.

It was in this everyday, domestic setting while reading the day's Atlanta Constitution, that the idea of hijacking for ransom first crossed his mind, an idea which would eventually take root and grow, leading him to commit a spectacular crime almost three years later.

It wasn't exactly an idea at that point in time, but that was when the two things, hijacking and ransom, first met in his conscious mind. As the bright sun coruscated through the large picture window throwing soft reflections on the pastel walls, he read about the latest hijacking and a spectacular kidnapping and wondered why no one had yet hijacked an airliner and demanded ransom. It seemed a natural next step to the hijacking craze that was fast becoming a plague on the house of the nation's air carriers.

Later, looking back on this day, he would speculate that even then he must have had larceny in his soul for the thought to have crossed his mind. An urbane and educated man, Cooper was aware that most people possess many-faceted personalities; that each of us display one side of our character at work and frequently reserve a completely different façade for exhibit to our loved ones at home. In between may lay a dozen variations of our public personality each of which may expose traits hidden adroitly from those who know us best. He recognized this characteristic in his own mental make up. On the job he was almost a zealot, an adamant perfectionist who had little tolerance for substandard performance or needless frivolity among his associates. But away from work he could relax and become just one of the boys. While he regarded the rules of the air and aircraft operating procedures as sacrosanct, he would violate minor traffic laws or smoke a joint with no compunction. Despite this recognition that many diverse traits lay hidden in his psyche, it didn't occur to him that he would be capable of hijacking. But later, in abject mental aberration during the autumn of 1971, he saw things differently.

In December of 1968 Cooper was still an unequivocal member of the establishment, a pilot flying for Eastern Airlines. Based in Atlanta, he was assigned as First Officer on a Boeing 727 run to Washington, Philadelphia, New York and back. That was one reason he took such a big interest in the latest hijacking.

Nineteen Sixty-Eight had been a climatic year for hijacking of American planes to Cuba. Twenty-four attempts so far with eighteen of them successful. Eastern had been hit five times. In September a Boeing 720 was hijacked over the Bahamas and flown to Havana. On the third of November a seventeen-year old boy had tried to hijack a DC-9 while it was on the ground in Birmingham. He had a shotgun but the pilot had managed to disarm him. Then on November 23, four armed men who had a woman and three small children with them, had diverted a 727 to Cuba. Only a week later a skyjacker, who said he couldn't stand life in the United States, forced a flight out of Miami to make an unscheduled stop in Havana. And now, yesterday, December 19, a black man had hijacked a company DC-8 with one hundred and forty-three passengers. He had his four-year-old daughter with him. This morning's Atlanta Constitution said that no one was harmed and the plane and its crew would be returning from Cuba today.

But that wasn't the only headline in the paper this Friday. An Emory coed, Barbara Jane Mackle, the daughter of a wealthy Florida real estate developer, had been kidnapped from a local motel on Tuesday night and held for ransom of five hundred thousand dollars. In a bizarre sequence of events the ransom was paid and Miss Mackle was found, buried alive in a box in Gwinett County, a few miles north of Atlanta. Today the paper was reporting the capture of one of her abductors and the recovery of the money.

Why, Cooper pondered as he lingered over his coffee, has no one hijacked an aircraft and demanded ransom. Eastern had sent a memo to its pilots instructing them to cooperate with hijackers and he assumed the other airlines had done the same. With this attitude prevailing it was a wonder some clever criminal had not already demanded some airline furnish him with a sizeable amount of cash to make his stay in Cuba more pleasant.

At the time his thinking did not burgeon beyond that point. It certainly didn't occur to him that he might be the first to successfully attempt such a caper. He was more concerned that any day his southbound flight might be diverted to Jose Marti Airport by some gun-waving incorrigible or a lunatic armed with a bomb. The man yesterday had boarded at Philadelphia only an hour or so before Dan's flight had made its scheduled stop there. It might just as easily have been him who spent last night in Havana. Like all professional pilots, Cooper felt the airlines and the FAA were dragging their feet in doing anything about the increasing number of skyjackings.

He had been flying with Eastern for more than four years. Coming out of the U. S. Air Force in 1964, he went right to work for the company. After training in Miami, he had been based for two years in Washington, D. C. before transferring to Atlanta in October of 1966. Now, just before Christmas of 1968, he was making a trip to New York one day then returning the following day, working five days a week. The schedule was a propitious one, leaving Atlanta at 11:37 AM and arriving in New York at 3:31 PM. The return trip the following day left La Guardia at 11:25 and was on the ground in Atlanta at 3:15.

Today he was in especially high spirits. Today he was going to shop for a special Christmas present for Helen. They had been married less than two months and he was desperately in love. At twenty-one his wife had classic beauty and youthful vigor, ingredients that had combined to topple the strong social defenses of a confirmed bachelor. At thirty-four he had succumbed to her fatal charms, felled unexpectedly like a tree in the forest chosen at random by the woodsman.

Only last year, in a moment of self analysis, he had concluded he might never marry. A man who had always suppressed his emotions and never experienced any deep romantic feelings, he was in love with his job and had been happy in the role of the perennial bachelor, the lady's man with no attachments. His work had provided him with the emotional stability and financial security he needed, while his occasional dates and infrequent affairs filled his social and sexual needs.

But Helen had changed all that. She had awakened an ardent passion, a yearning need for love that had been buried so deep within his parched psyche he had never known it was there. It hadn't been love at first sight, but she had made a powerful impression the very first time he had laid eyes on her.

Dan Cooper had been living in Atlanta for about nine months then. It was the sizzling summer of 1967, the year Detroit burned, and he had sought refuge from the scorching noonday sun in the cool confines of the Three Hearths Restaurant at the Air Host Inn. The Three Hearths, a watering hole popular with flight crews, was located on Virginia Avenue adjacent to Hartsfield International Airport. Working as the hostess that day, she greeted him with a raffish smile and bright, challenging eyes that aroused his interest, and when Ruby, his regular waitress, had come over he had asked about her.

"Her name is Helen and that's about all I know," snapped the always brusque Ruby.

"Isn't she sort of young to be working here? He queried persistently.

"If you ask me she is," huffed the waitress, a small homely woman with a whipcord body and shinny black eyes. "But I don't make the rules. Now whata ya want?"

Sipping his martini and waiting for lunch in the multi-colored ambience of the crowded restaurant, he watched her seating other customers and admired her youthful ebullience. Dan had always liked his women young and this gamine with her cameo body and inexhaustible supply of expressions enchanted him. In high school and college he had always dated girls two or three years younger than himself and as he grew older he found the difference in ages increasing. This girl looked to be around twenty but because he was confounded by her provocative beauty he didn't trust his judgment. Perky and alert, she exuded the boundless energy of a teenager but effectuated the refined look of a mature woman.

Her outfit was striking. She wore a white linen suit over a blouse of some diaphanous material in brown and russet hues. The suit was cut to accentuate her full bosom while her shapely legs were encased in sheer stockings over high-heel pumps of dark brown patent leather. An orange foulard in her breast pocket gave another touch of color to her ensemble. As she moved, her hips swayed in that erotic rhythm that is the delight of girl watchers everywhere.

With a smooth unblemished skin she used only a hint of makeup to accent her peaches and cream complexion. She had a warm, golden tan which contrasted pleasingly with the bright white of her clothing. Ash blond hair of medium length brushed her shoulders lightly as she moved about seating new arrivals.

But it was her face that bewitched him. It was a happy face, round and cherubic with dimples that winked coyly when she smiled, deep set eyes of a brilliant blue that sparkled wantonly, a broad, perfectly shaped nose, and a full red mouth with sensuous lips and two lines of perfect white teeth. Her jaw line was soft—perhaps it was lingering baby fat that gave it that smooth, rounded look—but she had a firm, well-shaped chin enhanced by a petite dimple. In repose it might have been a face of classic beauty, but it was rarely relaxed. An endless procession of pouts, smiles, and moue's, frowns and leers flicked rapidly across it as she scurried about seating diners, checking on the waitresses and visiting briefly with the customers.

"Enjoying your meal?" she asked solicitously with a look of real concern as she stopped by his table.

"Err, yes," he mumbled fatuously, at a loss for words. "The steak sandwich is very good today."

"Well you let me know if there's anything that's not right," she purred before she bounced away to greet more new arrivals.

She must spend a lot of time by the pool, Dan mused as he admired her retreating form. He'd certainly like to find out.

* * *

The Air Host was one of his regular stops and over the next few days Dan made several casual inquiries and found out a lot more about Helen Fairchild. He learned that she had only recently arrived in Atlanta along with a handsome young man by the name of Chuck Wade, the new assistant manager of the hotel. They had come from Daytona Beach where Chuck had worked for one of the big, beachside hotels. The word was that Wade was an enterprising young executive in his early thirties who would go far unless he allowed his penchant for teenage girls to get him in trouble. Rumor had it that he had met Helen some months earlier in Daytona where she had been working as a waitress in a hotel restaurant. They had immediately become lovers and when Chuck was offered the job at the Air Host he had asked her to come and live with him in Atlanta. She agreed to the arrangement but only on the condition he buy her a new wardrobe. Although everyone at the motel suspected she was less than twenty-one, the age she claimed, they were all taken with her good looks and pleasant personality. There were no objections when Chuck had given her the job as hostess in the restaurant.

Cooper was in The Three Hearths often and he saw her several times after that. He stopped in regularly for a late lunch and she always seemed to remember him, seating him at Ruby's station without having to be reminded of his preference. She made small talk about inconsequential things, but he had no opportunity to have a real conversation with her until one night some two weeks after their first encounter.

It was about ten on a Tuesday evening. Having just come in off a flight and still in uniform, he stopped at the bar at the Air Host for a nightcap before going home. He was putting money in the juke box when she walked up and started a conversation.

"How about playing something by the Supremes," she suggested brashly, nuzzling his shoulder.

"Sure, why not," he answered turning to give her a broad smile. "How about C-17, *You Can't Hurry Love?*"

"Great! Say, what's a good looking man like you doing in here by himself?"

"I'm just on my way home after a flight and stopped in for a quick drink. Why don't you join me?"

She did and they sat and talked for nearly an hour. Later it seemed strange that he couldn't remember what they discussed. When he left he knew little more about her than he had before, but he came away even more impressed by her ravenous beauty and captivating charm. And now he knew it wasn't just a superficial glamour. Despite her youth and innocence he found her intelligent and interesting—and very sexy. She definitely piqued his interest.

But Dan, a categorical Casanova with wings, had a lot going at the time and didn't follow through. He was left with the impression that she was still living with Chuck but wasn't completely happy there. He could probably have gotten her phone number from someone at the hotel but didn't. He went on about his business, but he didn't forget her.

Indeed it was more than a month after their meeting in the bar when he saw her again. It was a Sunday evening and he was at home alone watching *All in the Family* on Channel 5 when the doorbell rang. Dan had a comfortable one-bedroom apartment in The Landmark; a modern high-rise apartment house conveniently located right off the expressway near the corner of Piedmont and Cain Streets in downtown Atlanta. When he moved to the city, Alan Saxon, another Eastern pilot he had known in Washington, was living there, and Alan had persuaded Dan that it was the ideal place for a bachelor with good taste and sufficient income to make his base of operations.

Saxon, a husky blond with ruddy cheeks and crinkly, close-cropped hair, was Dan's age and the camaraderie between the two was of long standing. Sharing a room in the BOQ when they were undergoing pilot training at Spence Air Base in 1958 and 59, the two became immediate and close friends and afterward they managed to stay in touch during their Air Force years. Alan came with Eastern a few months after Cooper and when he was based in D. C., they renewed their friendship. But Alan, who had been born and raised in Atlanta, had transferred home at the first opportunity and then talked Dan into following him to Georgia and The Landmark.

A number of other bachelor fliers made their home there including Rod Kerry, a short, stocky red-headed Texan with sparkling blue eyes who was always full of banter and joviality; Jimmy Balmer, a Delta pilot in his early thirties with the conversational style of an express train; and John Bennett, dark-headed and handsome with large brown eyes who also flew for Delta but was a couple of years younger. David Barnes, a Captain with Southern, was good looking, breezy, and full of fun. He had sandy hair and little blue eyes which normally sparkled with friendliness but which would turn steely when he was crossed. In his mid-thirties and divorced, Barnes was a consummate actor who could tailor his act to suit the occasion. Popular with the ladies, he was always ready for a party or a trip to some exotic resort. And Dan Griffin, a flight instructor for a fixed base operator, was also among the carefree young airmen who called Atlanta and The Landmark home in 1967.

Prior to 1960, Atlanta had been just another sleepy southern city dozing placidly on the Piedmont Plateau. Made famous by Margaret Mitchell's novel, Gone with the Wind, it had briefly come to life when Clark Gable and Vivian Leigh came to town for the world premiere of the movie at Loew's Grand in 1939, but nothing exciting had happened since thirty-six people died in the tragic Winecoff Hotel fire in 1947. Up until 1960 the airlines there operated out of an oversized Quonset hut on the far side of Atlanta Municipal Airport, formerly known as Candler Field after the Coca Cola family and later renamed Hartsfield International for long-time mayor Bill Hartsfield. But that year a new, multi-million dollar terminal opened and at the same time the downtown area, under the aegis of a new progress-minded mayor, Ivan Allen, Jr., and an active Chamber of Commerce, began a renaissance that was still continuing.

During the sixties the downtown loop of the expressway, I-75 and I-85, was finally opened. It was routed just east of downtown through a former slum called Buttermilk Bottom. Overnight all the land between the expressway and Peachtree Street, the main street which straddles the ridge running north from Five Points, was immensely valuable real estate. On Peachtree Street John Portman build the new Merchandise Mart and began his Peachtree Center complex. Down the hill, next to the expressway, The Landmark occupied a small space kitty-cornered from the new Marriott Motor Hotel which took the entire block between Piedmont and Courtland and Cain and Ellis Streets.

In D. C. Cooper had shared a three-bedroom apartment in Alexandria, Virginia, with two other junior Eastern pilots, but in Atlanta he had opted to live alone. Alan had gone with him to The Store for Homes, part of the enormous downtown Rich's Department Store, where he had purchased all the furniture he needed to lavishly decorate his apartment. The Lackawanna leather sofa and easy chair in an olive color looked striking on the moss green carpet. A small walnut desk and three lighted bookcases added a stylish note to the spacious living room. Alan brought over John Sevierson, a decorator friend, who suggested painting the walls an off-shade of green and took Dan to Myron Dwoskin's where they picked out wallpaper for the kitchen and fabric for the living room drapes. He also helped select a large oil painting of a clipper ship to hang over the couch and a new console stereo to go under the picture window. Dan wasn't sure he liked the furry shag throw rug Sevierson found to go under the glass-topped coffee table, but he left it and in time became accustomed to it. But he was very pleased with the room as a whole. The smooth leather and knobby walnut, the various shades of green and brown, blended well to give it a warm, masculine feel. The round imitation walnut table and four black vinyl chairs he purchased for the dining area were not on par with the casual elegance of the living room, but they were adequate and would do until he could afford something better. He bought new drapes and a matching bedspread for the bedroom, already having a smart Thomasville bedroom suite in pecan he had bought in Washington.

Many of the tenants on his floor were airline employees and he had met most of those who weren't. They visited among themselves regularly so when his doorbell rang that Sunday evening he assumed it was one of his neighbors. When he opened the door and found Helen it startled him and the drink he was holding slopped over the rim. In a mild state of shock he invited her in.

Her appearance was striking as she stood in the open doorway, her small yet voluptuous figure silhouetted against the opaque darkness of the hall. A bright smile lighted her animated face, her eyes flashing, her lips wet and glistening. She was wearing a beige corduroy suit over an orange turtleneck sweater. Her lustrous blond hair was brushed to a fine sheen and it reflected the soft light coming through the door. She shook her head slowly as she made apologies.

"I hope I'm not intruding," she purred in a sexy, little-girl voice. "I can't stay but a minute. I'm looking for Bob Gordon, and he doesn't answer his bell. Do you know where he is?"

"Yes, he lives right across the hall in 801," Cooper stammered, unable to hide his agitation. "But I don't know where he is. I haven't seen him all weekend. He may be out of town. Is there anything I can do for you?"

"No, it's not important" she sighed, seeming to lose interest. "But maybe you could give him a message for me. You will see him won't you?"

"Yes, I'll be glad to. Give him a message I mean . . . . Let me get a pencil and paper."

He couldn't understand why he was so nervous around this girl. He should have invited her in for a drink or something, but he left her standing in the doorway and rushed past his desk to the night stand in the bedroom to get a pencil and pad. When he returned, flustered, she was still there.

"Here we are," he said rather breathlessly. "Now what is the message?"

"Just tell him to call Helen. My number is 639-8282."

"Okay, I've got that, Helen at 639-8282. Is that all?"

"Yes, I guess so. I had better be going," she said disinterestedly, making no move to do so. Instead she hung suggestively to the doorframe.

"Well, you don't have to rush off in the heat of the night," he mumbled lamely with a sly smile, beginning to regain his composure.

"No, I'd better go."

You're sure you won't come in and wait? I think I can scare up a drink."

"No, thanks a lot. I'd love to but I'm supposed to meet someone in just a little while. But thanks anyway. And thanks for taking the message. By the way, I haven't seen you around the Air Host lately."

He answered and she stayed for ten more minutes while they chatted inanely of unimportant matters standing in the door of the apartment. When she had finally gone Dan sat down and shook his head. What was that all about, he pondered? Her reason for stopping seemed so transparent. And yet she refused his invitation to come in and have a drink when he had finally gotten his act together enough to invite her—an invitation that might have led to other things.

He hadn't even known that she knew Bob Gordon. Bob, a senior rate clerk at Eastern Air Freight, hung out regularly in the bar at the Air Host so he guessed it wasn't that mysterious. But it still seemed strange.

And something else was strange—his reaction. He had been weak in the knees. Her appearance had turned him into a fumbling idiot. Normally he would have acted with a lot more cool. There was definitely something about this girl that messed his mind.

Later that night he went across the hall and finding Bob home, he delivered the message. Dan wanted to ask Gordon what he knew about Helen but wasn't the nosey type, didn't want to interfere in something that wasn't his business. Bob, a strikingly handsome bachelor who always had a couple of girls on his string, accepted the terse message without comment and thanked Dan for taking it. Somehow Cooper couldn't see Helen as Bob's type. She didn't come on that way. Dan kept the phone number. He put it in the drawer in his bedside table thinking he would give her a call some day and ask her out for a drink. But again, somehow he never got around to it. He was dating Frances Haverty regularly then and when he thought about Helen he always seemed to be busy. Several weeks went by and he didn't see her again. It was around the end of October when he asked Barry, the night bartender, about her.

"I heard she left town," Barry said. She went with Alma, who worked here nights as a cocktail waitress, and Alma's boyfriend, Big Sam Heard. They are supposed to have gone to DC or Philly or someplace up east.

Well, I guess that's that, thought Dan. I waited too long to call her. But he didn't throw her phone number away. And he didn't forget her.

* * *

It was a Thursday, the following February, when he stormed out of Frances Haverty's fashionable apartment at The White House on Peachtree. They had quarreled over his affection for her, or rather the lack of it. A shapely twenty-four year old legal secretary from a moneyed Macon family, she had confronted him with escalating demands, asked for more than he was prepared to give. By now, this was an old story to Dan. In the years since college it seemed that every woman he had dated for any period of time had, sooner or later, tried subtly, or not so subtly, to lead him to the altar. When he told them that for him their relationship was just a temporary affair, pleasure for the sake of pleasure, these women invariably became hurt, angry, and resentful. He could appreciate their feelings but could not change his own. He distrusted the conventional aspects of marriage, was not prepared to relinquish his freedom. Demands of eternal allegiance and declarations of undying love seemed foolish and insincere to him. And he lost patience with any girl who couldn't enjoy the pleasure of the moment, who must always seek assurances for the future. He knew he had no guarantees to give.

He wondered if perhaps his ability to love was somehow flawed. He had been a September child, born when his parents were already in their forties. There had been an older brother, born ten years before him, but he had died in 1933 at the age of nine, a victim of polio, that infamous killer and crippler of children that had since been almost wiped out by the Salk vaccine. He had grown up a shy lonely child; living in his dead brother's shadow, petted and pampered by loving but undemonstrative parents who never kissed him on the lips.

The family had been moderately well off when he was young. His father had owned and operated a general store in the little town of Woodland, Washington. It was a homey, small-town place where they sold groceries, dry goods and notions all in one big room, and where the local men gathered on rainy afternoons around the coke box to drink five-cent Nephi soda and root beer while they discussed the weather and exchanged gossip about their absent neighbors. His mother helped out at the store on Saturdays when people from outlying areas came in to shop, and so did he when he was old enough. He obediently went to church and Sunday school every Sunday at the Methodist Church and had dutifully joined the church when he was eleven.

The store had done well though the forties, but after the war, with the deluge of new automobiles and the opening of stores called supermarkets in the larger towns, people began traveling to nearby Vancouver and even to Portland to do their shopping. Dan had watched with dismay as his father became resentful and bitter realizing his business was dying. During those last years in Woodland, Ben Cooper had worked so hard and laughed so little his face had become as gray and weather beaten as the siding on the old store building.

When Dan finished high school in 1953, his father retired, closed the store, sold everything he owned in Woodland and moved the family to Seattle. They moved into a neat, white two-story house on 12th N. E., just west of the University of Washington campus and Dan enrolled there in the fall of that year.

He had been forced to work a series of menial, low-paying jobs to have spending money while he was at the University, but it didn't keep him from making good grades. He had majored in accounting and finished in four-and-a-half years with a B+ average. Like most young men in those days he was faced with a military obligation and so had opted to take ROTC in college. After graduation he had gone into the U. S. Air Force as a Second Lieutenant.

Living at home and spending all of his spare time working or studying, he had been a loner in college. While he had become friendly with many girls he met at school, he rarely dated because he had no car and very little money available for that sort of thing. He hadn't lost his virginity until he visited a whore house in Nuevo Laredo in September of 1958 while he was in preflight training at Lackland Air Force Base near San Antonio.

He had fallen in love with flying from the very first, and for almost six years he made the Air Force his home. He had done his primary pilot training at Spence Air Base near Moultrie, Georgia, and transferred to Webb Air Force Base at Big Spring, Texas, for basic training in single-engine jets. Graduating with his wings in the fall of 1959 he was assigned to Shaw Air Force Base in South Carolina for advanced training in tactical reconnaissance flying the RF-101 aircraft. From there he had been sent to Okinawa and the 45th Tactical Reconnaissance Squadron where he spent two busy years. Returning to Shaw early in 1962, he became part of the 20th Tac Recon Squadron and went with them on temporary duty to McDill Air Forced Base in Tampa at the time of the Cuban missile crisis in October of that year.

Cooper had never piloted a plane before he entered the Air Force, but he found he was a natural at it. The precision planning and execution of each flight appealed to his accountant's mind. The beauty of the sky and his country as seen from the air stirred the artist in him. He found he was comfortable in a regimented life with boundaries and discipline, and the wearing of a uniform with its rank and privileges was further compensation. It was only after he had been transferred to a desk job as Property Control Officer in Base Supply that he realized the limitations of a career in the Air Force, became disenchanted, and decided to get out. Fortunately the airlines were hiring in 1964 and he went straight from the service to the ranks of Eastern.

Both parents died of smoke inhalation when a faulty water heater set fire to the house in Seattle one cold night in October of 1961. Shocked and bereaved, Dan had taken emergency leave and flown home for the double funeral. His father had allowed all of his insurance to lapse and there was nothing left but the lot on which the house had stood. After it was sold and the funeral expenses were paid, he said goodbye to Seattle and closed the door on that part of his life.

The Air Force had been a lonely life, living in small towns and spending most of his spare time on extra duty or cross-country flights. He had been closer to his fellow pilots than to any of the girls he had dated in those fleeting years. Working for Eastern was a completely different experience. Making his home in big cities and traveling regularly between them he met hordes of eligible women on and off the job. In this new environment he had gradually shed his patina of aloofness and developed a new façade, becoming the typical flying rake, the hot shot pilot with a girl at every stop and ice water in his veins, the man with no attachments always out for a good time.

And so in early 1968, he was still single, his boyhood shyness covered by a layer of urban sophistication, his emotional growth stunted, his need for love buried deep under years of suppression and neglect. Despite his education and experience he had conned himself into believing that he could not fall in love, that he was immune to cupid's arrows. Living only for the pleasure of the moment, he didn't realize how vulnerable he was.

In March of that year he saw Helen again. It was a Tuesday night late in the month and the weather outside was serene; a soft seventy degrees, scattered clouds and just a breath of breeze. Inside Kitten's Korner, a popular go-go club near the corner of Peachtree and Sixth Street, the air was overheated, stale and fetid with cigarette smoke and perspiration. He had gotten in from a flight about eleven and after changing into casual clothes, had decided to check out the city's nightspots. The Korner had been one of the hot spots earlier that year but with the coming of spring the crowds had tapered off. That night it wasn't busy when he sauntered in and slipped into a seat on the end of the bar nearest the door. Against the opposite wall two shapely girls in scant costumes were gyrating in cages on either side of a small stage. A few couples were dancing to the raucous vibes of *Ramblin' Gamblin' Man* coming from the kaleidoscopic jukebox.

He ordered his usual drink, Wild Turkey and water, and looked around, his eyes gradually becoming accustomed to the smoky blackness. The long bar was about half full but only a few tables and booths were occupied. Several cuties in Kitten costumes circulated among those with languid movements, dispensing drinks. The jukebox changed and Otis Redding came on singing *The Dock of the Bay.* The go-go girls stepped back out of their cages and the dancers on the floor took up the slower rhythm. He decided to move to the other end of the bar to check the crowd and see if anyone he knew was there. He came here regularly and often ran into friends or acquaintances.

He was almost to the other end of he bar scrutinizing the sparsely occupied table area through the smoky gloom when a lyrical voice behind him cut through the busy hubbub of the room. "Hi Dan." it said, jerking his attention away from the table area like the sound of a gun shot. "What are you doing here?"

Surprised, he turned and there she was, looking like a figment of make-believe carefully superimposed on a real setting. She was wearing white again; this time a shapely pants suit. In the motley lights of the cabaret her soft blond hair and richly tanned complexion contrasted excitingly with the brilliant white of the bar. She wore very little makeup, just a little something around the eyes to make them look big and luminous, and a pale lipstick. His heart went to his throat.

"Hi," he stammered self-consciously. "I thought you left town."

"Oh, I did, but I'm back now," she replied laughing and keeping it light, her eyes shining coquettishly. "Are you still flying the big birds?"

"Yes, I just got in from Miami a couple of hours ago. What are you doing these days?"

"Not much. I'm staying with a friend who is the resident manager at the Lenox Grove Apartments. When she's at work at her regular job during the day I look after things. It's really been boring since I've been back. Do you come here often?"

"Maybe once or twice a week. Things are a little slow tonight"

"They sure are. I've been here nearly an hour and you're the first person I've seen I know," she said staring at him a long moment, clicking the rim of her glass against her gleaming teeth.

Smiling foolishly, he slipped onto the bar stool next to her and signaled the bartender to bring them both another drink. He felt very pleased at running into her. He had been extremely lonesome since breaking up with Frances and while he liked to have some time to himself, he'd missed having a regular girl. It was a propitious time to run into Helen. She had aroused a hidden and unspecified hunger in him from the first, and he was glad to hear she wasn't tied down.

They finished their drinks and he asked her to dance. She was a smooth dancer, effortlessly blending her steps with him. It was the first time he had held her in his arms and the feel of her warm, lush body through the sheer material excited him. She seemed to sense his excitement and reciprocated, snuggling closer and pressing herself firmly against him. He was disappointed when the song ended and a fast number came on. They returned slowly to their seats at the bar where he bought them another drink and they talked.

Wanting to somehow break the ice, he asked her if she'd like to go and check out some of the other nightspots or maybe stop somewhere and have a bite to eat.

"No," she sighed, a note of regret in her voice. "I've got to get on home shortly. I told Lynn I'd be in by one."

Can I give you a ride?"

"Thanks but I've got a car. But you can call me sometime. Do you still have my phone number?"

"No," he lied unctuously. "I don't think I do. What is it?"

"It's 639-8282. I'm usually there during the day."

"I'm usually gone during the day but I'm off on Thursday. Why don't we get together for dinner and go out and dance a little?"

"I guess that would be all right," she said with equivocation. "You can pick me up about eight. It's apartment number one at Lenox Grove Apartments on Lenox Road. Do you know where it is?"

"Sure do. I'll just plan on it, next Thursday, April 4th at eight." he replied with some eagerness. The idea of a date with her pleased him immensely, but he tried to hide his satisfaction. Shortly thereafter he excused himself and left.

* * *

When Cooper got off the following night he went straight home. On Thursday afternoon he made a special trip to the hair stylist and got the works, even a manicure. He spent a long time getting ready. Over a white knit turtle neck shirt and pale blue, belt-less trousers, he wore a new, bright blue sport coat he had bought recently in Florida. His alligator loafers were polished to a satiny shine. He wanted to look his best.

Ready early, he left in plenty of time driving the classy 1968 Lincoln Coupe he had purchased a few months previously. It was an impressive car with gleaming metallic paint of a dusty olive hue, matching leather upholstery, and all the options including an eight-track player, an accessory available only on luxury cars that year. The evening was beautiful and he circled through Piedmont Park on his way to Lenox Road. The fragrant spring air wafted through the open window, astringent as alcohol.

He was on time and she answered the door when he rang. She was ready and they returned downtown and had dinner at The Knight's Table on Luckie Street. The steaks there were always excellent and they served a cream garlic dressing that Dan swore was better than any he had tasted anywhere. Over dinner they began to talk of their pasts, revealing little bits and pieces of their lives, awkwardly maneuvering toward a relationship. He told her how he'd been born in Portland, Oregon, and had grown up in Washington State. He didn't dwell on his childhood, although it had been a happy one. Instead he talked a lot about his six years in the Air Force and his experiences flying for Eastern.

Helen also talked little about her childhood and he did not press her to do so. He did gather that her family lived in Daytona Beach, Florida, and before that they had lived in Virginia, somewhere near Washington, D. C. Her conversation was mostly about the present, how she wanted to get a job but was handicapped by not having a car. He wondered how she was supporting herself but was too much of a gentleman to ask. Apparently Lynn was giving her room and board for her help at the apartments. Beyond that she was vague.

After they finished eating they went next door to the Playboy Club. A popular four-man combo headed by a blind piano player named Ronnie Millsap was playing in the Playroom and they had to wait to get a table.

"Chain, chain, chaaain, chain of fools," the band moaned urgently as Dan and Helen took their seats and waited for one of the buxom bunnies to take their drink order. The crowd had that suave, urban, and slightly constipated look that seemed the exclusive province of the young executive types who frequented places like this. Dan had seen them often in the Playboy Club in New York and Miami as well as this one. Dressed to the nines, they were trying too hard to convince each other they were having a good time in the contrived party atmosphere of the pristine club.

But Helen seemed impressed. She said this was her first time here and busied herself scrutinizing the outfits worn by other women in the room. As usual she looked smashing, but then he thought she could make a garbage man's coveralls look chic. Tonight she was elegantly attractive in a tight-fitting, low-cut dress of off-white jersey with chocolate brown accessories. A simple gold necklace gleamed against the velvety tan of her ample bosom.

"How do you keep such a good tan, even in the winter," Dan asked, smiling.

"I get all the sun I can, silly," she replied with a short laugh. "But it's not hard. My complexion is naturally a little dark and I use a sun lamp on days when it's too cold to sit in the sun. That's one reason I like helping Lynn at the apartments. I've got plenty of time to lay by the pool or under the sun lamp."

He realized then that her skin did have a golden cast to it, a smooth unblemished texture that tanned easily and never burned. "Well I envy you," he said earnestly. "I spend a half-hour three times a week in the tanning room at the health club and it barely erases my greenhouse pallor."

Their bunny, Jean, finally arrived and took their order. By the time she returned with the drinks the band had taken a break. Dan wanted to ask Helen to dance, but it was quite a while before the musicians returned and they were on their second round. She said she'd like to go to the restroom before they danced and he was waiting patiently when she returned very quickly with a concerned expression on her pretty face.

"Dan, maybe we better go," she whispered breathlessly. "There was a black girl in the ladies room and she said Martin Luther King has been assassinated and the Negroes are rioting,"

"You mean here in Atlanta?" he asked, astonished. Atlanta was the headquarters of the SCLC, the organization the noble-prize-winning Doctor King used as his base for his non-violent crusades for civil rights for black people. Lately he had become even more controversial for his opposition to the Vietnam War.

"I'm not sure. But she was crying and they were talking about burning and looting on a little radio someone had in there."

"Well maybe we'd better," he acknowledged becoming concerned as he thought of his Lincoln parked on the street outside.

It took some time to get the check and settle up with Bunny Jean but they finally emerged into the cool evening air. Luckie Street had a life of its own and the usual quota of tourists, businessmen, hustlers and whores were moving back and forth between the bars, restaurants and hotels in the area, but there was no sign of violence. They quickly stepped off the half-block to where his car was parked, got in, and headed north.

"Turning on the radio they received the news first hand that Martin Luther King, Jr. was dead, shot down by a sniper at a motel in Memphis. The announcer said there was rioting in black sections of Washington and Chicago but none had been reported in Atlanta as yet.

Despite this news she insisted he take her straight home. He had been enjoying the evening immensely and was very disappointed at its being cut short. At Lenox Grove he walked her to the door where she quickly popped inside with only a short goodbye. He was left wondering about her with a hunger, an aching need to know more.

Cooper was flying during the next few days when dignitaries from all over the world descended on Atlanta for Martin Luther King's funeral, and Governor Lester Maddox barricaded himself in the state capitol. He missed the opportunity to join 150,000 people who on Tuesday marched behind the body of King in a mule-drawn wagon as it made the slow trip from the Ebenizer Baptist Church on Auburn Avenue across town to the grave site on the campus of Morehouse College.

On Monday morning he had called Helen and asked her out again that Thursday. She readily agreed and for the second time he drove out to Lenox Road feeling a mixture of excitement, curiosity and apprehension. His interest in her, aroused on their first meeting, had gradually mounted. Those intriguing incidents last year, then running into her unexpectedly at Kitten's Korner, followed by last week's aborted date had all served to increase her allure and challenge his masculine ego.

Her charms were both physical and mental. Her saucy smiles, her long golden hair, her sapphire blue eyes, the sensual way she moved; all were beguiling, but he was also captivated by the easy familiarity with which she had treated him from the very first. She was obviously intelligent, knew how to dress and how to act in public, and she had a freshness, a spontaneity of interest, that he had not found before in the women he had dated.

He found her tantalizing and wondered if there was something for him with this mysterious, enchanting girl, this subtle and complex woman, something significant, something beyond the usual dissolute banalities of the stale singles scene. She was full of challenging promise of great feminine warmth and he was eager to see where this attraction might lead.

The weather was warm and tonight she wore a summer frock in pastel yellow. He caught a waft of some subtle perfume as he ushered her into the gleaming Lincoln.

This time they went to dinner at The Round Table on Piedmont Road, but afterwards, instead of hitting the nightspots they drove around and talked. Helen was fascinated with the extravagant luxury of his car; the grand way it rode, the comfort of the roomy interior, the rich feel and smell of the leather upholstery. She was especially taken with the tape player. He had several good tapes but when she found *TCB* by the Supremes she played it over and over explaining that it was her current favorite recording. Afterward, whenever he heard it, he thought of her and that romantic night.

Their conversation was inconsequential but as before, she found out more about him than he did about her. She persuaded him to tell her about his early sexual experiences with women and probed and prodded enough to learn he had been through several short affairs but had never been married. He was a little embarrassed relating these intimate facts of his life he had never discussed with anyone before, but she was so relaxed, so easy to talk with, that he gradually dropped the mask and let her see behind his social façade.

Eventually they parked by the Ansley Park Golf Course, talked quietly, and listened to the music. A young moon hung in he east like half a golden egg.

"Why did you rush inside and leave me standing there looking stupid when we got to your apartment door last week?" he suddenly asked in a serious tone.

"I was afraid of you," she answered very quietly. "I was afraid I might get to like you and that's just what's happening."

He felt his chest tightening, his heart quickening. Her perfume tantalized him. Abruptly the force between them surged. His hand reached out and touched her hair, so silky and fine and sensuous. A little shiver and then they were kissing. He felt her lips soft and in a moment, welcoming, just a little moist, the taste clean and good.

Their passion grew. His hand moved to her breast and felt the heat through the silky material. Again she shivered and weakly tried to back off but he held her firmly, his heart racing, foundling her. Then her hands went to his chest and stayed awhile, touching him, then pressed against him and she broke the kiss but stayed close, gathering her breath.

"Dan . . . you . . ."

"You feel so good," he said softly, holding her close. He bent to kiss her again but she avoided the kiss.

"Wait, Dan. First . . ."

He kissed her neck and tried again, sensing her want.

"Dan, wait . . . first . . ."

"Your first kiss? I don't believe it!"

She laughed and the tension broke. "You're too fast for me Dan," she said, her voice throaty, arms around his neck. "Too strong and too attractive and too nice. Are all pilots like you?

"No, but most of us are a bit forward. But you! You really are a riddle."

"No, I'm not," she said shyly, her hand caressing the back of his neck seductively. "I'm just a little country gal trying to find happiness in the big city and I get a little jumpy if you move too fast."

"Then let's take it slow and easy," he said as he started kissing her again gently. Her lips parted.

"Let's go back to your apartment and have a drink," she said in a husky voice when he gave her a chance.

Back at The Landmark he fixed them a drink and then somehow, very quickly, they found their way to the bedroom. The reluctance, the hesitation, the holding back she had displayed in the car were all gone and she made it seem the most natural thing in the world. Maybe it was. He felt as if he had known her for years and wanted this from the day he had set eyes on her.

They shed their clothes languidly and he was in awe of her naked body; graceful, slender, silky smooth. He kissed her between the shoulder blades and ran his hungry hands easily over her firm, yielding body. He felt wonder and a kind of awe at being exposed to such beauty. She turned and drew him to her and they made love slowly and carefully again and again. She seemed to lead, but he felt always in command, masculine and strong as they sailed the erotic seas.

The best part was when, sated, they lay slackly in each other's arms, half asleep, cuddling and kissing. It was nice being warm and close. They lay there a long time laughing and joking and he kept kissing her in funny places that made her giggle.

He asked her to spend the night but she refused. She said she must be home when Lynn left for work the next morning and couldn't bear the thought of getting up at six and rushing home. But it was nearly four before they got there. On the way they stopped by the lake in Piedmont Park where they parked for a long time listening to the tape player and necking. Love was inevitable.

* * *

Things had gone swiftly after that. Looking back it was hard to remember where truth had ended and fantasy had begun. Those mad whirling days in the spring and summer of 1968 seemed to have had no endings and no beginnings. For the first time in his life Dan truly opened himself to love, an emotion as hot as fire with no more outline than a flame. Once, the preceding spring, he had gone with David on a canoe trip down the rushing Chattooga River, and had felt the same not unpleasant sensation of helplessness and surrender in the hands of luck and unknown gods as he was swept along, the world spinning. Once having started there was no way to stop, no way, until passion ran its course, the river finally flowed placid between broad banks, and risk was a happy memory.

They began dating three or four times a week. In May he bid a different schedule with Saturdays and Sundays off. This allowed them to be together on weekends and make trips out of town. One Sunday in June they drove to Chattanooga and spent the day on Lake Chickamauga swimming, boating and water skiing with Alan Hanson, a girl named Mary and some of Alan's friends who lived in Chattanooga. Another weekend it was an excursion to Panama City where they fell into the role of summer tourists, swimming in the gentle surf and sunning themselves on the blazing white beaches. It was a summer of torment for the country, torn apart by the Vietnam War and the Presidential Election. The murder of Bobby Kennedy in Los Angeles in June and the riots at the Democratic National Convention in Chicago in August shocked the nation, while the hijacking of airliners to Cuba became a regular occurrence. But they hardly noticed. For Dan and Helen it was a golden summer, a summer of fun memorable for so many delightful experiences shared, a time of catharsis and much emotion.

Helen seemed to be completely happy when she was with him. Anything he suggested was an adventure to her and this made him happy. Dan had lots of interests, but traveling and seeing new places and new things was his favorite, and it pleased him that she enjoyed that also.

And, after a time, it seemed they didn't need anyone else. Dan had many friends, men and women, but as he became more involved with Helen, he gradually quit seeing any of them. He just didn't need them. And she seemed to be the same.

One evening over dinner at Dale's Cellar she told him about her trip north the previous winter with her friend, Alma Austin, and Alma's boyfriend, Big Sam. Helen said she had gone to get away from Chuck, the assistant manager at the Air Host. They had broken up only a short time after she had come to Atlanta, and she had moved in with Lynn, whom she had known previously in Daytona. But Chuck wouldn't believe their affair was over, and he kept importuning her to come back until she felt she had to get out of town.

Although she didn't learn about it until the trip was underway, Sam was running from a bushel of hot checks he had dropped around town, and they left in an El Dorado the bank was trying to repossess. They had driven to Washington, D. C. where they had spent a few days with friends, stopped overnight in Philadelphia, and then gone on to Hartford, Connecticut. Sam was supposed to have connections there but after a couple of weeks his money ran out, and then, when he and Alma had a big fight, Sam ran out.

The girls had been forced to go back to waiting tables to eat. Helen made friends with an older man named Harvey Woodruff. Harvey was the dashing, man-about-town, playboy type. He was in the exporting business and made frequent trips to Europe: Paris, Rome, Athens and other exotic places. He drove a Coupe de Ville and smoked a pipe. Helen had liked him and he had helped make Christmas merry that year. But she told Dan that Harvey had been a little too old for her and maybe a little too Ivy League.

Later, Dan wondered if perhaps Harvey might have gotten a little tight in the pocket book with Helen before their friendship ended, but she never told him that. In early March, when Harvey had gone on a trip to Europe, she had caught a jet back to Atlanta and moved in with Lynn once more.

She told Dan about a winter coat trimmed in fur that Harvey had put on lay-away for her. It wasn't especially grand, but she didn't have a decent winter coat. In Hartford it had been on sale at the end of the season and Harvey had given her three hundred dollars to put down on it. Now, with cold weather coming again soon, they might sell it if she didn't send them the other two hundred that she owed on it. She talked about it so often that sometime in August Dan finally offered to lend her the money to send for it. After all, it would be a shame for her to lose it now.

On a weekend near the end of August he rented a small plane, a Cessna Skylane, and they flew to Savannah on Saturday morning. Flying fascinated her. She'd never been up in a light plane before and asked innumerable questions. Flying was both his profession and his hobby and her interest truckled to his pride and flattered his ego. He took great pains to explain the workings of the aircraft and the method of navigation he was using.

They stayed at the beautiful DeSoto Hilton Hotel in the heart of the ancient port city. A lot of hours were spent in bed that weekend, but they still found time to see some of the sights. Savannah was an enchanting place with its magnificent old trees, its stately buildings, its quaint little parks and squares. The dark green leaves of the great gnarled trees spread their cool shade over the bright green grass and pleasant benches. Amongst this effulgence they fed squirrels and snapped pictures.

She was wearing a white mini dress and a tiny white beret. An apple green belt and matching scarf gave highlights of color to the eye-catching outfit. In a small park behind the hotel he had her pose several times as he tried to get the light just right. It was a picture-postcard setting: bright sunshine splashed around them in puddles; an indifferent breeze stirring the glimmering leaves; Helen looking like the subject of a painting by Monet, her eyes so blue they matched the sky. It was a magic day, a day that would never die.

They had a splendid dinner in the hotel dining room that evening then went night-clubbing in the small intimate clubs down on the river front. On Sunday they drove their rental car to the beach, oiled their bodies and toasted in the sun.

* * *

The weekend they went to Savannah was the last of the summer. When he had to fly two extra trips on Labor Day weekend she drove to Daytona with her friend Juanita and two other girls. He missed her dreadfully that weekend and tried to persuade her to spend the night with him when she returned on Wednesday. But she said no. Lynn was already upset because she hadn't gotten back on Monday and might throw her out if she didn't go home.

She had continued to talk about going to work but just couldn't seem to make up her mind to do it. She complained about not having a car but seemed more concerned about Lynn's reaction if she wasn't there to look after the apartments during the day.

By this time Dan knew that he was truly in love for the first time in his life. But he hadn't wanted to admit it, at least not for a long bewildering time, even to himself. He'd been around a lot, had plenty of girl friends and a few affairs and he'd thought he was immune to maudlin sentiment. A methodical, almost plodding man, he had not needed marriage to find release from the passionate confusion of youth and had dated women only for the pleasure of their company. He had not needed women for the emotional stability of long term commitments.

But that had changed. Had he been a more romantic person familiar with the pathology of love he would have recognized the symptoms sooner.

But he had been agnostic on that subject for too long and it wasn't until Labor Day weekend when he had to go for almost five days without seeing her, that he was forced to the conclusion that his attraction to her was more than just another of his periodic affairs.

Lying in bed late that Tuesday night, the tension of the past few days weighing him down, he had tried to analyze his state of melancholy despair. He knew that when he was away from her he thought of her with wistfulness, a longing that was so sharp and hard he could have used it to cut glass. And that her presence banished loneliness and made him poignantly sensitive to the sensual, romantic aspects of life. But he didn't know why.

Of course there was her beauty, but he had gone with beautiful women before. Then there was her ability to be feminine and demure and yet remain confident and sure of herself. She was never nagging or demanding, taking him as he was and reinforcing his feelings of strength and masculinity by her loving acceptance of all his mental and physical baggage, good and bad.

One thing about Helen which made her so special was the way their personalities merged. She was enthusiastic about everything, interested in anything that interested him. She didn't mind listening to his stories about the things he did back in Washington when he was a boy or his flying adventures. When Cooper had learned to fly he had experienced the thrill of flying but had also learned that it was almost impossible to talk about it meaningfully with anyone other than another pilot. Someone who hadn't been there just couldn't relate to it, and after a few abortive attempts he had given up discussing his flying experiences with anyone other than his fellow airmen. But Helen was an exception, and while he knew she couldn't understand all the technical jargon, she was a good listener who seemed to be able to share his feelings when he talked about flying—the sometimes breathtaking panorama of the earth and sky from 35,000 feet, the dogging frustrations of traffic delays, the peccadilloes of his fellow pilots.

And he was also pleased that she wasn't too much of a good-time party girl. He had assumed when he met her in Kitten's Korner that she was the type who liked to hit the bright spots every night and drink it up. The quantity and quality of the clothes she wore suggested she was not unfamiliar with life in the fast lanes. But he now knew that this was not the case. She did enjoy it, but when he asked what she preferred to do her usual response was that she would just like to go to his apartment and be with him, watch television and make love.

Thinking about it coolly and logically, the way he had been taught to analyze a problem in math or a mechanical malfunction in an aircraft, he had concluded that, whatever the reasons, he was in love, deeply and truly, and if his feelings didn't change soon, he'd have to do something about it.

* * *

On the last weekend in September they drove to the mountains. There had been an early cold snap and the leaves were already beginning to turn. They left on a cold, pearly Saturday morning and headed north on U. S. 19. She had never been up into the North Georgia Mountains and was entranced by their beauty, a riot of color in fall hues. They ate a lavish picnic lunch she had prepared at Vogel State Park. She had fried chicken, made potato salad and brought beans, pickles, onions, and potato chips. They chased it all with cold beer and for dessert, a delicious lemon pie she had baked. They sat at a picnic table under a spreading elm in a little hollow while a cool breeze chased a few leaves as they picked over the remains of the meal. Surely he'd never been so happy, so contented.

In the waning afternoon they drove up onto Brasstown Bald and surveyed the scene. The mountain air was sweet and cool here on the highest point in Georgia. Then heading east on U. S. Highway 76, they soon came to Clayton.

They spent the night in Clayton at what appeared to be the only decent motel in town. The manager told them that if they hurried they could still make supper at The Dillard House, a well known eatery a few miles up the road. A deep dusk had descended by the time Dan and Helen got there, but they were still serving. The big family style restaurant was another first for her and she let him know how much she enjoyed it, eating voraciously, shoveling in the food. Dan wondered what kind of life she must have led before he met her. He took a lot of pleasure from introducing her to new things and watching her reaction.

There wasn't any nightlife in Clayton so they retired to the motel where they tuned in the Saturday night movie on TV and mixed a couple of drinks. She was in a playful mood and kept him jumping by sticking ice down his back, in his pants and in other uncomfortable places. He tried to get back at her, but she would skip lightly away and laugh. Before long the room was a shambles and it wasn't until he caught her, pulled down her pants and spanked her blushing bottom that she stopped bugging him and started to cuddle.

She knew how to cuddle and she knew how much he liked it. As she snuggled sensuously against him it awakened lascivious desires and he could not content himself with lying quietly. Slowly he began letting his wanton hands wander aimlessly over her warm, lush body, enjoying the illicit feel of her hot flesh. He was enraptured by the texture of her skin; fine pored, tight and soft, and his ardent passion soared. She felt the heat rise in him and responded by snuggling, nuzzling and squeezing until he could bear it no more. Rolling her on her back he kissed and fondled her blindly. As he moved she pulled him close, her fingernails digging insatiably into his hide like spurs, eyes open but glazed. It was sweet, oh so sweet, and as they rushed to a carnal climax he held his breath and heard her cry out his name again and again and again like a chant. Abruptly they reached the inalterable crest and tumbled over and hung there for a second in the splintered, blinding air then suddenly relaxed and lay still in each others arms.

"I love you. I'd do anything for you," she said quietly.

"Do you?"

"I truly do," she signed and snuggled closer as he held her tight.

Dan awoke early the next morning in a room full of ghostly light. Dawn loomed outside the motel window and Helen pressed warmly against the cambers of his naked back. Her arms encircled his chest and he felt her breath, slow and regular, on the nape of his neck.

He looked at his watch on the bedside table and read ten minutes past six. He lay there thinking and realized that sometime in the night he had reached a decision.

He wanted to marry her. He had been waiting long enough. He'd had his fun playing the field and was ready to settle down. He'd gone through a lot of one night stands and six month love affairs and he was ready for something different, something more. He'd been dating Helen almost six months now and their relationship was still growing, no sign of either of them tiring of the other. And he had met her over a year ago so it wasn't a spur of the moment affair. When she had told him the night before that she loved him he felt she really meant it. Girls had told him that before but he knew he could tell the difference between what was said in the heat of passion and the real thing.

"I've never told that to anyone else," she had said, her eyes glowing with a passionate fervor. "I lived with Chuck for almost six months and never told him I loved him. I liked him a lot but I didn't love him. I only had sex with him two or three times."

He hadn't been able to bring himself to tell her that he loved her, not last night. He had been afraid it was just their mood. But now, the next morning, when he felt the same, he knew it was true, he did love her. And she loved him. So why shouldn't they get married.

They were both loners. His parents were dead and he didn't have any brothers or sisters. And apparently she didn't put much store by her family in Florida. They needed each other. Right there he decided he should marry her.

But Dan Cooper was the cautious type. I'll wait a week, he thought. If I still feel this way then, I'll ask her.

He drifted back to sleep and only awoke when he felt her hair brushing his belly. Reaching down, he pulled her to him, up into a crushing embrace and a passionate kiss. He fought the urgency as she moved against him but he knew there was no need to hurry, no need for all the intricacies of acquaintance, arousal, and smoothing reassurances. They had been there and were past that point. Slowly, smoothly, he took her again and once more they soared to the heights of passion.

The maids were beating on the door in a fury before they finally quit the bed and began getting dressed. It took them another hour to shower, dress and pack, and the office called twice in an effort to get them out before they emerged into a bright and cloudless day. They were both in a jubilant mood and they wouldn't be hurried.

The weather was warmer than the previous day and Helen dressed accordingly. She wore a pair of tight white shorts and a blue denim work shirt. She left the second button unbuttoned displaying the swell of her breasts. Her shapely legs looked good enough to eat. White tennis shoes and the little white beret gave the finishing touch to her modish ensemble.

Dan wore a red golf shirt and white painter's pants. They laughed and said they were patriotic with their red, white and blue outfits. They ate a leisurely brunch there in Clayton at a local café where the tables were covered in oilcloth and the menus in scared plastic. He kept her in stitches by pointing out their fellow diners and telling her imaginary stories about them.

"You see the melancholy fellow in the back booth," he said, indicating a tall man in his late thirties with a lugubrious look on his long, lean face. "He's the local undertaker. He's got a long face because nobody died this week. He had an affair with the fat waitress last year. Did you notice how she keeps avoiding looking at him? Her BO and bad breath finally drove him away. I'm glad you aren't working in restaurants anymore, you might get fat like her!"

"No, no I wouldn't," she laughed uproariously. "You wouldn't let me. How about the lady with all the children?"

"Oh that's the widow Batterfield," he assured her, grinning. "Her husband died a couple of years back from her nagging. She inherited money from her daddy who use to be President of the bank. She's been making a play for the Baptist preacher, but she hasn't landed him yet.

After eating they drove further north, up into the mountains of North Carolina, before circling back. In Franklin they stopped at a convenience store and bought ice and paper cups. They had almost a full fifth of Wild Turkey left and as they drove on they sipped liquor and played the tape player. Helen had brought along a Janis Joplin tape and that afternoon she played it over and over. Dan didn't relate much to Janis then, or any other singers who were deep into the drug scene, but he enjoyed the music. It had a lonely, lost quality that seemed to reach down inside of him and touch a spot he hadn't even known was there.

It was about four in the afternoon when they came to Tallulah Gorge. They were both feeling very relaxed from the whiskey, not high but warm and pleasant. She didn't want to get out except to use the rest room, but he insisted they walk down and take a look at the gorge, and she reluctantly agreed. The view was spectacular. Hundreds of feet below the river smoldered in the afternoon sunlight, the water cascading over shimmering rocks as it raced turbulently along. Trees and shrubs of various kinds grew precariously out of crevasses in the sides of the steep cliffs. Walking a little way up into the park, they came out upon a lookout point that had been hidden as they approached by an outcropping of rock. A freshening wind brought the sweet smell of growing things, rank earth, and the brief stink of some small animal.

"This reminds me a little of the Cascade Mountains back in Washington," he mused with nostalgia as they admired the view. "I was quite a woodsman when I lived there. I didn't think anything about taking a fifteen mile hike up into the mountains and camping out for a weekend. I had a friend named Roy Andrews who was as crazy about it as I was. When we were in junior high school we camped on every mountain in Southwest Washington. I bet I could still find my way around up there better than most folks.

Unexpectedly it clouded over and a cool breeze blew down the gorge. She put her arm around him and snuggled close. "You probably could," she answered impishly. "I haven't seen much you can't do when you put your mind to it. Look at me! You've turned Miss Deep-Freeze of Daytona into Helen Hot Pants. You've made a fallen woman out of me."

"Oh, I don't know about that," he scoffed. "I think Chuck and Harvey ought to get some of the credit."

"You be quiet Dan Cooper! Chuck was a fumbling Freddie compared to you, Mr. Cool. And Harvey never laid a hand on me. He wanted to but he didn't!"

"Well I guess if it's my fault I'll have to take the blame," he lamented. "I'm glad to hear you weren't putting out to every stud in Daytona Beach. I'm glad I'm the one to blame. And since I am, I guess I ought to make an honest woman out of you. Will you marry me?"

He said these last words nonchalantly with all the cool detachment of an airline captain asking permission to land. She turned sharply and looked at him in amazement.

"Oh Dan, would I? Could I!" she gasped excitedly. "There's nothing I would like better. But you don't have to marry me. I'll just come and live with you if you'll let me. And I'll get a job and pay for my keep. Oh Dan I love you so much!"

So that was how it had happened. Overcome by felicity and prompted by the impressive surroundings, a few drinks and her unctuous comments, he had popped the question. He hadn't been able to wait that week. And of course he'd marry her. He wouldn't ask her to move in unless he wanted her to stay for good. And if she was going to stay for good it would be as Mrs. Daniel Benjamin Cooper.

They talked endlessly about the details as they drove happily back to Atlanta. The purple sky was stained with the bloody remains of the dying day as the big Lincoln on cruise control whispered along the Interstate at seventy. She cuddled lovingly next to him as the Supremes sang, "There's A Place for Us, Somewhere a Place for Us."

A small wedding both agreed. She didn't even want to invite her family. She thought she'd just have Lynn and one or two other friends as witnesses. He would see if he could get a week off at the end of October and if he could, they'd make it then. His apartment was only a one bedroom, but that wouldn't be a problem. She didn't own anything except her clothes and she said there weren't that many of those. Besides they could look for a bigger place in February when his lease expired. She wanted to buy a few new clothes, but she promised that as soon as they were married she'd get a job and pay him back.

* * *

And so on the last Saturday in October they had been married by the assistant minister of the First Methodist Church. Helen had asked Lynn to be her only attendant, and Dan asked Jim Parker, an Eastern Captain who had taken Dan under his wing when he had first gone to Washington, to fly down from D. C. and be the best man. Jim, forty and still a fine figure of a man, was a physical fitness nut who had persuaded Dan to join a health spa and gotten him into a skydiving club back in 1966. Helen's friends Alma and Juanita came, plus Jim's wife Ellen, and Dan's two best friends from The Landmark, Alan Saxon and Rod Kerry.

For their honeymoon they flew to New Orleans and spent four delightful days at the Royal Orleans Hotel. It was another new and exciting experience for Helen. Dan got the biggest kind of thrill out of showing her the town. He loved New Orleans with its quaint shops, its abundance of fine restaurants, and its different nightlife. He knew all the fun places to go, the fun things to do. She loved it too and when it came time to go home, she didn't want to leave.

She had bought quite an extensive new wardrobe for her trousseau and therefore, in the interest of economy, he had not bought her an engagement ring. They had gone to Meier and Berkley on Peachtree Street and picked out a simple wedding band of white gold and he had promised her an engagement diamond later, when his finances had a chance to heal.

Dan didn't want her to know about the fifteen thousand dollars he had stashed away in a savings account. He had started saving when he was in the Air Force and had managed to put something aside every month. He was making eighteen thousand a year now at Eastern and had saved more in the last two years than he had in all the years previous. His car was paid for as well as the furniture in his apartment. He could have taken the money out of savings and bought the diamond, but he didn't want to spoil her, giving her everything at once.

She was as good as her word about getting a job. The week following the honeymoon she went to work as hostess and relief cashier at the Hickory House Restaurant on Piedmont. She was beaming with pride when she brought her first paycheck home and gave it to him. It was only sixty-five dollars after deductions, but she was inordinately proud of it and so was he.

And so a new phase of Dan's life had begun and he was initiated into a contentment so egregious, a happiness so replete, it seemed that all life before had been a dream, a two dimensional play of shadows, half-remembered and having no bearing in the real world. Nor was he concerned with the future for he saw it only as a blissful continuation of today, an endless now, caught and held.

He marveled at the unique beauty of her body and during the long hours they spent together in bed he explored it minutely with eyes and fingers and tongue. Realizing that his body was less than perfect, he accelerated his physical fitness program at the Palm Springs and European Health Spa and watched his diet carefully until eventually his body too was exceptional.

Their lovemaking transcended anything he had known before. Her clinging, wanting kisses triggered a wild inexhaustible enthusiasm for sex he could hardly bear. Her body was warm and moist and deliciously sweet smelling and its silken touch against his own was so soft, so delicate it filled him with an unquenchable thirst, a need that no amount of sex could satisfy. The pleasure, the elation, the pure joy he felt, were indiscernibly sweet. At times when the sapphire blue of her eyes would darken to a near violet and she seemed far away, he would be overcome by a terrified bewilderment, an unbelieving wonder that he could be so blessed. For he had never before recognized how barren his life was, how lonely his existence had been, not until now. This realization would stun him, threaten to tear the fabric of his reality, but then, as he lay back in wonderment and peace with Helen's soft, sweet-smelling hair resting lightly against his shoulder, the anguish would fade and he would pass into a state of perfect happiness, feeling it roll over him in gentle waves. And he would love her with the passion of a drowning man clinging to a scrap of floating timber in a desolate sea.

He found new corners of himself, great sweetness and great tenderness. And eventually he became so enraptured he no longer needed to touch her in that fervid, compulsive way, but only to look at her: moving across a room, brushing her hair, or standing at the window. And she would turn and he would see the tenderness and gratitude flood her eyes and the contented smile of a woman radiant with love.

For there was no doubt she was also surfeit with happiness. She seemed to adore him, bringing him little presents and crazy cards, cooking for him and keeping the apartment neat and spotless, the way he liked it.

She was a good cook, not a gourmet or fancy cook, but a kitchen magician who could turn the simplest dishes into fare fit for the Gods. He had never liked liver and hadn't cared much for fish, but she could fix both in delightful ways that pampered his pallet and made him ask for second servings. Her homemade biscuits were so light and fluffy they would literally melt in his mouth and he had to restrain himself or he would eat an entire plate of them. And yet at first, eating her cooking he lost weight and felt better, more energetic and alive than he had felt in years.

Her working created some problems with the car. Since he had to be at the airport before ten and she went to work at ten-thirty, one of them had to get there by public transportation. He usually walked up to the Marriott and caught their airport bus, but it meant leaving an hour earlier than would have been necessary if he drove, an hour he could otherwise spend with her. When he got back the following afternoon she would be at work so he would have to ride the bus home. She got off at eight-thirty in the evening but she was also off from two until four and she would use that time to come home and make preparations for their evening meal. When she got in she'd finish it up and they'd enjoy an unhurried dinner, swapping stories of the day's happenings.

After a month of this he decided they could afford a second car. He didn't tell her what he was thinking, but one Saturday when he was off he took her to work, then went by Boomershine Pontiac on Spring Street and picked out a sporty Lemans coupe he knew she would like. It was a burnt orange color with a black vinyl top and interior, mag wheels, air conditioning and AM-FM radio. Quickly negotiating a deal, he gave a check for a deposit. The salesman promised to have it ready later that afternoon so after he had taken her back to work at four, he took a cab over and picked it up. He gave another check for the balance due but asked the salesman to hold it until he could go to his bank on Monday morning and make some arrangements. He could take the money out of his savings, but he thought he'd rather finance it. He was sure his bank would be willing to handle it for him.

She was waiting outside under the porch when he drove up that evening. She didn't recognize him at first in the new car and he had to blow the horn at her twice before she came over. When she saw him and realized what was going on she was shocked, thrilled, electrified.

"Where did you get this?" she exclaimed excitedly, jumping around like a nine-year-old kid on Christmas morning. "You didn't buy it did you? Not just like that . . . on the spur of the moment?"

He felt his own happiness choke him as he laughed at her animated exhilaration. To him it was worth the price of the car just to see her so happy. In a fever of excitement she raved on and on about how surprised she was. They rode around in it for what seemed like hours and in a maelstrom of passion she kept telling him how much she loved it and loved him for buying it. It was to be her car and she decided right then to name it Mauldene. He didn't know where she got the name, but Mauldene stuck.

That had happened earlier this month. He knew she wouldn't be expecting a big Christmas present after him buying her the car, but once or twice she had said something about not having an engagement ring, so he was going to buy her one for Christmas. He had withdrawn a thousand dollars from his savings account yesterday and this afternoon he was going to Tiffany's in New York and pick it out.

That was the reason he was sitting around thinking about hijacking this morning. It would be hell to get hijacked and loose this thousand dollars or to buy the ring and have it taken away. But he couldn't sit around worrying about it. Laying his paper aside, he went off to the bedroom to finish getting ready, leaving Helen to clean up the breakfast dishes and forgetting about the subject of hijacking for ransom.

And they didn't get hijacked. The flight that day was routine, landing at La Guardia on schedule. Dan had arranged for another pilot to take his place on the flight home today and the flight back tomorrow so he could spend the night in New York. Bidding goodbye to the other members of the crew, he took a cab into Manhattan. Inching along in heavy traffic waiting to cross the Tri-Borough Bridge he began to feel the excitement of New York. As always the grubby, hustling city had the ability to delight and impress him. It was a blustery day with the sun, dull and tarnished, glowing dimly through a high cloud cover.

At the Americana he checked in and left his things before hurrying across town to Fifth Avenue and Tiffany's. He was caught up now in the hustle and bustle of the city at Christmas time. New Yorkers were always at their best this time of year with everyone scurrying here and there, each bent on his or her own errand. The stores were full of people and the rudeness the natives often displayed was muted. As he pushed along through the crowds of holiday shoppers he couldn't help but reflect on how wonderful life was. He had a beautiful wife, a good job that he enjoyed, and money to burn. Well, not exactly money to burn, but enough to buy his wife something special for Christmas.

Tiffany's was crowded and he had to wait sometime before a salesman could help him. When he told the man what he wanted, a one to one-and-a-half carat stone in a solitaire setting, he was shown several impressive stones and settings. It took him close to an hour to make a decision. He was not given to grand gestures, either in thought or action, and he wanted this ring to be something special, unique and beautiful, that Helen could wear as a talisman, a daily reminder of his love.

The diamond he settled on was just over a carat and would look dazzling in the white gold mounting he chose. It came to nine hundred and eighty-six dollars with the tax and the salesman said he could pick it up the next morning. Today was Friday and he would be returning to Atlanta the next afternoon. He went ahead and paid for it because he didn't want to carry all that money around.

He returned to Atlanta that Saturday afternoon and then flew his regular schedule on Sunday and Monday so he could have Tuesday and Wednesday, the 24th and 25th, Christmas Eve and Christmas day, off.

Helen had to work the ten to two schedule on the 24th but the restaurant was closed on Christmas Eve. Before she got home Dan placed the small package with the ring partially hidden under the tree along with two other gifts for her. They dined out that evening at The Diplomat on Spring Street. Dressed in their finest they enjoyed a memorable meal in the soft candlelight. The polished silverware gleamed, the crystal sparkled, the white tablecloth and napery glowed. They sipped very dry martinis then relished a bottle of fine Merlot with their Chateaubriand. The waiter was especially attentive; the wine flowed. After a flaming dessert, they tarried over cocktails of white crème de menthe, basking in the rich ambience of the opulent restaurant. By the time they returned to the apartment they were both feeling giddy, full of Christmas cheer.

They had planned to wait until Christmas morning to open their gifts but now both were too excited to put it off. In addition to the ring Dan had bought Helen a white negligee and an umbrella. Both were wrapped in oversized boxes making it impossible to guess what they were.

She opened the negligee first. It took her several minutes with all the boxes and wrappings. When she finally extracted it she was tickled pink and made him wait while she ran to the bedroom and put it on. She came back modeling it, a vision in white, and instructed him to open the next package. It turned out to be a new piece of luggage, a large Hartmann attaché case. She had bought if for him to use as an overnight bag. It was large enough to take a suit, shirt, pajamas and a shaving kit.

Then it was her turn again and she opened the second package from him, the umbrella. He laughed and told her she might need it waiting at the bus stop on her way to work. She had complained about needing one a few weeks previously, but that was before he had bought the Mauldene car for her.

Opening his second package Dan discovered a suit, a grayish green single-breasted flannel with a vest. It wasn't what he would have selected, but it was nice and he thanked her with a hug and a kiss.

So then there appeared to be nothing left under the tree.

"How about some cake and lime sherbet?" she asked, never thinking he might have something else for her. "I baked a chocolate cake this afternoon."

"That sounds good," he murmured unobtrusively as she got up and started to the kitchen. "I believe I'll have a cup of coffee too. Oh wait, here's another present under the tree you must have overlooked."

Almost to the kitchen door, she turned sharply and looked back. When she saw the tiny package she almost knocked him over reaching for it.

"Dan, you foolish man," she exclaimed loudly. "What have you done now?" She tore the package open, slipped the ring on her finger and began to wave it around as she admired it. "Dan, it's gorgeous. And it's from Tiffany's! Dan you shouldn't. Where did you get the money?"

He didn't get a chance to answer as she grabbed him, wrestled him to the floor and laid kiss after kiss on him. "Oh Dan, you silly fool, I love you!" she shrieked between kisses. He thought she might rape him right there but then he wasn't fighting back very hard. You can't rape the willing.

"Here, here, stop that you silly woman," he countered laughing. "I'll buy you anything I like. And you let me worry about the money. After all, I'm the boss around here aren't I?"

"Oh yes Dan," she said, still kissing on him passionately, her eyes wide like big marbles rolling about and glistening like they had a coat of shellac on them. "Anything you say Dan. You're just too good to me. What have I done to deserve you and all this happiness?"

"Stop this weeping woman. Get me some food." He said gruffly in a mocking manner. "I'm just as happy as you. Now stop or you'll have me doing it too."

And indeed he was happy. Looking back later, he thought that Christmas was the high point of his marriage, of his life.

* * *

New Year's Eve had been fun too.

John Sweet, a pilot friend from Miami was in town and had a suite at the Regency Hyatt House. He invited them to come to a small party there beginning at ten that evening. It was a swinging crowd of attractive young people including Alan, Ken, David and John from the Landmark and several other flyers and their wives and girlfriends. Previously Helen had never been entirely at ease around Dan's friends, she had always been shy and unsure of herself. But this night was different. After a few drinks she loosened up and became just one of the gang. By midnight everyone was high and enjoying themselves thoroughly.

Just before twelve they went out on the balcony overlooking Peachtree Street. Cars were crawling along slowly in both directions like a huge herd of bugs. It was warm and there were several convertibles with their tops down. A police car, its blue light winking steadily, had stopped down the block. People in the hotel were throwing things off the balconies; confetti and toilet paper streamers came floating past.

"Dan you big beautiful man, I love you," she sighed affectionately as she snuggled next to him.

"I love you too Baby. Let's hope 1969 is as good a year for us."

"It will be Dan. I just know it will. You wait and see. Kiss me Dan. Let's start the New Year right!"

They stayed out on the balcony for another half hour embracing and watching the spectacle. On the stroke of midnight several firecrackers were thrown and someone on a lower floor fired off a Roman candle. The bright bursts threw flashes of green, yellow and red on the streams of cars inching along below, blowing their horns. It was an exciting time.

Dan couldn't recall any period in his life more free from strain than the early months of 1969. Nuptial happiness and a pleasant work routine seduced him into a complacent lethargy.

The lease on their apartment at the Landmark was up at the end of February and they had already decided to look for a bigger place. Dan wanted to buy a house. Ever since he had left home for the Air Force he had lived in furnished rooms or small apartments, and now that he was married and making good money, he wanted a house. It didn't have to be large, but it did have to be nice. Helen said she would be satisfied with a larger apartment.

They started looking in January. A lot of airline people lived in East Point and College Park, two suburban cities on the southwest side of Atlanta near the airport, and they looked first at several houses in that area. But Helen said she didn't want to move that far from downtown. Even though she didn't have a lot of friends in the city, the ones she had all lived on or near the north side and she preferred that area. Dan also liked that part of town but there was a problem. He had calculated that they could afford a purchase price of thirty-five to forty thousand dollars. On a forty thousand dollar house the down payment and closing costs would run about nine thousand and the payment around two hundred fifty dollars per month, about what he had been paying in rent. But in the areas they preferred, the only houses in that price range were older homes that would need extensive remodeling.

If they were willing to go out northeast, into DeKalb County, they might find something suitable in their price range, but here Dan balked about the location. He had to drive to work at the airport, and he didn't want to get much further away than he was now. The suburbs northeast of the city were too far out.

It was the last of January before they finally settled on something. They had just about given up on the idea of buying when they found a house they both liked. It was on Myrtle in midtown, a lovely street lined with great trees that would shade it in warm weather, and while the houses there were old, they were all in a good state of repair. This house had been remodeled by the present owner and he had done a very commendable job. It had a new kitchen with built-in cabinets and modern appliances plus central air conditioning with plenty of capacity. The owner was a wealthy bachelor who did a lot of entertaining, and the house was laid out well for that. It had a large living room and dining room, a small study, and a large enclosed back porch that overlooked the nicely landscaped backyard. There was only one bedroom but it was large with lots of closet space and a spacious bathroom adjacent. The study had once been a second bedroom and there was a second bath adjoining it. Dan and Helen liked the arrangement of the rooms and the way the house was decorated. The living room, dining room and study were carpeted in an avocado green plush and had harmonizing draperies. The bedroom had a shag carpet and was done in earth tones with accents of orange and white.

The lot sloped off in the rear and the backyard was on the basement level. Stairs led down to the basement and there was enough unfinished area there to add a couple of more bedrooms and a bath. A single garage opened off an alley in the back.

They liked everything about it except the price, fifty thousand dollars. The agent said he thought they could get an eighty percent loan but that still meant a down payment of ten thousand plus twelve hundred dollars in closing costs. Dan was also somewhat concerned about it only having one bedroom. That wasn't a problem for them now, but he knew it made for a limited market if they decided to resell it. There was space to add more bedrooms, but that meant more money.

Dan was more enthused about buying a house than Helen. She was interested and was quick to point out things she didn't like, but he had yet to see her get excited about anything they had seen. The more they looked, the more Dan decided he wanted to buy a house. But she remained noncommittal. She wasn't excited about the house on Myrtle Street, but said she liked it and would leave it up to him to decide whether or not they could afford it.

It was a Friday, the last day of January, when he finally reached a decision. He'd make an offer of forty thousand for the house and if the man took it he'd have what he wanted at a price they could afford to pay. If not, then they'd just find the bigger apartment and forget about buying until he had more money saved.

After lunch Dan called the real estate agent and told him he wanted to make the offer. The man was not enthusiastic, but said he'd present it and try to persuade the seller to take it. He filled out the forms and brought them by right away for a signature.

Later that same afternoon Helen came home bubbling with excitement. "Dan, I found a house today that I really like," she said fervently. "I was riding through Ansley Park a little while ago and I noticed a sign. It's a brand new development just off Piedmont near the Driving Club. There're a whole bunch of townhouses there but the agent said they were nearly all sold. The grounds are just beautiful and they're new, not something that's been remodeled."

"How much money was it?" Dan asked, interested but not showing any enthusiasm.

"I don't remember exactly but the lady said the down payment would be only sixty-two hundred dollars and when I told her you flew for Eastern she said she was sure you could qualify for the loan. I've got her number Dan and she said we could come back and see it anytime."

"I've made an offer on the other house, the one on Myrtle Street," he said, dismayed that he might have done the wrong thing. "I guess we ought to wait and see what happens on that before we look any further."

"I know you'll like it Dan," She importuned. "It's a townhouse with three floors. The basement has a garage in part of it and a big den and half bath. On the main floor it has a living room that opens out onto a terrace and a nice new kitchen with a breakfast area, and a large dining room. Upstairs there are three bedrooms and two more baths. It's also got an attic but it wasn't finished and I didn't go up there."

"It sounds nice but it's probably out of our price range."

"Dan you've got to at least look at it. It's the first thing I've seen that I really like. I think the fact that it's new is why I like it so much. All these old houses give me the creeps."

"Sure, I'll look at it. But I thought you liked the Myrtle Street house all right?"

"It's okay Dan. It's pretty and I like the way it's decorated, but it's still an old house in a mixed neighborhood. This townhouse is in a much nicer section and it's only a few blocks further out."

"You make it sound awfully good. When do you want to take me to see it?"

"Could we go tonight after we eat?"

"I guess so. Go ahead and call the lady and see if we can come tonight about nine-thirty."

Later, while they were eating dinner, the agent on the Myrtle Street house called. He said the owner had turned Cooper's offer down cold. He wouldn't even make any counter offer other than the fifty thousand he had been asking all along. Dan thanked him and hung up. Well, that was that. After what Helen had said earlier he wasn't too sorry. He didn't want to buy anything she didn't like. Maybe this townhouse was worth considering.

The night was cold and clear, the temperature near freezing, the sky an electrical blue-black with the stars hung low. They drove out Piedmont and turned onto Fifteenth Street. Helen was driving and she circled around and through the project first so Dan could see the entire development. It was built in a square with townhouses on all four sides. The drive entered the enclosed area on the southwest corner and circled to the left circumscribing a small, beautifully landscaped park in the center. The units on the north, east and south sides fronted this drive and faced the park. Those on the west faced a side street and their backs overlooked the square. They were all similar, being of a two-story Georgian design with two garages at or just below street level on either side of brick steps leading up to the main entrance on the first floor. Dormer windows protruded from the roof on the attic level. It was a handsome development, not showy or grand, but comfortable and solid, attractive and impressive.

Stopping the Lemans in front of the southern-most unit on the west side, Helen explained that this was the model where the agent lived. The only other unsold unit was three doors down on the same side.

The agent, a heavily fleshed, auburn-haired woman of about fifty with flashing blue eyes and a toothy smile was waiting for them. She introduced herself as Mrs. Court and first showed them through the unit in which she lived. She explained that while it was for sale, it was priced $10,000 higher than the other unit because it was an end unit and had several special features.

Dan found that he was even more impressed than he had been from outside. The completed unit was a truly magnificent home, elegant and luxurious with great attention paid to detail. Some of the rooms were small, but overall there was plenty of space. He liked the arrangement of the rooms also. He could use the room in the basement for a workshop or hobby room, and fit out one of the smaller bedrooms on the second floor as a study.

Three doors over the other unsold unit was completed except for the carpet and painting. Mrs. Courts told them it was left unfinished so the buyer would have the opportunity to pick the colors and carpet.

The layout was just as Helen had described it and was almost identical with the end unit. On the back the living room opened out onto a splendid terrace which was walled-in for privacy. The condominiums on the west side faced the street and thus the terrace was adjacent to the square.

It wasn't until they had looked it over thoroughly that Dan got up enough courage to ask the price. Mrs. Courts quickly explained that they were asking sixty-two thousand for this unit, but that ninety percent financing was available which meant that a down payment of sixty-two hundred dollars and closing costs of twenty-four hundred and eighty dollars were all that was required. The balance was payable over thirty years making the payments approximately three hundred seventy-five per month.

"See Dan," Helen put in, "it won't even take the ten thousand down, and I know we can afford an extra one-twenty-five a month. I'm bringing home nearly three hundred dollars a month now."

"Do you really like it that much Baby?"

"I really do Dan. It's beautiful and it's just what I want. Let's buy it."

"When could we move in Mrs. Courts?"

"We'd have to get your credit approved but that shouldn't take more than a week. Then we'll have to finish the painting and put in the carpets. I'm sure you could have it by the first of March and possibly sooner."

Dan wanted to think it over for a few days. He didn't believe in jumping too fast on anything, particularly something that involved so much money. But Helen was so anxious for them to go ahead right then that he had to consider doing so. Also he was tired of looking at houses and pretty well convinced they weren't going to find what they wanted for much less than sixty thousand dollars. What the hell, they did have her income now and he would be getting another raise next October.

"I'll tell you what Mrs. Courts," he said, flinging caution to the winds. "I'll give you sixty thousand for it providing we can get the thirty-year, ninety percent financing and that we can move in by March first."

"Well Mr. Cooper," the woman replied with a broad smile, her big blue eyes sparkling. "I'll have to present your offer to the builders, but I'll be happy to do that first thing in the morning. Now if you'll just come back over to my house we'll fill out the contract."

And so they bought themselves a home in Westchester Square. Mrs. Courts called the next morning and said the builders had accepted their offer. She was proceeding to get the loan approval. In the meantime would he and Mrs. Cooper like to meet with the decorator and select the wall coverings and carpets?

That started a round of conferences with the decorator, a short stout man named Sam Godwin. It seemed that there were certain allowances made for the remaining items, but these only covered painting the rooms in a single color and carpets of a standard quality. The decorator of course had suggestions for a more extensive decorating job and he quickly sold Helen on his ideas. Again Dan reluctantly went along. Since they were going to be living there for a long time they might as well have what they wanted he reasoned. By the time the loan was approved they had authorized the spending of an additional sixteen hundred dollars for special paint, wall paper, and paneling and carpet.

But it was going to be an opulent, breath-taking place. For the main floor they selected a cut pile carpet of top quality in the same shade of avocado they had liked so much in the Myrtle Street house. The drapes in the living room were in pale blue and the furniture they selected for this room combined these shades with hues of white and champagne.

The dining room had the same carpet and drapes. The dining room suite they bought—table, china cabinet and buffet—picked up the green in its finish, and the eight chairs had seats of green and blue stripes in hues that matched those in the carpet and drapes. The walls were papered in expensive green and white flocked wallpaper above the chair rail, and the paneling below was stained a harmonizing shade of pale green.

Upstairs they used a rich brown broadloom in the hall and two spare bedrooms and white shag in the master bedroom. Walnut paneling was added to one of the bedrooms to make it into a study. Draperies in dark rich shades added the quality touch to all the rooms.

The closing was set for Tuesday, February 25th. When they sat down with the attorney and the sellers Dan found out he was also committed for a seventy-five dollar a month fee which went to pay for the upkeep of the common land. The house being a townhouse he automatically had to become a member of the owner's association and contribute his share of the common expenses. In addition he was required to purchase homeowners insurance. With all the extras he had to lay out a little over ten thousand dollars and commit himself to a total monthly payment of four hundred fifty dollars, not counting utilities. He was upset over not being made aware of the clause in the sales contract about the common expense payment, but he couldn't back out now. They were all set to move.

Dan worried about the money but he couldn't remember when he had enjoyed anything more than he enjoyed the move into their new home. Of course Helen enjoyed it also and that added to his pleasure. They had decided to use his living room furniture for the study and his dining room table for the breakfast room. Therefore it was necessary to purchase new living room and dining room furniture and a second bedroom suite. He didn't want to part with any more cash just then so they went to Rich's and established a CCA account and bought the needed furniture. It was a convenient revolving charge plan with a modest monthly payment, but the balance could be paid off at any time. He figured as soon as they got over the cost of moving he could pay it off quickly.

But their expenses didn't stop when they got into the house. It seemed like they only began then. First, they had to buy pictures for the walls. Then they needed bed linens for their new king-size bed. Helen found a gorgeous quilted bedspread with a matching bench that went at the foot of the bed. Dan loved it until he found it cost two hundred and twenty dollars. But it was worth it, having her happy and having their own home. And of course he kept thinking this is all one-time expense.

They moved on the first of March but weren't settled well until late in April. Toward the end of February Helen quit the job at the Hickory House saying she just didn't have time to do all the things necessary to get them settled in the new house and work too. She assured Dan she would go back to work as soon as everything was done.

Other than his concern about the amount of money they were spending, Dan had few worries. His job continued to be interesting and satisfying. The first of February he had bid a different schedule working only three days a week. On Sunday, Tuesday and Thursday he got up at 4 AM to make a 6:30 departure on a 727 flight to New York. They left there at 10:30 flying direct to Miami International. The last leg of the trip back to Atlanta was scheduled out at 3:45 that afternoon and he usually was home and off duty by 6:30. That gave him four days each week to spend with Helen.

It was great fun decorating the house and as soon as they were settled they started having friends over. Helen was such a good cook Dan wanted to show off her culinary skills to his buddies and their wives and girlfriends. He was a little self-conscious about the grandness of the house, but he soon got over that. His friends' praise of his taste in selecting both a wife and a home helped remove any doubts he may have harbored. Almost all of the people who came to visit were his friends. She had a few girl friends over, usually in the afternoons on the days he was working, but she never invited them to dinner. Quite often she would mention going over to visit Lynn or taking Juanita to the doctor, but Dan never saw either of them. Alma, the girl who had been on the trip to Hartford with her, came over several times and raved about the house and how lucky Helen was to have married Dan. Helen seemed a little embarrassed by her company but never discouraged her coming. Dan, on the other hand enjoyed Alma's frank conversation. It was probably the fact that she was always saying nice things about him. Helen never invited her to dinner and when Dan mentioned it she said that Alma probably wouldn't mix well with Dan's friends. Even though she was never condescending, Dan suspected that Helen liked to show off her new house and new husband but really looked down on Alma now. She would occasionally make disparaging remarks about Alma's taste in men.

Dan turned into a real homebody. He almost quit going out at night. When they didn't have friends over he would usually go to bed and watch television. Most nights Helen would join him. Frequently she would run out and get pizza for a late snack or they would have ice cream and cake in bed while they watched the tube. They both gained weight and he started calling her "Pig named Baby."

She retorted by calling him "Hog named Danny." Helen loved to have her back scratched and while they lay in bed and watched television, Dan would scratch by the hour. This frequently got both of them turned on and terminated in an extended bout of love making.

When May came Dan casually suggested that it was about time she went back to work and helped him pay all the monthly bills they now had. She readily agreed, but asked him to let her wait until after the first of June. She hadn't been to Daytona to see her family since they had been married and she wanted to go Memorial Day weekend. He proposed taking a week's vacation and going with her. She didn't offer any objection, but said they'd have to stay at a motel since there was no room at her family's house. Dan put in for his vacation and when he mentioned to some friends that they were planning to go south for the holiday, two of them, David Barnes and

John Bennett, decided to go also. They brought their girlfriends along and everyone got rooms at the Holiday Inn on the beach.

They all drove down together in Dan's Lincoln and because one of the girls didn't get off work until late Friday afternoon, they stopped in Lake City, Florida, that night. They slept late and it was lunch time on Saturday before they reached Daytona. As they were checking in Helen spotted someone she knew. She brought over a bronzed young athlete and introduced him as Carl Chism, an old friend who lived in Tampa but came to Daytona regularly for the holidays. Chism introduced his traveling companion, another good looking young man named Ross Dawson. In the elevator Helen confided that Carl was married but seldom brought his wife with him when he visited Daytona.

That afternoon they had their first fuss. Helen wanted to take the car and go out and see her family. Dan had expected that he would be allowed to go along and meet her father, step-mother and younger brother, but she didn't want him to accompany her.

"I don't understand why you don't want me along," he said warmly. "When we planned the trip you didn't make any objection."

"Dan, honey, it's just that my folks aren't expecting you and I don't want to surprise them."

"Are they expecting you? They do know we're married don't they?"

"Yes, they know we're married," she said testily, her voice strained with exasperation. "But they're not expecting you and I want to wait until they are for you to meet them."

"Well it doesn't make sense," he replied with blatant anger. "It sounds like you are ashamed of me. Is that it?"

"No Dan. I just want to see them first by myself. Maybe you can go out there with me tomorrow."

"They'll know you are coming then. Now let me have the keys Danny and I'll be going."

"Oh, all right," he agreed reluctantly. "What time will you be back?"

"I'm not sure. I'll call if I can't make it for supper."

"Well that's a fine how-do-you-do. I take my vacation, come down here to be with you, and you run off and leave me."

"Please don't be mad at me Dan. I'll be back as soon as I can."

Feeling lonesome and a little foolish, Dan went down and joined the others on the beach for the afternoon. Carl Chism and Ross Dawson were there and he struck up a conversation with them. He learned that they were both employed in the public schools in Tampa. Carl was an assistant principal and Dawson taught high school English. When they found out Helen had gone to visit her family they invited Cooper to join them for dinner in the hotel's dining room.

Initially he turned them down saying he was sure she would be back for dinner and he couldn't make a commitment. But when she called about five to say she was eating with her folks he changed his mind. Dialing Carl in their room, he arranged to meet them downstairs at seven.

For a time he managed to forget his chagrin at Helen's deserting him and enjoyed himself. Over dinner Carl, who was a husky six-footer with a booming voice, dominated the conversation. Despite his piercing blue eyes and forceful manner he was not overbearing and Dan found him stimulating. Ross seemed mesmerized by his companion and contributed little to their discussions, being content to sit and listen.

But when Dan returned to the room after dinner and found that Helen still hadn't come in, he was extremely vexed. He resented the fact that she didn't want him to meet her family and was frustrated by the way she had just gone off and deserted him. David and John had rented a car, taken their girls, and gone off somewhere on their own. So he was left alone in the motel room with nothing to do. Impulsively he decided to leave a note in case she came in, go downstairs, and have a couple of drinks in the bar.

He was on his second Wild Turkey and water when Ross Dawson joined him at the bar. Ross looked to be in his late twenties and was attractive in a rugged masculine way. He had long chestnut brown hair which he kept neatly combed, and porcelain blue eyes inset in a chiseled countenance. His short body was muscular and he moved in a quick purposeful way. Despite his lack of conversation at dinner, Dan had found Dawson open and friendly and had taken a liking to him.

"What are you doing here all by yourself?" the younger man asked good naturedly.

"I'm not sure," Cooper replied ruefully. "Helen didn't say when she'd get in and I'm at a loose end. What happened to Carl?"

"He had a date and probably won't be back tonight. I'm just fixing to go out and hit a few bars. Why don't you come along?"

"If you don't mind I think I will. There's no use spending my vacation holed up in my room just because my wife is out visiting. You won't mind if I tag along for a while and then come home early will you?"

"No, come on. Anytime you want to come back just say so."

Hitting the hotel bars first they found them all busy, bustling with the holiday crowd. After a few drinks Dan began to forget about Helen and enjoy himself. It was then that Dawson suggested they go over to a club on US 1 called the Yum Yum Tree. He explained that a lot of gay people hung out there but you didn't have to be homosexual to go, and they had a very good show. Dan said it sounded all right to him.

But he wasn't quite ready for the crowd they found there. It was a big place and it was packed to the rafters. About half the crowd were young, good looking men—obviously homosexuals. The other half was a duke's mixture. Among them were a large number of attractive women who appeared to be between eighteen and thirty. Some apparently were dykes since they were holding hands and dancing with other girls. But there were several who definitely didn't appear to be that way. Then they were also quite a few men like Dawson and himself who were older and did not look gay. This group seemed to be clustered around the main bar drinking and watching the others.

The juke box was playing loudly over the frenetic buzz of the crowd. Aretha Franklin was grinding out Chain of Fools. They pushed their way through to a long bar set against the front wall and got a drink. Off to their right as they faced the dance floor was the main bar, a large four-sided affair with men packed three deep around it. At the far end of the building was a stage. The dance floor was just in front of this and had tables on its other three sides. About ten or twelve people, mostly attractive boys with long hair were on the stage dancing. They didn't have partners; they were just doing their own thing. The crowd on the dance floor was back to back and belly to belly as they twisted and gyrated, moving with and against each other as though they were all bound together by invisible strings. A revolving colored spot changed their animated faces from rosy red to livid green to glaring yellow.

Ross motioned Dan to follow and they pushed their way slowly through the churning crowd. He was apparently looking for someone and Dan followed obediently as they worked their way around the edge of the dance floor, finally stopping at a large table near the stage on the left side. Four people were seated there with eight empty chairs. Two comely women in their twenties were at one end and a younger couple at the other. Ross started a conversation with the two women.

"Hi Dora," he said, talking loudly in order to be heard over the raucous music. "I didn't know you were in town. You mind if we sit down?"

"No, go right ahead," replied the one on the right. She had long black hair parted in the middle and a lean, aristocratic face with large brown eyes under arched brows. "Who's your friend?"

"This is Dan Cooper. Dan, Dora Sears. She's a school teacher from Tampa like me."

"That's right Dan," she said smiling pleasantly. "Another school teacher who's gotten out of town to play. This is Janice Morris and that's Terry and Janie down there."

Dan nodded and said hello to everyone feeling a little strange. Dawson slid into one of the chairs and continued his conversation. "I came over with Carl Chism but he's out on a date somewhere. Dan's wife is off visiting relatives so we are just out bumming around."

"Just make yourself at home; we've got room for two more. Do you know Tommy Irwin and his lover, Bob Smith? They are out there somewhere dancing."

Dan sat down next to Dawson and tuned the conversation out. When the dance ended they were joined by two androgynous young men in their middle twenties who were introduced as Tommy and Bob. They took seats on the other side of the table, opposite the dance floor. A limp-wristed waiter came by and took everyone's order for fresh drinks.

Dan sat quietly watching the noisy activity that swirled about them. He couldn't remember when he'd seen a place quite so packed. It was almost midnight and the crowd was still growing. Except for the people on the stage no one had room to dance but somehow they shifted around and up and down with great gusto in the psychedelic glare of the revolving spot.

He was beginning to feel the effects of the liquor. He'd had about a half-dozen drinks, his usual limit. But he was enjoying himself and couldn't see any harm in one or two more, particularly since he wasn't driving. He felt a little out of place here with all these gay people, but it had taken his mind off of his fight with Helen and that was good. One thing was sure; everyone was having a good time.

"How about dancing with me?"

Coming out of his reverie he realized she was speaking to him. It was the girl named Janice. "Sure, I'd love to," he answered quickly, wondering what he was getting into.

They pushed their way onto the crowded floor as the juke box thundered out Choo Choo Train. She was a pretty girl with short brown hair, a clear complexion and a triangular shaped face that produced long dimples when she smiled. She threw herself into the dance with wild abandon and Dan found himself watching her with envy. He was a good dancer but nothing to compare with Janice.

They were leaving the dance floor when he caught sight of Carl Chism sitting at a table on the other side of the dance floor with his arm around a vapid, dark-haired, effeminate young man in his early twenties. Dan was shocked and stopped and looked again to be sure he wasn't mistaken. When Janice saw where he was looking, and sensed his dismay she smiled broadly and urged him to come along.

"You didn't know Carl swings both ways did you?" she said knowingly with a big grin.

"No," Dan replied with bewilderment. "I thought Helen told me he was married."

"Oh he is. And back in Tampa he's straight as an arrow. But when he comes over here he lets it all hang out."

"Well he sure had me fooled," Dan confided, shaking his head in disbelief.

They sat down and ordered another round of drinks. He didn't know how the waiter got through the crowd but he was keeping them well supplied. Other people drifted up and chatted, then drifted away. Janie now sat on his right and they carried on a sporadic conversation while he pondered the complexities of human nature. The noise of the music was so great it was difficult to be heard without screaming and this prevented them from becoming better acquainted.

Dan's attention was caught by a young blond girl sitting at the next table. That is, she was sitting there between dances. The minute a tune she liked came on, she would jump up and rush to the stage to dance alone to the driving music. Although she was a little shorter than Helen, this gamine reminded Dan of his wife in many respects. She was wearing a dazzling white outfit: white pullover shirt, white shorts, white knee socks, and tennis shoes. A beautiful, beautiful girl, her clear cheeks were flushed from dancing, red lips open, blue eyes clear and sparkling. And that long blond hair, bouncing sensuously every time she moved.

"Do you know the blond girl there dancing by herself on the stage?" Dan asked Janice.

"No, I don't really know her," she replied in a breathless voice. "But her name is Nicole and I've been told that while she's as beautiful as the beach at sunset, she's as ruthless as a hurricane. She's from Jacksonville and is supposed to have a rich lover."

Intrigued, Dan wondered if her lover was a man or a woman. He was tempted to go over and ask her to dance but she seemed to be having such a good time by herself he decided against it. Everyone here seemed super friendly but in spite of all the liquor he had consumed, he still felt extremely shy and out of place.

Just before the show started they were joined by another party, four guys who looked like aging incorrigibles, the bottom four students in the remedial class at reform school. But after Ted, Tom, Jim and Richard had been introduced, Janice told him that two of them were medical students, one was the high school football coach where she taught, one owned a service station, and they were all gay as geese. Dan shook his head in disbelief.

It was nearly one o'clock when the show finally got underway. There was such a crowd by then that about a hundred people sat on the dance floor. The first act was a blond named Allison doing an old Eartha Kitt number. Dan thought at first she was actually singing but then realized it was only pantomime. It really was Eartha Kitt singing and you had to watch Allison closely to realize she was only mouthing words into a dead microphone.

She got a big round of applause, then introduced Rhonda, a big girl who was obviously a man—no woman had shoulders like that. She did a comedy act that was entertaining, and then gave up the stage to a pair of buxom ladies who sang "Bosom Buddies" from *Mame*. By this time Dan was thoroughly drunk and enjoying himself immensely.

"Stop . . . . In the name of love . . ." The familiar lyrics of the Supremes hit introduced the finale, an act dubbed Daytona's Own Diana Ross and the Supremes. It wasn't the real Diana Ross of course, but the three willowy black girls in clinging dresses certainly looked a lot like the originals. And their pantomime and movements were rhythmic and natural, an extremely good imitation of the stars they impersonated. When they swung into a medley of Supremes favorites the crowd went wild. Dan could easily have believed that the three on stage were singing if he hadn't known the music well enough to recognize the songs they were doing as Supremes recordings. The Supremes had always been one of his favorite groups, and

Helen loved them too. He found himself singing along on many of the numbers. They must have sung for forty minutes and when they closed by singing, "There's a place for us, somewhere a place for us," it brought down the house. Dan found the lyrics so powerful they were cloying. A lump came in his throat and he found he was crying, soundless, wordless, unassaugable tears as he remembered that he and Helen had listened to this very song on the way back from the mountains last fall, the day he had asked her to marry him. Cogent emotions washed over him. Missing her and wishing she was here to enjoy the show with him, he was imbued with love and transfixed with longing. Later, looking back, he wondered what it was about that show that had touched him so deeply. It was only pantomime done by three black drag queens in a dumpy club, but their poignant performance had ravaged and devastated him emotionally leaving him emasculated and wrung out. He thought it must have been a reaction caused by his argument with Helen, a recrimination of sorts. The song reminded him of how much he loved her and the fact they had argued was like sandpaper roughening his nerves, ravaging his mind. For a while he had forgotten her and their argument, but only for a little while. She was too much a part of him now to be forgotten long

The Daytona Supremes sang two encores to thunderous applause and it was well after two o'clock when the show finally ended. Dan indicated to Dawson that he was ready to go and they bid goodnight to Dora, Janice and the others.

"I hope you had a good time," Dawson said as they drove away.

"Yes I did," Dan replied honestly." "It was my first visit to a club like that, but I enjoyed it. I was a little uneasy at first but everyone was so friendly I got over it. And the show was very good. I really enjoyed the Supremes."

"They were good weren't they? I had heard about them but this was the first time I had seen them. We don't usually get anyone that good at the clubs in Tampa."

"Do you have clubs like the Yum Yum Tree in Tampa?"

"We have three where mostly gay people hang out, but we don't have anything as big as the Yum Yum."

"I'm surprised there are that many gay clubs."

"Yes, most straight people don't realize how many there are. They don't advertise except by word of mouth. There are three in Tampa that are almost exclusively gay and two or three others that are mixed, one of which has drag shows on weekends."

Dan wanted to ask Ross if he was a homosexual but couldn't bring himself to do it. He was sure the answer was yes, and he felt that Dawson wanted him to ask. It would probably be an opening to a lot of explanations that Dan didn't want to hear. He didn't have anything against queers and he had enjoyed himself tonight with Ross and his friends, it just wasn't his bag. And so he kept his thoughts to himself as they drove slowly back to the Holiday Inn.

When he got in it was nearly 3 AM. Helen was curled up fast asleep. Dan wondered how long she had been there. He felt bad then at having stayed out so late. He should have come home before they went to the Yum Yum Tree.

The next morning she gave him a hard time about staying out all night but did it in that good natured way that let him know she really wasn't mad. They slept until noon and upon awakening made love with passion and tenderness. Afterward they had breakfast sent up to the room, then joined David, John and their girls around the pool. Helen made no mention of her family and when John asked casually how she found them, she made some vague comment that left Dan with the impression she didn't want to talk about it. He didn't bring it up again. He had decided that if she didn't want him to meet them, then that was her business and he wouldn't insist. With that cloud removed from the horizon, their relations were back on their usual high level.

That night they all had dinner together at Martin's Steak House and afterward went to a party on the beach south of town. A bright three-quarter moon bathed the beach and the sea in white ethereal light. They drank a few beers and danced in the sand, thoroughly enjoying themselves. Later Dan and Helen slipped off amongst the dunes and made love to the drowsy hum of insects and the distant sound of breakers on the shore. By the time they were ready to start home on Monday, the unpleasantness of Saturday was forgotten.

Back in Atlanta, Helen kept her promise about getting another job. She began looking that Tuesday and on the following Monday she started at Sears as a clerk in the shipping department of the catalog sales store on Ponce de Leon Avenue. The pay was a little more than she had made at the Hickory House and the hours were better. She went to work at eleven in the morning and got off at seven in the evening. This allowed her to get home for supper with Dan on nights when he was in town. He was very pleased and let her know it.

Around the nation that summer was not as chaotic as the previous one yet it was one of momentous events. The Vietnam War raged on despite Nixon's election, tearing the country apart. In June a group of drag queens routed New York's Finest from a gay bar on Christopher Street in what became known as the Stonewall riots, and the gay political movement was born. In July Buss Aldrin and Neil Armstrong planted the American flag on the moon, culminating ten years of escalating triumphs for the United States in the infinity of space. And the same week Teddy Kennedy lost his way leaving a party on Chappaquiddick Island and Mary Jo Kopechne lost her life. Four hundred thousand young people gathered for two days in the rain at Woodstock, New York, for a music festival that would make history, and actress Sharon Tate, her unborn baby and four other people were cruelly murdered in a posh house hidden in the Hollywood Hills.

But it was a happy summer for Dan and Helen. He continued to fly the three-days-a-week schedule and even then he was home most nights by seven-thirty. She threw herself enthusiastically into her new job at Sears and found she truly enjoyed working there. The work was not difficult, she didn't have to get up early, and she was always home at a convenient time. She usually cooked supper after she got in.

On the Friday night of the Fourth of July weekend they dressed and went out on the town. After dinner at Fan and Bill's, they went to the Sans Souci and ran into several people they knew including Dan's old neighbors from the Landmark, Alan and Rod, who were there with twin sisters named Ruby and Sapphire. When the bar closed at two they invited about twenty people to come home with them and continue the party there. Everybody came and the merry-making continued until almost five in the morning.

The Sunday night the astronauts made their moon walk Dan and Helen invited a dozen people over to party and watch it on television. Everyone gathered in the master bedroom, sitting on the bed and on the floor, to see Neil Armstrong step down onto the moon.

Having enjoyed themselves so much on these occasions, Dan and Helen decided to have a big party to celebrate Helen's twenty-second birthday on August 23rd. She made a list of those she wanted to invite and Dan was surprised when he saw they were all people she had met through him. There was no one from her past or from her job.

The birthday party was a big success. More than fifty people showed up. They had told everyone not to bring presents but many did. Helen opened them all at once around midnight. She had several very nice gifts including a gossamer chiffon negligee in a peach color from the Balmers, a big bottle of perfume from Alan Saxon, and a lovely pearl necklace from John Bennett and his girl, Cecile. In addition she received a number of welcome gifts for the house; bookends, a collection of china mushrooms, serving dishes, and an ice bucket shaped like a big beer mug. No one had given her a shower or any parties at the time of their wedding, and they had received only a few wedding presents, so it was all a big thrill.

Their house proved to be a great place to give a party. The weather was warm but not sultry, and they threw open the doors to the terrace and let the crowd drift in and out. They had the stereo connected to speakers outside and after the crowd departed they sat out there reminiscing and listening to B. J. Thomas singing about being hooked on a feeling.

"Dan, it's been a wonderful party," she sighed as she gave him a bear hug.

"You're right, it really has," he agreed. "I didn't realize giving a party could be so much fun until we had that crowd over July Fourth. We'll have to do it again. I wish they hadn't all felt they had to bring presents."

"I don't mind that at all," she chortled. "I don't know when I've enjoyed anything as much as I did opening those presents. So many nice things! But I didn't notice anything from you?"

"Well I thought the party might be present enough," he said craftily. "Were you expecting something else?"

"Oh Danny, you don't need to get me something else. The party was really great and it's all I need. But I was kind of hoping you might buy me one thing I wanted."

"Okay, come on. Out with it.," he teased. "I know you have something in mind. You might as well tell me what it is."

"Well I just happened to be driving by the Cadillac place last week and they had this gorgeous white convertible in the window. You know white is my color and I just had to go in and look at it. There was this nice young salesman named Stu Ellis and he showed it to me and told me all about it. He looked at Mauldene and said he'd be glad to trade. He said you wouldn't have to put any money down, just start over on the payments."

"Did he say how much the payments would be?"

"He said they probably wouldn't be much more than you are paying now. But I don't need it Dan. It was just so pretty and it being my birthday and all, I just thought I'd check in case you did want to buy me something special, something I really wanted."

"I'll tell you what," he said expansively, again disregarding his lifelong habits of frugality. "If that is what you really want, we'll get it. I don't suppose the payments will go up much and you're making good money now. I've always wanted a Cadillac convertible too. And white really is your color. We'll go down Monday and buy it."

And they did. The first thing Monday morning they drove to Capital Automobile and made the trade. It was a grand car with bright red leather upholstery and a white top. The payments did go up, about double what they had been on the Lemans, but by the time Dan found that out it was too late to back out.

On October 1st an AWOL Marine, Lance Corporal Raphael Minichiello of Seattle, Washington, commandeered a TWA Boeing 707 at gunpoint on a domestic flight between San Francisco and Los Angeles and forced the crew to fly him to Denver. There the nineteen-year-old who had escaped the previous day while en route to a court marital at Camp Pendleton, California, allowed thirty-nine passengers and three stewardesses to debark. With the Captain, First Officer, Flight Engineer and one stewardess as hostages, the plane continued to New York's Kennedy Airport where FBI agents tried to board. When the skyjacker fired his carbine into the roof of the cockpit and threatened to shoot spectators unless they moved away, the FBI gave up. He permitted two overseas pilots to board, and after refueling stops at Bangor, Maine, and Shannon, Ireland, California Flight 85 landed at Rome's Leonardo da Vinci airport some twenty hours later.

With the airport police chief as hostage at the wheel of a police car, the young marine, a Vietnam veteran decorated for gallantry, headed for the Rome countryside where he was captured a few hours later. Minichiello spent November 1st, his twentieth birthday, in Rome's Queen of Heaven jail. He was indicted in New York for piracy, kidnapping and other offenses, but Italian officials, who held him with charges of their own, were reluctant to give him up. His sixty-nine hundred mile odyssey was the longest and most bizarre skyjacking on record at the time.

PART III

"Raindrops Keep Falling On My Head"

Monday, ***October 20, 1969***

On October 7, 1969, Atlanta elected its first Jewish Mayor, Sam Massell, and its first black Vice Mayor, Maynard Jackson. Their election heralded the dawn of a new era in the south's most progressive city, one that was already known *as The City Too Busy to Hate.*

Meantime Dan and Helen Cooper approached the calamitous period of their lives that began the same month not as an old married couple, safe in their many years of shared experience, but as amorous lovers still drunk with passion and desire, ill prepared for adversity.

Although Helen and Dan had both experienced their share of life's ups and downs, in their pasts the undulations had been small, the highs only briefly removed from the lows. And neither had ever been caught up in such bliss, such complete happiness as they had experienced during the preceding year. Perhaps that bliss, those months of delightful discovery and romantic adventure, had formed the groundwork for real love—that magical stuff from which most lifelong marriages are forged—but Dan and Helen still lacked the perception, the real understanding that comes only with the mutual sharing over time of both triumph and tragedy. Their love had not been tested, either by the winds of adversity or the tides of time. Now suddenly it became subjected to stresses and strains neither had expected nor were prepared to cope with.

The first shock came on this blustery Monday in mid-October. As Cooper drove downtown to the Medical Arts Building, a raw northwest wind swirled the colorful leaves in small tornadoes and lifted the skirts of secretaries scurrying to work along Peachtree Street. Like all Airline Transport Pilots, he was required to undergo two rigid physical examinations each year. Now, reporting to the sixth floor offices of Dr. Norris T. Henderson for this semi-annual chore, Dan had no premonition of the ineluctable string of events which, like a row of dominoes, would be relentlessly set in motion today. Because he had just turned thirty-five, this October for the first time, he would be required to have an electrocardiogram made. But he was not concerned. As far as he knew his health was perfect.

Except for the electrocardiogram, the exam was routine. When the tests were complete Cooper dressed and took a seat in the doctor's drab waiting room where he leisurely flipped through an old issue of *LIFE*. After a short wait the buxom receptionist smiled at him and purred solicitously, "Doctor will see you now."

Dan nodded, returning her smile, and with cheerful abandon, moved into the doctor's private office. Dr. Henderson rose from behind his oversize desk, holding out a large freckled hand. He was a tall solemn man in his late forties who rarely smiled. Why, Dan pondered as he shook the proffered hand, does someone so grim and somber surround himself with such a young and nubile staff.

"Mr. Cooper," the doctor said sonorously. "Have a seat."

"Well Doctor, how'd I check out?" Dan replied with alacrity as he settled into a worn leather chair. "I hope that new blond nurse you have didn't get my blood pressure up over two hundred. She's very unsettling."

"I'm afraid it is a little more serious than that Mr. Cooper," Henderson answered in measured tones. "Although we can find nothing amiss otherwise, the electrocardiogram indicates you have a slight aneurism, what we generally refer to as a heart murmur. It's nothing serious, nothing to worry about medically, but it is disqualifying. I can't reissue your medical certificate, at least not at this point."

"You mean I'm grounded, it's that serious?" Dan asked incuriously, not wanting to believe what he had just heard. For all these years he had trusted the system and it had repaid him in kind. Now suddenly, on this pleasant October morning, he felt betrayed; a terrible premonition seemed to uncoil in his body like a hideous snake abruptly come to life.

"No, I'm not telling you that you can't fly," Dr. Henderson continued his voice a flat monotone. "In fact your present certificate is good until the end of the month and you could probably continue to use it longer as a Second or Third Class Certificate, but I can't issue you a new First Class Certificate, not without a waiver which I will request from the Flight Surgeon's Office in Washington. I'll see that it gets out of here today but I doubt we'll have an answer before your present medical expires. Of course you'll need to notify your company."

"Are you saying the problem I've got isn't serious enough to worry about but that you can't issue me a new First Class Certificate without a waiver from Washington?" Dan asked, still in shock but regaining a little of his usual aplomb.

"That's correct," the doctor replied in an oleaginous voice. "It's really nothing to worry about. But we will have to have authorization of a waiver from Washington before we can issue the certificate. I will send them all the information immediately along with my recommendation that the waiver be granted, but don't expect to hear back too quickly. They always take their time about such matters."

"Then you do think they'll issue the waiver, that I won't lose my medical?"

"I'm recommending that they do. Of course they may not take my recommendation. I can't issue you a new certificate unless they do grant the waiver."

Cooper left the doctor's office in a daze, his normal confidence shattered. Flying was not just a job but a way of life he had enjoyed for over ten years now. Those who flew were members of a special fraternity and those who flew for the airlines were an even more select group. He couldn't envision what life would be like if the FAA medical people in Washington refused the waiver and he had to give it up. Of course Dr. Henderson seemed to think the waiver would be granted, but it wasn't a sure thing. The possibility that he might have a real medical problem didn't concern him at all compared to the worry that he might lose his right to fly and thereby lose the job he loved and the lifestyle he enjoyed so much.

Returning to the house, he found Helen had left for work. As reaction set in he felt dejected and alone. It was such a stunning shock. All afternoon his mood shifted between ice cold anger and vivid anguish. He eased his tension with whiskey but there was no way to block out the feeling of dread that seeped into his soul that day.

That evening when he told Helen he didn't voice his worst fears, only told her that there was a problem and that he might be grounded for a few weeks. She was stoic about it, accepting his explanation that it was only a temporary thing that would be cleared up soon. But sensing that he was very down, she did what she could to cheer him, cooking his favorite dishes, being especially attentive to his physical needs.

When the first of November came and the airline grounded him, she was full of suggestions of things to do to fill his day; books to read, movies to see, friends to be invited over for dinner or a drink. He continued to be depressed but gradually quit brooding about it knowing there was nothing he could do but wait.

Then, out of the blue, she lost her job. She told him she got into an argument with her boss and he asked her to leave. It wasn't until several months later that Dan learned the truth; that she had quit. Then Alma, who was also working at Sears at that time, told him that some of the other girls had teased Helen about coming to work in a new Cadillac convertible. They said that she didn't need to work for $2.60 an hour if she had that kind of money. And poor Helen, always very sensitive to what other people said, got her feelings hurt and quit.

At first it upset him, seeming to come as another stroke of bad luck, but then Dan found that, in a way, he didn't mind. Since he wasn't working it was nice to have his wife around all the time. With no jobs to go to they slept late, went to the movies in the afternoon, and had friends over for dinner. Then, often as not, they'd go out to one of the clubs and party till after midnight. December the first came and went with no word from the FAA Medical Review Board. Dan was still drawing his pay from the airline (it would continue for six months if he was grounded that long) so he wasn't too worried about money. But he was very worried about his job.

On December fourth Dr. Henderson's office called. The FAA was requesting more tests. Dan went down that same day and had them done.

Despite his growing doubts, Helen continued to be optimistic. She could see there was nothing wrong with Dan and she couldn't understand what the problem was. And with childlike faith, she believed him when he told her it would all be straightened out in a month or two.

The week before Christmas they flew to New York for a festive holiday. Accompanied by John and Cecile Bennett who had been married in October, they saw the play *HAIR* and heard Oliver sing at the Copacabana. Ensconced at the Plaza, they did their Christmas shopping along Fifth Avenue at Saks, Bloomingdale's and Tiffany's with time out for lunch at Twenty-One and drinks at the Top of the Sixes. Everyone had a marvelous time and Dan completely forgot his worries for a few fleeting days.

But Christmas itself was a big letdown after the gay time in New York. It certainly wasn't as merry as it had been the year before when they had just been married. Nevertheless they enjoyed being in their house rather than an apartment. They put up a large tree, decorated the house, and had friends over regularly until Christmas Eve. Helen gave Dan an elegant new overcoat—she said the old one he had worn in New York looked out of style—and he gave her a mink stole. She had complained about not having one on the trip.

It was on the Tuesday after Christmas, a miserably crude day with cold rain driving in gusts, when Dr. Henderson called personally to give Dan the bad news. The Medical Review Board had decided that they could not reissue him a first class medical certificate. While they didn't think his heart condition was serious, it did have the potential of a heart attach at any time. And airline pilots could not be allowed to fly if there was the slightest chance of a heart attack.

The news came as both a stunning surprise and, at the same time, an almost predicable event. Even though he had been mentally preparing himself for this possibility for more than two months, Dan was devastated by the decision. It was just too big a blow, coming like it did with so little warning. For days he wandered around in a blue funk feeling frightened, helpless, furious. It was almost a week before he could bring himself to face up to it. Only after the airline called him in and gave him the official notice did he truly begin to understand that he would have to find another career. They were as nice as they could be about it. He would receive his regular pay through the end of April; he had his equity in the company's profit sharing and retirement plans which he could draw out or leave to grow until he was sixty, the normal retirement age; and he could convert his hospitalization insurance policy to a personal one if he so desired. But that was all they could do. There was no way he could continue flying.

Looking back later he would realize that this was the point in time when he first began to feel a deep resentment, an indigenization toward the system, the establishment as the malcontents called it. He had been brought up to believe in the system, been taught and come to have faith that in the long run right would always prevail, that those people who worked hard and did their best would be rewarded with prosperity and happiness. He knew that everyone must suffer occasional trials and tribulations but was not prepared to assign his present troubles to that category. To Dan it seemed incredible that he had to lose ten years experience and the work he loved because some petty official in bureaucratic Washington had arbitrarily and capriciously decreed that such a heart murmur would disqualify him as a pilot. He never flew alone. There was always another pilot plus the flight engineer on duty on all his flights. And Dr. Henderson, a Class One FAA Examiner, had admitted that the chances of an attack were like one in a thousand. To Dan it just didn't make good sense. It seemed the system was picking on him.

Helen did what she could to east his pain during this difficult time but she soon found there was nothing she could say and little she could do to exorcise the despair and bitterness he felt. Finally she withdrew and left him to his own devices.

He seemed beyond help, sunk in the blackest depression. Liquor did little to lift the gloom but he used it as a balm for his fear and disgust, shutting himself in his study and drinking for hours while listening to sad music. What had happened was just too big a shock for him to handle and he was left utterly despairing, savagely embittered, anxiety and doubt gnawing at his stomach. He had possessed it all; a lovely wife, plenty of money, a career he loved. And now, with one of these gone, he wondered how long it would be before he lost everything. He had noted how some charmed people skated effortlessly through life with never a spill while others less fortunate seemed to lurch shakily from crisis to crisis, always just steps short of disaster. Had he joined this latter group, those whose luck had run out?

The idea terrified him. He couldn't tolerate failure, had never failed at anything in his life, and had forgotten the mental anguish of those terrible years when his father's business had faltered and gradually failed; eventually putting the college education he yearned for in jeopardy. But now, in this shock and anger, those anxious memories came flooding back, adding to his apprehension.

It took days for this mood to pass. Yet it did as, little by little, his despair and incredulity were replaced by resignation, weary acceptance. To escape his bitterness, he buried it deep in his subconscious mind where it would fester and grow until, with other insults added to this injury, it would again surface.

Fortunately Cooper was a positive thinker. Deep in his heart he had always believed in looking on the bright side and knew that good can often result from even the worst adversity. This inherent optimism finally overcame his rage at the inequity of fate, the humiliation he felt at losing his job, and he began to count his blessings. He was a college graduate, only thirty-five years old, and in spite of the heart murmur, enjoyed good health. He had a loving wife, a nice home and lots of friends. There was no reason he couldn't get busy and find himself a new career.

On a shinning Sunday when a bold January sun filled the house with golden light, he began studying the help-wanted section of the paper. The next day, nourished by hope, he started calling for interviews and making the rounds of the personnel agencies. But he soon discovered that there were few jobs he was qualified to fill. The country was going through what the economists called "A Mild Recession", and jobs of any kind were hard to find. His degree was in accounting, but he had no experience working in that field, in fact no experience of any kind other than the Air Force and flying with Eastern. Any job that paid any money worth while required experience, usually in a specific area, and of course that was something he didn't have. And because of his age, education and salary history, he was considered over-qualified for almost everything else.

One employment agency suggested he go in business for himself and open a personnel agency. They had a franchise available in Macon, Georgia. Cooper considered this but it required an investment of several thousand dollars and he didn't know if he'd be successful or not. He might spend six months at it, lose all his money and then have to start all over looking again. Besides, he didn't want to leave Atlanta. He and Helen both now thought of it as home. Their house was here, their friends were here, and they just didn't want to move to a smaller town.

Finally, on a cold and rainy Monday in early February, one of the agencies sent him for an interview with Massachusetts General Life Insurance Company. He wasn't enthused about the idea of selling life insurance, but it was one job for which he qualified. All they were looking for was a college degree and an ability to meet and talk to people. He took an aptitude test and endured three separate interviews before they offered him a job. By that time he had become interested and decided he might enjoy the work. Because his father had died without any insurance Dan was very aware of what life insurance could and could not do. He had purchased a $25,000 whole life policy from a retired Air Force officer turned agent when he was at Shaw in 1962, and in addition had taken out a $100,000 convertible and renewable term policy in December of 1968, soon after his marriage. He also had a $54,000 reducing term policy designed to provide money to pay off the mortgage on their home should he die, and his group policy at Eastern had provided another $25,000 in life coverage until his termination there. Along the way to purchasing these contracts he had been exposed to the spiels of several agents, analyzed their product for himself, and learned a great deal.

And he liked the idea of working his own schedule, being his own boss to some extent. Tom Vaughn, the manager of the agency, emphasized in the last interview that he would in effect be in business for himself. Because, even though the company had a compensation plan that gave him enough to live on from the first month, his earnings in the end would be strictly commission. He must build up a sufficient volume of sales within a few months to equal his draw or he would be dropped. The draw they agreed to give him, eight hundred dollars a month, was considerably below what he had been making at Eastern, but he was getting his severance pay and he had some savings left to help tide him over. Vaughn insisted that if he was any good at selling life insurance, he should be making eighteen to twenty thousand a year by January of 1971. And besides, there didn't seem to be any other job available.

When he tried to talk it over with Helen she didn't seem to have much opinion one way or the other.

"Dan, I don't know what to tell you," she said testily one gloomy February afternoon as they sat in front of a blazing fire, savoring its warmth, watching the rising tongues of flame. "I do still not believe you got laid off at Eastern! You had me thinking you'd be going back to work in January and the next thing I know you're fired and out looking for a job. I know you're smart enough to do all kinds of things but I don't know what you should do. Hell, I can't even keep a job in the warehouse at Sears. I'm sure not qualified to give you advice."

"I know Baby," he replied, trying to be sympathetic but wishing she would help him make the decision. "But I've got to find something that will bring us enough money to live comfortable. I think this insurance job might work out but I don't have to take it. I've got two more month's pay coming from Eastern and a little money still in savings. I can keep looking."

She reached for a cigarette, lit up, sucked the smoke deep, and huffed it out before replying. "Dan do what you think is best," she said looking stern. "I've enjoyed having you around but if you think it's time to go back to work that's all right with me. And as soon as you do I'm going to get out and find another job."

After much soul searching he decided to take the job. In six weeks of looking he hadn't come up with anything else that looked promising. He went to work at Massachusetts General on March second.

Once the decision was made, Dan threw himself into the new job with assiduity and zeal. The company had a three week training program he had to complete before he could start selling. During that time he studied insurance manuals, rate tables and numerous company publications, learned a canned approach talk, and took the state insurance examination for his license.

Throughout this training period Cooper was supervised by Herman Clark, the Assistant Manager. Clark, a slim and impeccable man in his late thirties, radiated an aura of confidence. He never seemed to doubt that selling life insurance was a high calling, one demanding hard work and sacrifice but returning both financial rewards and those of a more intangible quality. If you wrote down the things Clark said and studied them later, you'd find the errors, but listening to him talk, you'd become convinced of anything. He spoke in a rich, fruity baritone and knew all the buzz words and phrases to motivate his men to sell, sell, sell.

Clark's considerable abilities were complimented by those of Tom Vaughn, the manager. Another life insurance zealot, Vaughn spent most of his time working with the more experienced agents, but the new men also got the benefit of his talents. In his early forties, the handsome manager resembled nothing less than a flashy high roller with his seven-hundred dollar suits and diamond encrusted fingers. But this sleek façade hid a keen mind, a strident vitality, a ruthless desire for success. When he addressed the assembled agents at the weekly sales meeting, crowing over their successes and urging them on to greater efforts in a vibrant voice, his face took on a high, hard look of excitement, enthusiasm burned in his eyes, showed in his clenched fists.

Most of the technical instruction was given by Phil Hunter, the third member of the office's ruling triumvirate. A pale, worried pencil of a man, Hunter also held the title of Assistance Manager, but his specialty was the design of the intricate tax plans the agents recommended to their more affluent clients. A CPA and expert on corporate and estate tax law, Hunter knew all the angles. He was the systematic kind of man who never gave answers out of sequence because he felt it led to confusion and disorder. With his disciplined, steely mind, he was methodical and neat in everything he did but never dull. He too was enthusiastic about their work, about the many ways a knowledgeable life insurance agent could help professionals and business owners protect their earnings and estates from the tax man. He rejoiced in the lingo of the trade ("Survivorship," "Inter vivo trust," "Joint Estate," "Buy-Sell Agreement," "Keogh Plan") and barked his lectures with the vigor of a gung-ho platoon sergeant.

These three men were experts at the art of selling and at motivating those under them, so it was no wonder Cooper soon put away his bitterness, forgot his doubts, and became enthusiastic about Massachusetts General as a company and sales as a career.

When the time came to start selling he was ready and eager to begin. He launched his effort with people he knew—other pilots, Eastern executives and administrators based in Atlanta, small businessmen who were friends or acquaintances. And almost immediately he met with some success. In April he wrote two life policies with a face amount of $50,000 and first commissions of five hundred and sixty dollars. The following month he sold a $100,000 life policy with a first commission of thirteen hundred-fifty dollars and a disability policy which paid him another hundred and sixty-five.

The same week Dan started at Massachusetts General, Helen began looking for another job. He was relieved she was going back to work. He knew they couldn't live on his present income. The monthly payments on the house, her car, and the furniture ate up his entire eight hundred dollar draw. After two weeks of looking she landed a position as a clerk at the GEX store on I-85 North. She insisted she didn't have the right clothes to wear for such a job so Dan reluctantly shelled out two hundred dollars for some new ones. Everything started out fine, but after only five weeks problems developed. Her supervisor, who she liked a great deal, transferred, and a new supervisor moved in to take his place. Helen couldn't get along with the new man no matter how hard she tried, and so after a week under him, she quit. For two weeks she couldn't bring herself to tell Dan about it. He was enthused about his work and she didn't want to depress him with bad news. On those lovely spring days she spent her time in Grant Park, where she wasn't likely to encounter him, idling away the hours she was supposed to be working. She waited until the night in early May when he came home jubilant with the news that he had sold the $100,000 policy on which he would earn thirteen-hundred and fifty dollars commission, to tell him she had quit her job. In spite of his good humor he got cross with her.

"Gee, Baby," he said with asperity, "what's the problem? You left Sears because you couldn't get along with your boss and now you've done the same thing at GEX. And after we spent two hundred dollars on new clothes! Are they making passes at you or something like that?"

"No Dan, it's not that," she explained. "Ferris at GEX was just a bastard. No one else could get along with him either. It's just that I had the guts to quit and tell him off when no one else would. You know I can get another job with no problem. I don't have to put up with a boss like him. And I did earn enough to pay for the clothes I bought and now I've got them to wear on the next job."

"When you get the next job you may decide you need something different to wear. I know you've got to dress right for the position, but what I'm saying is that I wish you'd find something and stick with it. Things are working out all right with my new job but it's going to take a year or two before I'm really established and I don't think there'll ever be the security there I thought I had with Eastern. That's why I wish you could keep a job and help me pay the bills and build up our savings. After what happened with Eastern I'll never feel financially secure again. If you can just net a hundred dollars a week that'll give us an extra five thousand a year,"

"I know Dan," she replied humbly. "I'll start looking again tomorrow."

But their relationship was already in the grip of change and somehow she avoided going back to work.

During the four months he was out of work they had been together almost constantly. Even before, while he was flying for Eastern, he had considerably more time to spend with Helen than most men have to spend with their wives. As a result of this and the fact they were newlyweds still very much in love, they were extremely close, engrossed in each other, and did not need other people to fill gaps in their lives. On numerous occasions they had discussed the possibility of having children, and while both agreed they wanted a family someday, neither was eager for a baby. They savored their time together and did not feel they needed children to make their lives more complete. Even when they were working, both had been able to forget their jobs when they were away from work and devote their time and thoughts to each other, their home and their mutual activities.

With Dan's increasing involvement in his insurance job, their relationship began undergoing a gradual but definite change. During the three weeks he was training he began bringing work home with him, things to read and study. Once he began selling he often had to work late which meant he frequently wasn't home for supper. And now he also usually spent most of the day on Saturday at the office doing paperwork or out talking to prospective clients. He realized that to get results he must get out and see people and because he wanted so desperately to succeed, he did just that, leaving Helen with lots of spare time on her hands.

At first she did spend a lot of this time looking for another job. But as the weeks passed without success she gradually lost interest. She began to spend her days visiting friends or sitting in Piedmont Park talking with whoever happened to be there. That year, 1970, was the first year of the big hippie migration to Atlanta. With the warm weather they came in droves from everywhere. Most of the disreputable looking young men and women congregated in Piedmont Park and on the strip, a stretch of Peachtree Street between Tenth and Fourteenth Streets. During the day Helen enjoyed rapping with them in the park—sitting in the swings around the lake or under the trees. And frequently in the evenings when Dan was out calling on prospects, she would go down on the strip and drink with these new found friends in the bars or smoke pot with them in her car.

Dan didn't like her hanging out with the hippies, but he didn't exactly know what attitude he should take. He wanted her to get another job and help him with the bills and he told her so. But when she came back day after day and told him she had tried and failed to find a satisfactory job there was little he could say. He knew from his own recent experience that finding a job wasn't that easy. Of course he knew too that she wasn't spending all her time looking. He occasionally drove through the park during the day and more than once found her there talking to her long-haired friends. He would stop and visit for a short time and if he mentioned job hunting she would say yes, she had been looking and had just stopped for a few minutes on her way home. If he knew what time he would be in that evening he would tell her and she would have supper for him, but when he didn't he often came home and found her gone.

As the summer arrived Dan became more and more embroiled in his new job. He realized that the only way he could build his income up to the level he needed was to sell more and bigger policies. His early successes encouraged him to work harder, and in June he sold seven policies with a total first commission of just over eighteen hundred dollars. After that he worried less about money and quit bothering Helen about getting a job. He had decided she wasn't going to get one until she was ready anyway, and he might as well forget it. She still did an excellent job of keeping the house clean and neat, and her cooking was as good as before when he was there to eat it. But they had little leisure time together and rarely had friends over as they had done so often prior to his taking the insurance job. She spent more and more time with her new friends, the hippies. She befriended both men and women, most of them between the ages of eighteen and twenty-five. Sometimes when Dan dropped by the house in the afternoon he would find her there entertaining two or three. They were always courteous and friendly but some were none too clean. He never met the same one twice and she rarely talked about any of them, so he assumed she was not emotionally involved.

In July she drove the Cadillac to Daytona to spend a week visiting her family. The first day, before she even reached her father's house, she parked the car on a downtown Daytona Street and someone slit the top and stole two suitcases and all her clothes. She called Dan crying and upset. He didn't know what to say except to promise to wire her money to buy a few new things. It was a small loss but nevertheless it upset him a great deal. A couple of hundred dollars meant a lot more to them now than it had a year earlier.

In 1970 the hijacking of airliners was over shadowed in the news only by the continuation of the unpopular war in Vietnam and the protests against it. The national tragedy was exacerbated on May 4th when confused and frightened National Guardsmen fired into a group of protesters at Kent State University in Ohio, killing four students.

The skyjack epidemic, which had grown to startling proportions in 1969 (eighty-nine successful and unsuccessful attempts), continued unabated in 1970. For the most part the hijackers consisted of an assortment of homesick Cubans, jobless misfits, criminals on the run, and lost souls suffering from various degrees of mental illness. But this year the phenomenon took on a new twist with the proliferation of purely political hijackings. On March 31st nine militant Japanese students wielding samurai swords took over a Japan Air Lines 727 with one hundred twenty-two passengers and seven crewmen after takeoff from Tokyo on a domestic flight. After a three day battle of wits in which attempts to trick them into debarking at Seoul, South Korea failed, they were flown to Communist North Korea. The crew and hostages returned April 5th.

On July 22nd six Palestine commandos hijacked a Greek Olympic passenger jet after takeoff from Beirut and after negotiations with Greek officials in Athens, agreed to let the fifty-five passengers and crew off in exchange for a promise to release seven Arab guerillas in Greek jails. The hijackers, identified as members of the Popular Struggle Front, were flown to Cairo and the jet returned July 22nd.

There were many such incidents but the use of hijacking as a military tactic reached its zenith in September of 1970. On September 6th Palestine Commandos hijacked the first three of four Western airliners bound for New York in the skies over Europe and precipitated a world crisis which endangered the fragile ninety-day Mid-East ceasefire and sparked a civil war in Jordan.

All the planes were bound for New York. A fourth attempt by a man and woman to take over an El Al 707 shortly after takeoff from Amsterdam was foiled by security guards who shot the man and overpowered the woman. She was Leila Khaled, a veteran of an earlier hijacking, who was turned over to British authorities in a brief stop at London.

A Pan American World Airways 747 jumbo jet, also out of Amsterdam, was forced to fly to Cairo, where the plane was blown up only minutes after the one hundred forty-two passengers and seventeen crew members were rushed off and freed.

A Trans World 707 with one hundred fifty-five passengers grabbed shortly after leaving Frankfurt, Germany, and a Swissair DC-8 with one hundred forty-three aboard, taken minutes after leaving Zurich, were both flown to a dessert airstrip, twenty-seven miles north of Amman, Jordan's capital city, and their passengers held as hostages. There they sweltered in their desert prisons as the governments involved sought desperately to free them and the guerrillas threatened to blow up the planes. A seventy-two hour deadline for release of all guerrillas held in Israel, West Germany, Switzerland, and Britain was set September 7th by the Popular Front for the Liberation of Palestine, the Marxist group responsible for the hijackings. The Jordanian army stood by helplessly as guerrillas mounted guard around the planes.

Some passengers, mostly women and children, were sent to Amman, but on September 9th, a British Overseas Airways VC-10 with one hundred seventeen passengers on a Bombay-London flight, was pirated over Lebanon and forced to join the other two planes on the commandos' "Revolution Airfield." International Red Cross negotiators were working against the destruction deadline as the ordeal worsened for the hostages, suffering their desert confinement with sparse food and water.

The desert phase of the hijack drama climaxed September 12th when their captors blew up all three jetliners, only minutes after the last of the four hundred twenty-nine passengers and crewmen were removed and taken to Amman, where all but fifty-four were freed.

The fifty-four, hidden in various hideaways, were released unharmed in three separate groups, September 25th, 26th, and 29th. Release of the last six, all Americans, cleared the way for seven guerrillas in European jails to be freed September 30th.

In July of 1970 Dan Cooper met Louise Haddock. It happened when he approached one of his friends, a young Eastern pilot named Jim Carpenter, about insurance. Jim suggested that Dan come over to the house and meet Louise. If she would give him the money he might buy something.

Dan was not surprised that Jim was living with a woman who wasn't his wife and was not shocked that Jim might ask her to give him money to buy insurance. But he was quite taken aback that muggy July evening when he went to the old house on Sixth Street and met Louise.

Carpenter was twenty-six years old, extremely handsome and quite the lady's man. Dark curly hair framed his soft, wide-eyed, sensuous face, and his well-built, nicely proportioned body was always nattily attired in the latest fashions from Anthony's or Kicks and Lids. He had a deep mellow voice of great power and a sparkling personality that appealed to both men and women. Bursting with life, motion, vigor and bright gaiety, he possessed great charm and even the realization that it was contrived was no defense against it. A native of Atlanta, born and raised in the suburb of Doraville, Jim had used his unctuous charm to wrangle an assignment there immediately after completing his training with Eastern. Dan had known him about eighteen months, seeing him occasionally around the airport and frequently in the city's livelier night spots. Jim had been to Dan's house on several occasions, always accompanied by a young, attractive woman: a willowy model, buxom stewardess, or vivacious secretary.

So Dan was amazed when he found Jim living with a forty-year-old woman who had little or no sex appeal.

Louise Haddock was definitely not physically attractive. She stood just over five feet and had coarse, corpulent features. While her face did have some pleasing lines, it was doubtful that she had ever been pretty.

The night Dan met her she wore no makeup and the unkempt condition of her hair gave her the look of a harridan. She was overweight and the loose fat bulged. She was engirdled in a straining black knit dress with a ripped seam gaping. Dan could not imagine what Jim saw in her until the story unfolded.

It developed that Louise was rich. At least that was the impression Dan got that night from the things Jim said as they sat around a tiny living room crowded with furniture which obviously had been purchased for a much larger house. Carpenter let drop the fact that Louise was the beneficiary of a huge trust fund left by her father, a Pittsburg banker. He explained that she got a large dividend from it every quarter plus several smaller monthly checks which were the proceeds of her father's life insurance policies. While one certainly wouldn't think she was well-to-do from her appearance or the way her house looked, Jim assured Dan she had plenty of money to do with as she pleased and she confirmed his statements with knowing nods.

Avariciously Dan suggested that Jim buy a $50,000 whole life policy even though the only justification he could give for the purchase was that it was a way for Jim to put aside some money and at the same time buy insurance which would be more expensive later. Jim readily agreed and without hesitation Louise wrote out a check for the first year's premium. After completing the papers for Jim's policy Dan tactfully inquired as to what type of insurance Louise carried on herself and her three children and was not surprised to learn she had none at all. He recommended she start an insurance program with a hospitalization policy for herself and the children. She agreed she needed it but said it would have to wait on her October check. The bills, Jim's insurance, and other expenses she explained, had about decimated her July check and she had to use the monthly checks for food.

When he was ready to leave Louise walked to the car with him. She was cordial but nervous, guarded and reserved. "It's been a pleasure meeting you Dan," she said timidly as he opened the door and slid into the Lincoln.

Her pleasant manner had effectively erased his earlier negative impressions and he answered her warmly. "It's been nice meeting you too Louise. If I can help you with your own insurance or any of your other business affairs please feel free to call on me."

"Dan do you know anything about wills?" she suddenly asked in a hesitant voice as she stood beside the car. "I've got to do something about a new will."

"I don't write them but I can give you some advice and put you in touch with a good attorney who can help you," he answered encouragingly.

"Could you come back one afternoon soon and let me tell you about it?" she wanted to know.

"Of course," he said smiling. "I'll call you on Friday and make an appointment for one afternoon next week. How'll that be?"

"Oh that would be fine. I also need some advice about buying a house. Can you help me with that too?"

"Possibly. I'm no expert but I know a little about houses. I spent two months last year shopping for one before I purchased the townhouse where I live."

"Call me then and we'll get together next week. Make it some afternoon and we'll have plenty of time to talk without interruption."

He did call the following Friday and she suggested he come by on Tuesday afternoon. She explained that Jim was scheduled for a trip that day and the children would also be gone giving them the house to themselves.

Away from Jim, Dan found the rotund Louise a lot more talkative and he began to take a real liking to her. After being sure he was comfortable and getting them both a cup of delicious coffee, she began a long incisive explanation of her problems.

In a sonorous voice she described in detail how her father and then her late husband Charlie had taken exemplary care of her business affairs in the past. Now, since her husband's untimely death from cancer the previous November, she, an intrepid but untrained housewife, had been forced to shift for herself. Married to Charlie for seventeen years, she had three children, a girl fifteen and boys twelve and thirteen. The family had made their home in Ft. Lauderdale for eight years where they had owned a large but not ostentatious home on one of the canals and her husband had earned a good living as a salesman for a yacht broker.

With a touch of pride she described how there had been enough money for a full time maid, their own boat docked in the back yard, and frequent travel. But after Charlie's illness, which had been unexpected and short, everything had changed. They had no savings or insurance and she had been forced to sell the boat and take out a second mortgage on the house to pay off the hospital and funeral bills. Paul DeVories, the churlish young man who had been named executor in Charlie's will, had been no help. He had treated her niggardly, railing at her about her spending habits, and she had grown to dread his frenetic calls. Only her income had saved them from penury.

The previous spring she had met Jim Carpenter aboard a friend's yacht docked at Pier 66, and when they had become close he had suggested she sell the Florida house, pay off her debts and move to Atlanta to make a new start. It had been a simplistic solution and while she sometimes harbored doubts, so far she did not regret it.

"We're only renting this place on a month to month basis," she said deprecatingly. "It's not nearly big enough but it was available without my having to sign a lease and it is within walking distance of a few stores and the bus line. I don't drive and the kids aren't old enough yet to get a driver's license and that has been another problem. I've got a 1970 Coupe de Ville that Charlie bought just before he got sick and I let Jim drive it. He chauffeurs me when he's around but of course he's gone a lot."

"I can see that you've gone through a very traumatic experience in the last nine months," Dan replied sympathetically. "But how can I help you?"

"I want to buy another house, something bigger than this and in a better neighborhood. The kids have to start back to school in the fall and I'm told that Grady High School, where they'd have to go, is largely black. But we've spent all of the money I got out of the house in Lauderdale paying off debts and moving, and now I don't have anything for a down payment. I think the bankers in Pittsburg who control my trust fund might agree to give me money out of the principal for a down payment—they did something similar one time years ago—but I don't know exactly how to approach them. Jim would be happy to do it for me but I think we need someone more professional or else they might not give our request the proper consideration, you know, just brush it off. I could hire an attorney but after my experience with DeVories in Lauderdale I'm not anxious to put myself at the mercy of another lawyer. That's why I wanted to talk to you. Do you think you could help me out?"

Dan was complimented that she would consider asking his advice on her financial affairs, but he felt some trepidation when he considered what she wanted him to do. Still he felt he owed her something. After all she had already spent several hundred dollars with him and would probably spend more, particularly if he could help her out with her house problems. "Louise I don't know if I can do what you want or not," he replied cautiously. "But if you like I'll take a closer look at your situation and give you my opinion. If I can help you I will, and if I decide I can't, I'll recommend someone, a lawyer or accountant, you can trust to help you and not rip you off the way DeVories did."

"That's all I could ask Dan. Now here is a copy of my father's will and the trust agreement for you to look over."

She also had copies of her will, her last three year's income tax returns, and the closing statement from the sale of her Florida home. He asked a few questions but withheld any opinion until he could take the papers back to his office and study them.

Cooper found the will and trust agreement of Louise Haddock's father to be straight forward and easy to understand. From reading them he learned that the trustees, a bank in Pittsburg, could advance money from the principal of the trust for anything relative to the health and welfare of Louise or her children. It was a broad clause designed to give the trustees some discretion in passing out the principal, and he felt certain that they would be willing to give her money for the down payment on a house if the situation were presented in the proper light. He discovered that while her income was large, it was not as great as Jim had led him to believe. Louise was getting about twelve thousand dollars a quarter from the trust but about three thousand of this was being deducted as an estimate on her federal income tax. The small checks she received monthly totaled only about five hundred dollars. To Dan, with his accountant's mind and frugal habits, this seemed like enough for her to live well and still bank lots of money, but he had already learned in his insurance work that everyone wasn't as careful with money as he was. And he assumed that Louise, being from a wealthy family, was used to spending lots of money on clothes, vacations and the like. After carefully examining all the information she had given him, he went back to her with a detailed proposal.

"Louise," he said confidently, trying to convey his assurance but avoid any hard sell, "if you want me to do so I'll agree to act as your financial advisor. That doesn't mean you have to take my advice but of course if you don't take at least some of it we are both wasting our time. For doing this my fee will be one hundred-fifty dollars a quarter plus the commissions I will make off whatever insurance you buy from me. We can raise or lower the quarterly fee depending on how much time it takes and how much I'm making on the insurance, but I'll not raise it without your approval. To begin with there are three things we need to work on. First is the buying of a house. I'll write the trustees informing them that I am advising you now and inquire about getting money from the principal for the down payment and moving expenses, etcetera. We'll have to decide what kind of house you want and have a fairly close idea of the price before I approach them on this but that will only require a little looking on our part.

"The second thing we need to get done is get you a new Georgia will. Did you realize that if you die without a valid will the principal of the trust fund reverts to charity? You have a will that was drawn in Florida before your husband's death and it needs to be revised in accordance with your current wishes and with Georgia law. I'll set up an appointment with an attorney to have that done right away if you approve.

"The third thing I want to do is get you started on an insurance program. As soon as you have the money I'd like to see you buy the hospitalization policy we discussed and then some life insurance. With the proper will the proceeds of the trust can pass to your children without estate taxes so I don't know if you need any great amount of life insurance on yourself, but it might be a good idea to get the children started with small whole life policies on each of them."

"Well, what do you think," he said pausing for breath. "Do you like my ideas?"

"Yes Dan I do," she replied with some enthusiasm. "I think you're being very reasonable in what you're asking and all three of these projects are things I've wanted to do. Let's go ahead and get started."

They did and so within two months Louise and her family including Jim Carpenter moved to a forty-thousand dollar house in Garden Hills. It was an older section of town but the home they purchased had been recently renovated and was in excellent condition. On the main floor it had a large living room, a dining room, kitchen, three bedrooms and two baths, and the basement had another bedroom, a bath and a roomy den. The trustees sent her thirteen thousand dollars which she used to make the twenty percent down payment buy some new furniture and get moved.

During this same period he took her to meet with Sam Levy, an aging, erudite attorney. Levy, an expert in the drafting of complicated wills and trust agreements, agreed to draw her new Georgia will. It took four visits over a period of several weeks to iron out all the fine points, but by October it was completed and signed.

And in September he took her application for the hospitalization policy he had recommended although the money to pay for it would not be available until her next quarterly check came.

It arrived on Friday, the ninth, a glittering day in early October. Dan was at the office doing his usual Friday morning chores when an excited Louise called to tell him it was there in the day's mail. He already had a full day planned but promised her he'd drop by late that afternoon for a drink and discuss how she should use the money in meeting the myriad financial obligations still facing her.

During the past three months Cooper had devoted a lot of his time to Louise, her family and her affairs. The paltry one-hundred-fifty dollar fee and the commission on the health policy would not begin to properly compensate him for the inordinate amount of time he had spent with her, but he had enjoyed doing it. Seeing the joy she and the kids obviously felt when they moved to the new house had been reward enough for what he had done. Perhaps that was why he felt a keen sense of disappointment that evening when he stopped at her house only to find she had left with Jim Carpenter.

"I don't know where they were going," Janie, the fifteen-year-old daughter, told him laconically. "Jim came in about four and right away they changed clothes and left."

"Well tell her I came by. She can call me at home if she needs me," he replied tartly, making no attempt to hide the chagrin and frustration he felt.

During the period since July, Dan's friendship with Carpenter had cooled perceptibly. Dan had hoped to avoid this but when he repeatedly saw Jim take advantage of Louise's timidity and her obvious affection for him to rapaciously feather his own nest with no regard for her ultimate welfare or that of her children; he couldn't help but feel contempt for the younger man. Although Jim had continued to live with the Haddocks, he had taken little interest in the details of what Dan had been doing for them.

Dan was puzzled by the relationship between Jim and Louise. He knew for instance that Jim had an apartment of his own and was keeping a girl there. Yet he continually drove Louise' car and spent a large part of his free time with her. For a time Dan had thought Louise didn't know about Jim's girl, Debbie, but just recently, one evening when they were having a drink and discussing her financial problems, Louise surprised him by bringing it up. She told him she knew Jim was keeping another woman. He had even bought Debbie an expensive outfit for her birthday and charged it to Louise's account at Saks. And she didn't like it but she didn't know what to do. She said she didn't want to alienate Jim, she felt he needed her.

As they continued to talk about it Louise surprised Dan further with her stunning candor; telling him that although Jim slept with her frequently, they never had sex. In some ways she was just mothering him, but there was more to it than that. She had three beautiful children of her own and at the same time she seemed to neglect them, especially the boys, while worrying about Jim. Dan felt it was none of his business and yet it seemed to do Louise so much good to discuss things with him. He did steer clear of giving advice on any matters that were not of a financial nature, but he found that when she discussed other things she took his noncommittal to be an endorsement of her expressed feelings and actions.

So he was appalled when she called the next morning to apologize and tell him where she and Jim had gone.

Apparently, unbeknownst to Dan, Jim had also been eagerly awaiting the arrival of Louise's quarterly check. He had immediately whisked her off to Capital Automobile and convinced her to trade her 1970 Coupe de Ville for a shinny red and white, 1971 El Dorado. She had so little equity in the 1970 Cadillac that she had to put up another one thousand dollars in additional down payment and her monthly payments jumped from two-twenty-five to three-thirty.

Dan didn't learn the baleful details until he went over to her house that Saturday afternoon. Then, when he saw how thrilled she was with the new car and Jim's pleasure in it, he didn't have the heart to scold her for buying it. Instead he got her to write checks for the health insurance and the bills he knew must be paid, and admired the new car.

Despite the time he spent with Louise and her affairs, Dan's business had continued to improve during July and August. In September Tom Vaughn asked if he'd like to go on straight commission and audaciously he decided he would. After the second month he had consistently earned more than his draw, and while he had been allowed to draw some of this excess, the company had held back several hundred dollars which he could now get by going on commission. In spite of his success with selling insurance, his savings had continued to dwindle. He knew he must reverse this ominous trend.

Now, in the autumn of 1970, when Dan thought about his wife and their relationship he still felt a warm glow. It was true that the first bloom of marriage, the excitement of the first year, had faded. But he had developed a strong dependence on her and his love for her gave him the courage and strength he needed to overcome his regrets at the loss of his flying career. Even though he spent much less time with her than he had when he was with Eastern, he valued their time together more highly. And as this need for her strengthened and grew through the months of anxiety, spreading its roots through his subconscious as he tenaciously pursued his new career, he ceased talking about her going to work. She obviously didn't want to work and he knew it. Even when she had worked the amount she brought home after taxes was small. After the trip to Daytona in July, she had not asked for money for any extras and compared with the way they had lived the year before, they were misers. Helen still had her Cadillac convertible, but it was her only extravagance. She hung around with her long-haired friends from the park and although they sometimes drank up all the liquor in the house or made a raid on the refrigerator, Dan thought it a small enough price to pay to keep Helen happy.

Their future seemed even brighter when, in October, Dan scored his largest insurance sale to date—four policies with a total face value of $400,000. It was a business sale, the policies funding a buy-sell agreement among the four Burson brothers who owned Burson Aviation, a prosperous light aircraft fixed-base operation at Fulton County Airport. Charles Burson, the oldest brother, was an Eastern pilot and Dan had made the successful approach through him. The commission was over five thousand dollars and it brought Dan's first year commissions to more than thirteen thousand and qualified him for company honors for the year. He took the applications for the Burson policies in October, but it was early December before they were issued and placed. Between worrying over this sale and looking after Louise's affairs, Dan didn't get other new business working and ended the year with few additional sales. Still, he had done very well for his first ten months in the business and he began to believe Tom Vaughn when the dynamic manager optimistically predicted he would earn twenty to twenty-five thousand dollars in 1971.

In December, riding the euphoria of this success, he traded his Lincoln for a new Continental Mark III. Helen, who always got off on new cars, had importuned him to trade ever since he had made the big sale. She felt their financial problems were behind them and they could afford to loosen up a little in their spending. Dan's 1968 Lincoln, now three years old, had nearly fifty thousand miles on it, and was beginning to need regular repairs. So he was able to rationalize that payments on the new car would not cost anymore than repairs on the old. The new Mark was a dark metallic shade of brown with rich-looking, saddle brown leather upholstery and a sun roof. It sold for something over nine thousand dollars, but they gave Dan thirty-five hundred for the sixty-eight and the bank allowed him to borrow six thousand dollars on a ninety-day note. By arranging the financing in this manner he realized a few hundred dollars in cash and avoided monthly payments. He convinced the bank to allow him to borrow this way by explaining that his commissions varied a good bit from one month to the next and while he might have trouble making a large monthly note he could probably make a ten percent reduction and pay the interest when he renewed the note every ninety days. He could possibly pay more when he had a big month. When the deal was closed he instructed the salesman at Colonial Lincoln-Mercury to list the bank as mortgagee on the title application, but somehow it was not done and when the title arrived in the mail in January it showed no lien against the car. He prudently considered sending the title on to the bank, but decided instead to just hold it. If they wanted it they'd tell him.

As the New Year began, Cooper became more and more involved with Louise Haddock and her intractable affairs. He seldom saw Jim Carpenter, but the handsome young pilot was still living with Louse and her children, still driving her car. In December he had persuaded her to purchase two vacant lots, one for him and one for herself, in Big Canoe, a second-home development north of Atlanta. She called and asked Dan's advice about it—after it was too late to back out. Personally he thought it was a foolish thing to do given the state of her finances, but there wasn't any point in berating her for it once it was done. Besides he realized, it was her money. If she wanted to throw it away on her recreant boy friend that was her business.

But Dan did worry about her children, especially the boys, Pete and Joey. She often spoke of how they needed clothes but there was never any money left to spend on them. Like most kids that age, the Haddock boys weren't too concerned about what they wore, but when they used the lack of shoes as an excuse to skip school, it was getting serious.

The very same day her January check came, Dan sat down with Louise to help her decide how it should be spent. After paying her estimated tax she still had close to ten thousand dollars, but she had already written a check for thirteen hundred to pay for a new diamond wrist watch for Jim. She explained that it was a belated Christmas present. So after making the three monthly payments on the house, the car, the car insurance, her accounts with Rich's, Sears, Davison's, Saks, Lord and Taylor, Averts, Bank Americard, Master Charge and Richway, and paying a two thousand dollar, unsecured note at the C. & S. Bank, there was nothing left. She still had payments to make on the lots they had recently purchased including a one-thousand-dollar note that was part of the down payment, and a welter of small bills. Dan patiently went over everything again, pointing out that she could easily work out of her troubles in just a few months if she would stop her excessive spending and concentrate on reducing her outstanding bills. Categorically she agreed that this was what she should do, and the next day Dan introduced her to a loan officer at the Trust Company Bank where she borrowed three thousand dollars on an unsecured, ninety-day note to tide her over until the next quarterly check came. Afterward he insisted she go to Richway and buy the boys some clothes. To Dan it seemed peculiar that Louise didn't spend much money on herself. He wasn't sure whether it was just because money was short and therefore she held off, or that she just didn't want anything for herself. But she seemed to have no way to say no to anything that Jim Carpenter suggested. Several times Dan had to loan her small amounts of money to buy groceries when her monthly checks were late or when Jim needed a little extra money for one thing or another.

Then unexpectedly, in the latter part of January, Jim was fired from Eastern. Dan never found out the exact reason for the dismissal, but Louise quickly told him the underlying cause—Jim had become a heroin user. Coming as a big surprise, this news confounded Dan. He knew Jim smoked marijuana regularly and occasionally took LSD and other drugs, but he had no idea he was into heroin.

In telling him about it, Louise related that during the last two months Jim had become strident and quarrelsome and more demanding about money as opposed to his usual charming personality. She said she had suspected he had a problem but had assumed it involved Debbie or his always pressing money worries. She was stunned when he came home one afternoon and tearfully told her of his addiction and the loss of his job.

Her first reaction was to rally to his support like an old mother bear protecting a cub. In the weeks that followed she did her best to help him as he tried to kick the dissolute habit. He gave up his apartment and his other girl friend simply because he could no longer afford them. Lethargically he hung around Louise's house sleeping most of the time and taking a variety of other drugs in his attempts to end his addiction to the heroin. When he became physically ill Louise took him to the doctor or the hospital and when he couldn't stand it any longer she went with him in the skulking search of a pusher for "just one more fix."

The effect of all this on Louise was gradual deterioration. She, who had worried before, now became obsessed with worrying, and like many fat people, she compensated by eating constantly, aggravating her already overweight condition. As the execrated weeks became months with no solution to Jim's addiction, she became more and more dependent on Dan for his help and advice.

For a time Dan didn't realize how much his involvement with Louise was hurting his insurance work. In January and February he put in long tortuous hours working two new business prospects that had the potential of big sales similar to the one he had made to the Bursons. But when neither of them closed and March came around, he began to worry. He had sold a few small policies and he would soon start getting some renewal commissions, but his income was below five hundred dollars in February and he had nothing working that was likely to break this sales slump. In March he worked furiously trying to find new prospects in any category, business or individual, large or small, but the results were meager. He worked so hard and so long trying to sell insurance it was almost a relief to spend a little time with Louise and her obdurate problems. At least he felt he was accomplishing something by helping her.

In March she managed to get Jim enrolled in a methadone program and her house returned to a more normal routine. He left each morning to go to the clinic on Eleventh Street for his shot and counseling, usually returning in time for dinner. He looked bad, having lost more than twenty pounds, but his confidence had returned and he was talking of looking for a job.

Spring arrived suddenly in early April. Almost overnight the trees turned green and the dogwoods bloomed. And with it came Louise's next quarterly check Dan had hoped that with its arrival she would be able to catch up her bills but now, with the added expense of looking after Jim, she was in worse shape than she had been in January. Dan recommended she pay the bank loans first, the three thousand at the Trust Company and the two thousand she had re-borrowed from C. & S. in February, and then make only one payment on each of her bills in April. Even doing this the check ran out before everyone was paid. He advised her to send a token payment on each of the charge accounts and then plan to borrow again from the banks in May and June.

At the same time Dan worked up her 1970 income tax return and by itemizing deductions—taking advantage of all the money she had paid out in interest-he computed her tax to be several hundred dollars less that the estimates she had paid. By making a small reduction in the 1971 estimates and deducting the refund due on the 1970 taxes, he cut her April tax payment by more than twelve-hundred dollars.

Working with his insurance prospects Dan was learning more and more about other people's financial and tax situations. His college background in accounting helped his understanding of what he was seeing and in addition his company had given him considerable training in the fields of income and estate taxes. He knew a great deal more about these matters than the average individual or small businessman and so was able to give this type of customer valuable advice. But the more he saw of the federal income tax and the way it was viewed by the majority of people, the more confused he became. Dan had always thought of the paying of taxes as black and white situation. If the law applied to you, you paid your taxes and that was it. But as he became familiar with different businesses and different circumstances, he found that many tax situations were not black and white. In one of the simplest situations, the commission salesman like himself who paid his own expenses, it was difficult to decide how much of his expense was personal and how much was for business. His car, for instance. He used it almost exclusively for business; that is if he considered trips like visiting Louise as business. But the law said the mileage going to and from the office was not deductible as a business expense and therefore had to be considered personal. He was supposed to keep a record, a diary, to support his deductions, but how should he log a trip that included a visit to his office, a stop at a prospect's office on the way to Louise's house, a hop to the grocery story and back with her, and then the drive home with another stop at a liquor store owned by an established customer? Most of Dan's daily trips were like this and he thought it would take a Solomon to reach a fair decision. He knew he could not.

He was surprised to find that many businessmen went out of their way to pay more taxes than they thought they fairly owed just to avoid trouble. Others pushed things to the limit in the other direction knowing that if they were checked they would probably compromise and still get away with deducting more than they would have if they had started with a strict interpretation of the rules. Dan found himself in agreement with the latter. Why not take all the deductions that seemed in any way feasible and then if you were challenged you could back down on anything the auditor wouldn't buy. He followed this plan in filing Louise's return and also with his own.

The manner in which his peers viewed the paying or avoidance of taxes was only one of the things that were causing Cooper to reevaluate the concepts of right and wrong that had been with him since childhood. The country was undergoing a catharsis of change and so was he.

The sixties had been a decade of protest. Blacks had opposed unfair and oppressive laws with sit-ins and mass demonstrations. The hippies had done the same by dropping out and turning on. And the hippies weren't the only ones who were turning on. Dan estimated that fifty percent of his friends smoked marijuana, at least occasionally, and many used LSD and other drugs that were against the law. He could understand prohibiting the indiscriminate use of something as terrible as heroin, but he thought it was ridiculous for the government to attempt to outlaw anything people wanted as much as they seemed to want pot. It was no more harmful than liquor or cigarettes and they were going to get it one way or the other. The intransigence of the moss backs in power only benefited the lords of organized crime at the expense of legitimate businessmen and government which should be taxing this growing industry.

For that matter Dan thought it silly that the police wasted their time hassling prostitutes and pornographers. It wasn't the government's business to stamp out sin, and laws against these and other so-called victimless crimes only offered further opportunity for organized crime to subvert the police, the courts and other public officials. When the police tried to enforce unpopular laws they only promoted disrespect for the law and increased the possibilities of graft and corruption.

And then there was the morality of big business, or rather the lack of it. With his book, *Unsafe at Any Speed*, Ralph Nader had focused attention on the unconscionable automobile industry and the way they had sold automobiles they knew to be unsafe or defective. Environmental groups pointed out how other business practices were endangering the general population with all types of pollution. And Dan knew personally how banks and insurance companies film-flamed their customers with such things as add-on interest and hidden charges. They used meretricious advertising to get the suckers into the tent, and then hired the sharpest attorneys to draw up air tight contracts with lots of fine print to confuse and short-change the customer. So accepted was their integrity, few people even realized they were being fleeced. The Truth-In-Lending law was supposed to curb some of these abuses but all it really did was generate more work for the rapacious lawyers. Woe be it to anyone, individual or small businessman, whose interests should conflict with these powerful groups. They had no compunction about forcing you to the wall. The doctrine of fairness was outdated in the higher echelons of many big corporations; all they were concerned with was the bottom line.

Finally there was the war in Vietnam. It had undermined the credibility of the government and divided the country like no issue since slavery with sincere men of good will as well as a profusion of hot heads on both sides of the question. Dan had served in the Air Force with fierce pride and could not understand young men who would run off to Canada to avoid their military obligation. And he couldn't comprehend why the unpopular war couldn't be brought to an immediate halt, the killing stopped. In 1968 he had voted for Nixon assuming the Republicans would find some quick, honorable way (as Eisenhower had done in Korea in 1953) to end the conflict and bring the troops home. But more than two years had elapsed and things had only worsened. The war had escalated and events like the Kent State massacre last year had further exacerbated emotions and rhetoric without suggesting any solution. It was obvious the U. S. had lost the war, but it looked like the military—industrial complex was prolonging it for its own selfish reasons.

And all of this—the protests of the blacks and other disaffected groups; the corruption in government; the chicanery of big business; the agony of the Vietnam War—were brought into the home every night via the evening news on television. Was it any wonder many people, young and old, were questioning their definitions of right and wrong?

Although he was older than most of those who were actively rebelling against the system, Dan was in sympathy with many of their grievances and had begun to question the simple values he had grown up with. When he saw the law abused and misused he lost respect for it. When he saw the doctrine of fairness ignored by greedy business interests with devious motives, he wondered where his priorities lay. When he saw his country writhing in agony, torn between continuing an unpopular war to uphold the nation's honor or losing face by pulling out and stopping the senseless waste of men and money, he despaired of ever knowing the answers. Lacking any deep religious faith, he gradually abandoned the teachings of his youth and became a moral agnostic.

Dan's relationship with Helen, which had undergone many changes during the last of 1969 and the first of 1970, had stabilized during the latter part of that year. Now, in the early months of 1971, it was again changing subtly. They saw less and less of each other and whereas at first Helen hadn't objected to his long working hours, she now seemed jealous of his work. During the entire time they had been married she had suffered from occasional fits of baleful depression. In the early months of their marriage these were usually triggered by small things such as her burning the supper or a cross remark by Dan.

But now, like a bad omen, they seemed to become more frequent and ominous. Dan didn't really know what caused them. Sometimes when she was in one of these moods she would lie comatose on the couch for hours and listen to melancholy music. One night in February when a cold, northwest wind whistled around the house and lashed the barren trees, she played the B. J. Thomas *Raindrops* album over and over and over until it got on Dan's nerves so bad he lost his temper and dramatically broke the record in half.

Dan knew she occasionally took drugs and he wondered just how much her minatory moods were caused by them. One weekend in the late summer of the previous years, she and two of her hippie girl friends had gone to the Holiday Inn at the Airport, gotten a room, and tripped on acid. In a recalcitrant mood she had called Dan about midnight to tell him she wouldn't be home until morning. He was upset but she assured him she was all right and told him not to worry. He was upset but she assured him she was all right and told him not to worry. When she had returned the next day about noon they had a long talk. Fervidly she told him how much she had enjoyed the experience, describing the relaxation and the esoteric beauty of the airport at night as seen in vivid, drug-induced colors. But when she saw how upset he was she had promised not to do it again.

More recently, at the Sans Souci last New Year's Eve, one of her friends had slipped her a couple of downers. She had taken them on top of several drinks and then told Dan about it just before she passed out. He took her home and put her to bed. The next day she apologized abjectly and again promised not to take any more drugs.

But several times she brought pills home and in March, when he was trying ardently to get some new insurance sales on the books, she persuaded him to try speed. Dan found the little yellow capsules a big help in giving him the energy he needed to get through a long, onerous day. And while he didn't take them to get high, the pleasant feeling of well-being they induced was welcome in those discouraging days. He became a regular user although he rarely took more than one a day. Later that summer, when he complained that the capsules weren't as effective as they once had been, Helen brought him some tablets she called spotted dogs which were much stronger.

She also took speed occasionally and they both drank more than they had in the past. They began to have occasional disagreements—Dan wouldn't call them quarrels. She was dissatisfied with the way things were going (was it a reflection of his own worries about his job and their financial future?) and she would begin by berating him for not closing some sale or for not working harder. Then she would change her tune and claim that he didn't love her, that he was looking at other women who were prettier or more sophisticated or who had money.

Dan tried to reason with her when she was in these fractious moods but he finally came to the conclusion that it accomplished nothing. It seemed to be a form of deep insecurity she had, and his blatant reassurances did little to relieve it. Like the fits of depression, these saturnine moods of insecurity had to go away by themselves.

Often, after they had one of these fatuous disagreements, she would go out and drive around all night, returning home only in time to fix his breakfast. One stormy night in early April after one of their scenes she went out driving in Dan's Mark III, as she often did when he was in bed, and had a freak accident. She told the police she was coming west on Cheshire Bridge Road when a large dark car suddenly shot out of a side street and almost hit her. She claimed she swerved to miss it and accidentally hit a concrete island in the middle of the street that was there to separate converging traffic. The Continental, traveling at high speed, struck the island at an angle and turned turtle, flipped completely over, and skidded along the roadway on its top.

Luckily Helen had her seatbelt fastened and she was not badly hurt, only bruised and shaken up. But the car was ruined. Dan didn't want it back and besides, he couldn't do without a car for the weeks it would take to repair it. He agreed to settle with his insurance company for seventy-four hundred dollars, their estimate of the car's current value less the deductible.

When the check came it was made out to Dan only. He still owed the bank six thousand dollars on it but they had not discovered that they did not have the title. When he had renewed the note in March he had told the banker that his business had been a little slow and had been allowed to pay the interest only. They had not pressed him to reduce the principal since he still had good equity in the car. Now he had the check to pay it off. But he didn't. His savings had dwindled to almost nothing during the last three months and because he was hoping for a good commission check in May, he perfidiously decided he would just deposit the seventy-four hundred, use a little of it if he had to do so, and if anything was said, immediately pay off the six-thousand-dollar note. He used five hundred dollars of the money to make the down payment on a new Chevrolet Impala Custom Coupe which he financed with GMAC.

Now Cooper knew that what he had done was chicanery. He had arrantly sold mortgaged property and not paid off the loan. But in the throes of his own insecurity he rationalized that he could come up with the money to pay off the note at any time. Like a speculator watching the market fall, it gave him a great sense of security to know he had money in the bank, and this security made it easier for him to continue his selling efforts in the face of those recent demoralizing results.

His commission check the first of May was only eight hundred dollars. This was enough to pay his monthly bills without having to touch any of the sixty-nine hundred dollars in his savings account, but his daily and weekly expenses went on and he flagrantly began to dip into it.

About this time Dan realized he had run out of friends to contact about insurance. He was reduced to trying to get referrals from his present customers to strangers. In some cases this was not hard but even when he was directed to good prospects he found he was thwarted in achieving his goal because he wasn't nearly as effective with strangers as he had been with friends. Selling insurance was largely a matter of getting the client's confidence. Few people really understood life insurance and almost no one bought it for practical reasons. Like a daughter's wedding or a father's funeral, they dealt with it emotionally. If the salesman could arouse their sense of responsibility enough they would buy. Therefore when working with people who knew him well, Dan was much more effective. They knew he was not a con artist, not trying to sell them something they didn't need, and they bought from him. True, his success varied somewhat from one individual to another, but in most cases when he took the time to go into a man's insurance program carefully and give him an honest appraisal, he could usually convince the man to buy the additional coverage he needed. But with strangers it was different. While they might listen and might cooperate to the point of giving him the information he needed to make his analysis, he found it harder to win their confidence. The result was that when he presented his recommendations, instead of buying they procrastinated, confounded him by saying they would think about it, or that they would buy sometime in the future. While he was making a lot of new friends and doing a lot of work, he wasn't making near enough sales or enough money.

In early April he received a referral to Mike McKnight, a highly successful real estate developer, who qualified as a prime prospect for a large amount of life insurance. McKnight, a big chested, balding man who had about him an air of friendliness and undeniable charisma, welcomed Dan's questions and stated frankly that he wanted to review his life insurance program. He had purchased large amounts of coverage in the past—a good sign—and he had the ability to pay for anything he decided to buy. It was largely on the prospects of a good sale to McKnight that Dan held back the money he should have used to pay off the note on the Continental. By the time he got the check from his insurance company he had decided to recommend McKnight buy an additional $200,000 life policy on himself and a similar one on his junior partner. While he had no commitment of any kind, the remarks McKnight had made led Dan to believe he would buy, even if he opted for a smaller policy. Early in May Cooper had his presentation ready and tried to make an appointment with McKnight. But the real estate man was busy and then two weeks later he left on a three week vacation to Japan, so it was the middle of June before Dan was able to sit down with him again. By this time McKnight's mind had become occupied with a new apartment project he was considering, and he was less concerned with his estate plan than he had been back in April. Although he gave it his full attention the afternoon of the presentation and appeared to be impressed by Dan's reasoning, he didn't buy. He told Cooper he would think about it, talk it over with his lawyer and his partner and get back with him in a couple of weeks. Dan knew this was the kiss of death. When the prospect didn't buy at the presentation the chances of his buying later were very small. But Dan needed this sale so badly he wouldn't let himself believe that was the case with McKnight. He kept telling himself the man really meant what he said and that a sale would result in the next few weeks.

In this frame of mine he slowly began dipping into the money in his savings account. After all he had to keep up the payments on the house and the cars or lose them. He paid the June and July bills and a share of their living expenses from this money and by the end of July, even with his best efforts; the balance in the bank had dropped below forty-five hundred dollars. When the Continental note came up for renewal again in June he paid six hundred dollars on the principal plus the interest, but that left a balance of fifty-four hundred owing.

Although he was still in the methadone program, Louise suspected Jim Carpenter was using heroin again. In early May when he went to the hospital with a severe case of infectious hepatitis, she asked Dan to sell the El Dorado for her. He cleaned it up, put an ad in the paper, and moved it quickly. After paying off the note there was no cash left, but at least she got out from under the three-hundred-and-thirty-dollar monthly car payment and the one-hundred-dollar a month insurance payment.

She had borrowed twenty-five hundred dollars from the C. & S. Bank at the first of the month and now Dan took her back to the Trust Company where she signed a new ninety-day note for another thirty-five hundred. They used this to make the monthly payments due in June on her bills and made a two hundred dollar down payment on a new, light blue Pinto which she financed with Ford Motor Credit. Janie had recently gotten her driver's license and the plan was for her to drive the new car.

Dan still did not like to tell her so, but he could see that if the vulnerable Louise didn't extricate herself from her abortive relationship with Jim Carpenter she would never get out of the dire financial straits she was in. In fact there might be trouble paying her monthly bills as early as August. After Dan's success in getting the money for her house, she felt he could persuade the trustees in Pittsburg to give her more money from the principal of her trust fund. But he was reluctant even to try. First, he felt it would be hard to justify any outlay from capital when her quarterly income was so high. If it were one of her children who had the drug problem it might be possible to use this as a reason for needing additional money. But Jim Carpenter was not related by blood or marriage. Secondly, Dan was sure that if Louise got any extra money now, the incorrigible Jim would just figure some way to get it away from her. Dan felt some sympathy for Jim, but he was distressed at the effect the young addict had upon Louise. She was a nervous wreck—never sleeping; constantly eating, drinking, and worrying.

In June the solution to the problem of Jim finally presented itself when he was arrested for burglary. After being released from the hospital in late May he had arrogantly declared himself cured of his addiction and had indeed stayed straight for a few days. He looked healthy again and thus encouraged, Louise let him use the new Pinto to go out to look for a job. But he found no job and within a week, like a bear going back to a honey tree, he went back to shooting heroin.

At this point Louise was penniless and even if she had wanted to give him money, she had no cash. So Jim began taking things from her house and selling them to get money to feed his habit. First it was a black and white TV they kept in their basement. Then it was a portable sewing machine that belonged to Janie. The next day Louise came home and found the big color console gone from the living room. When she asked Jim about it he mendaciously said it had quit working and he had called a repairman to pick it up but he was vague about which repairman.

Dan, who was wrestling with his own financial worries at the time, was treated to a heart-rending review of Louise's problems at least once every day and several times on some days. Her maudlin recitals depressed him but she didn't seem to have anyone else she could talk with and he felt he had to do what he could to help her even if it was only lending a sympathetic ear to her constant recriminations.

It was on a warm hazy May morning when he was discussing selling the El Dorado over breakfast that Helen, who had previously made little comment about his involvement with Louise, spoke up angrily. "Louise Haddock, Louise Haddock, that's all I ever hear! If she wasn't so fat and old I'd think you were having an affair with her. I just don't understand what it is going to get you!"

"Baby, I just don't know how to explain it," Dan said with a pusillanimous sigh. "It's partly that she is already a customer. I've made about a thousand dollars off the policies she bought, but it is also that she's someone who truly needs help and advice and I can supply these. And she is still paying me the hundred and fifty a quarter to be her financial advisor."

"But Dan if she has ten thousand dollars coming in every quarter she ought to pay more than a lousy hundred-fifty dollars considering all the time you are spending with her. I believe you see more of her than you do of me," she asseverated, a note of envy creeping in.

"I may have the last week or two with all the trips to the hospital to see Jim and trying to sell her car, but it is just a temporary situation. If she ever gets any money ahead she has said she'll buy more insurance."

"But why do you have to be the one to take her to the hospital every day. Why can't she get her daughter to drive her or take a cab?"

"I guess she could cab it but she can't really afford that right now. And Janie just got her license and isn't insured to drive the El Dorado. That's one reason I'm trying to sell it, so she can buy something Janie can drive." Look, he said in a flash of inspiration, "she wants to go to the hospital to see Jim again this afternoon. Why don't you take her? You don't have that much to do. It'll leave me free to work and maybe you'll get to know her a little better and begin to understand the situation."

"All right I will. I don't dislike Louise. I just think she is taking advantage of you and I don't like that."

That was the start of the specious friendship between Louise and Helen. During that May and June there was so much happening that Helen and Dan both spent a lot of time chauffeuring the fat woman here and there. When Dan sold the El Dorado and Louise bought the Pinto they all thought it would stop, but it didn't. As soon as Jim was home from the hospital he was using the Pinto and when he wasn't Janie had it visiting her friends. So Helen began going out to Louise's house almost daily to drive her to the grocery store, to the bank, and on other errands. She was as concerned as Dan when Jim started taking things out of Louise's house. However Helen was considerably more outspoken about it than Dan. She told Louise that she had to get rid of Jim. She said she had known people on heroin before and she felt there was nothing that could be done. Louise seemed to agree but did nothing and as they turned the corner into June things had only gotten worse. It was a bright sullen day during the first week of June when Jim was first arrested. This time it happened around noon. He called Louise just after one. He had been caught red-handed bringing a TV out of an apartment on Buford Highway. For once he hadn't been in Louise's car but with one of his friends from the clinic. His bond was only a thousand dollars and he told Louise to get up a hundred and get in touch with a certain bondsman who would get him out.

The first thing Louise did was call Dan. He told her to let Jim stay in jail. It would force him off the heroin since he couldn't get it there, and maybe it would make Jim realize that there was a limit to what Louise could afford to do for him. Dan hung up the phone feeling a small sense of relief. He told Helen about it and she agreed that leaving Jim in jail for a few days was the thing to do.

But later that evening Louise called again. Jim was out. When Janie had come home and Louise had told her about it she had felt they had to get him out. She had come up with twenty dollars she had made baby sitting and contributed that toward the bond money. The boys had come in from school and Janie had persuaded them to contribute a few dollars also. Just then the mailman arrived with one of the monthly insurance checks that Louise normally used to buy groceries. So they loaded into the Pinto and after cashing the insurance check at the grocery store, had gone to the DeKalb County Jail to wait while the bondsman did his thing and arranged for Jim's freedom. When Louise called she was in good spirits. Exuberantly she said Jim was chastened and contrite, had learned his lesson, and was determined to kick the habit for good. Everything was going to be all right.

But in three days he was shooting again and in two weeks he was back in jail. It was another burglary charge. This time he was caught trying to sell a TV that had been stolen the day before. He had been in the Pinto and it had been impounded by the police.

When Louise called this time Helen answered the phone. Dan was out so Louise asked her what she should do. "Helen I just don't have any money to bail him out again," she expostulated in her unmitigated misery. "I've got less than fifty dollars and no money coming in until the quarterly check early next month and we don't have hardly any food in the house either. He said the bond was twenty-five hundred this time so I'd need two-hundred-fifty dollars for the bondsman. Maybe I could get a cash advance on my Master Charge card. I haven't charged anything on it lately and we did make payments on it the last two months."

"I don't think you should do that Louise. Why don't I come over and pick you up and you can come here and stay until Dan gets home. Then you can talk it over with him."

Reluctantly Louise agreed and Helen went to pick her up. Before leaving Louise told Janie that if Jim called again to tell him she had gone out to try to raise some money.

It was late before Dan got in. By that time Louise and Helen had consumed several drinks and Louise was feeling much better. After telling Dan about it she surprised them both by dolorously confessing, "Dan I really can't help him any more. You've told me that before and Helen has told me again this afternoon and I realize it's true. But what can I do when he calls and I begin to feel sorry for him?"

"You just can't afford to feel sorry for him anymore. You've done your share. You have tried to help him over and over and you're right back where you started. You've got to just let him sit it out in jail for awhile. Maybe when you get some money you might want to hire him a good lawyer who can get him into a drug hospital instead of prison. That's where he needs to be."

"I know you're right but when he calls I get all upset."

"Why don't you just not answer the phone?" Dan asked plaintively.

"I could try that but when the kids are there they answer it and call me without telling me who it is."

Without hesitation Helen spoke up saying, "Why don't you just come over here and stay for a couple of days. We've got plenty of room. You could even bring the kids. Then he won't know how to reach you and he'll eventually stop trying."

"Oh, I couldn't impose on you like that," Louise replied in vehement protest.

"Helen just said she'd be glad to have you and I think that might be a good solution. Why not?"

"Well if you're sure I wouldn't be imposing I might do it for a couple of days. I think the kids could manage without me. The boys are both working and Janie is going to summer school."

So it was arranged. They all drove to Louise's house for her to pack a bag. She told Janie she was going to a motel for a couple of days to get some rest and that she would drop by the next afternoon.

She stayed with them for more than a week. Dan was out most of the time trying to get his lagging insurance sales back up, but Helen enjoyed embroiling herself in entertaining Louise.

The day after Jim was arrested they took Janie with them and picked up the Pinto from the police impoundment so she would have a way to get around. The children seemed to take it all in stride although Janie felt unequivocally that her mother should do something to get Jim out.

Languishing in jail he continued to call daily and like a spoiled child spewed out his choleric diatribe on whoever answered. But after not being able to talk to Louise for several days he got the message that she couldn't or wouldn't bail him out again. It was the sixth day before he happened to call when Louise was at home.

"Louise, this is Jim. Why haven't you gotten me out?" he chided her belligerently.

"Jim I just can't raise the money. You know how broke I always am this time of the month."

"Then why don't you borrow it from Dan? He'll loan you that much until your check comes."

"I can't ask Dan for any more money Jim."

"Well he'd give it to you. I know he would. Now hang up and call him and get the money," he demanded rabidly. Then pleading he continued, "I can't stand this place any longer. You don't know how sick I've been. Louise, you've got to help me!"

"I'll see what I can do Jim. Bye now," she replied hastily, ringing off.

The call upset her but Louise didn't change her mind about getting him out. Just having Helen there gave her a great deal of strength. But after that she was careful not to answer her phone.

She had, by this time, told Janie where she was staying, and it was the next day that she called her mother at Dan and Helen's with the news that Jim was free. "Mom he came by and picked up his clothes. He said his parents had gotten up the bail money and that he was going to their house and stay. He wants you to call him there."

"Okay Janie, thanks for calling," Louise said. "I'll be home in the morning. I guess I'll see you then."

"He's out," Louise told Helen tersely. "Janie said he picked up his clothes. He wants me to call him at his folk's house."

"I don't think you should. He'll just start on you again."

"You're right. But I guess I should move back home."

"Stay as long as you like," Helen replied earnestly. "I'm enjoying having you."

"Well one or two more days at the most. I guess he realizes I can't help him anymore."

Dan had enjoyed having Louise there to visit. Getting her away from the duplicitous Jim had made a different woman out of her. She lost her haunted look and began to smile and laugh again, even displaying a fine dry wit. Dan had always found her an intelligent and charming person when she wasn't worrying about Jim or one of the children, but he was amazed at the propitious change that took place in those few days. She and Helen did some shopping, all on credit of course, at Rich's and Saks, and opened a new account at Penny's. Dan didn't approve of this but he felt it would be parsimonious to object too strenuously. Without Jim Louise could probably work out from under her debts in a few months. And after all, it was her money, not his. She bought Helen three new outfits explaining that she had to repay her in some way for her hospitality. They were striking clothes and because Dan hadn't been able to give Helen any money for new clothes in several months, he was pleased.

One night they took her out, had dinner at the Coach and Six, and afterward went dancing at the Sans Souci. Another night Alan joined them and after dinner at The Midnight Sun, they all went to see Phil and Nancy Erickson's latest show at The Wit's End. Louise loved it. Yet another evening they had dinner in Underground Atlanta, then partied at Ruby Red's and The Burning of Atlanta Bar.

She went home on the ninth day a different woman. Jim came by one day shortly afterward and gave her a hard time, berating her for not helping him, but somehow she found the courage to endure his fulminations without making any concessions. Dan's opinion was that she really had convinced herself finally that she couldn't afford to do anymore for Jim. She was depressed by his visit but that evening she came to their house for dinner and after a few drinks she was back in good spirits.

When her quarterly check came in July they sat down and tried to figure how to spread it around. Repaying the bank loans took the biggest part of it but there was enough left to make the minimum payment on all the charge accounts for one month.

"Dan, I've got to get out from under these bills so I can have a little money to spend," Louise fretted. "Do you realize the kids haven't been on any kind of vacation for two years? And those clothes Helen and I bought last month were the first new things I've had in nearly a year!"

"Louise I don't see how you can do much this quarter or next. But by January you should be able to start using the charge accounts again."

"Dan, I just can't wait until then. You know we don't have a TV in the house. Jim sold them all, even the old used set the boys had. And I need a dryer. I have to stay up half the night drying the boy's jeans over the stove so they'll have something clean to wear to work."

"I suppose you could put a black and white TV on the CCA at Rich's and some clothes for the boys on the new account at Penny's. But you're paying an awful lot of interest now and the longer you take catching up the bills the more interest you have to pay."

"Dan, why don't you write the trustees and see if they will give me an extra ten or fifteen thousand to pay off these bills? You can tell them we were all sick or something. You got money from them for the house."

"Yes I did, but that was a little different. I'm afraid they would say no and I hate to be told no. Besides if I ask for money now to catch up bills and then you really did have an emergency you might not be able to get any help when you need it most."

"I can't think of any financial emergency that would be any worse than my present situation. How would it be if we flew up to see them? I've got a new credit card from Eastern."

"It would be better than writing. Let me ask you this. If we did and were successful in getting ten thousand, do you think you'd be able to go ahead and buy those life policies we talked about on the kids? I hate to push it but my business is off and if I could make that sale it would justify my taking the time to make the trip."

"Yes, I'd be willing to do that. I know the one hundred and fifty dollars a quarter I've been paying you doesn't properly compensate for the amount of time you've spent with me."

"I don't want you to think I've only helped you for the money involved, but right now I'm in a financial hole myself and I need to be out stirring up insurance business. And I know you haven't had the money to buy any more insurance. But if we could get ten thousand from the trustees and you used a thousand of it to pay the first year's premium on a $10,000 policy for each of the kids it would be a big help to me. I don't only need the money; I need to sell the insurance."

"Let's do it then. I'll pay the cost of the trip if you'll go and do most of the talking. If we get the money I'll buy the insurance."

So it was arranged that on the first Wednesday in July they flew to Pittsburg to confer with the trustees of Louise's trust fund. Like wise old owls the bank officials sat across a table, nodded sympathetically, and gave sage advice—but they did not come forward with the money Louise was hoping for. They said they were glad she had made them aware of her situation. They would henceforth manage her money in such a way as to increase her current, after-tax income as opposed to concentrating on long term capital growth as they had been doing. They explained that while they were empowered to give her money from the principal of the trust for medical emergencies and for reasons connected with the children's education, there was no way they could advance her funds to pay her current bills. They had justified the outlay of the house money on the basis that it would enable her to move to a better neighborhood, North Fulton High being considered a superior school to Grady.

However, they did come up with one suggestion that Dan thought worth considering. They said they saw no reason why she couldn't cash in one or more of the insurance policies that paid her the monthly payments. There were eight of these of different face amounts and as far as the bankers knew, Louise could elect to draw down the principal in one lump sum rather than taking the monthly settlement option payments she was now receiving. In the twenty years since her father's death interest rates had gone up considerably and she could probably reinvest a portion of the money in bonds or savings certificates and receive as much income as the entire amount was now paying and use the balance to pay her current bills.

Dan had thought about this possibility before but had not suggested it because he feared that with Jim around the entire principal would be spent as quickly as gambling winnings and Louise would just be left with a reduced income. However now that the trustees had brought up the idea, he couldn't refuse to check into it for her. Besides he had begun to think that without Jim's profligate influence Louise would use good judgment in spending her money and not get back into the kind of financial panic she had experienced for the last few months.

Upon their return he wrote the eight insurance companies on her behalf and inquired if the policies could be cashed in. It took several weeks to hear from all of them and most of the news was discouraging. It developed that her father had elected to have interest only paid to her from these policies during her lifetime with the principal passing to her heirs at her death. However one company, Mutual of Ohio who was the one who sent the largest monthly check, advised that while their instructions were the same, with their policy she had the right to change these instructions.

They received this propitious letter on the second of August. Dan immediately wrote back and asked the company to send the forms for Louise to sign to withdraw the principal. He calculated it to be approximately fifty thousand dollars. If she deposited thirty thousand in a savings account paying only five percent it would return something close to a hundred thirty a month, almost as much as she was getting from the entire fifty thousand now. And he thought she could probably get a much higher return by purchasing a Certificate of Deposit. That would leave twenty thousand she could use now. He figured it would take close to eleven to pay off her charge accounts. The remainder would be sufficient to pay back the three thousand dollars she had just borrowed from the C. & S. to see her through August (they had not had to re-borrow from the Trust Company yet but would doubtlessly have to do so if the fifty thousand didn't come by early September), buy the insurance he was proposing, and see her through until the October check came. In fact he thought there would be enough to pay off her car as well, but that wasn't necessary.

With prospects of the sale to Louise, to McKnight and to others, Dan went back to his bank to borrow money again in early August. He got two thousand dollars—this time on a ninety-day, unsecured basis. After paying his August bills he again had enough in the bank to cover the Continental note should it become necessary to pay it off.

By the summer of 1971 the belated efforts of the world's governments and air carriers to stop the hijacking of airliners was beginning to show results. In the first six months of 1971 there were only twenty-seven attempts compared with forty-seven during the same period of the preceding year.

And there were far fewer which were successful. Only seven made it from the U. S. to Cuba between January 1st and July 24, 1971. At that point the anti-hijack program consisted of a three-pronged effort: the behavior check; the frequent use of manometers to check passengers and their carry on luggage; and the stationing of sky marshals on certain flights.

The behavior check program was just that, a check of the behavioral characteristics of those purchasing tickets, and it was successful in weeding out many of the Cubans, the misfits, and the mentally ill who came to the airport with hijacking on their mind. While the details of the program were not revealed, obviously appearance and dress were high on the list of characteristics to be observed. Additionally, the amount and type of luggage, the method of payment for the ticket, and the general demeanor of the individual were factors which might cause a departing passenger to be stopped and questioned by a security guard.

In 1970 manometers began to appear in many terminals and all passengers entering certain areas or boarding certain flights were required to pass through these metal detectors. Undoubtedly these discouraged other would-be hijackers who got by the behavioral check.

The sky marshals were special agents trained to thwart hijackers without endangering the aircraft or its passengers. Immediately after the Arab skyjacks two hundred civilian government guards were rushed into skyjack duty and the force was quickly increased to about two thousand. They rode selected flights in the disguise of ordinary passengers and were occasionally successful in preventing a hijacking. On July 18, 1971, Bobby White, an emotionally disturbed young man who boarded a Piedmont 737 at La Guardia and demanded to be flown to Cuba, was overpowered by two sky marshals.

But these measures were only partially successful as some hijackers continued to slip through the net. On May 28, 1971, ex-policeman James E. Bennett commandeered an Eastern 727 en route from New York to Miami and ordered it flown to Nassau where he allegedly demanded $500,000 ransom—for donation to the Irish Republican Army.

He was overpowered upon landing at Nassau.

June 11 the first passenger fatality aboard a U. S. aircraft was recorded with the death of Howard L. Franks who was shot by a hijacker shortly after the latter had seized a TWA 727 at the boarding gate in Chicago. After a bullet-punctuated flight to New York, Gregory White, 23, was arrested on charges of murder and aerial piracy. He had asked to be supplied with $75,000, a machine gun and a free ride to North Vietnam.

A cliffhanger began on July 2 and ended forty-four hours later and seventy-five hundred miles from the point of origin to establish a new record for lengthy hijackings. Robert Lee Jackson and Ligia Lucrecia Sanchez-Archilla took over a Braniff 707 on a Mexico City-San Antonio flight and ordered it flown to Buenos Aires—by way of Monterrey, Lima, and Rio de Janeiro. While in Monterrey they demanded and received $200,000 in ransom money for the release of a passenger hostage. Argentine police took the cash away from them when they arrested the pair.

On July 23rd an FBI marksman armed with a high-powered rifle took aim at Richard Obergfell, hijacker of a TWA jetliner, on a Kennedy Airport runway where Obergfell expected to board a plane to Italy. After forcing Chicago-bound Flight 335 to return to La Guardia, he had demanded ground transportation to Kennedy and taken a stewardess hostage along with him. The FBI agent's aim was accurate; the stewardess was uninjured, but the suspect, wounded in the shoulder and stomach, died twenty-five minutes later. This was the first time an American hijacker had been slain on U. S. soil in the course of a hijacking.

The next day, July 24th, brought more bloodshed. In the years seventh skyjack to Cuba, a man armed with a small caliber pistol and a stick of dynamite took over a National DC-8. On the way to Havana he opened fire and wounded a male passenger and a stewardess.

From the first the hijacking issue had been complicated by the sympathetic feelings Americans felt for those who used it as a method to escape from communist-dominated countries. But the biggest problem delaying the implementation of truly effective measures against hijacking was the cost. The airlines wanted the government to pick up the tab and vice versa. Naturally the airlines that had been hardest hit were the ones who had the best security. National and Eastern, who had experienced twenty attempts each since January of 1968, had very fine operations as did TWA (sixteen attempts) and Delta (twelve attempts). But American, Braniff and Continental with only one hijack each over this period were less concerned as was Northwest who had been troubled by skyjackers only twice since the craze began May 1, 1961, when a Cuban calling himself Elpirati Cofrisi used a gun and a knife to divert a National Convair 440 to Havana.

During that spring and early summer Dan Cooper was like a student pilot on his first solo cross-country flight. He thought he knew where he was and where he was going, but occasionally he would experience terrifying doubts. In an iconoclastic mood he had thought again about the possibility of an aircraft hijacking for ransom. While no one had gotten away with it yet, a few hijackers had demanded and been given money. It wasn't that Dan was seriously considering doing it. But as his money had gotten short he began to think of some way he could raise a considerable amount of cash. Thus it was natural that the idea, dormant for two-and-a-half years, should surface again in his mind.

Criminals often become criminals by first committing small infractions of the law then gradually becoming inured to the notion that crime (at least some types of crime) is acceptable. The suggestion he had passed into his subconscious mind by association now had come back as auto-suggestion. At this point of course Dan was not a criminal. At least he wasn't a criminal type. But in the early summer of 1971 he found himself harboring thoughts of possible crimes. A man is what he is because of the thoughts he permits to occupy his mind, and so when Dan

Cooper allowed himself to contemplate illegal ways of raising money he took the second step toward becoming a criminal. He had taken the first step the previous spring when he didn't pay off the loan on the wrecked Continental. It had been an accident, the bank not asking for the title, but it had given him the opportunity to commit a crime undetected when he sold the car to the insurance company without paying off the note. True, it was a minor crime, and as long as he could come up with the money at any time it would probably go undetected. But it was a crime nevertheless. It had taken a great deal of rationalization on Dan's part before he could bring himself to take that step. But once he had done it, had committed the crime of selling mortgaged property, he had crossed the boundary where it was no longer a question of "would I be capable of committing a crime?", because a crime had been committed. Instead the question now became "how far would I go in committing a crime?" So although Dan, in his conscious mind, did not admit that he had even committed a crime, subconsciously he knew he had and now admitted to himself that he might have to commit others to extricate himself from his difficulties.

So, although he didn't believe he would seriously ever consider hijacking an aircraft, he let himself think about it. He considered it an intellectual puzzle, something to occupy his mind.

As he saw it, the biggest problem all hijackers faced was that they couldn't get away from the airplane once they commandeered it. Most ended up going to Cuba where a doubtful reception awaited them, while a few had gone to Egypt and other third-world countries. But in every case the hijackers were at the mercy of the officials in whatever country they chose as their destination. If a way could be found to get away from the airplane without the crew being aware of it, this monumental problem would be solved. Dan's experience immediately suggested the idea of using a parachute. He had been an amateur jumper when he lived in Washington, D. C. in 1965, and had made some twenty jumps from light planes. Having flown the Boeing 727 he knew that it had a rear stairway which could be lowered into the slipstream without serious consequences to the airplane. He believed a man could easily parachute out of a 727 using this rear stairway as an exit. While it might not be necessary, it would certainly be better to have the aircraft going as slow as possible when the jump was made.

This much had probably crossed his mind before that fateful summer. But now he reviewed it and proceeded with the other questions that naturally followed. Would it be possible to carry a parachute or parachutes aboard an airliner? Probably not, but if you could coerce the airline into rounding up and bringing ransom money to the airport, you could probably get them to bring you a couple of parachutes also.

The next problem was how to jump from the plane without the crew knowing you had left. Obviously you would have to release the passengers and lock the crew in the cockpit in order to have the cabin to yourself when you got ready to bail out. It was possible the authorities would scramble other aircraft to follow the hijacked plane to see if anyone bailed out. Therefore it would be better to make the jump at night or in weather where a following aircraft could not get close enough to see you leave. Of course there was a disadvantage to this. If a following aircraft could not see the airliner then the parachutist might not be able to see the ground at the time he bailed out. It would be essential that when he bailed out he know exactly where he was going to land. Because he must be able to get to the ground, get transportation, and hole up somewhere before the authorities could figure out where he had gone and start combing the country looking for him. But the pinpointing of the spot to jump was not as difficult as it appeared. As a pilot Dan knew that there were several ways to pinpoint an aircraft's position. The first and most reliable was simple dead reckoning. If an aircraft left point A on the hour flying at a speed of 360 knots (six nautical miles a minute) you knew that twenty minutes later it would be 6 x 20 or 120 miles away from the starting point in whatever direction it was flying. Assuming the crew followed his instructions, he could calculate where they would be at any time. Of course there were a few variables such as wind and the time required for takeoff and climb, but an experienced pilot knew how to allow for these and should be able to put himself within a few miles of his position at any time.

A second way of locating one's self in the air was by observation of landmarks on the ground. Darkness was not a problem in a populated area in good weather. Small towns, cities and highways were good checkpoints, especially in the early evening when houses were lighted and traffic was on the roads. Bad weather was something else again. But if a man was familiar enough with the general area in which he intended to jump, even occasional glimpses of landmarks while he was descending might give enough clues to his location to tell him which way he must travel to reach his destination.

Radio navigation is a third way to keep track of the aircraft's position. Modern aircraft carry several radios which enable the crew to pinpoint the aircraft's location at any time. Except when instructed to do otherwise by the FAA controllers, airliners always travel on the airways, a set of invisible highways in the sky. These are plotted on charts and if the hijacked aircraft should be instructed to fly a particular airway that went over the point at which he wanted to jump, it only remained to pinpoint the time at which it would cross that point. Of course the plane might wander off course but modern airline pilots were professionals and prided themselves on their proficiency. The chances of being off course were small. There is also a radio navigational device carried by all airliners which can tell the pilot when he is over a certain point on the airway. This is called DME, distance measuring equipment. It continually gives a reading in nautical miles of the distance the aircraft is from any given station within range. The normal procedure is to keep the DME tuned to the navigational station behind the aircraft until it is halfway to the next station and then tune it to that station. If the hijacker could know the airliner was flying down the specified airway and watch the DME until it told him that the aircraft was over his predetermined jumping point, he could jump exactly where he planned. Dan wasn't sure just how this could be done but he felt reasonably certain that using a combination of navigational methods, he could jump into a given area with accuracy.

There were some other considerations about the jump. It should be made from an altitude high enough to give him some chance to determine his exact position visually while he was descending. But he didn't want to be too long in getting down because that meant there was a greater chance of his being spotted by a following plane or someone on the ground. Of course a night jump would minimize this possibility.

It was absolutely essential to jump into an area he knew well. Once on the ground he would have to determine his position and immediately make his way to some mode of transportation. On reflection he realized the only safe mode of transportation would be a private car or truck. One could be left almost anywhere for a day or two without arousing suspicion and if he could parachute close enough to be able to walk to it without being noticed, he could make a quick, safe getaway. Therefore the choice of where to jump was a very important consideration.

There were a lot of other things to consider but Dan had gotten this far in his thinking about the hijack by late July. He certainly wasn't planning to go through with it when he was doing this thinking. He was merely speculating on what the problems would be and considering how they might be solved.

On Tuesday, August 3rd, the day after he wrote Mutual of Ohio to send the papers for Louise to sign to withdraw her $50,000, Cooper took applications for a one-million-dollar life insurance policy. When issued and paid for it would earn him first commissions of more than ten thousand dollars, by far his largest sale to date.

Everything had happened quickly culminating with his taking of the applications that afternoon. It had begun only the previous week when Dan had once again called on Mike McKnight, the charismatic real estate developer. McKnight, in his redoubtable way once again put off a decision concerning his own insurance needs, but attempted to compensate Dan for his trouble by telling him of a friend who had mentioned he was considering purchasing a large policy. Without hesitation McKnight picked up the phone and called this friend, a contractor named George Burnett whose company had built some of the McKnight apartment projects, and let Dan talk with him. The result was an appointment with Burnett the following morning.

The contractor was a big man, almost six-four, with broad shoulders and chest. However he moved with a relaxed grace as he came bounding from behind a huge walnut desk to greet Dan with a hearty handshake and a warm smile. After they were seated he explained in his garrulous way that he and his partner, Terry Jennings, had already decided to enter into a buy-sell agreement and fund it with life insurance. Jennings had an agent and he was right now in the process of working them up a proposal. But Burnett didn't particularly care for this agent and wanted someone else to give them some figures. With barely concealed elation Dan exacted the necessary information and promised to be back with a competing proposal the following Tuesday.

The very next day Dan sat down with Phil Hunter, the design man in the Massachusetts General office, and worked out a compelling presentation based on a joint whole life policy covering either partner. It was cheaper than two whole life policies and would serve their purposes as well.

He met Jennings for the first time when he arrived to present his proposal on the third. A small dark man, sword-thin with jet black hair, he remained imperiously behind his desk when the bombastic

Burnett introduced Dan. But as Dan went carefully through his cogent presentation, Jennings followed his arguments closely and asked several provocative questions. When Dan was finished both partners seemed to be sold on the fact that his product was a better proposition for them than what had been recommended by the competition. However there was still some hesitation.

"These rates you have quoted us are for a standard policy aren't they Mr. Cooper?" Jennings asked in lugubrious tones.

"Yes sir that's right. Do either of you think you might be rated?"

"No, but of course it is a possibility. Is there any way we can find out without a final commitment to buy?"

"Yes of course. If you go ahead and make application for the policy and it isn't issued standard, you have the option of declining to take it and you get your binder back."

"How about if we just made the application and didn't give you a binder until we are sure about the rates?"

"That would be all right too. Of course you wouldn't have any coverage until you did put some money on it."

"How long would it take to find out?"

"If there is nothing wrong they can usually let me know within a couple of weeks after you take the physical. If there are any questionable areas then the underwriters will have to contact your doctors and it will depend on how fast the doctors answer them. On the amount of coverage we are talking about the underwriters will be thorough and cautious but I will push them all I can. We should make the application for the largest amount you are considering even if you later decide that you don't want all of it. Shall I make it out for a million?"

"What do you think George?" Jennings asked agreeably. "We need to be sure of the price and I don't see we have anything to lose by making the application and taking the physicals. If they come back with a rate we can't live with we can shop elsewhere."

"Yes, Terry," Burnett replied in a firm voice. "I think we should go ahead. I'd like to give Dan the business if he can sell us this joint policy at the rate he has quoted."

"Okay then, let's see those applications."

Dan was ecstatic. The first year commission on this million-dollar joint whole life policy would be more than ten thousand dollars. And while it wasn't sold until he had the policy back from underwriting and the premium check in his hand, he was past the biggest hurdle. Once the customer signs the application he has committed himself to a large degree. Both Burnett and Jennings took the physical examinations that same week and Dan got his hopes up that he would have the policy delivered and paid for by the first of September.

Life had been grim for him for the last few months. Starting with the sales slump the first of the year nothing had gone right. There had been Louise and her increasing troubles with Jim Carpenter and with her money. There had been his problems with Helen. There had been the wreck of the Mark III and his failure to pay off the note. And there had been his ever increasing need for money. All these problems had ground him down, but now it appeared this time of tribulation might be past. Jim had faded from the scene and when Louise got the fifty-thousand from Mutual of Ohio she would be on easy street. If this sale went through it would make up for all those slow months and put him back on target for a good sales year. And of course ten thousand dollars would neatly solve all his financial problems. That only left Helen, and Dan felt that getting the other problems off his mind would allow him to concentrate on improving their relationship.

Of course he told Helen and Louise about the big sale to Jennings and Burnett. To his chagrin Helen was almost indifferent, not at all enthused the way she had been when he sold the big Burson policy the previous year. It seemed as though she didn't have confidence in him anymore and this took a lot of the fun out of the sale.

Louise, on the other hand, had nothing but accolades for his performance. When he told her about Helen's reaction she was sympathetic. "Dan, don't let it get you down," she said. "When the policy is sold and you have the commission money she'll get excited.

She just doesn't want to get her hopes up and chance a big let down if something happens."

"Do you think that's all it is? I get the feeling she just doesn't care anymore one way or the other."

"Oh she still cares. It's just that the honeymoon is over and the two of you haven't gotten completely readjusted."

"Yes things are a lot different than they were the first year we were married when I had plenty of time and plenty of money. But I love her even more now than I did then. You know, like the song, I've grown accustomed to her face."

"She loves you that way too Dan. But she feels insecure. She's young and doesn't have your faith that things are always going to be rosy."

"Sometimes I don't have that faith either. But I do have confidence in myself. Confidence that I can be defeated and still come back. Losing my job with Eastern was a bad shock but I came back from that all right. But Helen is my biggest reason for wanting to succeed. She's my reason for living."

"Just don't lose that faith Dan. Just keep plugging and she'll be with you. You know I get the impression talking to her that she led a very insecure life up until the time she met you. She lived with different sets of parents and then drifted around with various men, none of whom she really cared for."

"Yes she doesn't talk about it much. I think she's ashamed of her family. But that doesn't matter to me."

"I know it doesn't matter to you. The point is she had been insecure all her life up until she married you. Then for the first time she found real security and happiness. But she's not entirely sure it will last. So she has started worrying about it. She just needs some reassurance."

"This big sale has reassured me. Even if something were to happen to it I'd still feel reassured because I did get this far with it. There are not that many life insurance salesmen who have even taken an application for a million dollar policy."

"You know what you need to do is take Helen on a short vacation. Go somewhere and show her a good time, spend a little money. Isn't her birthday coming up the last of this month?"

"Yes, it's the twenty-third. That might be a good idea but I hate to spend the money until I'm sure the policy is going through."

"When I get my big check I'll be glad to lend you ten thousand for a few months. If this deal were to fall through there'll be another one coming."

"Would you really?" Dan replied enthusiastically. "It's not that I have to have money right now, but if I knew I could borrow it if I needed it, that would make things easier on me. You know my income in this business is so erratic."

"Yes I'll be glad to lend it to you when the Mutual of Ohio check comes or later if you need it. You can count on it. So go ahead and spend a little money on Helen. It will do more for her spirits than three million-dollar sales."

"I'll suggest a trip somewhere, maybe to New Orleans. You know we went there on our honeymoon and she loved it. Have you ever been there?"

"No, but I've always wanted to go," Louise replies suggestively.

"Then why don't you come along too? We could invite another man to make it a foursome and all have a grand time. You've been saying you needed a vacation."

"I don't know if I could go before my check comes. It may not be here by the twenty-third."

"I can lend you a few dollars to make the trip if the check isn't here by then," Dan countered. "It's my reserve but since I know you'll be willing to make me a loan if the big sale doesn't go through, I don't mind dipping into it."

"Well okay then. But you talk it over with Helen first. She might not want me along."

"I'm sure she'll want you to go. You know how much she likes you."

When he brought the subject up with Helen that same evening, she was thrilled. "Oh Dan, that would be loads of fun! You know what a good time we had down there on our honeymoon."

"I hope you don't mind but I invited Louise to go along. In fact she was the one who suggested the trip."

"No, I'd love to have her come with us. Then I'd have someone to drink with me when you poop out."

"I thought we could ask another man to go along too. Harold Collette would probably be interested. He used to always be game for a trip to New Orleans."

"Do you think he and Louise would hit it off?" she asked mischievously."

"If you mean do I think they'd fall in love, I'd say no. But Harold is the attractive, easy-going type of person who fits into any group and I'm sure he would add to the party. Besides it would give me somebody to drink with when you poop out," he teased.

"You won't see me pooping out Dan Cooper! Not in New Orleans. You better be careful if you don't want me going to bed with one of those good looking French guys."

"You might be disappointed."

"I might just take my chances," she replied coyly.

It seemed like old times for the next few days around the Cooper household. Helen was floating on cloud nine. She insisted she needed just a few new things for the trip so Dan dipped into his dwindling savings account and gave her three hundred dollars.

She took Louise shopping and they both bought smart new outfits. Louise was running up her accounts at Saks and Lord and Taylor again but Dan didn't let it worry him. She should be able to pay them off as soon as the big check came.

He immediately contacted Harold Collette and persuaded him to join them on the trip. Harold, a quiet, almost beautiful young man with sparkling blue eyes and dark wavy hair, worked as a salesman at Brooks Brother's downtown. While he was as handsome as Jim Carpenter, he was older, just over thirty, and displayed a much more solemn demeanor. He kept an apartment at The Landmark on the same floor where Dan had lived before his marriage, and they had made a couple of trips together in years past. With his subdued, scholarly personality, Dan thought Harold would be good company for Louise. He didn't expect any romantic interest to develop but should that happen he was sure it would work out better than Louise's involvement with the predatory Jim.

On a Friday night a week before their scheduled departure, they had Louise and Harold over for dinner just so the two of them could get acquainted. While she didn't seem impressed by the taciturn clothing salesman, Louise was relaxed and gracious and within an hour she was acting like she had known him for years.

The papers which Louise had to sign to cash in the policy came on a steaming Saturday, the fourteenth of August. They got them signed, witnessed and airmailed back the same day. Dan told Louise not to expect the check before the first of September but that didn't reduce the excitement in any way.

By this time their plans for the New Orleans trip were complete. Leaving the following Saturday, August twenty-first, they would drive down in one day. They had reserved a suite at the Monteleone for Saturday through Tuesday night and would be there to celebrate Helen's birthday on Monday, the twenty-third. They planned to return home on Wednesday, the twenty-fifth.

On the morning of Wednesday, the eighteenth, Dan received word from his underwriters about the policy on Burnett and Jennings. Jennings was standard but Burnett had high blood pressure and his part of the policy was rate 150%. That wasn't much of a rating but it did up the premium an additional one thousand dollars a year on the million dollar policy. Dan was apprehensive but he decided the best thing was to take the bull by the horns and go see them immediately. At their office he found Jennings out but was able to talk with Burnett.

"George I hope this won't affect your decision to buy the policy," Dan said unctuously after explaining the rating. "It is only a minor problem but one they couldn't completely ignore. And it is always possible that if the high blood pressure goes away you could get the rating removed down the road somewhere."

"I don't think it will Dan. I'll have to talk it over with Terry naturally but I'd still prefer to give you the business. I didn't tell you about it but we took physicals for his agent's company and they have come back with a rating also. I don't have the figures but I think he said it was 150%. When will you have the policies?"

"Probably the first of next week but of course I know the premium now if you want to go ahead and give me a check. That way coverage can begin immediately," Dan urged blatantly in an unconcealed effort to close the sale on the spot.

"I'd better not do that without talking it over with Terry. He is out of town until the middle of next week. Why don't you plan to come back a week from Friday. You should have the policies by then and we'll have had a chance to talk about it."

Cooper knew instinctively he should get back to see them as soon as he could talk to both together. But he was planning to be gone from Saturday until the following Wednesday so the Friday after that would work in well with his plans. That was probably the first day they would see him anyway. If Jennings wasn't returning until the middle of the week he would probably be busy with other, more pressing company business for a day or so before he could turn his mind to the insurance policy. And from what Burnett said, it looked like Dan was home free. So he agreed to come back and see them both on Friday the twenty-seventh.

Helen had been dropping hints for several weeks about what she wanted for a birthday present and Dan had been ignoring them. What she had in mind was a new car. Her convertible was two years old and while it was still a very stylish car, she was tired of it. She said she didn't care for another convertible but instead wanted a roomy sedan. Earlier that month she had dragged a reluctant Dan down to the showroom at Capital and shown him exactly what she had in mind, a dark blue Fleetwood Brougham. She knew Dan was in favor of their next car being a four-door sedan. While he liked his Chevrolet coupe he did not feel it was comfortable enough for four people on a long trip, and likewise Helen's convertible was best suited for trips around town. He hoped they could start traveling again regularly and he realized a big car would be both pleasant and practical. Overcoming his reluctance, he decided to go down and see what kind of trade he could get.

On Thursday morning he told Helen he was taking her car to be serviced since they planned to leave in it on Saturday. But while it was getting its oil changed and lubrication he was doing a little figuring with Stu Ellis, the polished, low-key salesman who had sold them the convertible in 1969. Ellis offered a big allowance on the convertible and a reduced price on the new car. He convinced Dan that now was the perfect time to trade by explaining they could offer top dollar for the rag-top during the good weather and had now reduced prices to move their remaining 1971 models because the 72s were coming out the following month. Dan had been paying on the convertible for two years and by putting a thousand dollars with his equity in it he was able to keep his monthly payment about the same. Agreeing to the deal, he took care of all the paper work that day, but made arrangements to pick up the new car late on Friday evening. He wanted to keep it as a surprise for Helen until the last possible minute even though she would have to see it before her birthday. As he started home that afternoon he was enraptured, excited as a kid with a new toy. It would be fun to have a new car to drive to New Orleans and double fun because he knew Helen would be thrilled with it also. He was so ecstatic he had to tell somebody about buying the car, so abruptly he decided to drive out to Louise's house and confide in her. When he showed her the car she smiled broadly and said it was a great idea. She knew Helen would be happy with it.

They planned to depart for New Orleans early on Saturday morning. On Friday night Dan had to attend a dinner meeting of the insurance agent's association at the Marriott. He left early taking Helen's car on the excuse that he would fill it with gas so they wouldn't have that chore to worry about the next morning. She was a little perplexed at his taking her car since he almost never did this, but didn't seem to suspect his intentions. Swapping cars at Capital, Dan went to his meeting, and then afterward rode around until late to insure Helen was in bed when he got home. Arriving a little after midnight he left the new Cadillac in the driveway.

For some reason they both awoke very early that Saturday morning. They made love, something they rarely did in the morning, then lay in bed talking quietly. "Dan, I'm so excited about the trip I don't know what to say," she signed, giving him a big hug. "I guess that's why I woke up so early this morning. It's just five-thirty now. Say, what time did you get home last night? I waited up until after the eleven o'clock news and you still weren't here."

"I got in around midnight. I was late because I had to go by and pick up your birthday present."

"My birthday present! I thought the trip was my birthday present?"

"You know better than that. You've been dropping hints all month about what you wanted."

"Maybe I did drop one or two but I didn't expect you to buy me anything big. You haven't closed the deal on the big policy yet have you?"

"No, but I think it is as good as closed. And I figured we ought to have your birthday present to take to New Orleans with us."

"Can I have it now or do I have to wait?" she asked with flagrant aplomb.

"I guess you can have it now. There isn't much way I can keep you away from it until Monday. It's outside in the driveway."

"Ooooh Dan," she screamed as she ran through the hall to the front window in the study to look out. "It's beautiful. Is it the one we looked at last week? Let me get some clothes on and we'll go down and check it out."

She snatched on some clothes and he was right behind her. It was just getting light out but she insisted on going for a drive. In the brief void between the retreating night and the crouching morning they rode regally through the quiet streets of Ansley Park in the big blue Cadillac.

"Does Louise know about it?" Helen asked as they swung smoothly onto Westminster Drive. The dawn was growing increasingly bright as she expertly maneuvered the big car.

"Yes, I was so excited I had to tell somebody so I told her Thursday when I bought it."

"Dan would you mind if I dropped you back at the house and rode over to Lynn's and showed it to her? I'll be back in about an hour. We've still got plenty of time don't we?"

"Yes, go ahead. Louise and Harold probably won't be ready before nine o'clock anyway. I'll fix myself some breakfast. Just be careful. I love you."

She dropped him at the house and raced off, zipping through the early morning traffic like a fox running from whippets. It was more than two hours before she returned. She had not only been to Lynn's, but to see two other girl friends to show off her expensive new car. As Dan had predicted, Louise and Harold were running behind schedule so it was ten before they finally got loaded and on the road. They had to stop and get gas before leaving town. Helen had burned up a whole tank riding that morning."

The trip down was fun. Dan and Helen took turns driving. When they decided to stop in Montgomery for lunch Harold suggested a drive-in. But Helen wouldn't allow them to eat in her new car. She insisted they find a restaurant and go inside. Arriving in the Crescent City a little before six, they immediately checked into the hotel and got ready for a big night on the town. They were given a corner suite with a sitting room which had a nice view of Royal toward Canal, and three bedrooms, two of which opened directly into the sitting room.

That night they had dinner at Antoine's and then began a leisurely tour of the clubs on Bourbon Street. Louise was like a new person. She seemed to be having the time of her life. Harold however, complained of a headache and left them to return to the hotel shortly after dinner.

When they tired of listening to the musicians at Preservation Hall, Louise insisted they go see the exotic dancers at the 500 Club. Helen said she didn't really care to see that show and if they didn't mind she would go to Pat O'Brien's and listen to the piano players. They could catch up with her there. Dan didn't like leaving her but was stuck with Louise since she didn't want to go to the exotic's club alone. The show there lasted nearly an hour and then, arriving at Pat O'Brien's, they encountered a long line of people waiting to get into the main lounge where the piano players performed. They waited their turn and when they did get in Helen was nowhere in sight. Louise was having such a good time Dan felt he had to stay with her but was concerned about Helen. He went out and called the hotel. There was no answer in their bedroom or the sitting room. They continued their round of the clubs, staying out until nearly two, but when they got in she still wasn't there.

Dan was troubled and didn't know what to do. He and Louise were sitting up drinking bourbon and discussing it when she came bouncing in around two-thirty. Before he could ask where she had been she burst out, "Dan you'll never guess who I ran into at Pat O'Brien's!"

"No I don't guess I will," he replied tersely in a strained voice not trying to hide his displeasure. "Who was it?"

"Harvey Woodruff, my friend from Hartford, Connecticut. Remember the one I met up there the summer Big Sam left Alma and I stranded?"

"Yes I remember your talking about him. Why did you run off?" Why didn't you wait on us there?"

"We did wait Dan nearly an hour. I figured you two had changed your mind and gone somewhere else and Harvey wanted to show me some of the other clubs so we went on. I hope you're not mad?"

"No, I'm not mad, but I wish you had waited on us. Of course we were a long time getting there."

"See there, I wasn't at fault. Come on now and let's go to bed. I haven't had an opportunity to thank you properly yet for my birthday present," she said with ardent affection as she put her arms seductively around his neck.

"You're a wicked woman Mrs. Cooper," he replied teasingly. "Staying out all night with strange men and then coming home and trying to seduce me. You're damn near irresistible. Come on, let's go."

The next day they slept late, but everyone got together for breakfast in the sitting room. From then on it seemed they did things in pairs: sightseeing, shopping, drinking and eating. Harold took Helen sightseeing to the old cemeteries and the Garden District of the city. Dan and Louise went browsing through the shops and ended up drinking coffee at the French Market. Then they got back together long enough for Louise and Helen to head back to one of the shops where Louise had spotted something she thought Helen would want, while Dan and Harold went downstairs and had drinks at Le Carousel Bar. When it came dinner time Harold cancelled out pleading another headache and Helen brashly claimed she wasn't hungry. But Louise had been planning on a big dinner at the Rib Room at the Royal Orleans so Dan was trapped into spending the evening with her again. After dinner she begged to go see Al Hirt and since Hirt was also one of Dan's favorites, they went. Helen met them momentarily when they had finished dinner, but since she didn't care to see Al Hirt's show, she went her own way promising to meet them later back at the hotel. Rain was falling in a solid wall of water when they left

Al Hirt's Club, and it took them quite some time to get back to the room. When they arrived they found Helen in bed asleep.

Monday was Helen's birthday and they celebrated by all having a long lunch at the Court of Two Sisters. They had martinis before lunch, a dusty Beaujolais with the meal, and several after-dinner drinks. By the time they finished it was two-thirty and everyone was high. Dan went in for a nap and left the others having more drinks in the sitting room. When he got up an hour later Helen had gone out alone for a ride in her new car and Harold had gone sightseeing on foot. Louise was still there drinking and watching a soap opera on television.

"How do you feel by now?" Dan asked, mixing himself a Wild Turkey and water.

"Real great! This trip has been the most fun I've had since my husband died. I really want to thank you and Helen for bringing me along."

"You don't have to thank me. The whole thing was your idea. I'm the one who should be thanking you."

"Well you've gone out of your way to be sure I had a good time and I appreciate that."

"You know you're perfectly welcome. I've enjoyed everything we've done. I wonder though. Do you think Helen is having a good time? She keeps running off from the rest of us."

"I think she has been enjoying herself. You know she's a very independent person. She likes doing things on her own. I'm not that way. I have to have company or I just sit."

"Where has she gone now?"

"She said something about going for a ride in her new car. It is a pretty day out. We should do something besides sitting here and getting drunk."

"I wish she had waited on me. I would like to have gone with her. I haven't done any sightseeing outside the quarter."

"She'll probably be back in a little while."

It was only a few minutes later when the phone rang. Dan picked it up and said hello.

"Hi honey, are you up?" Helen asked craftily.

"Yes, I've been up about half an hour. Where are you?"

"I'm at the Touche Bar at the Royal Orleans. Dan I want you to do me a favor. Will you?"

"That depends on what it is."

"Dan I want to use the sitting room for about an hour. Do you mind going out?"

"You want to use the sitting room?" he asked in a puzzled way. "What on earth do you need the sitting room for?"

"I want to invite an old friend over to have a couple of drinks is all," she answered unequivocally in a level tone of voice, giving nothing away."

"Then go right ahead but I don't see any reason I should have to leave. Louise is here too. Do you want her to leave?"

"Yes if she doesn't mind. Why don't you take her somewhere and buy her a drink?"

"I just don't understand what it is you want to do that you don't want us here. Are you ashamed to have him meet me or is it the other way around?" Dan replied sourly, starting to get mad.

"It's not that. It's just that I want to sit and talk to him for a while someplace other than in a bar. I thought you'd probably have gone out sightseeing anyway. You said you were this afternoon."

"Yes I had planned to go out with you but you keep running off. Now you want to bring some man here to our room. I just don't understand what's going on," he said resentfully, now really getting worked up.

"Please don't get your feelings hurt Dan. I didn't mean it to be the way you make it sound. I just wanted to use the room for a little while. Never mind. We'll visit here a little longer and then I'll bring him up and let you meet him. I guess you've figured out it is Harvey I'm with."

"I don't give a damn who you're with. If you want to use the room come ahead. I'm going out and look up some of my old friends. Goodbye," he said flamboyantly slamming down the phone.

"What was that all about?" asked Louise meekly.

"It's Helen," he replied hotly feeling aggrieved and stultified. "She wants us to clear out so she can bring Harvey up here for a drink. I don't understand why she wants us to leave. After all I am her husband. Oh to hell with it! I'm going downstairs and get drunk."

He stomped out of the room and went downstairs to the bar. He sat where he could see out into the lobby and about thirty minutes later he saw Helen walk by with a slim, attractive, blond-headed young man who didn't look a day over thirty. Dan kept his seat and they didn't see him as they moved toward the elevator. Helen looked happy. Apparently she was having a good time in spite of the harsh words they had exchanged on the phone. She wasn't letting Dan's feelings interfere with her fun.

Disgusted, Dan got up and walked out. Emerging into the afternoon's heat, he turned right and walked up to Conti before crossing to Bourbon Street. As he turned right and pushed his way through the afternoon crowd, a good looking blond just ahead caught his eye. She was a small, short girl with full luxuriant hair the color of ripe wheat cascading below her shoulders. She looked smashing in a starched, blue cotton shirt, tight white shorts, and sneakers without socks. As she moved her lean feline body seemed to be bursting with life. Dan momentarily forgot his bruised feelings as his eyes lasciviously followed the provocative switch of her firm round bottom as she threaded her way smoothly along the busy sidewalk. When she disappeared into the Downtowner he continued on and stopped at a café on St. Peter Street called the Fatted Calf. There he ate a hamburger and had two drinks before returning to the hotel. By then it had been over an hour since he had seen his wife with the handsome young stranger and he hoped Harvey, or whoever he was, had left.

When he arrived only Louise was there. She still had the TV going and the usual drink handy. "Did you get to meet the mysterious Harvey?" he asked dejectedly.

"I saw him but she didn't introduce me. I excused myself and went to the bedroom until they left. She knocked on my door as she was going out and said she'd be back in a little while to go to supper."

"I've already eaten. I'm going to have another drink and go to bed."

And he did just that. When Helen returned about seven he was in the bedroom with the door shut. She and Louise sat around drinking for a while, then called room service to bring up supper. When she joined him in bed about midnight Dan was sound asleep.

The next morning he was the first up. She found him in his robe drinking coffee and reading the paper in the sitting room when she came out.

"Hi. Are you feeling better this morning?" she asked solicitously, giving him a warm smile.

"Yes, I'm in a much better mood thanks. Do you want coffee?"

"All right. Look Dan, I'm sorry about yesterday afternoon. I was expecting you to be here when we came up. Louise said you just slammed out. I told you over the phone you didn't have to leave."

"Let's just forget it. I got my feelings hurt at the time but I'm all right now."

"Gee I didn't mean to upset you. I didn't think you'd mind my bringing Harvey up here to have a drink and I thought you might want to meet him."

"No I don't guess I did want to meet him. And I don't really mind you entertaining him. It was just that you hurt my feelings," he said with a petulant frown. "I brought you down here to celebrate your birthday and we haven't done hardly anything together. I have been stuck with Louise most of the time while you've gone off on your own. I spend enough time with Louise in Atlanta."

"I didn't mean for it to work out that way Dan. I couldn't help running into Harvey. And I did enjoy seeing him. I guess I wanted to impress him by bringing him up here and giving him a drink. You remember I was working as a waitress when he met me three years ago."

"You didn't want to ruin the impression by showing him your husband though did you?" he retorted disagreeably.

"Dan that's not fair! I just didn't think you'd want to meet him. And then I thought you were going to be here when we came up and you were gone."

"Well let's not talk about it anymore. It's over with. Do you want to order breakfast here or go out?"

"Let's eat here. I'm hungry and I don't feel like getting dressed just yet."

Breakfast came and they ate. About ten Louise came in and a little later Harold was up. He had gone out early for breakfast and a walk. They began the day's drinking and talked about what they were going to do. Since they had all eaten except Louise who claimed she wasn't hungry, they decided to skip lunch and have a festive dinner that night at Brennan's. Dan suggested they ride out to the lake that afternoon and maybe take in the attractions at the Pontchartrain Amusement Park. Helen dressed quickly and left saying she had an errand to run but would be back in a short while. The others drifted off to get ready to go.

When Dan came back to the sitting room after getting dressed, there sat Helen with the biggest flower arrangement he had ever seen outside a funeral home. It has Mums and Glads and several other kinds of flowers and a big card attached that said, "To the Best Husband in the World, Love Helen."

Dan didn't know what to say. He already felt like an ass for making so much fuss about Harvey. The flowers were beautiful but it was the poignant realization that she really cared that she had hurt his feelings that made tears come to his eyes. He grabbed her and gave her a big hug so she wouldn't see he was crying. "Damn, you really know how to get to a fellow don't you," he swore ardently into the soft fragrance of her hair.

"I couldn't let you stay mad at me. Please say you're not mad at me anymore Dan," she replied softly in contrition.

"I'm not mad at you anymore. All is forgiven. You're about the sweetest wife a guy could have."

"I'm so glad!" she exclaimed. "I didn't mean to hurt you. Aren't the flowers pretty? I told the florist I wanted the biggest arrangement he had that I could carry."

"Is that where you went?" he joked. "Out spending my money on flowers"

"I had to get you back in a good mood didn't I? I couldn't let anything spoil our trip."

"I'm glad you did. I feel better now. Let's get the others. I want them to see how much my wife loves me."

Louise and Harold came in and cooed over the flowers. Dan felt better than he had at any time since the first night when they lost Helen. They finally got away and drove out to the lake. They took some pictures but decided against going to the amusement park. About five they returned to the hotel to dress to go to Brennan's for dinner.

Dinner was superb. They had several courses with drinks and wine and everyone was in good spirits again. The air was cool and pleasant when they came out and Harold suggested they walk down to Jackson Square. They strolled for nearly two hours before Louise complained of being tired and said she was going back to the hotel and go to bed. When Harold excused himself and drifted off on his own, Dan and Helen stopped at Pat O'Brien's where they sat on the patio drinking hurricanes for a long time. Afterward they wandered slowly up and down Bourbon Street unsuccessfully looking for a place where they could dance.

About one they walked back to the hotel. Dan wasn't sleepy but his feet hurt from so much walking. As they turned into the lobby Helen stopped him. "I want to ask you a favor, Dan," she propositioned coyly.

"Okay, what is it?"

"I want to take the car and just drive around for a while. You know how I am when I get restless."

"Can I go too?" I think I would enjoy going for a ride.

"No, I want to go by myself."

"What would you do if I said no?" he asked frankly trying to exact the truth.

"I'd keep on asking until you said yes," she importuned without apology.

Dan didn't want her to go but he knew if she had her mind made up there was no use arguing about it. She was impervious to his feelings, and after the trouble yesterday he didn't want to start another fight. So he just said okay and shut up. She left and crossed the lobby toward the garage while he turned and sidled into Le Carousel.

The crowd there was sparse, but near the door, sitting at the revolving bar, was the same striking blond he had followed down Bourbon Street the afternoon before. Nonplused, he sat down next to her and struck up a lively conversation. Her name was Donna (he never found out the rest) and she was from Dallas. She had come to New Orleans for a week's vacation with two other girls who worked with her at University Computing, but tonight they had dates and she was alone. She was quite drunk and very friendly.

"Was that your wife you were talking with out there in the lobby?" she asked dissolutely, her eyes wide and shinning. She was obviously astute despite her inebriation.

"Yes it was. I didn't see you out there."

"I walked in right behind you and came on in here when you stopped to talk. She's very attractive. Did she go up to bed?"

"No she took the car and went out for a ride. I didn't want her to go but she can be very pigheaded at times."

"I know what you mean," she said laughing felicitously and displaying a dazzling set of antiseptically white teeth. To Dan it seemed hers was a profile that deserved to be described as classic. She had sparking blue eyes, a proud forehead and a mouth that was ripe and full. Tonight she was wearing an eggshell white blouse that clung hungrily to every indentation of her braless breasts and a bright red skirt. As they exchanged small talk the smoke from her cigarette made blue coils in the dim bar light.

Soon it was two o'clock and the bar was closing. Finishing their drinks, they moved slowly out into the empty lobby. "I'd invite you up to my room for a drink but one of my friends is there entertaining," she cooed, giving him a beautiful open, searching look. "I guess I will have to walk the streets for a while longer.

"We could go up to my suite," Dan volunteered hesitantly, his heart thudding, his mouth dry as dust. "I think there is still plenty of liquor up there."

"What about your wife? What would she say if she came back and found me there?"

"I don't think she will be back for some time. But suit yourself," he replied offhandedly, unsure whether or not he wanted to involve himself further with this provocative blond. She had a roguish buoyant sparkle to her that intrigued him but his conscience warned him to beware.

"If you think it is all right I'd love to come up. I really don't want to go out again. I'll give Sally a few more minutes and then I'll call her and tell her I'm coming up."

In pregnant silence they hastily made their way to Dan's suite. He hadn't meant to invite the girl up, but a combination of being mad at Helen, an attraction to this sexy young woman, and a general lack of caring brought on by too much liquor, had resulted in his hesitant invitation which she had snapped up. He felt it didn't really matter. He was just going to give her a drink and then send her up to her room.

When they got to the suite they found Louise still up watching TV. Dan hadn't expected this after all her talk earlier about being tired and going straight to bed. She was in her robe with curlers in her hair. When Dan came in with Donna she quickly excused herself and scuttled off to her bedroom without asking questions.

"Who was that?" Donna asked when Louise had gone.

"A friend who is along on the trip. I didn't expect her to be up."

"Well I'm just going to have one little drink and then call Sally. What have you got to offer a tired Texas girl?"

"It looks like we've got bourbon and scotch. Plenty of ice but not much to mix with. What are you drinking?"

"Scotch on the rocks will be fine. Maybe just a little water."

He mixed two strong drinks and handed one to her. "Here's to it," he said suggestively as he flopped down in a big chair. "It's been a long day and I'm still not sleepy."

It had been over three years since Dan had been to bed with any woman other than Helen. But all of a sudden he found himself lusting after this petite blond. Her small tight body and clear smooth skin awakened licentious desires within him. He knew her body wouldn't have the fleshy fullness of Helen's, but yearned to caress the cool freshness of her well proportioned limbs. He doubted she was a virgin but she seemed youthful and unspoiled. And he could tell she wanted to make it with him. The dissolute way she had maneuvered him into inviting her up was evidence enough of that. Still he might have let the whole thing pass if she hadn't spoken up. "Is that your bedroom in there?" she inquired seductively indicating the connecting door.

"Yes, that's it."

"Why don't we go in there?"

"Let's do," he said unemotionally, a sense of reality now eluding him as he got up and followed her into the darkened bedroom.

They never got the light on. She sat her drink on the dresser just inside the door and turned to face him without comment. He put his down beside it and took her in his arms. They kissed passionately, her hot tongue expertly exploring his eager mouth while he ran his rapacious hands ardently over her firm young body. Making urgent cooing sounds she dragged him down onto the bed and began fumbling at his clothes in a frenzy or ardor. He kicked the door shut as she rolled him off the bed and attacked him on the floor. It had been a long time since Dan had experienced such fervor and voraciously he indulged himself in the debauchery of love making, the sweetness of the sampling of forbidden fruit.

In a few minutes their passion was spent. She dressed hurriedly and left without touching her unfinished drink. She said she had better get on up to her room but she didn't bother to call her friend Sally. Satiated, Dan methodically gathered up his scattered clothes, poured out the untouched drinks they had left on the dresser, and went to bed. He didn't think about Helen.

About four o'clock the phone rang. It was Helen. She was in Gretna, across the river, and she was in jail. A policeman had stopped her and when she couldn't show him her driver's license he had pulled her in. She had apparently lost her wallet with her money and identification. He had allowed her to lock the car and leave it sitting on the side of the road. Would Dan come get her?

He started to say, "It serves you right, I asked you not to go," but he didn't. He said he'd get a cab and come after her. He got up, dressed again, and checked his money. He had ten dollars in small bills plus two one-hundred-dollar bills. She hadn't said how much her bond was, but he guessed it wouldn't be more than a hundred dollars. Downstairs he was lucky and found a cab right away.

It took hours to get her out. First the cab driver had trouble finding the Gretna Police Station. When they finally got there the desk sergeant said Helen was asleep. The bond was only twenty-five dollars but he couldn't make change. After some discussion the sergeant told Dan where the car had been left and suggested a place where he could get a one-hundred-dollar bill changed. So Dan took the cab on to pick up the Cadillac and then had to try three places before he managed to get change. By the time he finally got her out it was seven o'clock in the morning and the sun was already reflecting hotly off the dirty pavement.

She didn't have much to say. She had gone up and crossed at the Huey P. Long Bridge and was coming down the West Bank Highway when the cop had stopped her. He had probably wondered what a woman was doing driving around at three in the morning in a new Cadillac in that part of town. Because she hadn't had any identification on her, he had become suspicious and taken her in. Dan didn't criticize. He knew she knew he wanted to say, "I told you so," but he felt guilty about Donna and he didn't want to make waves. Back at the hotel they ordered breakfast and while they were waiting she snuggled up to him and let him know she wanted to make love. He felt a strange detachment but managed to carry on as usual. She didn't seem to suspect that while he was in bed with her he was thinking of another woman.

Neither of them had gotten much sleep so after breakfast they went to bed for a couple of hours. Getting up at eleven, they were on the road home before twelve. At a truck stop near Slidell, just outside New Orleans, they stopped for gas and a late lunch, and it was after eleven that night before they made it to their home in Atlanta. No one had much to say on the trip home. Dan was glad. He had enjoyed himself part of the time, but it wasn't the kind of trip he had expected.

They slept late on Thursday morning. That afternoon Dan went to the office to check on the Burnett-Jennings deal. The policy had arrived and the rates were as Dan had been told. All he had to do now was get the check. When he called Burnett to confirm their appointment for the next day, the hypertensive contractor was out so he talked with his secretary. She didn't have any notation of the appointment but she knew Mr. Burnett was planning to be in on Friday morning. He asked her to check on Jennings also and when she came back on the line she said he was also out but would be in the next day. Dan left word that he would be there at ten and if that wasn't convenient for Burnett to call him at home when he returned.

Not having heard anything, he was at Burnett's office the next morning at ten. He was kept waiting a half-hour before finally getting in. Burnett, who had previously always been very animated, now put on a long face and Dan got a sinking feeling.

"I have your policy here Mr. Burnett," he said without flinching. "I would like to go over it with you and pick up a check."

"I'm afraid I have some bad news for you Dan," Burnett replied stonily. "I discussed it with Jennings when he got back on Tuesday. He was upset about the rating as he had hoped you might be able to write us both standard. When I told him you couldn't and gave him your prices he called Hank McWhorter, his agent, and asked him to come over. We compared policies and we ended up buying from McWhorter. The price break wasn't that much and we do get two separate policies with McWhorter's deal."

"I wish you had given me an opportunity to go over my policy again as I think you would have felt it was a better deal for your money as you did before," Dan responded resentfully, embittered that he hadn't been there on the critical day.

"Dan I tried to reach you when Jennings called McWhorter but your office said you were out of town until Thursday."

"Thanks for trying," Dan replied tersely with no enthusiasm. "I appreciate your letting me quote. If you decide to buy any more life insurance I'd appreciate the opportunity to talk with you then."

"Of course. Thank you again for your time and trouble. I'm just sorry it didn't work out for you to make the sale. I would have preferred to buy from you but the decision went the other way."

Dan was shattered. He felt so low he couldn't go back to work. Instead he went to the Steak and Ale and had four martinis for lunch then went home and went to bed. Fortunately Helen was out. At supper he told her what had happened.

"Gee Dan I'm sorry," she said with little feeling. "I know you were counting on selling it. Have you got anything else working?"

"There is the five hundred dollars I'll make on Louise's children's policies when she buys them and McKnight is still a possibility. But I'm afraid to count on him."

"I don't think Louise really wants to buy those policies on the children. You really shouldn't pressure her on it."

"I haven't pressured her on it," he snapped back crossly, his eyes wary and hurt. "I presented the proposal back when I first went over her affairs. She said she would like to do it but she didn't have the money right then. When she got me to go to Pittsburg with her she agreed that if we could get as much as ten thousand dollars she would buy the policies both because she wanted them and because it would be a way to pay me for my services. Has she said something to you about not wanting to buy them?"

"Not in so many words but I don't think she does. She resents you telling her how to spend her money."

"God knows I've tried to steer clear of telling her what to do," he exclaimed bitterly in an exasperated voice. "But she asks for my advice and that's all it is, advice. She doesn't have to take it. In fact she doesn't take very much of it."

"I don't care what you say, I don't think you ought to badger her about how she spends this money she is getting. Let her do what she wants to do with it and enjoy it."

"When did you become her champion?" Dan asked sarcastically, his eyes dark and glittering. "I can remember when you gave me a hard time for spending so much time trying to help her."

"I didn't know her that well then. I realize now that when Jim was there she needed someone to give her some sound advice. All he was after was her money."

"I'm not so sure of that. Jim was very good for her for a while. It was only after she reached the point where she couldn't tell him no that the trouble started. And of course the big problem came when he got hung up on drugs."

"I don't think he was ever good for her. He bossed her around and took her money and left her a nervous wreck. What I'm trying to tell you is that you shouldn't boss her around. Let her make up her own mind on spending the money, even on buying insurance."

"Well if she doesn't want to buy insurance she doesn't have to but she should pay me in some way for what I've done for her other than the hundred-fifty a quarter. A lawyer would have charged her five thousand dollars to do what I have done."

The sardonic discussion stopped there. It left Dan with an ominous, uneasy feeling about his relationship with Louise. Maybe he had been bossing her around although he certainly had tried to steer clear of doing that. It looked like he was going to have to ask her for a loan now that the Burnett-Jennings policy had fallen through. He had less than thirty-five hundred dollars left and nothing worthwhile sold. In addition he might be in danger of losing his job. He had only forty-five hundred in first commissions for the year and eight months gone. He needed to sell the children's policies for reasons other than money.

Dan didn't feel much better on Saturday. He stayed home and washed his car while Helen took Louise shopping. She came home with another new outfit. When Dan asked her where she got the money to buy it she said Louise bought it for her as a birthday gift. Dan wasn't pleased about it but he didn't say anything not wanting to poison the belligerent atmosphere any further.

On Sunday night they invited Rod Kerry and Alan Hanson over for dinner. The two pilots had been over often during the first year of Dan's marriage but only occasionally since. Alan had become an especially close friend of Helen's and they both knew Louise also. After supper the four of them played a lively game of Monopoly and drank. Dan was still depressed and he drank more than usual. In spite of that he was leading at Monopoly when the phone rang about ten o'clock. Helen answered it and called to him. "It's Louise," she said stridently. "Janie and one of her friends have wrecked the Pinto. She's all upset and wants you to come over."

"Hell why can't she call somebody else," Dan complained bombastically as he got up and started to the phone. "I've told her she should not let those girls run wild with that car but she doesn't listen to my advice. She just calls me to come and pick up the pieces."

Helen stood glaring at him as he picked up the phone and said hello.

"Dan, Janie and Mira had a wreck in the Pinto," Louise wailed pitifully. "Can you come over and take me to see it?"

"Was anybody hurt Louise?" Dan asked in a gruff voice.

"No, no they weren't hurt, but I think the car is totaled. And Mira's stepfather has called and blessed me out and threatened to sue me and I don't know what to do."

"Have they towed the car in yet?"

"I don't know. The police brought Janie home a few minutes ago and that was the first I knew about it."

"Well I don't think there is anything to do tonight. We'll have to call your insurance company in the morning. I wouldn't worry about Mira's stepfather. If he does sue your insurance company will defend you."

"Oh well, all right," she replied dejectedly. "I just thought we ought to go see what the car looks like. I'm so upset I want to do something."

"Listen Louise, if there was anything I could do I'd be glad to come over tonight. But I've had several drinks and I don't really want to get out and drive or go around the police. And there is nothing that can't wait until tomorrow. I'll come over then and do whatever you want."

"All right Dan. I'll talk to you tomorrow."

"Goodbye," he said, pleased at himself for putting her off so adroitly.

"You mean you aren't going over there?" Helen, who had been listening to his end of the conversation, asked incredulously.

"No, I've had too much to drink to go out tonight. I'll go over tomorrow and see what I can do."

"Would you mind if I went? She really was upset and needs somebody there. Those kids are enough to drive her up the wall without any accidents."

"No, go ahead if you want to. I really don't give a damn tonight."

So, in a flurry, Helen left. Dan finished the Monopoly game with Rod and Alan and when they departed he went to bed. It was late when she came in and it wasn't until breakfast the next morning that he found out what had transpired.

Helen had taken Louise and Janie back to the scene of the accident so Janie could show her mother just what had happened. Apparently she had come around a curve too fast on wet pavement and lost control. The little car spun around and was traveling down the road backwards when it slammed into the front of a blue Dotson coming the other way.

The Dotson had tried to avoid the out-of-control Pinto and was almost stationary by the time they collided. But the impact had bashed in the rear of the Pinto all the way up to the back of the front seat and ruined the front end of the blue car. The man in the Dotson wasn't hurt but Mira's stepfather claimed she had whiplash and had taken her to the hospital. They had gone out to Northside Hospital but it was too late to get in to see Mira. The car had been towed to a wrecking yard in Chamblee. Louise had been so nervous by the time they returned to her house she had asked Helen to drive her to the Riviera Motel where she rented a room. She was going to sleep until noon. If Helen could pick her up about one, they'd go visit Mira then.

Dan was a little sorry now that he hadn't gone the night before, but he still didn't see where his presence was necessary. He called Louise's insurance company and gave them what information he knew and told them where they could contact Louise and the other people involved. He went to his office but told Helen he would be available if Louise needed him for anything.

About two o'clock Helen called sounding very excited. "Dan, the check's here," she exclaimed gleefully. "Fifty-thousand two-hundred dollars and ninety cents. What do we do with it?"

"Why don't you and Louise meet me at our house? I have all her files there on what she owes, etcetera. I can be there in about thirty minutes," he replied happily, pleased that something good was happening. It gave his sagging spirits a big lift to know the check had arrived. He hadn't worried too much about it, but then he hadn't worried about the Burnett-Jennings sale either and that had fallen through. At least one thing he had done that summer had worked out right. Now he could write those children's policies and have something to keep his boss happy.

He got Louise to sign the applications and the check for the first year's premium that afternoon. He advised her to deposit twenty-five thousand dollars in her savings account and the balance in checking. He wanted to ask her to go ahead and lend him five thousand dollars but decided that he wouldn't bring that up immediately. It could wait and he might decide he needed more. When he got the loan from her he was going to pay off that note on the wrecked Mark so he could quit worrying about it. Maybe he should get enough to pay his unsecured note also.

Louise and Helen hurried off to the bank so they could make the deposits before closing time and left him at the house to write out checks to pay the accounts that were due or past due. He thought she should go ahead and pay everything up completely but remembered Helen's little tirade about letting Louise spend the money the way she wanted and didn't push it. If she didn't want to pay them all now, that was her privilege.

The women were so excited when they left they didn't say when to expect them back. He finished writing the checks and fixed himself a roast beef sandwich for supper. Soon he started drinking Wild Turkey and was beginning to get a buzz on by the time they finally returned a little before nine. Twilight was invading the house with gray shadowy fingers when they burst in.

"Dan, Dan, look what Louise bought me!" exclaimed Helen exuberantly as she flashed a large diamond dinner ring under his nose. "She got one too and we bought you something."

Dan was shocked and taken aback. The diamond was huge and to his way of thinking, vulgar. Louise had one very similar and they had bought him a new briefcase, an electric shaver, and a gold money clip. He didn't need any of the gifts but he thanked Louise profusely and mendaciously admired their rings. They had been to Elman's Wholesale Jewelry and it appeared they had tried to buy the place out. In addition to the rings and the gifts for Dan, they had bought several presents for the kids and a new set of luggage for Louise. Dan didn't ask them how much they had spent but he heard Helen mention three thousand dollars.

Louise signed the checks he had written and insisted on paying him the money she owed for her share of the New Orleans trip then and there in cash. He thought again about asking her for a loan but decided to wait for a more propitious time—some time when Helen wasn't around. They had a couple of drinks and then, since Louise and Helen hadn't eaten, they decided they would hurry to the Steak and Ale before it closed. They invited him to accompany them, but he declined. He just couldn't get as excited about the money as they were.

After they left Dan sat and thought about it carefully. He wasn't sure what it was that was troubling him but he surmised that it was a combination of things. First he was still upset over losing the big insurance sale and the poor showing he was making on his job. Then he was miffed at Louise for being such a wastrel, for going on an immediate spending spree after all her poor-mouthing and crying over the last several months. Finally he was jealous because she was buying gifts for Helen. Like always, thinking the thing through made him feel better. As his thoughts traveled on Louise's affairs he became more optimistic.

With fifty thousand Louise could afford to throw away ten thousand and still have plenty. With twenty-five thousand in savings bringing in five percent her income would be only about thirty dollars a month less than she had been getting with the entire fifty thousand in the hands of the insurance company. And if she could purchase a seven-percent CD she would be getting more. If she blew ten that would leave fifteen thousand to pay off her bills and the bank note. Of course in that situation she might not have any money left to lend him, but he decided he could borrow part of the twenty-five and pay her as much interest as the bank.

It was after midnight before Helen returned. Dan was still up drinking and watching a movie on Channel 17. "Hi," she said gaily as she came bouncing in. "I didn't expect you to still be up but I'm glad you are. Louise wants to take us both to dinner tomorrow night, anyplace you want to go."

"That's nice of her but she really doesn't have to do that," he replied churlishly.

"Oh come on Dan. Don't be a wet blanket. Help her enjoy spending her money," Helen said happily as she slid onto his lap and gave him a big hug.

"Sure, okay. I don't mean to be a wet blanket. Forgive me," he answered meekly as his arms enfolded her and he buried his face in the gossamer chiffon of her expensive mauve blouse from Saks that had been a gift from Louise.

The next day Dan had an appointment to see Mike McKnight once more. It proved to be another inconclusive interview. McKnight said he still hadn't met with his attorney but as soon as he did he was going to make some kind of decision. He indicated he still planned to buy some insurance. It left Dan with a better feeling than he had before the interview, but not with any high hopes of a quick sale.

Helen spent the day with Louise buying more clothes. She brought them home and put them away in her closet without mentioning them to Dan. When he got in he found her and Louise still in high spirits sitting around having their first drink of the day. About five-thirty David Barnes called. He was having a party at his apartment in The Landmark on Friday night and was calling to invite Dan and Helen. A lot of their old friends were coming and he wanted them to be sure and be there. Helen had answered the phone and she had to tell him about her new car, the New Orleans trip and her new diamond ring. When she mentioned Louise David suggested they bring her along to the party also.

They decided to have dinner at Gene and Gabe's Restaurant on Piedmont and called for reservations for nine o'clock. There was some delay in being seated and the service was slow, but the food was excellent and they thoroughly enjoyed themselves. Dan steered clear of Louise any advice about the money. He complimented her on she looked and how much more fun she had been since she worrying all the time. Afterward they went back to the house and had several more drinks before Helen finally took Louise back to her motel. She hadn't moved back home and said she didn't plan to for another couple of days. She explained that she found it very relaxing to get away from the children and the problems of keeping house.

Helen hadn't done anything about getting a duplicate driver's license since losing hers in New Orleans, so the next morning Dan insisted she go to the driver's license bureau and take care of it. When she told him she had promised to take Louise out to look at the wrecked Pinto that afternoon, he volunteered to do it. He didn't want to have to make another trip to get her out of jail.

Louise didn't seem to mind that he had come in Helen's place. She was up but not dressed when he got there about one in the afternoon. She had already been drinking and he had to have two drinks with her before she finally got ready. They drove out to Chamblee and viewed what was left of the battered blue car. The trunk had been mashed up into the back seat but forward of that it was undamaged. Louise was aghast at how it had folded up. She kept saying that it was certainly a blessing that there had been no one in the back seat at the time of the crash. Afterward they went back to her house to see how the children were making out. They had been there by themselves since Sunday. The house was a mess but then it usually was, even when Louise was home. Janie was there but both boys were at work.

They stayed until nearly supper time. Helen called and suggested he bring Louise home for supper. Dan wasn't enthusiastic about the idea but hated to just dump her at the motel. He again felt depressed and frankly wanted to see a little less of Louise for a few days. But he took her on home for supper. Helen fixed one of her better meals and he volunteered to clean up afterward if she would take Louise to the motel. He hoped by getting them off early that Helen would be back soon and would spend some time with him that evening. But it was not to be. The women stopped off at Sugar Daddy's and had several drinks. It was midnight before Helen returned.

Thursday morning Dan slept late. He decided if he couldn't see his wife at night, at least he would see her in the morning. They were both in good spirits and made love, the first time since their return from New Orleans. Afterwards Helen cooked a big breakfast and Dan went off to the office around noon. He came home at five to find the house empty. He figured she was out with Louise. He called and got no answer at the motel and when he called the Haddock house, Janie said she hadn't seen her mother or Helen. About a half hour later Helen called to say she was with Louise and they were shopping. They were going to shop a while longer, then grab some dinner. Did he mind getting his own? He said no, he could manage, but he was disappointed that he had to eat alone.

He didn't hear anymore until sometime after one in the morning when his wife called again. "Hi Danny," she purred coquettishly. "I hope you're not mad but we had dinner and then we stopped at the San Souci and had some drinks and it got late before we realized it. We're over at the motel now. I'm a little high and I don't think I should drive. If you don't mind I'll just spend the night here and see you tomorrow."

"I wish you had called earlier," Dan replied peevishly. "I've been worried about you. I was afraid you'd had a wreck or gotten arrested again. I wish you would come on home."

"Dan honey I'm too drunk to drive. If I try you might really have to come to the police station and get me."

"Then I'll come over and pick you up. We can get the car back tomorrow."

"No, don't do that. I'm dead and I'm going to bed right now and you should too," she replied insistently. "You've got your Friday morning meeting at the office tomorrow and you better go."

"I don't want you spending the night over there," he snapped with ill humor. "I'm coming to get you."

"No damn it," she shot back defiantly. "I'm staying over here. Now go to bed and I'll see you tomorrow afternoon. You know we are supposed to go to that party at David's tomorrow night," she continued in a more normal voice.

"You're the most stubborn woman I've ever met when you want to be," he said resignedly. "I'll see you tomorrow afternoon."

Every Friday morning Dan was supposed to attend a sales meeting at his office. That morning he got up and fixed his own breakfast and left early. After finishing there he made a couple of calls and arrived home at three. Helen had apparently been there because there were new clothes laid out on the bed. He looked in her closet and was surprised to discover a lot of other new expensive things. He just couldn't understand H hang-up about clothes. She had more than any three womer now, and she kept buying more. He was sure Louise had pa and he didn't like it at all. It was all right for Louise to buy Helen the ring or a few clothes for all the chauffeuring she had been doing, but there was no point in going hog wild. There must have been two thousand dollars worth of new things there. He felt tired and discouraged. The events of the last two weeks had wrung him out, emotionally and physically. He got the liquor out and started drinking early.

Helen showed up about six o'clock. She had brought Kentucky Fried Chicken for supper. He started to say something about the clothes but restrained himself, deciding it was not the best time. He didn't feel up to a fight and he could tell she was already on edge expecting some criticism for staying out the night before.

Dan and Helen had both been taking amphetamines for months. Helen got them from some of her hippy friends down on the strip. Dan frequently took one in the morning to get going, but rarely used any at night. But tonight he felt depressed and tired and decided he had better take another spotted dog if he was going to the party. He swallowed one just before he left to pick up Louise. He failed to notice that Helen had already taken two and had put two more in her purse.

Louise had not been ready and he had another drink while waiting on her. They swung back by the condo for Helen and made it to the party just before ten. A lot of their old friends were there and they were quickly separated in the crowd.

David was serving a punch called Transparent Death. He told Dan confidentially that it was almost pure liquor. Each full bowl contained one gallon of Pink Catawba wine, two quarts of ginger ale, a fifth of vodka, a fifth of gin and a pint of 190 proof grain alcohol. It wasn't even diluted by having ice in the bowl. The ingredients were chilled before they were mixed and then ice was put in the cups before the punch was ladled in. It tasted delicious for such a deadly mixture. Everyone was drinking it with great gusto.

The party was supposed to end at eleven-thirty. About eleven-fifteen someone proposed they all go out to Uncle Sam's, a huge nightclub located in an old warehouse off Peachtree Road where a lot of the swinging singles were congregating that summer. Dan, although quite drunk, had cornered Chuck and Peg Sanders, a couple who had bought insurance from him the previous year, and was trying to persuade them they should buy another policy. When Helen told him she and Louise were ready to go to Uncle Sam's, he bombastically insisted they go ahead without him. He'd get someone to drop him off at their house where he'd pick up his car. He said he'd meet them at Uncle Sam's a little later. Helen didn't want to leave without him, but rather than start an argument, she said all right and left.

He had one more cup of the potent punch and got Chuck and Peg to drop him off to pick up his Chevrolet. It was close to one when he reached Uncle Sam's. The place was packed but he had no trouble finding the group from David's party at a big table in the back. Louise was holding court, buying drinks for everybody. Rod Kerry, Alan Hanson and several other men were clustered around her laughing and drinking. They found him a chair and told him Helen was on the dance floor with David. He finished two drinks, compliments of Louise, before they returned to the table. Both seemed to be having a very gay time and even in his drunken state Dan recognized there was a mild flirtation going on between them. He chose to ignore it however. A lot of men were attracted to his wife. Instead of worrying about Helen he struck up an intimate conversation with a pretty brunette with the unlikely name of Mazoo who was there with Brad Wellman, another of the pilots.

Dan was too drunk to want to dance but David and Helen kept it up until close to closing time. Louise was drinking with Rod and Alan and appeared to be having the time of her life. Just before two Dan went to the rest room and washed his face in an attempt to sober up a little. He knew things were close to getting out of hand and he didn't want that to happen. Wesley Thomason, another young pilot who was with the group, came in just as Dan was getting ready to go back out.

"Hi there Dan," he said with a drunken smile. "How's it going?"

"I'm loaded Wes. Too much punch."

"Say, you must be! I'm not giving advice Dan but you shouldn't give Helen so much cash when you're coming to a place like this. Someone might steal her pocketbook."

"Whada ya mean, so much cash?" Dan asked unpleasantly, slurring his words.

"Why she must have had five thousand dollars there when she was buying drinks for everybody right after we got here. She flopped it all out on the table and let the waiter take what he wanted. Everybody saw it."

"It must be Louise's money. I didn't give her that much," Dan growled as he slammed out.

What in the hell, thought Dan, is my wife doing carrying five thousand dollars around and buying drinks for everyone in sight. I don't like it in the least.

When he exited the rest room he found Helen at the table. Dropping into a vacant chair on her left, he suggested they leave for home. She looked over at David who was seated on her right and asked clearly, "What about Louise? Who is going to take her home?"

"I'll see if Rod or Alan will drop her back at the motel," Dan answered with little grace. "They all seem to be having a big time together."

"Okay, do that while I go to the lady's room," she said still looking at David. "I'll be ready to go in a minute."

Louise and her group of revelers were surprised that it was near closing time. Rod spoke up and said he would be glad to see that Louise got home and she made no objection. Dan walked over and waited just inside the front door. He watched Helen come out of the lady's room and get into what appeared to be a serious discussion with David. Finally she seemed to say goodbye to him and joined Dan. Without speaking, they made their way out into the stifling heat of the parking lot. Later Dan found it hard to remember who started the argument.

"Where did you park the car?" he asked stridently.

"It's over there on the back side," she replied. "What are you going to do about your car?"

"We'll just come back and get it tomorrow. I want to drive you home so I'll be sure you get there and not get lost."

"It was a stupid idea bringing two cars anyway," she said in a scathing voice, matching his fractious mood. "I don't know why you didn't come with us."

"I was talking a little business and you and Louise were in such a big hurry to go," he said cuttingly. "Don't you remember?"

"I don't know what you thought you were going to sell. You can't sell insurance sober. How do you expect to sell it drunk?" she castigated him wantonly raising her voice.

"Well I have to keep trying. I don't want Louise to have to take you to raise."

"Just what do you mean by that?" she asked harshly, stopping and turning to face him.

"I'm damned tired of you letting her spend so much money on you. She needs to use her money for other things and I can buy you anything you need," he asseverated, his boisterous voice rising to meet hers.

"That's a God damn lie!" she yelled at him. "You're so tight with money you squeak. If it wasn't for Louise I wouldn't have a single new thing to wear."

"I don't see anything wrong with all the old things you have to wear," he replied caustically in a somewhat lower voice. "You must have bought three thousand dollars worth of clothes since we got married."

"So what if I have?" she stormed back at him. "Women's clothes get out of style fast and if Louise wants to buy me a few things I don't see why you should care!"

"I wouldn't care if it was only a few things. But she must have bought you two thousand dollars worth this week on top of the ring and all the stuff you bought before we went to New Orleans."

"How do you know how much she bought me?"

"I saw it all in your closet."

"What were you doing snooping in my closet?"

"I just wanted to see how much you were taking Louise for. Apparently you didn't want me to know."

"Hell no I didn't. I knew you'd just get on your high horse like you're doing now and I didn't want a fight."

"You knew I'd find out sooner or later. Here you've been giving me all these lectures about not telling Louise how to spend her money and you're out every day getting her to buy you rings and clothes and God knows what else. And what about all that cash you were throwing around here tonight? Don't tell me you didn't get that from her!"

Dan was livid with rage. They were standing in the middle of the fetid parking lot screaming at each other, sweat streaming freely down their contorted faces. Suddenly all of his fears and frustrations of the preceding days and weeks and months came welling up from inside him and vented themselves in his fury. "You don't need all those damn clothes and next week you're going to return them," he blatantly asserted. "You can keep the ring but you're not to take another thing from Louise."

"I'll be damned if I will," she answered sneering and sarcastic like a schoolmaster. "You're just jealous because Louise is spending a little money on me instead of doing whatever it is you want her to it. Well I've got news for you. Next week she and I are goir and she's buying me a new fur coat and a new set of luggage and then we're flying to Daytona for a few days. And after that we might go on the Miami and Jamaica for a long holiday. What do you think of that mister know-it-all?"

Grim faced and trembling, Dan was at the point of going berserk. It was all he could do to keep himself from hitting her. He wasn't a violent man and had never struck a woman, but he was seized with an intractable urge to belt her one. Fighting for control he gulped three or four times without being able to speak and blinked back salty tears that welled up into the corners of his burning eyes. Finally, clenching and unclenching his fists, he mastered his emotions and spoke quietly to Helen who was still standing there belligerently glaring at him, hands on her hips. "Look, we're both tired and a little drunk. Let's go home and go to bed and talk about it tomorrow."

His capitulation punctured her belligerence like a balloon pricked by a pin. Her shoulders dropped and wearily she turned and started on toward the car. "Come on. I'll drive," was all she said.

Dan followed her through the muggy night and without saying anything further, got in on the passenger's side. The argument had sobered him considerably but he still felt woozy and light-headed. He opened his window and as they pulled out onto Peachtree Road and turned south, the cold blast from the air conditioner drove the hot air from the car and some of the cobwebs from his head. Without comment Helen pushed a tape into the eight-track player and they listened to B. J. Thomas's *Raindrops* album as they drove slowly along. Ahead, in the distance, summer lightning flicked angrily across the black sky, a harbinger of approaching storms. In silence he ruminated balefully on the events of the evening. At the house she parked the car in the garage and followed him upstairs.

"Do you want a drink?" she asked, going to the kitchen for ice.

"No, I think I'd better go to bed. I've had too much to drink." he replied quietly, all of the fight gone out of him.

"I'm wide awake. I took two hits of speed before we went to the party and two more at Uncle Sam's."

"What did you do that for?" he asked irately. "It's no wonder you're all keyed up."

"How do you think I've kept up with Louise these last few days?" she answered mildly without rancor. "She goes all day and all night and I've been run ragged trying to keep up. Without speed I would have crashed long ago."

"Well I think we better let her look after herself from now on."

Helen made no comment but went on fixing her drink. Dan had collapsed in a chair in the living room. In spite of his statement about going to bed, he sat and watched her sip her vodka and tonic. When she had about finished he spoke up. "Come on and bring your drink. Let's go to bed. Even if we can't sleep. I can talk to you better in bed and I think we need to talk a little."

Immediately Helen became tense again. In an argumentative tone she replied angrily, "I'll come to bed but I don't want to talk about anything tonight. There has been too much said already."

"Have it your way, but let's go to bed."

As they got up and moved toward the stairs he heard a nearby thunder and realized the storm was upon them. In the bedroom a lightning flash showed rain slanting in streaks on the window just as he closed the drapes.

Dan was feeling some remorse now. It wasn't that the things he had said didn't need saying. It was just that he realized he had picked the wrong time and place to say them. Almost all their shouting matches developed late at night when they both had drunk too much. He knew things would be better in the morning and he felt they could talk then.

They both undressed and got into bed. He wanted to cuddle but she refused, saying she was hot, and moved all the way over to the edge on her side of the big bed. For a few minutes he lay there listening to the thunderstorm now raging outside but he soon dozed off. It seemed he had just gotten to sleep however, when the telephone shrilled angrily. He came abruptly back to wakefulness when he realized it was Louise.

"Hello Dan," she chirped in a drunken voice. "Is Helen there?"

"Yes but she's asleep," Dan lied as Helen turned over to give a scathing look.

"Then wake her up," the fat woman demanded bellicosely. "I want to talk to her."

"She's asleep. You can talk to her in the morning. Where are you anyway?"

"I'm at Rod's apartment and I got worried about Helen," Louise persisted with great pomposity. "I want to talk to her."

"You can't tonight and that's all there is to it," Dan snapped back, losing his patience.

"Give me that phone," snarled Helen as she came around the bed and snatched the phone out of Dan's hand. "Hello Louise. What is it?" she said sharply into the phone.

"I just wanted to be sure you were all right. David said you and Dan had a fight in the parking lot after you left Uncle Sam's," Louise wailed over the wire.

"Yes we did but it's none of his business."

"Dan didn't hit you did he?"

"No, he just made a lot of noise and said I had to give you the clothes and the ring and everything back."

"You don't have to do that honey," Louise replied fervently in her drunken slur. "I gave those things to you. They're yours. It's my money and I'll spend it any way I want to. You tell that to Dan."

"I already have. Are you all right?"

"Oh yes, I've been having a fabulous time. I'm over at Rod's apartment but I think I better come over and see you. I don't want Dan to beat you up."

"He isn't going to beat me up. But come on over if you want to. I'm wide awake."

Dan, who could hear both sides of the conversation, was seething by this time. In a blind fury he snatched the phone roughly away from Helen and shouted at Louise," Don't you dare bring your fat ass over here Louise. This is between Helen and me and it is none of your business." And then, without waiting for an answer, he brusquely hung the phone up and turned on his wife.

Helen jumped back when he snatched the phone. Now she sneered at him maliciously saying, "You sure are a gentleman tonight aren't you!"

"It's my house and you're my wife and I've had enough of her interfering. Get back in bed and let's go to sleep."

"I'm not sleepy. You go to sleep. I'm going down and getting another drink."

"You don't need another drink. Get back in bed," he screeched in vengeful rage.

Ignoring him, she stomped out of the room as he shouted imprecations after her. Wide awake now, he trembled on the edge of hysteria. The more he thought about it the madder he got. The gall of Louise, calling up at four in the morning and interfering further!

The storm had momentarily abated. Through the closed drapes he saw a flash of lightning. Still fuming, he slipped on a robe and followed her downstairs. He found her sitting stonily in the living room, a drink in her hand. When she didn't offer any comment, he went to the portable bar and splashed a large slug of Wild Turkey over some ice. He drank it quickly and was pouring another when the doorbell peeled ominously. "Who in the hell can that be out in this rain at this hour of the night!" he growled cholerically.

"It's probably Louise," said Helen unemotionally as she got up.

"Don't let her in," Dan railed at her in a hoarse voice, beside himself with the enormity of his animus. "I won't have that fat bitch in this house. Not tonight or ever again!"

Without looking at him, Helen stalked toward the door. Dan took three quick strides and grabbed her roughly by the arm. His face was bright red, his eyes wild and staring as he spun her around and thundered irrevocably, "If you open that door and let that cow in here, you're going out. For good!"

Coolly she shook off his grasp and in three quick steps reached the door and flung it open. Like a drunken lord Louise swayed arrogantly on the doorstep, oblivious to the rain pouring down. Rod, in a raincoat, held an umbrella ineffectively over her head while Alan huddled close behind trying to stay dry. Stepping forward dramatically she threw her arms around Helen in a protective embrace.

"There you are," she gurgled. "I was so afraid we wouldn't be in time. Has he beaten you?"

Rod, who followed her in, looked nervously down the hallway at Dan who was standing there scowling and said quickly, "She insisted we bring her over here. She said you were beating Helen."

Dan stepped forward and savagely grabbed Helen by the arm again, jerking her away from Louise' embrace. "Get the hell out of here, every damned one of you, before I hurt somebody," he screamed, his eyes bulging, his face a sick shade of gray

"You shut your God damned mouth Dan Cooper," Helen retorted sardonically giving him a hateful look and wrenching her arm free once more. "They're my guests and they're welcome."

Without another word Dan slapped her hard across the face. It stunned the entire company. They all looked at Dan with wide-eyed, startled expressions. Helen let out a sharp cry, then turned and ran up the stairs sobbing.

"Now you've done it Dan," Louise said virulently, recovering her voice. "I knew you were a wife beater and now everybody knows it." With a flamboyant gesture she pushed past him and hurried up the stairs after Helen. Dan turned and walked dejectedly back into the living room where he finished mixing his drink. Rod and Alan followed him not knowing what else to do. In the silence they all heard the rain slashing against the windows. Thunder pealed.

"I'm sorry Dan," Rod avowed apologetically. "I wouldn't have brought her here if I'd had any idea what was going on."

"Gee Dan; is there anything we can do to help?" Alan prated helplessly.

Dan, who had slumped in a chair, looked up sadly. "It's too late," he said miserably. "There's nothing you can do. It's all my fault. I'm a failure and Helen is fed up with me. She deserves better."

He put his face in his hands and began crying softly. Rod and Alan incoherently stammered a few words but embarrassed, they soon fell silent.

"I got jealous because Louise was buying her a lot of presents and I told her to take them all back," Dan confessed in despair. "Louise has been such a good friend to both of us. I don't understand why she has done all these things to turn Helen against me."

"I'm sure she didn't mean to come between you," Rod offered.

"You're all just drunk," Alan contributed. "Things will be all right in the morning."

"No, you don't understand," Dan cried abysmally, his face slack and struggling. "I told her if she opened that door and let Louise in here I was throwing her out. She's upstairs packing now."

"Oh I'm sure you're mistaken," Rod replied. "She's hurt because you hit her."

"She wants to leave me. She maneuvered me into the position where I'd drive her out. She goaded me into it," he said imploring them. "Don't you see? She's fed up with me and wants Louise to protect her."

"You're just making something out of nothing Dan," Alan said, trying to be encouraging. "Maybe Rod and I can get Louise to leave. You go to sleep down here and try to patch things up in the morning."

"I tell you she's up there packing. I just don't understand how Louise can do this to me. She knows how much I love Helen. I don't think I can go on without her."

As thunder boomed again they fell silent. Dan took out a handkerchief and dried his eyes, then took another sip of his drink. After a few minutes Helen came briskly down the stairs wearing a smart new black hooded raincoat and carrying an overnight bag. Louise followed doggedly in her wake dragging a larger suitcase.

At the door to the living room Helen paused and looked across at Dan. "Do you mind if I take the Cadillac?" she asked in a haughty voice, her eyes flinty. "Louise is going to buy a new car next week and I'll bring it back then. I'll send for the rest of my things."

"Yes I do mind! If you leave you're not leaving in my car! You can take a cab or walk," he declared adamantly as he jumped up, his face streaked with tears, his voice breaking.

"Rod, will you take us to Louise's motel?" Helen asked calmly, turning to him.

"Ah, I guess so," Rod replied hesitantly as he eyed Dan with apprehension.

With determined movements the women stalked out the front door into the still-raging storm. Rod and Alan followed sheepishly. Dan walked swiftly to the front hall closet and took out a briefcase in which he kept most of Louise's financial papers. He followed them out the door and as they reached the glistening sidewalk he hurled it after them. "Here, take this along," he cried acrimoniously. "Since you are looking after spending big mama's money, you might need it."

As a streak of lightning zigzagged across the sky and the rain beat down harder, he turned on his heel and stepped quickly back into the house, closing the door with a crash.

PART IV

"If You Go Away on This Summer's Day, Then You Might As Well Take the Sun Away"

Sunday, September 4, 1971

DAN SLEPT UNTIL three o'clock the next afternoon. He awoke groggy, with a hangover as mean as insanity itself and fuzzy memories of the night before. Getting up and gingerly making his way downstairs to brew coffee, he tried vainly to reconstruct the chain of traumatic events that had climaxed with Helen's leaving. His still-muddled mind could not recall exactly who had said what, but he remembered Helen and Louise dramatically stalking off in the rainy night. How could he have let it happen? "I must have really been out of it," he thought ruefully.

Slowly his thoughts began to arrange themselves in logical order. He recalled how he and Helen both had been fractious and on edge for weeks. Long before the New Orleans trip she had become restless, and recently she had been more critical of him than she had ever been during the first two years of their marriage. The trip to the Crescent City hadn't helped at all, and the few days since their return had been an unmitigated disaster.

As it fell back into place a piece at a time he realized that this week's tumultuous events had further aggravated the situation causing tensions to grow and misunderstanding to spread like a malignant tumor. His loss of the Burnett-Jennings sale and the arrival of Louise's check had been the twin triggers that, like two concealed bombs timed to go off in rapid sequence, had blown his marriage apart. The loss of the sale had devastated him and must have convinced Helen, as nothing previously had, that he was a failure. And with the arrival of the check Helen and Louise had gone hog wild. Like reformed drunks falling off the wagon, they seemed to have lost all sense of proportion, all power to think logically.

Going back over it now soberly, he knew he was to blame for the final blowup last night. He shouldn't have issued any ultimatums. When he told Helen she had to leave if she opened the door he threw down the gauntlet, put himself in a bad position from which there was no retreat. Particularly in the frame of mind he knew her to be in. She had admitted taking four hits of speed and had drunk a lot of booze. He shouldn't have issued any ultimatums last night. He was certainly in the wrong there.

But on the other hand he must draw the line somewhere. Louise had just taken his wife over, bought her with gifts and attention. He had to assert himself somehow. But last night had definitely been the wrong time.

And what about Louise? What was her motive in all of this? He just couldn't believe she could turn on him after all he had done for her in the past year. After helping her get the money and buy her new home he had provided a shoulder for her to cry on during the early stages of her financial woes and her problems with Jim Carpenter. Then he had actively tried to help her manage her money so she could pay her bills and not have to worry. He had done her income tax and spent hours discussing what to pay and what to defer and where she could borrow money to make it through until the next quarterly check arrived. He had sold the El Dorado for her and gotten at least a thousand dollars more than she would have gotten if she had been forced to sell it herself, and he had driven her to the hospital when Jim was sick, and to the one-hundred-and-one other places she had to go. True, he had received some compensation in the form of insurance commissions and the one-hundred-fifty-dollar-per-quarter fee, but if his pay was computed on an hourly basis it couldn't be more than a few cents an hour. No, he just couldn't believe Louise bore him any ill will. Surely she must have just drifted into this situation as he and Helen had done. She had been drunk last night too and maybe he shouldn't try to read anything into her actions and the things she had said. In fact, the more he thought about it, the more he was convinced that the whole episode was caused by too many pills and too much liquor. The punch David had served at the party had been extremely potent despite the fact it tasted so good. And Dan knew that speed changed his personality. He was more aggressive and argumentative when he took it. Was it any wonder Helen had been intractable and difficult to reason with when she had taken four hits?

But that was no excuse for his slapping her. He had never struck a woman before in his entire life. He hadn't had a fight with anyone since he was a school boy. Yet he had struck Helen, the dearest person in the world. He remembered a quotation from something he had read which said that people killed those they love more often than those they hate because only those you love can truly make life unendurable. Maybe that was the case here. But it was no excuse.

As he poured a second cup of coffee and gazed out at the sun baked patio he wondered how she was feeling today. Was she having second thoughts? He felt sure she was. In spite of everything that had happened he was certain she still loved him. But of course her pride had been hurt. She would realize as he was doing that it never would have happened if they hadn't all been drinking excessively and taking speed. But she had her pride and it might be harder for her to admit it. He would have to be the one to apologize first.

And how would Louise feel this morning, or rather this afternoon? Would she be willing to charge it all off to whiskey and pills and forget it had happened? He hoped so. After all she was a lot older than Helen and she should have the maturity to recognize that people often said things they didn't mean, even when sober, and that while things said under the influence of liquor were sometimes the truth, they were usually better off forgotten.

He knew that there would have to be changes. Even if last night could be forgotten completely he and Helen needed to stay away from Louise. It wasn't that she meant to come between them. But she had and if she cared for them both as she claimed she did, she would be willing to let them live their lives and develop some new interests of her own. After all, she had plenty of money now, thanks largely to him, and she could travel or go out and mix socially. They had helped her get out of the unfortunate relationship with Jim and she was free to find her another man who would treat her better. They could still be friends but they had to get away from the everyday relationship that had built up during the summer.

The more he thought about it the more encouraged he felt. Surely both Helen and Louise would recognize today that what was said last night was just liquor talk. He would have to be the one to make the first move, to apologize for his words and actions, but once he had done that he thought they would be willing to forget what had happened.

He decided the best approach would be to call first. If Louise answered he could apologize to her and then ask Helen to meet him so they could talk face to face. He wanted to talk about changes—changes in their life pattern and in their relationship with Louise—but this wasn't the moment for egotistical indulgence and these things could wait if necessary. The first thing was to apologize for last night and get her to come home. He could talk about changes later. Maybe they should take another trip, just the two of them. That would give them a chance to get away from Louise and all the other things that were a bad influence here. He picked up the phone and called the motel. The clerk told him curtly that Mrs. Haddock had checked out.

He called Louise's home next. The phone rang for several minutes but no one answered. Where could they be? Surely they hadn't gone on another shopping trip today. Not after last night. Maybe they had moved to another motel to get a bigger room. He decided to call Rod and Alan and see if they knew anything.

There was no answer at Alan's number but Rod picked up on the third ring. Yes he knew where they were. Alan was gone right now taking them to the airport. They were flying to Daytona this afternoon. It seemed that they hadn't even gone to bed. They had kept Rod and Alan at the Riviera talking until noon. Helen had been sullen and withdrawn while Louise had fulminated about the change that had come over Dan, how she couldn't understand it. Rod said he and Alan had tried to tell her it was just liquor talk but she had been too overwrought to hear anything they were saying. Apparently she and Helen had already been thinking of going to Daytona and in the frenetic aftermath of the fight at the condo, they had decided to leave immediately.

Dan was taken aback. It killed his idea of meeting Helen today to apologize. He asked Rod if he knew where they planned to stay. Rod said he didn't but he would have Alan call when he returned. He might know something Rod didn't. Dan hung up and went to fix himself a sandwich and rethink the situation.

His mind was still full of recrimination when Alan called an hour later. "Hello Dan," he said cautiously. "Rod said you wanted me to call when I got in."

"Yes Alan, I wanted to apologize for last night. I had entirely too much to drink and frankly I just didn't know what I was doing."

"That's all right Dan. I understand."

"And I wanted to get in touch with Helen and Louise and apologize to them. Do you know where they were going?"

"They were flying to Daytona. They didn't know where they would stay but promised to call me tomorrow."

"Alan, I'd like to sit down with you and talk the situation over. I know I was in the wrong to start a fight last night and start issuing ultimatums. I've got to decide what I'm going to do."

"Okay Dan but not tonight. I've got to get some sleep. Besides I think you should let things cool for a few days before you do anything. Tell you what. Why don't we get together and have dinner tomorrow night?"

"That sounds fine," Dan answered quickly, feeling a little better. "I'll come by your place about seven if that suits you."

"Right. I'll see you then."

That evening Dan continued to review everything that had happened, not only the events of the past days, but going back several months. It seemed that the real problems had begun when his business fell off in the early months of the year. His anxiety must have communicated itself to Helen and her feelings of insecurity, which had abated somewhat, had then begun growing again.

He thought of the time last spring after she wrecked his car. She had stayed in bed for two days straight, too miserable and depressed to get up. It was only after much assurance and display of affection from him that she had returned to normal. Things like that hadn't happened in the early stages of their marriage.

Of course she had always attached a lot of importance to material things: clothes, jewelry, cars. He didn't believe she had ever owned much of anything before they were married and now she felt a need to continually accumulate these things. They helped her control her insecurity. He couldn't remember when he had recognized this need of hers, but thinking back realized that buying the new Cadillac for her birthday had been in part an effort by him to truckle to this compulsion for material possessions. Even their house to some extent was part of this scenario. Helen had commented several times that she didn't need that big fine home, that she'd love him just as much if they lived in a one bedroom apartment. But once or twice, when he had mentioned selling it in hopes of reducing their cost of living, she had changed her tune and said that wasn't practical, that the cost of moving would eat up any savings they would realize. Now it seemed that clothes and rings and cash money were the things she wanted and Louise was willing to supply all of them in large quantities.

There wasn't any way he could compete with Louise in that department even if he wanted to do so. The principal thing he had to offer was his love and affection. He realized he would have to show Helen how much he cared. His drunken display of jealousy and male chauvinism the night before had been exactly the wrong approach.

Still feeling wrung out, mentally and physically, he stayed home and watched television alone that night. He had trouble getting to sleep and still felt awful the next day. Summer air lay over the city like a wet blanket, breathless and sultry. He spent the afternoon roaming the shimmering streets in the Cadillac, rolling the same thoughts over and over in his mind in a vain attempt to make some sense of it all. The inaction was chafing and it was with a sense of relief that he met Alan at seven.

"I haven't heard from them today," Alan said as they sat down for dinner at B. Morley's Mousetrap on Cain Street. "Helen will probably call tonight."

"Alan I don't have to tell you how much I care for my wife," Dan said fervently, plunging directly into his prepared speech. "I think you realize that I am deeply in love with her and am just lost without her. Somehow I've got to get word to her that the things that happened Friday night were an accident, a result of too much booze and too many pills coming on top of a traumatic two weeks for both of us. I think she still loves me and I'm hoping that if she realizes that what happened Friday was a freak occurrence that it couldn't ever happen again, that she'll forgive me and come back. Do you think she will?"

Dan's appearance was wretched. With blotchy grey skin and large bags under his eyes, he looked sick. Alan sympathized with him but didn't know what to say. He took a sip of his martini and tried to answer in a way that would not wound his friend further. "Dan, she's badly hurt by it all. I don't mean physically. I mean she acts like she's in a state of shock. I'm sure she still loves you but she is going to need a little time to come out of this shock before she will be able to see it."

"I suppose you are right," Dan replied unenthusiastically in a small voice. "I know the worst thing I could have done was start issuing ultimatums and that's exactly what I did. Do you know Alan; I think maybe Helen knew me better than I knew myself. At least twice before she has begged me not to throw her out. First when she wrecked my car and again in New Orleans. I had no thoughts of throwing her out on either occasion but Friday night I didn't waste words. I told her if she opened the door she was going out."

"I agree it was the wrong approach to take," Alan said sympathetically, nodding his head. "Louise being there gave her a place to go."

"That's another thing," Dan continued, pleading his case. "I don't understand what has provoked Louise to turn against me. We've been the closest of friends. There were times during her trouble with Jim Carpenter when she told me I was the only human being she could talk with freely and frankly."

"I don't know Louise that well," replied Alan. "Saturday morning she was upset as much as Helen but she reacted differently. She kept asking Rod and I if we thought you had lost your mind, gone off your rocker. We assured her that it was mostly the liquor talking. I think she'll calm down in a day or two and you'll be able to talk to her."

"Yes, my first thought was that I would have to apologize to Louise before Helen would even talk to me. If she is against me it will make things much more difficult."

"I'd say damn near impossible," Alan agreed caustically. "She was clucking over Helen like an old mother hen yesterday."

"I wonder where Louise got the idea I was mistreating Helen?" Dan asked. "I never laid a hand on her until after you all showed up."

"I think she got that idea from David," replied Alan curtly. "When he came back to our table after you two left he told us you and Helen were having a fight in the parking lot. I don't think he said you hit Helen but he definitely left us with that impression."

"That was another thing that bothered me Friday night," Dan said bitterly. "The way Helen kept hanging on David. I don't think I ever said anything but it was one of the things that got my dander up."

"I don't think there was anything between them if that's what you mean. Helen was just having a good time and David was enjoying paying court to an attractive woman."

"I hope that was all there was to it," Dan confessed. "I thought I knew my wife pretty well but the last two weeks have left me wondering."

"I wish I could be of more help Dan. My only suggestions are for you to keep your cool and let things work themselves out."

"If I wasn't so much at fault I'd probably be able to do that, but I feel I've got to get in touch with both of them and tell them I was wrong, that I'm sorry; and then try to work things out from there. Listen Alan, when you talk to Helen, when she calls, tell her I said that; that I'm sorry and I want to apologize. And if she shows any signs of wanting to see or talk to me, tell her I want to see her to apologize and see if she'll let me call her."

"Of course Dan," Alan reassured him. "I'll do all I can. But don't get your hopes up too soon. She was in a bad state of shock when she left here and I think it will have to wear off before she will talk to you."

When they finished their dinner and left the restaurant Dan went home and Alan promised to let him know when he heard from the women. When he didn't call Sunday night, Dan placed a call to him the next morning. It was Labor Day and neither of them was working.

"Alan this is Dan. Have you heard anything?" he asked apprehensively.

"What did she have to say? Did she mention me?"

"She told me they are staying at the Shady Rest Motel in Daytona and they've rented a new Pontiac Gran Prix, a maroon one. They slept all day yesterday. That was the reason she didn't call until so late. And Helen was going out to visit some of her folks today. I didn't talk to Louise."

"Did she mention me Alan? Did you tell her I wanted to apologize?"

"Dan she doesn't want to talk to you," Alan said in a frank tone, not pulling any punches. "I told her I'd eaten supper with you and you wanted to see her to apologize and she got all upset. She said to tell you to stay away from her, that she was happy and she didn't want to talk to you."

"Do you think she meant it Alan or was it just a front?"

"I think she meant it Dan," Alan replied, his voice growing grave. "She was very emphatic about it. I think you should let things lay for a while. She said she'd call me back tonight and I'll let you know if there is any change by then."

"Well thanks Alan," Dan replied unenthusiastically, feeling a new sense of depression set in. "I don't know what to do. I'm going crazy sitting here worrying. I feel like I've got to do something, make some effort to get her back."

"Get drunk and go to bed," Alan said laconically with a laugh. "Things will look better tomorrow."

Dan didn't return the laugh or get drunk but he did have a couple of drinks. Later he took a cab to Uncle Sam's and picked up his Chevrolet which had been there in the parking lot since Friday night, then rode around for hours. Out by the airport, he stopped near the approach end of runway Nine Left and watched the big jets land and takeoff, the words from *Early Morning Rain* running through his mind. It had been popular in 1968 when he had first dated Helen and they had parked at this same spot to watch the airliners departing for distant places.

His thoughts moved on to Louise. If Helen wouldn't talk to him perhaps he could talk with Louise. If he could apologize to her and get her back on his side he could eventually talk to Helen. After all, Louise had nothing to gain from their estrangement. She had enough places to spend her money without supporting Helen. Maybe the thing to do was to try and see Louise when Helen wasn't around and talk to her. If she really cared for Helen she would realize it was in everyone's best interest for them to work their problems out.

He thought about calling her tonight when he got home. He could dial direct and just ask for Louise's room. Helen would probably have a separate room and if she should be in Louise's room and answer he could disguise his voice and quickly say something like, "Sorry wrong number," hang up, and call back later. It was late now, almost midnight, and Helen would surely be in bed or out visiting her family; but Louise was such a night owl he knew she would still be up watching the tube and sipping bourbon.

Spurred by the idea, he cranked up and drove home quickly, going over it again and again in his mind. Louise wouldn't know where he was calling from, and he hoped she would be impressed enough by his tenacity in tracking her down to offer his apology that she would accept it gracefully—accept it and become his ally in his efforts to make peace with his wife. He became so enthused by the idea of finally taking some action he hardly paused to consider any but a positive outcome.

The minute he was in the house he went straight to the phone, got the number from information, and dialed the call. He felt the excitement build as he heard it ring several times. By the time the motel operator finally answered his throat was so tight and dry he found he could hardly speak. "Mrs. Haddock's room please," he croaked in a voice like a dying bullfrog.

"Hello." It was Helen's voice. Panic overwhelmed him. Suddenly he found he couldn't say a word; just sat there frozen, holding the squawking phone.

"Hello, hello! Hello, who's there?" Helen cried stridently in a voice that was beginning to shriek.

The motel operator came back on the line. "Mrs. Haddock I had a call for you. It sounded like a man. He must have hung up."

"If he calls back don't ring," Helen screamed hysterically. "We've gone to bed."

Dan quietly replaced the phone in the cradle. His throat felt like it was going to split, his heart was thumping furiously. He rushed to the kitchen to fix himself a stiff drink.

There, sitting and sipping, he began to relax. He was dismayed by his inability to speak—to make some excuse and hang up when Helen came on the line—but he was appalled at her hysterics. She was definitely mentally affected by their separation. That was all the more reason he needed to talk to Louise and affect some kind of reconciliation.

Thinking about it further he decided he should fly to Daytona and attempt to see Louise in person. He would go to his office the first thing next morning and put things there in shape so he could be gone a few days. Then he'd catch a plane around noon. If Helen was going out to visit her parents she'd leave Louise at the motel. That would be his chance to see her. Maybe he could catch her by herself on the beach or by the pool.

Arriving at this decision made him feel better and he slept soundly that night. Early Tuesday morning he went to the Massachusetts General office and made his arrangements. Back home he packed a small bag and called Alan.

"Alan I've decided to go to Daytona and try to talk to Louise," he blurted.

"I'm not sure that is wise Dan." his friend cautioned, obviously disapproving of the idea.

"I don't see how any harm can come of it," Dan argued ardently. "I won't even see Helen or let her know I'm there. If Louise won't talk to me I'll just get on the plane and come back.

"Don't let her know I told you where they are staying," Alan advised him tersely, apparently giving up any attempt to dissuade Dan from making the trip. "I told Helen I wouldn't tell you."

"I won't," Dan agreed. "I'll just say I called all the motels until I found them. Did you hear from Helen last night?"

"No, she didn't call. I was out for a while so I might have missed her if she did. Dan, I wish you would wait another day or two until things cool off a little more," Alan continued, pleading with his friend. "If Helen finds out you are there she is going to be more upset than she is already."

"I've got to do something," Dan replied earnestly in explanation. "And as I said I don't think this can do any harm. I've got to find where I stand with Louise and I think this is the way."

"Well good luck then. Call me and keep me informed."

He got a noon plane out to Daytona. At the Avis counter he asked for the newest and nicest car they had available and was given a Coupe DeVille, silver with a blue vinyl top and blue leather upholstery. He looked up the address of the Shady Rest Motel in the phone book. It was on the south end of the beach, a rather old and shabby area as Dan remembered it. He wondered why they had chosen to stay there. It didn't sound like the kind of place either of them would pick.

It was hot but the air conditioning quickly cooled the big, comfortable car. He had brought along a pair of sunglasses and an old hat he seldom wore and now he put these on. They weren't enough for a good disguise but if he ran into Helen accidentally they would keep her from recognizing him immediately.

The sky was a deep azure blue and out over the ocean puffy white cumulus were lined up like sentries facing the beach. He found the Shady Rest, right where he thought it would be. It was an old motel but it had been through a face lifting. Fresh paint and a modern looking lobby set it apart from its nondescript neighbors. It was two stories high built in an L shape. The pool and parking were within the L. The driveway entered at the front off Atlantic and exited on the side street that ran along the north side of the property. It backed on the beach. He drove past once, looking for a maroon Gran Prix. Not seeing it, he came back, turned in, and drove slowly through to the exit. He spotted a few people around the pool but no one he recognized. The motel didn't have a restaurant and he wondered of they might have gone out to eat.

His next move was to drive down on the beach and carefully check out the people there, particularly those in the immediate vicinity of the Shady Rest. Still seeing no signs of either woman or a maroon Gran Prix, he returned to the street and parked where he could watch the entrance to the motel. He wasn't sure how he should proceed. He definitely wanted to see Louise without encountering Helen. She could be there but he didn't know which room she was in. Since the car was gone, Helen must be out. He thought he might call and if he found Louise in, try to get her to go out somewhere with him and have a drink. On second thought he decided it would be better if he could just knock on her door. She didn't know how to be rude and she'd have to invite him in. After thinking it over thoroughly he decided that would be the best approach. He'd just drive up in front of the office, go in and ask for her room number. He was a reputable looking person and he thought they would give it to him. He cranked the car and swung into the motel, stopping so the clerk could see what he was driving. He walked in quickly and smiled pleasantly at the young man behind the counter.

"Could you tell me which room Mrs. Haddock is in please?" he asked in an authoritative voice. "I'm sorry sir," apologized the clerk. "Mrs. Haddock checked out about an hour ago."

"Do you know where she was headed?" Dan asked hastily, trying to hide his chagrin.

"No sir I don't. She didn't leave any forwarding address."

Dan turned and left cursing his luck. He had missed them by only a few minutes. And now they could be anywhere. He cruised back up Atlantic Boulevard slowly, scanning every motel parking lot for a maroon Gran Prix. He almost got hit twice by impatient motorists. Finally he decided the only thing to do was to check into a motel himself and start calling the larger, nicer places. The Shady Rest was probably the best they had been able to do on a Saturday night, but now that the holiday weekend was over they would have moved to better accommodations.

But he had trouble getting a room. Most places were full and those that weren't didn't want to take him unless he was planning to stay at least three days. He finally took a room at an older motel out north on U.S. 1 called the Blue Bird Inn. The room was comfortable enough but Dan didn't discover until he looked for it that there was no telephone there. Having already paid sixteen dollars for one night's stay, he was upset to find that it didn't have the one thing he needed. But feeling tired and wrung out from the stress he had been under, he lay down on the bed and immediately dropped off to sleep.

He awoke around five feeling refreshed and his mind began to function again. He decided he'd call Alan. Helen might have been in touch with him. She had promised to call last night. She might have called today after they moved. Inquiring at the office, he was told the nearest phone was a booth out on the street in front of the motel. He got some change from the desk clerk, a balding little man with a big voice, and put through a call to Alan.

"Hi, it's Dan," he said sounding better than he felt. "I'm in Daytona but I haven't talked to anyone. They've moved from the Shady Rest."

"I know," Alan replied ominously. "Helen called a little while ago. She said somebody called last night and then hung up. It got Louise spooked and they moved first thing this morning. Were you the one who called them?"

"No," Dan lied anxiously. "I don't want to upset either one of them. I just want to hang around until I can talk to Louise by herself."

"I told her you didn't know where they were staying. How's the weather down there?" he asked, changing the subject.

"It's hot and sticky here in this phone booth but it was nice on the beach. Why don't you fly down and join me if you're not working? You might be a big help."

"I'll think about it. What are you going to do now?"

"I'd like to keep trying to see Louise. Did Helen tell you where they had moved?"

"I don't know if I should tell you. She was very emphatic that I not do so. She was convinced it was you who called last night."

"Well it wasn't and I'm not going to cause any trouble," Dan replied petulantly. "I'm staying completely sober and being very careful what I say. If you tell me you'll just be saving me a lot of time and trouble."

"Oh all right," Alan agreed reluctantly. "They are at the Deauville. She didn't tell me the room number."

"Thanks Alan. Let me go and I'll call you back a little later, I think I'll go over and reconnoiter the Deauville."

"Please don't do anything rash Dan," Alan pleaded. "By the way where are you staying?"

"I'm at a dump called the Blue Bird Inn out on US 1," Dan replied. "It was the best I could do for one night. If you decide to come down maybe we could get a room at one of the better places on the beach. Just getting out of Atlanta has made me feel better and maybe it would be wise to just hang around for a day or two before trying to talk to either of them."

"That's the way I feel," Alan volunteered with alacrity. "I'll tell you what. If you really want me to come, I'll catch a plane later tonight and stay until Thursday. I don't have a flight scheduled until Friday morning."

"That would be great," Dan replied enthusiastically. "Why don't you check on the flights and pack your bag and I'll call you in an hour or so to find out what time you'll be in."

Dan hung up and headed for his car. It was getting on toward six and traffic was heavy as he headed south then turned left to cross the Sea breeze Causeway. A late afternoon thundershower had washed the city and now the air was sweet and heavy. Steam rose from the pavements and misted his windshield. He felt more relaxed than he had in days.

Reaching Atlantic he turned left and headed north, his tires hissing on the wet street. The Deauville was one of the newer, larger hotels just north of the central part of the beach, and as he approached it he felt his nerves begin to tense once more. He didn't have a plan of action but was again wearing his hat and sunglasses.

Driving into the hotel garage, he circled upward checking out the cars that were there. On the third level he spotted a maroon Gran Prix with small hub caps and a rental tag. That meant Helen was probably in the hotel. He drove back out and parked across the street at a meter. Getting out he noticed a small tavern called The Surf Bar and decided to stop there for a drink and think the situation over.

Coming out of the sun into almost total darkness he could barely see. He slid his sunglasses down on his nose and stood for several moments just inside the entrance waiting for his eyes to adjust to the gloom. To his right stood a large rectangular bar with stools on all four sides. Prism spots gleamed down on the bald pate of the blond bartender, on shinning glassware, on the padded bar rim, on the black Naugahyde stools with brass nail heads. On the left a minuscule dance floor with small tables clustered about it was lit only by the light from a large, garish jukebox now spilling out a Carpenter's tune.

Slowly, for he was still having trouble seeing, Cooper made his way around to the back side of the bar, away from the entrance, opposite the dance floor. There were only a half-dozen patrons and the blond bartender, a lethargic man of about forty who wiped the bar with half-hearted strokes and asked what it would be. Dan ordered Wild Turkey and water.

He was sitting and sipping, his sunglasses still low on his nose, his hat cocked back, when his attention was caught by a flash of light as the outside door opened and closed. Glancing up, he was startled to see Helen standing just inside, peering about the darkened room. She was wearing clothes he had never seen, a white mini-skirt and a sky-blue blouse. Her long blond hair was hanging around her shoulders like a golden mist. She was smiling and talking rapidly to a girl, an attractive brunette about her age who had a full figure and a soft round face. His heart skipped a beat as he sat in stunned amazement.

At first he thought she would surely recognize him. But then he realized they were blinded just as he had been when first coming in out of the bright sun. Quickly slipping his sunglasses in place, he pulled the hat down over his forehead and held his drink in front of his face in hopes she wouldn't notice him. She looked his way, but then she stepped forward and the other girl followed as she went to speak with two men who were lounging at the back corner of the bar near the juke box. Helen appeared to be introducing the dark-headed girl to the two men but Dan couldn't catch what was being said. He gulped down his drink and while her back was turned, slipped around the front of the bar and out the door. He wasn't sure she hadn't seen him, but he didn't think she had.

Back on the street his heart was still beating a fast tattoo and his palms were sweaty. But he immediately realized this was his opportunity to talk with Louise. Chances were good she was back in their room, so he crossed the street and entered the elegant lobby of the Deauville. When he asked at the desk for Mrs. Haddock's room number the clerk, an efficient looking young man in a blue blazer, refused to give it out, but suggested Dan call on the house phone. He knew it would be much better to see her in person, but now that he was here, he decided to go ahead and call.

It rang several times before she answered. He was about to hang up when she finally said hello.

"Hello Louise, this is Dan. How are you?" he said cheerfully, trying to make his voice sound natural.

"Dan!" she exclaimed in a shocked voice. "Where are you?"

"I'm downstairs in the lobby," he said, plunging into the little speech he had been rehearsing. "I saw Helen go into a bar down the street and decided to take the opportunity to call you. Louise, I want to talk to you without Helen knowing I'm here. I want to apologize to you for what happened Friday night. I've been miserable ever since it happened and must have your help. I wondered if you would meet me somewhere for a drink or maybe for dinner this evening?"

"What are you doing here Dan? How did you find out where we were staying?"

"I came down from Atlanta today. I just had to try to talk with you. I called motels until I found where you were staying. Look Louise, I know Helen is upset and has said she doesn't want to see me. But I thought maybe you and I could sit down nice and quiet and talk it over and you could advise me what to do. I still love her Louise and I've got to let her know how sorry I am about what happened."

"She said she didn't want to see you."

"I know and I'm not asking to see her just yet. I don't even want her to know I'm here. But I would like to see you. Will you come down and meet me in the bar or would you rather I came up there?" Dan asked using an old salesman's trick called the fatal alternative. Agreeing to either alternative would commit her to doing what he wanted but Louise avoided his trap by not answering at all.

Dan had planned and rehearsed this conversation in his mind several times and in these rehearsals he anticipated some affirmation from her at this point. In his eagerness he didn't realize that she wasn't responding, that she had just been mumbling replies. He waited a few seconds, and then unable to restrain himself, he rushed on. "If you can't come now I could meet you somewhere later for dinner."

Seizing on the can't, Louise finally answered. "I can't come now. Helen is supposed to be back any time."

"Then how about meeting me for dinner later this evening?" Dan pressed, a little desperate now.

"I don't know what Helen's plans are for this evening," Louise whined childishly. "I'd better not."

"Well how about tomorrow?" he asked anxiously. It was beginning to dawn on him that she was giving him the brush-off and he felt he couldn't let that happen. It had taken him too long to locate her and get her on the phone.

"Maybe I could call you tomorrow after Helen goes out?" Louise said hesitantly.

"That will be all right. I'm staying at the Blue Bird Inn on US 1. I don't know the phone number but it is in the book. If you call before noon I could meet you for lunch. On second thought couldn't we just plan on lunch and then if something comes up and you can't make it you can call."

"We'd better not plan anything. Helen said she might want to fly on down to Miami tomorrow. If we don't I'll call you when she goes out. If we do I'll leave a message for you at the desk here."

Dan didn't like it at all, but it looked like that was the best he was going to get out of her. He didn't want to be too pushy and as they talked he belatedly realized he wasn't getting the reaction he had hoped for from her. Obviously she was shocked at his being here. At the end she had sounded rational so maybe she would call him tomorrow. And if they didn't run off to Miami he could always try again. Reluctantly he agreed and left the Deauville to get his car.

Driving slowly back to the Blue Bird he went over their conversation in his mind. Getting his wife back now looked like it was going to be a slow and difficult proposition, but the fact that he had made a start made Dan feel better. At least Louise hadn't been hostile to him. He had expected her to be more sympathetic but he wouldn't let her reticence discourage him. Surely she realized by now that what had happened Friday night was a freak occurrence. As long and as well as she had known him surely she couldn't think that he really wanted to be rid of Helen. It was probably just the shock of finding him here in Daytona that had caused her to be so hesitant. It probably was best to give her until tomorrow to get her thoughts together.

It looked like he would be here for a while. That thought made him think again of Alan. He had promised to call his friend back to see what time his plane was getting in. It would be good to have Alan down here to help. He was friendly with Helen and Louise both and it seemed that Helen was confiding in him a great deal.

Returning to the Blue Bird he parked the car in front of his room and walked back to the phone booth on the street. He was short of change but persuaded the operator to charge the call to his Atlanta number. After a few minutes he had Alan on the line and was telling him of his encounter with Helen and Louise.

"You don't think Helen saw you?" Alan asked incredulously.

"If she did she didn't give any sign of it. It was awfully dark in there and I slipped out when her back was turned."

"Do you think Louise will tell her you called?"

"Gosh I don't think so," Dan replied uncertainly. "I didn't specifically ask her not to, but I told her I wanted to talk to her before Helen knew I was here. I hope she won't tell Helen."

"I hope she doesn't too. Helen was mighty upset on the phone both times she called me and if she found you were there now I'm not sure what she might do. I checked and I can get a plane out at eleven tonight and be there a little after midnight. I think it makes one stop in Jacksonville."

"Good, I'll meet you at the airport. I guess we can both sleep here at the Blue Bird tonight and tomorrow we'll find a better place. The bars here are open until two or three so we can go somewhere and live it up a little after you arrive. I'm beginning to feel a little more human and get my hopes up slightly."

The phone booth in which Dan was standing was located between the sidewalk and the street on the north edge of the motel property. Traffic flowed past steadily in the gathering dusk. As he was talking he noticed a Gran Prix come to a stop at the traffic light half a block south of the motel, and suddenly he became alarmed. "That looks like Helen's car!" he exclaimed, interrupting Alan's goodbyes.

"Where Dan?" Alan responded.

"Waiting on the light down the block. It's changing now and she's coming this way. You don't suppose Louise told her where I was? It is her Alan!" he shouted, now really excited. "She's turning in at the motel!"

Sure enough it was Helen. She wheeled into the far drive of the motel, about thirty feet from where Dan was standing in the phone booth. He was profoundly shocked. It hadn't been more than thirty minutes since he had talked with Louise. The fat bitch must have told Helen the very first thing when she returned that he was in Daytona, staying at the Blue Bird. And she had come rushing out here, probably looking for a fight. Before he had time to consider all the implications, Helen threw the Pontiac into reverse and the tires squealed as she backed recklessly back out into the street, then screamed ahead to the next light. Grasping the phone tightly Dan breathlessly described the scene to Alan in Atlanta. "She pulled into the driveway, then backed out and screeched off down the street. I've never seen Helen drive like that. She must be mad as a hornet!"

"Louise must have told her where you were," Alan said, echoing Dan's thoughts.

"She sure didn't waste any time either. I guess she was looking for my car. I didn't tell Louise I flew down and rented a car. I'm glad she didn't see me standing here in the phone booth."

"Do you still want me to come down?"

"Yes, I'll be there to meet you at midnight," Dan replied, a little calmer now. "I'll stay away from here until you get to town and then we can decide what to do. Good Lord! She's coming back. She just made a U-turn down the block. She must have seen me when she went by. Hold on a minute. I'm going to leave the phone and get out of sight," Dan shouted as he dropped the phone and quickly exited the booth.

While they were talking the crimson car had made a U-turn at the light half a block north of the motel. She got rubber again as she accelerated southward on the far side of the divider going back past the point where Dan stood talking in the booth. Catching a green at the next light she swung another wide U-turn and headed north once more. Dan dropped the phone, left it dangling in the booth, and ran along the north side of the motel to duck behind the office building. He stood there a moment, hidden from the street, waiting to see if she would turn into the motel parking lot again. When, after a couple of minutes, nothing happened, he peered furtively around the corner expecting to see her stopped on the street by the phone. But there was no one in sight. He waited a couple of more minutes and then walked slowly back to the booth, looking carefully in both directions for the red car. When he picked up the phone Alan was still there.

"God, that gave me a fright when she turned around and headed this way," Dan confided shakily to his friend. "I've never seen Helen drive a car like that. She must be fighting mad and I sure don't want her to find me while she's feeling that way. The last thing I want is another fight."

"I told you how upset she was on the phone when she talked to me," Alan said reprovingly.

"Yes you did but Alan I don't understand it. Don't you think she still loves me?" Dan pleaded, feeling shaken and puzzled.

"I'm sure she does Dan, but you've got to give her a little time to realize it," Alan counseled. "She feels you made a fool of her in front of Louise and Rod and me the other night and she hasn't gotten over that yet."

"Well you go ahead and come down here," Dan said resignedly. "You can talk to her tomorrow and if she still feels that way I'll go back to Atlanta without seeing her. I'll meet your midnight plane."

"I'll see you then. But stay out of her way in the meantime."

"I will. Goodbye."

Dan hung up the phone and walked slowly back toward his room. He couldn't figure where Helen and her shiny red car had gone. He had seen her making the U-turn at the light south of the motel and from where he had hidden he could see the street going north. Since she didn't pass the Blue Bird or turn in she must have changed her mind and somehow wheeled around and continued south.

It was now close to eight o'clock and he hadn't eaten since breakfast. Leaving his hat and sunglasses in the room, he got in the rented Cadillac and drove south until he found a Bonanza Steak House open. His mind was in complete turmoil and he ate slowly, trying to sort out his feelings.

It looked like Louise had betrayed him. She must have told Helen immediately when she came in that he was in Daytona and had tried to see her. That was the only explanation for Helen showing up at his motel. There was no telling what might have happened if she had found him there. Somehow everything looked pretty hopeless again, but maybe when Alan arrived he could get them calmed down enough to talk. Dan still felt that if he could sit down with Helen in a sober, quiet mood, he could straighten things out.

He didn't want to go back to the motel and it was still more than three hours until Alan's plane came in. He drove back over to the beach and turned north on Atlantic. It was cooler now and a lot of people were churning up and down the busy streets in cars and on foot. He wanted a drink to calm his nerves and decided to return to the Surf Bar. It was convenient and it wasn't likely Helen would turn up there again tonight.

Business had picked up since his earlier visit. The bar was about half filled and there were several couples on the dance floor. He made his way around the bar and sat in the same seat he had occupied that afternoon. The heavyset blond bartender had been replaced by squat young man with short dark hair who obviously lifted weights. He served Dan his usual quickly and efficiently.

From his vantage point there on the far side of the bar Cooper had a good view of the crowd. Several more people came in and he strained in the darkness to see if there were any familiar faces. After a few minutes, satisfied that there was no one there he knew, he began to relax. He ordered a second drink and when it came he thought of playing the jukebox. Picking up his change, he worked his way around the bar and spent several minutes flipping through the selection cards on the machine. He had pushed the buttons for two and was looking for a third when something caused him to turn around.

And there she was again, still wearing the white mini skirt and the blue blouse. She glared at him with a look of fierce determination on her face. Their eyes locked.

"Just what in the hell are you doing here," she asked in an icy voice. "I told Alan to tell you not to follow me that I don't want to see you. Why did you come?"

He was shocked by the way she looked. Her face was waxy white and covered with a sheen of sweat. Her eyes seemed to jerk uncontrollably, and there was a tremor to her chin. Her lips met and drew apart spastically.

Surprised at seeing her and taken aback by the verbal punches she was throwing, Dan could only stand there with his mouth hanging open, struggling to find his voice.

"I want you to leave me alone," she cried, snatching at his left sleeve and shaking it. "You threw me out. Now leave me alone. You've got no damn business following me here. Why did you do it? Why?"

Her voice grew shrill as she shook his sleeve crazily and repeated her question. Words tried to form in his beleaguered brain but they would not come. Abruptly she dropped his arm and stepped back.

"We're leaving," she said in a more controlled voice, her panic seeming to subside. "We're leaving and this time I won't tell anybody where we are going. I won't have you following me."

There were tears stinging her eyes as she turned on her heel and pushed her way rudely through the crowd. Dan continued to stand, rooted to the spot in front of the juke box until she had disappeared through the street door. He had wanted to say something, to try to explain, but the suddenness of her appearance and the ferocity of her attack had immobilized and left him speechless.

A terrible sense of depression engulfed him. Alan had told him that Helen didn't want to see him and Louise had echoed it this afternoon, but optimist that he was, Dan hadn't really believed them. He had been sure they were mistaken. But now he had seen it for himself. This afternoon she had been happy and carefree when she came into the bar with her friend. Tonight she had been entirely different—so cruel and harsh—and yet at the same time frightened and panicky. Of course he hadn't planned on meeting her this way and it must have been as great a shock to her as it was to him. He still didn't know where she had come from, whether she had just walked in while he was at the juke box or had been back over in a corner where he had missed her in his scanning of the place. But he knew he had done nothing to deserve the viciousness with which she had attached him.

He finished his drink quickly and left. Outside, he breathed great gulps of salt-smelling air as he cranked his car and headed for the airport in a somber mood. He knew now the trip down here had been a mistake, a waste of time. Apparently Louise wasn't going to be any help to him and Alan had certainly been right when he said Helen needed a few days to cool off. He had never seen her in such frenzy. Even last Friday night at the height of their argument when she had told him she was not returning the clothes, she had not displayed such viciousness. He had made a mistake by coming. He might as well get on a plane and go home before he did any more harm.

Arriving at the airport he parked the car and went to the Eastern counter to check on flights to Atlanta. There was one leaving at eleven-fifteen, an hour away. He bought his ticket, then remembered that Alan was flying down and would be arriving after his flight departed. He rushed to a phone booth to try to call and head his friend off.

No one answered at Alan's or at Rod's apartment. Dan called Eastern operations in Atlanta and checked the departure time of the flight. It was scheduled to leave in thirty minutes. They wouldn't allow him to talk with the gate agent but they took a message and promised to get it to Alan before he boarded. The message he left was short and said simply: "Change in plans. Do not leave Atlanta. Am returning tonight and will call you when I get in. Dan."

It was only then that he thought about his bag which was still at the Blue Bird. He hadn't checked the car in so he retrieved it from the parking lot and drove hastily back to the motel. It took him only minutes to pack and he was on his way back to the airport by twenty of eleven. Not rushed now, he was cruising along at thirty-five when a maroon Gran Prix swept by on his left. He recognized Louise sitting in the passenger seat.

Now it looked like he was running into them everywhere he turned. Of course Helen had said they were leaving but he hadn't expected them to clear out tonight. He wondered if maybe they were just going to the airport to get tickets, but as he pulled in behind them he saw the back seat piled high with luggage and knew they were on their way somewhere.

When they turned into the airport he hung back to see what they would do. The Pontiac pulled into the rental car return area so he turned aside into the parking lot and parked where he could watch. They got a skycap to carry their luggage to the Eastern counter where they checked in and bought tickets. He wondered where they were going. He seemed to remember that there was a plane to Miami that left just prior to the one to Atlanta. That must be where they were headed. He really didn't care. He was so heartsick over the whole affair all he could think about was avoiding them now. He waited in the parking lot until they disappeared in the direction of the loading area before cranking up and driving his car to the check-in area. He checked his bag quickly and ducked into the men's room to wait until his flight was called for boarding.

The Eastern flight to Miami was called first, then his flight to Atlanta. His watch jerked away the minutes as he paced up and down, waiting until the last call before finally leaving the obscurity of the men's room and heading for the gate. It was still five minutes until departure but he didn't want to risk getting left. The handsome young gate agent pulled his first class ticket and waved him through. At the next gate the Miami flight was firing up as he climbed the front boarding ramp of the 727. The stewardess glanced at his boarding pass and directed him to the forward cabin. As he turned to start down the aisle he got his umpteenth shock of the day. Louise and Helen were sitting in the last two seats on the left in the first class cabin.

Coincidence had been the order of the day today. Wherever he went there she was. If he had been trying to follow her he couldn't have done much better. Fortunately they weren't looking up when he turned into the cabin and he was able to drop into one of the front seats without their noticing him. He was again wearing his hat and once he was seated everything else was hidden from their view. He sat there trying to catch his breath and wondered what would happen next.

The cabin door was closed and the stewardess came by and took his drink order. He spoke quietly so his voice wouldn't carry in the back of the cabin. He needed a drink after the series of shocks he had undergone in the last few hours. She moved rearward taking orders and Dan could hear Helen and Louise laughing merrily as they ordered double bourbons. Apparently Helen had recovered from her bad temper and was once again in high spirits.

There was a short delay in leaving the gate and he had a moment of panic when he heard Louise tell Helen she had to go to the ladies' room. The rest room was up front, next to the cabin door, and she would pass him both going and coming. Dan grabbed a big magazine from the rack in front of him and slumped low in his seat as she passed. The hat and the magazine did the trick and she paid him no attention when she returned to her seat a few moments later.

After takeoff the stewardess brought the drinks. Dan sipped his slowly and once again the wheels in his mind began to turn, shifting possibilities, trying to fathom the day's events, the motives of the two women. What were they doing on this flight to Atlanta? Helen had said they were leaving Daytona but he had expected them to head for Miami or other points further south. Yet here they were returning to Atlanta in good spirits.

Could it be that she had experienced a change of heart? Maybe she had been shocked by seeing him but then had reconsidered and decided to return to Atlanta and maybe to their home. His emotions had been on a roller coaster all day and now they started to climb once more. Maybe fate meant them to be on this plane together, he rationalized. This was the fifth time he had run into her today and in all cases except the first one, he had been actively trying to avoid her. Yes, it looked like fate wanted them together.

His craving for a reconciliation and the relaxing effects of the liquor combined to embolden him once more. When he heard Helen order another round of drinks he decided to try an experiment. While the stewardess was up front getting them, he opened his briefcase and removed a card he had purchased at the gift shop in the Atlanta Airport that morning. He had bought it on the chance that Louise would think Helen would be receptive to an apology from him. It was a large, rich-looking card with a photograph of the sun seen through clouds reproduced in an array of yellows and golds on the front. The caption began there saying: "You may not always see my love . . .", and continued inside with: "but like the sun, it's always there." He signed it "Love Dan" and addressed it to Mrs. Helen Cooper, Eastern Flight 212.

When the stewardess started back up the aisle with the drinks he stopped her. Speaking in a low voice he handed her the card and said, "Please give this to the young lady who ordered those drinks. Tell her it was handed on just before takeoff with instructions to give it to her before landing."

The stewardess looked puzzled but took the card. "You understand, I don't want her to know it came from me," Dan whispered conspiratorially.

"Yes sir, I'll give it to her," the stew replied. Dan wasn't sure she had understood exactly what he wanted but it was too late to say anymore now. He scrounged down in his seat and strained his ears to hear what was said.

"Here are your drinks and I believe this is for you Mrs. Cooper," the stewardess said brightly. There were a few moments of silence. Dan thought she must be opening the card. He anxiously awaited her reaction. It wasn't long in coming and it wasn't what he had hoped for. "Where did this come from?" Helen blurted out in an angry voice.

"Oh, err, a gentleman gave it to me and said it was for you," the embarrassed stewardess mumbled.

There was another moment of silence before he heard his wife's voice cut through the cabin, loud and harsh. "Then you just give it back to him and tell him not to send me any more notes."

Dan was both deflated and embarrassed. The stewardess hadn't said anything about it being handed on board before they left and Helen had immediately put two and two together. She might even have seen him hand it to the stew. He had been a fool once again as he had so often in the past few days, acting on impulse without giving due thought to the possible consequences of his actions. If she chose to make a scene or start a fight he had no place to go. He could hardly leave.

The stewardess came forward and handed the envelope back to him unopened. She covered her embarrassment by asking if he wanted another drink. He quickly replied in the affirmative and slumped lower in his seat.

Fortunately the women kept their seats. Helen made a couple of loud remarks about being followed but did not attempt to speak to him directly. He was thankful but was uneasily conscious of a cold feeling in the pit of his stomach and a compulsive urge to look over his shoulder. They ordered a third round of drinks just before the captain came on the cabin speaker to say they were approaching Atlanta.

Dan didn't look back when they parked at the gate. He just got up and out of the plane as quickly as possible. As he left he glanced over his shoulder and saw they were still in their seats. He decided to get his car first and then come back for his bag, giving them time to leave without another confrontation. He had left it parked in the remote lot and had to wait a few minutes for the bus. While he was waiting he checked his pockets for the car key. It wasn't there. He tried to remember what he might have done with it. The day had been so long and so full of traumatic experiences he was at a loss to come up with any memory of the key. He rode over to the lot on the chance he had dropped it around the car somewhere. The Impala was locked and the key was not in the ignition. Circling it, he carefully checked the pavement without success. Not knowing what else to do, he caught the bus back to the terminal and called Alan.

"Hi," he said in a dejected voice when Alan answered. "You won't believe all that has happened since I talked to you a few hours ago. Now, on top of everything else, I have lost my car key. Can you come to the airport and pick me up?"

"Sure. Rod's here and we'll come right on out and get you," Alan replied without hesitation. "I got to the gate on the way down there and got your message. Rod had brought me out there and luckily had walked me to the gate. We started to hang around and wait on you but we weren't sure which flight you'd be on."

"Good. I'll be downstairs. I'll tell you all about it when you get here. I ran into Helen in a bar and then of all things I got on the plane and there they were."

"You mean they came back to Atlanta on the same flight you did?" exclaimed Alan.

"That's right," Dan sighed. "I've run into Helen every time I turned around today."

"Well hang on. We'll be there in a few minutes. I want to hear all about it."

Dan waited a few minutes before going down and claiming his bag. He wanted to be sure Helen and Louise had plenty of time to get their luggage and depart. He wasn't up to another encounter. It should take Alan and Rod about ten minutes to get there from the Landmark and he timed it perfectly. They were pulling up as he came out of the terminal on the lower level. He got in and told them the story on the way back to town.

"Would you mind if I got my extra set of keys and then you took me back out there tonight so I can get my car?" Dan asked.

"No," Rod replied. "We're both wide awake and don't have to work tomorrow."

When they arrived at the Ansley Park townhouse Dan rushed in, left his bag and got the keys. Rod and Alan waited in the car and as soon as he was back they started for the airport again. As they emerged onto Peachtree Dan had another idea. "Why don't we stop at the Sans Souci and get a drink," he suggested. "It isn't out of the way and I think we've got time before they close."

"Okay by me," said Alan, and Rod quickly agreed.

It was late and there wasn't a big crowd in the Sans Souci. They walked in and took seats around a table about halfway back. As they sat down Alan happened to glance toward the front of the club and exclaimed, "Good Lord, there's Helen and Louise!"

Sure enough there they were, sitting at a table against the wall to the left of the door. The men had walked past without noticing them in the dim light of the cabaret. As Rod and Dan turned uncomprehending eyes to look, Helen left her seat and started toward their table.

"I don't want to talk to her," Dan said nervously, getting up and making a fast exit. "I'm going to the rest room."

What now, he thought in desperation. Would this terrible day never cease throwing surprises at him, taking his good intentions and turning them back on him in bizarre ways. He threw cold water in his face in an effort to pull himself together, to prepare his defenses for the next attack which he feared was awaiting him. Combing his hair, he squared his shoulders and returned to the muted atmosphere of the almost empty bar. As he emerged he saw Helen was moving back toward her table. He crossed and slid in next to Alan.

"Dan, she's terribly upset," Alan confided in alarmed tones. She said you had followed them to Daytona and bugged them so bad they had to leave and then when they got on the airplane there you were. I tried to tell her it was a coincidence but she wouldn't believe me.

"I've run into her everywhere I've turned today," Dan replied with asperity. "It has gotten past the point of being funny. Look, let's leave. She's all upset and I sure don't want a scene here."

When Helen had turned to sit down she had noticed Dan and now she started back across the room. Without giving Alan and Rod time to answer his question, Dan got up and hastened toward the door, the others following reluctantly in his wake. He was halfway there when Helen intercepted him. Her voice was high and tight and she was almost crying. "Why are you following us like this?" she wailed, half pleading, half demanding. "All I want is to be left alone and everywhere I look, there you are."

"Look, I'm not following you. It's all a big coincidence. Now I'm leaving," he said quickly as he dodged around her and continued toward the door.

But she was beside herself by now. She followed him out the door shrieking accusations while Alan and Rod followed in stunned disbelief."

"Yes you are," she charged. "You came to the Surf Bar looking for me and then you followed us onto the airplane and now you have followed us here. I was having a good time in Daytona and you spoiled it. You're trying to spoil everything. I hate you Dan Cooper, I hate you, hate you, hate you!" Completely losing control she started hitting at Dan with her balled-up fists.

He tried to grab her arms to stop her hitting him and they danced around on the sidewalk in front of the club. Alan came up quickly and grabbed her from behind in an effort to subdue her. "Helen stop!" he cried excitedly. "Get a hold of yourself. We didn't know you were here. We just stopped for a drink."

She was crying now, big tears rolling down her cheeks and suddenly she stopped fighting and allowed herself to be led back toward the door by Alan. "He hates me Alan," she sobbed. "He's been following us all day. He doesn't want me to be happy. He wants to spoil it all."

"No, no, that's not true," replied Alan in a soft voice, trying to sooth her.

"Yes it is," she said loudly, her temper flaring again. "Let me go. I'm going over to his house and wreck it. I'm not going to let him get away with this."

Dan had backed off when Alan pulled Helen away. He now turned and started toward the parking lot. "I'll wait in the car," was all he said.

"You better leave damn you," she screamed after him. "And you better not follow me anymore. I'll come over and wreck hell out of that beautiful house of yours." She subsided into a crying jag and laid her head on Alan's shoulder as she sobbed. Rod watched in stunned silence.

"If he doesn't leave me alone I'm going out of my mind," she whispered hoarsely to Alan. "I'll go over and wreck hell out of that house if he comes near me one more time."

"Helen get control of yourself," chided Alan, still trying to calm her. "I've tried to tell Dan to stay away from you but he's still very much in love with you and hurt about this whole thing."

"He's hurt!" she cried indignantly. "He's the one who slapped me and threw me out of the house in the rain. I ought to go over there right now and wreck hell out of his house for him."

"No, no," he answered in a soothing voice, still holding her.

"I'm going for a ride Alan," she said, now breaking away. "Do me a favor and tell Louise I'll be back in a little while."

With that she darted across the street and drove off in a green Chevelle coupe. Alan turned and joined Rod and they went back inside to find Louise sitting like a stone Buddha soaking up scotch.

"Helen went for a little ride," Alan told her. "She said she would be back to pick you up in a few minutes."

"She didn't leave with Dan did she?" Louise asked sharply, coming to life with a jerk.

"No, he's waiting in Rod's car. She tried to slap him and I pulled her off and he left."

"Well I hope so," she said emphatically. Alan had always thought her controlled, even phlegmatic, but new she was twanging, fiery, alive. "He's about driven us both out of our minds following us. First the hotel, the bar and by God I thought I'd die when he turned up on the airplane. When he walked in here it was the last straw!"

"We had no idea you were here or we'd never have come Louise. I better go and take Dan home. Helen said she'd be back in a few minutes."

"I hope she's all right. I'm half crazy myself," she signed, returning to her scotch.

Back at the car, Rod and Alan found Dan sitting quietly in the back seat. As they got in he spoke up. "What's going on Alan," he asked incredulously. "I've never seen her like that. She was mad when she ran into me in the bar in Daytona, but she was completely crazy just now."

"She's very drunk and she's almost hysterical," Alan replied grimly. "I'm glad you had sense enough to leave."

"Hell, I've had a couple of drinks but I'm sober enough to know that a fight is the last thing I want. That was what got this whole thing started—both of us getting drunk and getting in a fight. Has she calmed down now?"

"I don't know. She left and went for a ride. She was still upset and talking about going over to your house and wrecking it."

"I don't understand what's come over her. Why would she want to wreck our house? It's as much hers as mine."

"I think that is just it. It is something you had together, something that went with your marriage. Now she wants to smash it."

"Maybe we better forget about picking up my car tonight." Dan said with a sigh. "She still has her key to the house and she might go over there and do some damage. I don't want that to happen."

"Yes we better do that," Alan agreed. "Rod are you still with us?"

"I guess so," Rod replied smiling. "I don't want to miss any of the excitement."

As he spoke a nocturnal thunderstorm broke over the city and rain began pelting down in giant drops. They headed north on West Peachtree in a somber mood.

Hurrying in out of the rain they found the house quiet and cool. Dan put on some coffee and they were sitting around the breakfast room table drinking it quietly when the phone rang. Alan answered. It was Louise.

"Alan is that you?" she inquired drunkenly. "I hoped you'd be there. Helen never has come back and they are fixing to close up here. She's not over there is she?"

"No, I haven't seen her since she drove off from there about thirty minutes ago."

"Well I'm stuck here and I don't know what to do," she wailed. "Wait a minute, here she comes now. I'll talk to you later."

Alan came back to the table and flopped down wearily. "It was Louise and she really sounded out of it," he chuckled. "She first said Helen hadn't come back, but apparently Helen walked up while she was talking to me."

"That's good," Dan commented. "I was worried about her running off in the car like that. She was so overwrought I was afraid she might have an accident with the rain and all."

"Apparently she's back there to pick Louise up now. I don't know where they are going."

It wasn't long before they found out. They were on their second cup of coffee when they heard the front door open. It was Helen with Louise right behind. Before any of the men could get out of their chairs, Helen was standing in the door eyeing them. "I won't be here long," she said in a detached voice. "I just came to get some of my clothes I left. You can just keep your seats."

With that she headed up the stairs. Dan rose and invited Louise to have a seat and a cup of coffee. She accepted and subsided wearily into the closest chair. Alan went out and up the stairs after Helen. Catching up with her in the master bedroom he offered to help.

"I don't know if I need any more of your help Alan," she said cattily. "Whose side are you on anyway?"

"I'm on both sides Helen," he replied with sincerity. "You're both my friends."

"If that's the case then tell Dan to leave me alone. He scared Louise to death following us to Daytona."

"He didn't mean to do that. He only wanted to talk to her and find out what her feelings were. He mainly wanted to apologize to both of you for last Friday night."

"He's got a funny way of apologizing, following us around like a private detective!"

"He didn't mean to get on the plane with you. I know. He talked with me on the phone after he had talked with Louise and I was going to fly down tonight. Then, after he ran into you at that bar and you said you were going to Miami, he decided to come back home. I had already gotten to the airport when I got his message not to come."

"I wanted to go to Miami but Louise thought she should come home and check on the kids. We'll probably take them and go on a vacation later this week."

While she was talking she was rummaging in the closet and piling clothes on the bed. "Be a dear Alan and take these down and put them in the car," she requested without pausing.

In the meantime Dan and Rod were talking with Louise downstairs. "Louise I'm sorry everything has worked out this way," Dan said apologetically. "I don't understand why you had to go and tell Helen I was there in Daytona."

"I didn't tell her Dan," Louise replied quickly. "I didn't see her from the time you talked to me until she came rushing in the room a little after nine and said you were in town. She was in a rage and insisted we leave immediately. I called and the first plane out to Atlanta was the one we took."

"If you didn't tell her what was she doing at my motel ten minutes after I got back?" Dan exploded accusingly. "You must have told her almost the minute you hung up talking to me."

"I'm telling you I didn't see her again until after nine," Louise reiterated. Her reply was precise, so firm he began to have doubts again.

"Then how in the hell did she know where to come looking for me at seven o'clock?"

"I don't know but I sure didn't tell her."

I don't know why you want to lie to me about it," he said doggedly, still not convinced she was telling the truth.

"I'm not lying Dan," Louise replied with exasperation.

"Both of you stop arguing," broke in Rod. "It's over anyway."

About that time they heard Alan coming down the stairs. "Alan come in here a minute," called Dan.

Alan appeared at the door carrying an armload of clothes. "What is it?" he asked.

"Tell Louise about Helen coming to the motel," Dan urged. "She is trying to tell me she didn't tell Helen where I was, but Helen was there at seven o'clock looking for me. You know, I was talking to you on the phone when she drove up."

"That's true," Alan agreed, looking at Louise. "At least it's true you were talking to me at seven o'clock. You said she drove up, turned into the motel, and then squealed off."

"That is exactly what happened," Dan said determinedly. "And if you didn't tell her Louise, I don't know how she could have found me so quickly. She didn't see me in the bar."

"I thought she did see you in the bar?" said Louise, now puzzled. "That was when she came home and made me pack."

"No, that was later, the second time," he said, trying to explain. "I went back to the bar after I ate and she saw me then. That was when she said all those nasty things and didn't give me a chance to answer, just walked out."

"Well I didn't tell her you called," Louise repeated, glowering, "even after she had seen you."

"I'm going up and ask her," Dan said, now determined to find out the truth.

"Let me put these clothes in the car and I'll be right back," put in Alan hastily. "Don't start another fight Dan," he warned.

Dan took the steps two at a time. He found Helen surveying a half-empty closet. She turned and gave him a disdainful look as he came in. "I don't want these other clothes," she said. "You can give them away or do whatever you want with them."

"I'll just let them stay there until you come back," Dan said somberly. He realized suddenly that this was his first chance to talk with her in a normal tone of voice since Friday night.

"Do whatever you want," she replied flippantly. She showed signs of nervousness but seemed to have control of herself, just barely.

"Listen, I don't know that it's important now, but I want to ask you something," he said proceeding cautiously. "How did you know where I was staying in Daytona?"

"I didn't. In fact I still don't," she replied flatly, now standing, hands on hips, staring directly at him. "What are you talking about?"

"I know damn well you did," he flared, not believing her. "I saw you. Louise must have told you the minute you walked into the room where I was for you to get there so fast. You're just covering up for her."

"I'm doing no such thing. When I got back to the room I told her to get packed, we were getting out of town on the first plane, I never went near your motel."

At that point Alan appeared in the doorway. Glancing at him Dan continued. "I was talking to Alan on the phone when you drove up. Didn't you see me in the phone booth?"

"That's true," said Alan glancing from one to the other.

"I don't know what either of you are talking about," she replied testily, her voice rising. "I never knew you were in town until I saw you at the juke box at the Surf about nine-fifteen."

"If that's so what were you doing out at the Blue Bird Motel on US 1 about seven o'clock then?" Dan shot back in unbelieving tones.

"Oh, then. I was just taking Patsy home."

"Who's Patsy?"

"A girl friend of mine in Daytona. She lives in an apartment right behind the Blue Bird. I didn't know you were staying there."

"Oh, come on now. You can invent a better story than that," Dan stormed at her. He grew red in the face and began stuttering as he continued to accuse her. "You tu-tu-turned in and when you didn't see my ca-ca-car you backed out and squealed off up the street."

"It's a good thing I didn't see your car," she thundered in return, her dull anger igniting into sudden fury. "It would have been smashed right there. But I turned into the wrong driveway. The one I meant to make was an alley just before the Blue Bird. I had to go around and come back."

"I can't believe you'd drive that way unless you were very mad and upset," Dan said more quietly, contempt in his voice.

"Well, I don't care what you believe. After the way you treated me last Friday night and your following and hounding me all over the country I'm going mad." Her eyes were suddenly huge and feverish and her voice became harsh and guttural. She waved her hands excitedly.

Dan ignored her theatrics and replied contemptuously. "I still think you are lying, you and Louise both."

"Alan will you take the rest of these clothes down for me. I can't stand to stay here another minute," she cried as she rushed from the room in tears.

"Dan lay off her for God's sake," pleaded Alan.

"You don't believe that story do you Alan?" Dan sneered. "She wouldn't drive like that unless she was terribly upset."

"I don't know. It doesn't make any difference now . . . What's that noise?" he said jerking around at the sound of a crash nearby. "What's going on?"

The noise seemed to come from the room across the hall, Dan's study. They both rushed from the bedroom and through the hall into this room where they found Helen throwing papers and books in every direction. A large planter that had been on the desk had been smashed down on a glass coffee table that stood in front of the couch. Both the planter and the table had broken and dirt, plants and glass were strewn everywhere.

"Helen stop that!" cried Alan in alarm.

"There you son-of-a-bitch," she screamed at Dan. That'll teach you to slap me and throw me out." With one wide sweep she sent everything that remained on the desk cascading onto the carpet. His insurance files, rate books, and scraps of paper with cryptic messages only he could read were mixed with the dirt and glass.

"I wouldn't have slapped you if you hadn't acted like such a cheap bitch," he raged back at her. "Getting Louise to buy you diamond rings and clothes and give you money to flash in the bars."

"I don't give a damn about this ring," she said weeping openly. "I wish you'd shut up about it. Here, take it, I don't need it." Pulling off the ring she threw it at Dan then fell to the floor crying in loud gasping sobs.

Dan picked up the ring and dropped it in his pocket, then went over to her. Kneeling on the floor, he put his arms around her and spoke softly. "I'm sorry Baby," he said, now trying to console her. "I didn't mean it. I love you so much. I'm just jealous. Please forgive me."

"You don't love me," she said still crying. "You've been planning to throw me out for a long time. I saw a chance to get a few things I wanted and you resented it so!"

"I haven't been planning to throw you out at all. I was just drunk last Friday night and you were so nasty to me I lost my temper. Please forgive me."

"Yes you have. You worry about your job and you take it out on me. And Louise told me about that girl in New Orleans."

"Oh, Lord," he said with a loud sigh. "Why did she have to tell you about that? It wasn't anything. She just came in for a drink. She was living down the hall from us."

"You don't have to lie Dan. I know you don't love me anymore," she mewed, crying again.

Deciding it might be best to leave them alone, Alan returned to the breakfast room where he found Louise and Rod talking and drinking coffee.

"What happened up there?" Louise inquired in a querulous voice.

"Helen got upset and broke a few things," Alan replied depreciatingly in an effort to belittle the incident. "Dan's with her and I think she has calmed down now."

"I better go see about her," Louise exclaimed starting to rise from her chair.

"No, just keep your seat," Alan said with some finality. "She's all right. Why don't you let Rod and I take you home?"

She lapsed back into her seat but seemed to do so unwillingly. "I can't leave without Helen," she whined. "I wouldn't leave her here alone with Dan."

"She might decide she wants to stay with Dan. You wouldn't object to that would you?" Alan asked sternly.

"I don't think she wants to stay here," Louise retorted with more vigor. "I'm not leaving without her. I didn't want to come but she said something about needing some clothes that were here."

"I think she wanted to talk to Dan or at least give him a chance to apologize or something like that," Alan replied defensively. "But I'm giving up. I don't know how I got in the middle of it."

"I think you both would do well to get out of the middle of it if you can," Rod said decisively, looking at Louise. "I think it would be best if we all left now and let them try to work things out."

"I'm not leaving without Helen," Louise said again with feeling

Alan and Rod relapsed into silence and they all sat drinking coffee quietly for several minutes. When Dan descended the stairs and reentered the breakfast room they looked up inquiringly. He crossed to Louise and rested his hand lightly on her shoulder, speaking in a subdued voice. "Would you mind letting Rod and Alan take you home or wherever you want to go? Helen can bring you the car tomorrow or whatever you want."

Shaking off his arm abruptly, she rose and prowled the room, her heavy body balanced improperly on bare feet. "I'm not leaving without Helen," she said, stopping to face them. A tic jerked her face furiously and she nodded her head often as she resumed pacing.

"Louise I promise no harm will come to her," Dan pleaded. "She's upstairs and I think it would be best to just leave her there until morning. She's still a little drunk and so are you. We can talk things out better in the morning."

"I'll just stay here until she's ready to go," the big woman replied belligerently, pausing and facing them again. "If she wants to sleep a little while that's all right. I can wait."

"Louise please go on home. I'll just put her to bed and if she wants to leave in the morning she'll still have your rental car and I won't stop her."

"I don't think I ought to go without her."

They were still arguing about it when Helen came down the stairs. Her face was red and tear-stained, her clothes dirty and disheveled. The air of arrogant self-righteousness she had displayed earlier was replaced by a meekness that twisted Dan's heart. She spoke in a quiet tremulous voice. "Dan, what happened to my ring?" she asked.

"I don't know Baby," he replied sympathetically. "You threw it at me. I don't know where it went."

"I can't find it," she mewed helplessly. "Will you come help me look?'

"Sure, anything you say."

They all trouped back upstairs and spent several minutes searching the wrecked study for the ring. Dan had it in his pocket all along, but he pretended he didn't know what had become of it. When it became apparent they weren't going to find it he turned to Helen. "Why don't you let Alan and Rod take Louise on home and we'll find the ring in the morning," he suggested in a flat monotone, not blinking, looking at her directly.

"I'd like to find it now Dan," she whined in reply. "It's here somewhere."

"We can clean up the mess in the morning Baby and I'm sure it will show up then. It's after four o'clock. We ought to go to bed."

"I can't stay here Dan," she said resolutely. "Have you got my ring?"

"No, I haven't, but I'm sure it's here somewhere. Let's wait and find it in the morning."

"Oh all right," she agreed reluctantly. "Come on Louise. Let's go."

She turned and slowly made her way down the stairs with the others following single file. Dan didn't say anymore but trailed them out the door. He stood on the porch in the fogged dawn and watched dejectedly while they got in the car. They sat there for several minutes talking before finally cranking up and driving slowly away. He came back inside drained, light-headed with tiredness, his anger spent.

Alan and Rod were waiting in the hallway. "You've got the ring don't you?" Alan asked matter-of-factly.

"Yes, I thought maybe she'd stay if she didn't find it. After she did all the damage and all the crying she talked a little sense. I think she still loves me. If only Louise hadn't been here it would have worked out all right."

"We tried to persuade Louise to let us take her home before you came down," Rod explained. "But she was adamant that she wouldn't leave without Helen."

"Somehow they seem to feel they are responsible for each other," contributed Alan dolefully. "If you could get Helen alone and sober you might be able to talk to her."

"That's one reason I kept the ring," he admitted. "Maybe she'll come back for it. I think I'll tell her you found it in the dirt on the floor after she left if you don't mind Rod."

"Sure, that's okay. I guess we should go Alan. It's getting on toward daylight out there."

As soon as they left Dan went upstairs craving sleep like an addict. He didn't go in the study but headed straight to bed. He had just turned out the light when the phone rang.

"Dan honey, I want to apologize," Helen said in a normal tone of voice. "I don' know what made me smash your planter and coffee table but I feel real bad about it. I guess I just lost my mind for a few minutes. If you will let me, I'll come over and clean it up tomorrow."

"Sure, that will be all right. I'd appreciate it."

"Did you find my ring after I left?"

"Rod found it. In the pile of dirt that came out of the planter. I don't know how it got there."

"You had it all along didn't you? Don't lie to me." This time her voice was calm and displayed no malice toward him.

"No, no I didn't," he lied convincingly. "He sifted the dirt and found it."

"Okay I'll get it when I come over sometime tomorrow to clean up," she continued apparently accepting his explanation. "If you go out just leave it on your desk. I've still got my key."

"If you know what time you're coming I'll be sure and be here," he said eagerly, sensing a further opportunity to breach the wall of intransigence she had erected to shut him out of her life.

"I don't know. It's nearly six and we haven't gotten to bed yet. We are at the Squire Inn. I'll have to see what Louise wants to do and then come over. It may be late afternoon but I'll clean up the mess."

"I was just hoping we could talk a little. I've still got a lot of apologizing to do."

"Okay, I'll try to get there around five but don't hold me to it. I'll see you then."

"Okay. I love you. Bye."

"I love you too Dan," she said meaningfully as she hung up.

She called at five the next afternoon and said she couldn't make it. "I was planning on coming Dan but Louise wants to go on home and we will have to go to the grocery store and run some errands and I just can't get there this afternoon. Will it be all right if I come tomorrow?" she ran on hurriedly. "I can probably make it shortly after lunch."

"I guess that will be all right," he answered unenthusiastically.

"You still have my ring don't you?"

"Yes. It's here whenever you want it."

"Good. I'll be there tomorrow after lunch. If you are out you can leave it on the desk. I'll clean the house up good for you."

It was a reeling disappointment. Tuesday night and Wednesday morning had been such a circus he wasn't at all sure where they stood. Now that they had at least reached the point where they could talk to each other again without losing their tempers he was anxious to go further, to sit down and have a realistic discussion about their problems and their future. But if nothing else, the previous day's unbelievable string of startling events had taught him to be cautious and not trust his feelings. On Saturday he thought everything would be smoothed over by now, that she'd be back home and they would have written off Friday night as a bad experience, a drunken debacle best forgotten. Sunday and Monday he had been optimistic that all he had to do was apologize and everything would be back like it had been. Now he realized that, addicted to the belief that Friday night's trouble was an isolated incident, he had consistently underestimated the complexity of the situation. He had been, and to some extent still was, out of touch with his wife's fears and desires, her emotional state of mind. Last night he thought she was going to stay but again he had been wrong. If she had, he believed it might have led to some frank talk and a settling of their differences. If only Louise had let Alan and Rod take her home!

Louise! What was with her? What complicated motives, what half-acknowledged needs were driving her? She was acting as if Helen was hers—her responsibility or something more. Dan thought of the strange relationship that had existed between the fat woman and Jim Carpenter and wondered if somehow Louise had shifted those protective, motherly feelings she had shown for him to his wife. Or could it be something more ominous? He didn't think Louise was a lesbian, she'd never given him any reason to suspect her of any homosexual tendencies, but around Helen she was acting just like a bull dyke protecting her fluff. Last night when she had refused to leave without Helen she had looked like any angry frog, croaking at him, defending her territory.

Restless and worried, Dan called Alan to see what he and Rod were doing. They had slept most of the day and were ready to go out. After discussing it they agreed to pick him up and take him to the airport to retrieve his car, then go to the Crossroads for dinner. Dan was very appreciative of their doing so much to help him. He hadn't realized until Helen was gone how much he had become separated from his friends in the years since his marriage.

At dinner Dan told them about Helen's call the night before and the postponement today of her cleanup visit.

"I don't know whether she is coming back because she's sorry about the mess or because she wants that damn ring," he said jokingly.

"It's probably both," Alan replied. "But I think she also wants to reestablish communication with you even if she isn't ready to come back home just yet."

"If it hadn't been for Louise being there she would have stayed last night," Dan remarked with bitterness.

"You know the hardest thing for me to figure out about the whole thing is Louise's attitude," Rod said in puzzlement. "I haven't known her that long or that well, but up until last night she didn't strike me as the type who would purposely aggravate this kind of situation. She's mentioned to me before how much she liked you Dan and how much you had done for her, and she has always appeared to have plenty of decency and common sense. She kind of acted an ass Friday night but then again some other people did too. Now, I'm beginning to wonder about her."

"I know what you mean," said Alan, nodding in agreement. "If she would encourage Helen to sit down with Dan and talk the whole thing out it would probably blow right over. But she seems to be doing the opposite. By the way Dan, did you ever figure out who was lying about her telling Helen you were in Daytona?

"Not really. They both swear she didn't tell Helen I was at the Blue Bird. Helen said she was taking some friend to an apartment next door to the motel. I could believe that except for the way she was driving. Of course if it's true then I have misjudged Louise to some extent."

"I think you ought to give her the benefit of the doubt," said Alan. "What I don't understand is how she can run off and leave her children for days at a time."

"The kids have learned to take care of themselves," Dan explained. "That isn't necessarily good, but that's the way it is. I didn't like it at first but I came to the conclusion that it didn't make much difference whether she was at home or away. The kids do pretty much what they please."

"Well I thought you handled yourself very well last night Dan," Alan said encouragingly. "If you can keep your cool and keep hanging in there, everything will work itself out in a few days."

"I hope so," Dan sighed. "I can't stand riding this emotional roller coaster much longer without a crash."

Helen showed up the next afternoon about three. Dan stayed home most of the day so he would be sure and not miss her, but just before lunch he made a quick trip to the Kroger store at Ansley Mall to replenish his dwindling supply of milk and sandwich ingredients. While he was there he decided to leave the ring at the jewelry store in the mall to have it cleaned. It didn't really need it but that would lend credence to his story about finding it in the dirt.

She looked sensational in a pair of tight jeans and a denim shirt. The worn fabric of the pants caressed the curve of her thighs and accentuated her ample bottom while the shirt, worn with the tails out and tied in front, displayed a wide strip of tanned flesh. She had dyed her hair hot silver blond and wore it in a pony tail. Her fingernails and toenails, displayed in open toed sandals, were painted a flame red which matched her lipstick. Her carefully made up face showed no signs of the ravages of Tuesday night. Dan's heart was twisted by the sight of her, and it was all he could do to restrain himself from taking her in his arms. But he had learned something from the troubles of the past few days and kept his emotions in check.

He carried out the pieces of the broken coffee table and she went to work on the dirt. He had already picked up his papers she had scattered everywhere and spent hours putting them back in order. He could have cleaned up the rest but had left it for her. Her wild actions of Wednesday morning had done a little to offset his drunken behavior on the preceding Friday night and he didn't want her to forget it too soon.

It didn't take long to get the study straight. She didn't have much to say, just worked away quietly, and Dan held back, waiting for the right moment to suggest they sit down and talk. When, about four o'clock, she said she needed some vacuum cleaner bags and other cleaning supplies, he volunteered to go for them. But she refused his offer saying she had another errand she needed to do anyway and that she'd be back a little later. He was apprehensive but reluctantly agreed, then sat around worrying until she came back just before six. "I didn't mean to be so long," she apologized. "I stopped in the park and got to talking."

In another hour she was through. Dan had followed her around like a lost puppy but she hadn't once given him the opportunity he wanted to sit down and talk things out.

"I guess that's got everything," she said as she put the vacuum away. "I had better be going. Can I have my ring now?"

"Oh, damn," Dan exclaimed in genuine regret. "I left it down at the jewelers at Ansley Mall this morning to have it cleaned and I forgot to go back and pick it up this afternoon."

"What did you do that for?" she asked crossly.

"It got dirt all in it and I wanted to give it back to you clean," he explained. "I'll get it for you tomorrow."

"Why don't you just give me the ticket and I'll pick it up," she suggested, holding out her hand.

"Okay if that's what you want," he replied reluctantly as he dug in his pocket for the ticket. "I've already paid for it. Here's the ticket but look Helen, I need to talk with you. Can we sit down for a few minutes?"

"I could Dan but I don't want to," she said without emotion, putting the ticket in her jeans and surveying him with a cool expression. "You've got me all mixed up and I need time to think."

"Baby I know you're still upset over what happened last Friday night. I was entirely in the wrong and I'm willing to admit it and do anything I can to make amends if you'll only agree to come home."

"Dan I just don't want to talk about it right now. You hurt me awful bad and your following us to Daytona didn't help any. Poor Louise is still all to pieces. Give me a few days to get her taken care of and maybe we can sit down and talk."

"She doesn't need you to take care of her Helen. She's a grown woman."

"Dan she wants me to help her with her money. She is still mad about the way you threw her papers out the other night. And she thinks you gave her some bad advice in the past."

"Baby I never claimed to be omnipotent. I just tried to help her to do what I thought she wanted to do. But I don't see how you are so qualified to help her. If she is willing to pay the price she can get a lawyer or an accountant to do what I was doing."

"She can't afford that Dan. Anyway a man can't understand her like I can."

"Have it your way. But let's don't let Louise break up our marriage."

"If our marriage is breaking up Dan, it isn't because of anything Louise has done. It's because of the way you have acted."

The cool detachment with which she cut him down made his blood boil turning his face a bright shade of crimson. But he steeled himself to control his emotions and answered matter-of-factly. "All right," he said, accepting failure for his plans for today. "I won't argue about it. Please stay in touch."

He didn't see her again until Sunday. She called that afternoon and wanted to know if she could come over and talk. He said of course he would be glad to talk and was waiting eagerly when she arrived a little after three. She refused the offer of a drink and went straight to the point.

"Look Dan, before we start I want to get one thing straight. I don't want to talk about the fight we had the night of David's party or what happened here the other night. I'm getting Louise's affairs in order and I want a little help from you about some things you've had her do in the past and so forth. Is that agreeable?"

He found it hard to conceal his disappointment. It had been more than a week since she had left and wrecked his life and now all she wanted to discuss was Louise's financial affairs. A wide range of emotions played across his face. A wave of hostility gave way to a look of resignation as he fought to quell his inclination to tell her to forget Louise and her money. Finally he nodded in agreement and she plunged ahead.

"First, Louise wants to buy another house. That thing you got her to buy is just all to pieces. It is like a pigpen. The kids started painting the rooms over but I think it's a lost cause. She's got enough money now to buy a better place and she's going to do that as soon as we can look around. I wondered if you could tell me anyone that we could get to buy her present house. In the condition it's in she'd sell it to someone who would just take over the payments as long as they gave her time to find a new place and move. She doesn't want to have two house payments."

Dan didn't like the sound of this kind of talk at all. It sounded like Helen was planning to work Louise back into the same financial hole she had just escaped from. He felt bad vibrations but he sublimated his personal feelings of annoyance and answered her as if she was any other client. "I don't know anyone right off," he said shaking his head. "But I'm sure she can sell the house without any trouble. If it were me I would hire someone to come in and do the painting and repair anything that needs it, and then list it with a good real estate agent. If you get a good one and at the same time let him know that you're in the market for a new house when that one is sold, he'll probably find you a buyer in a hurry."

"We've already been out looking because I think she is going to have to move before they can get that house cleaned up. You wouldn't believe the way those kids live. The place is the worst I ever saw!"

"Well of course she could do that. She might have to make two payments for a couple of months. On the other hand she might not be able to get another house financed if she still has her present one."

"Is there any way around that Dan," she asked in a controlled, businesslike voice.

"If she finds something she likes that already has a large, assumable mortgage on it, it could probably be worked out," he replied cautiously. "How much down payment are you thinking about making?"

"The house we were looking at yesterday was in the low sixties and they said they needed twenty percent down. I think she could handle that all right."

"Yes I suppose so. But I thought she was going to keep twenty-five thousand in savings to offset the loss of income from the insurance policy she cashed in," he inquired reprovingly.

"Oh I don't think she needs to keep all of that," Helen said airily. "Besides you always said houses are good investments that they increase in value didn't you?"

"Yes that's true," he counseled. "But only in the long haul. You can't generally buy one this year and sell it next year and plan to make money on it. Particularly when you give it the kind of treatment she has given that house she's in now."

"That was such a cheap house to start with. You let her pay too much money for it. And if we get a new one we're not going to let those kids make a pigpen out of it like the one they are in now."

"It sounds like you are taking over completely," he rebuked her. "Have you started to discipline the kids yet?"

She ignored the disapproval in his voice and answered as dryly and as dispassionately as if she was discussing a grocery list. "I don't have any problem with Janie, we get along just like sisters, but I have had to say a few things to the boys. That Joey got plain smart with me Friday night and I told him off in a hurry."

"What did you say?"

"He was just using some filthy language in front of his mother and I told him to stop. He called me a dirty name too and I told him off good. Afterwards he came and apologized. I think we are going to get along fine now."

"Helen why don't you let Louise take care of her own problems and come back and take care of your husband?" Dan said plaintively, shaking his head. "He needs you a lot worse than Louise does."

"I probably will Dan," she replied softly, starting to get up. "But give me a few days. I want to get Louise a better house and we've got to buy a car. That rental car is running us a fortune. That's something else I wanted to ask you about. We had a wreck in it last night."

"You had a wreck in it?"

"Not a bad one," she laughed and tossed her head. "I ran into the back of a Volkswagen bus coming out of the parking lot at Uncle Sam's. Louise and I both had been drinking and we didn't want to call the police so Louise just gave the girls in the bus two hundred dollars to pay for the damage. But what do I do about the rental car? Do I have to get it fixed?"

"No," he replied easily, picturing in his mind what the scene must have been with the two of them drunk, plowing into the back of a bus whose occupants were probably also inebriated. "Just take it back to them and get another. Did you take full coverage insurance?"

"I don't know. Here's the rental agreement," she said pulling it out of her purse. "Louise signed it."

He looked at it quickly, then handed it back. "Yes, you've got full coverage. Just take it back to Avis and tell them you came out and found it in the parking lot that way and that'll be all there is to it. What kind of new car are you planning on buying?" he asked remembering Jim and the El Dorado that had been such a stone around Louise's financial neck such a short time ago.

"I'd like to see her get a Gran Prix but she hasn't decided yet. She's not going to get another one of those little cars," she said, scornful now. "She thinks you steered her wrong by insisting she buy that Pinto. She still worries about the way it folded up in the accident."

"At the time she bought that Pinto it was all she could afford," he shot back defensively. He was getting tired of her condescending attitude and depreciating remarks about his advice to Louise. "And I still think something like that is what she should have if Janie is going to drive it. It won't be but a few months until the boys have their licenses and then they'll all be driving."

"Then she may have to buy two cars," Helen replied flippantly as she headed for the door. "But what if she does. She's got plenty of money."

The weather had been pleasant when she arrived with only a few puffy clouds floating above the trees, but now it had turned dark to match his mood. As he watched her departure from the dining room window, rain began pelting down. Returning to the living room, he resumed his seat wearily and tried to think.

Reviewing their conversation he felt a little heartsick about the whole thing. It sounded like Helen was taking over at Louise's and enjoying every minute of it. It upset him to hear her talk so callously about Louise's money and the way they were throwing it around. He remembered how only a few weeks ago Louise had borrowed twenty dollars from him to buy groceries and here she was spending twenty or thirty a day on a rental car and paying out two hundred because she and Helen were out drunk and had a wreck.

It appeared that Louise had made a complete about face, that the arrival of the fifty thousand dollars had made her forget all those problems of the past few months and throw caution to the winds. And what was even worse, that same money was corrupting his wife. In Dan's opinion Helen had always been very careful about spending their money. At times she had spent a good bit for clothes and she had encouraged him to buy new, expensive cars, but she had always seemed concerned about the amount they were spending and had made him feel that he was the one making the decisions. It shook him to see her callously talking of spending large amounts of Louise's money for cars and houses with no more regard than she previously would have shown for the purchase of a new skirt or an extra bottle of booze. It especially hurt him to hear her laugh about having a wreck and having to pay out two hundred dollars because they were drunk and didn't want to call the police. When she had wrecked his car she had stayed in bed for two days worrying about it.

He had considered offering her the use of the blue Cadillac. He didn't need two cars and it might be the kind of gesture that would convince her he was sorry and meant what he said. But the story about the wreck killed that idea. If she and Louise were driving around drunk and having wrecks he wanted it to be in someone else's car. His insurance couldn't stand another wreck. Besides, it was something she would have without question if she came back. If he gave it to her now she might be that much longer coming home.

On Monday he went back to his office and piddled around. He hadn't worked regularly in over three weeks. And he couldn't seem to get himself psyched up to a new effort. He did what he had to do and no more. He knew he needed to do something to get moving again, either at this job or at a new job. He thought of going job hunting but he just didn't feel it was the time to change jobs. He needed to get things settled with Helen first.

So it was on this Monday, September 13, sitting in his office and pondering his options that his thoughts again turned to hijacking for ransom. He still wasn't seriously thinking of doing it but working out the details of a plan was a good antidote to thoughts of his marital problems.

He reviewed his previous plans and considered the problems that remained. In his prior deliberations on the subject he had been thinking in general terms, working out a possible scenario but not bothering with any details. Now his thoughts turned to one of the specifics that was a detail yet was vital to the success of the venture—the pinpointing of the place to bail out.

In his mind he listed all the things it should and should not be. First it must be in a somewhat remote area—he didn't want to come down in someone's back yard—but not so remote that he couldn't reach civilization and disappear before the authorities could figure out where he had bailed out and start looking. With the crew locked in the cockpit they wouldn't know exactly when he left the plane and if he jumped at night, as he was now thinking of doing, the chances of anyone seeing him coming down were very slim.

Secondly he would have to be familiar enough with the countryside to locate himself once he was on the ground and make his way undetected to a car or some means of public transportation that would carry him out of the general area within a fairly short period of time. The terrain could not be too rugged to prevent his traveling a few miles on foot carrying a bag of money.

Thirdly it would be preferable if it was on an airway or very close to a navigational fix so that the pilot could be directed there without giving away the fact that this particular spot was his destination.

With these factors defined he realized immediately that the area where he had grown up, the country around Woodland, Washington, would probably qualify. Woodland was a small town on I-5 between Portland and Seattle. He didn't remember exactly but he felt sure the airway between the two large cities passed within a few miles of the town. Once you got out of town the countryside was sparsely settled but there were roads and logging trails aplenty and when he was a kid he had gone hunting and camping in those woods. He hadn't been there in several years but didn't think things would have changed that much.

The more he thought about the Woodland area, the more he became convinced it would be suitable. In fact it was the only place he could think of that would meet the criteria he had outlined if he was to be the hijacker. At lunch time he left the office and went by Peachtree DeKalb Airport where he bought a sectional aeronautical chart of the Portland area. Sure enough, the airway did pass about ten miles east of Woodland, directly over countryside he remembered from his childhood. He took it home and studied it that afternoon.

Without seeing the terrain first hand he couldn't be sure, but from the map and from his memory he thought this area where the airway passed east of Woodland would be an acceptable location. The airway appeared to go directly over the Lake Merwin dam.

It would be an excellent checkpoint, easily spotted even at night. North of the lake the terrain was very rugged, but on the south side it improved rapidly as the airway approached the Columbia River and Portland.

Several roads crossed the area but it was sparsely inhabited. Much of it was still in forest but he remembered several places where the land had been cleared. If he could locate the proper spot and somehow manage to leave a car near there, all he had to do was bail out at the right time, walk to the car; then drive out quickly, hopefully before the alarm could spread even if they did figure out where he left the aircraft. He started thinking about making a trip to Washington to take a close, first hand look at the area.

When he went to the office the next morning he found the policies on the Haddock children had arrived. He decided to call Louise and ask if it would be all right to bring them by. Janie answered the phone but when he asked for Louise, Helen came on the line. "What do you want with Louise Dan?" she asked in a suspicious voice.

"The policies on the kids are here and I wondered if it would be all right if I came by sometime today and delivered them. I'd like to go over them with her," he explained.

"She's not feeling well," Helen answered with a firmness that left no room for argument. "Why don't you take them home with you and I'll come by around five and pick them up. You can explain them to me and I'll tell her. Does she owe any more money on them?"

"No, they are paid for in full."

"Then I'll see you around five."

He hung up the phone feeling only a pinprick of bother. He was still upset at the way Helen was involving herself in Louise's financial affairs, but that was outweighed by the elation he felt realizing she was coming to their house again that afternoon.

He went home at lunch and spent the afternoon giving more thought to the idea of flying to the West Coast. He checked the airline schedules to Portland and Seattle and between the two cities. Despite the fact he had grown up in that part of the country, he had not visited there in several years. He thought it might be a good idea to make the trip even if he didn't bother going to Woodland. It would be a change from Atlanta and God knows he needed a change. He decided to sleep on it.

Helen arrived just before five looking seductive in a white dress with miniskirt and red accessories. She was still wearing her hair in the pony tail. He had consumed several drinks by this time and when he invited her to have one with him she readily agreed.

"We bought a new VW bus today," she volunteered while he was fixing the drinks. "We didn't have to put but five hundred dollars down and the bank financed the rest. We're going to let Janie have it and buy another car for us to use, probably a Gran Prix or a Rivera," she continued happily.

"You're sure having a good time helping her spend her money aren't you?" Dan said without rancor as he passed her a bourbon and water.

"Yes, I guess I am."

"Well," he said, sitting down and smiling warmly at her, "what I want to know is when you are going to come home and look after your old worn out husband. He's in pretty bad shape. He can't work or do anything constructive—just sits around drinking and feeling sorry for himself all the time."

"Oh Dan," she said smiling, her dimples winking at him coquettishly. "Don't make it sound so bad. I know you can take care of yourself. I'm coming back. I still love you. Just give me a little time."

"Baby do you really?" he said finding it hard to believe his sad little speech had reached her after so many of his efforts had proven futile. Moving quickly, he came to sit beside her on the couch and put his arm gently around her shoulders. "Baby you don't know how I've missed you, how miserable I've been." he continued in a voice thick with emotion, an opaque film covering his glistening eyes. "You must know that it was all a big mistake and that I'll make it up to you the best way I can."

"Oh Danny, you big baby," she sighed as she embraced him. Suddenly both his arms were around her fierce and stiff, a clasp of possession. Clumsily he found her lips and kissed her tenderly. When they separated he had tears streaking his face.

"Darling you just don't know how good that makes me feel," he said in a weepy voice.

"Don't cry Dan," she said softly cuddling his head on her breast. "Things are going to work out all right for us."

"Helen I've tried so hard to do the right thing," he whispered hoarsely. "It hasn't been easy trying to learn a new job and we have both gotten used to living pretty good. It hurts me when Louise can buy you things that I can't afford. But if you come back I promise I won't be jealous of her."

"That's all I can ask Dan," she said trying to comfort him as she stroked his hair.

They sat quietly holding each other for some time. She kissed him and continued running her hand slowly through his hair. Finally she spoke. "I hate to leave Dan, but I better go. We are taking the kids to the beach in the morning for a holiday and there are a million things to be done."

"All right Baby," he said, his voice more composed now. "But when are you coming back to live with me?"

"It won't be long Dan. We're going to Panama City for a few days. When we get back I'll call you."

"I've been thinking of going out of town too. I may fly up to Seattle and look up some old friends."

"I think that's a good idea. How long will you be gone?"

"Oh I'll probably leave tomorrow and be back this weekend," he said suddenly making up his mind to definitely make the trip. "I just want to get away for a couple of days like you do."

"That'll work out good then," she said cheerfully as she got up to leave. "I'll call you Monday."

"I'll be expecting it. Hey wait! Let me give you these insurance policies. That was what you were supposed to be here for," he said, smiling now.

After she left he was so elated he felt he had to tell somebody about it. Alan was out on a flight but he got Rod on the phone. He was pleased to hear Dan's news and congratulated him. They ended up getting together for dinner at The Knight's Table, then doing a little bar hopping. It was the first time Dan had been happy since the Friday night fights.

His feelings of guarded optimism about their future were still with him the next morning and Dan whistled as he dressed. His face no longer wore the strained restless, reckless look that had been so prevalent the past few days, and though it appeared thinner, the eyes under the thick blond brows were quiet and contented. He decided he would fly to Portland, have a look around Woodland, then consider what to do next. He checked in at the office, told them he would be out of town until the following Monday, then caught a noon flight westbound.

Arriving in Portland he rented a Ford from Avis and checked into the Cosmopolitan Airtel, a large motel on NE 82nd near the airport. When he went out for dinner at Sylvia's, an Italian restaurant on Sandy Boulevard, he stopped at a service station and picked up a road map of the Woodland area, and later that evening he sat down to study it.

Using the aeronautical chart as a guide, he drew the airway on the road map and scrutinized the terrain it passed over, particularly in the vicinity of Woodland. It showed two roads running east out of Woodland. State Route 503 ran northeast for twenty-one miles along the north bank of the Lewis River, through Ariel where the Lake Merwin dam was located, to the little town of Yale. There it turned south, crossed the river, and continued south-southeast along the eastern edge of the airway. The town of Amboy was on 503, ten miles south of Yale.

The other road going east from Woodland was not numbered. It was a short spur which connected the town with a whole network of county roads south and east of the Lewis River. Once across the river, it immediately split, one leg bearing northeast along the southern bank of the river, and the other going south-southeast to La Center. From there this road went almost directly east through the hamlets of Highland, View, and Fargher Lake where it rejoined State Route 503.

The northernmost county road, the one which followed the river's southern bank northeastward toward Lake Merwin, eventually found its way to Amboy, some sixteen miles east. Cooper seemed to remember all of these roads as being gravel, but from the map it appeared they were now paved. Amboy and La Center had been very small towns in the days of his youth and didn't appear to be any bigger now. Highland, View, and Fargher Lake were little more than wide spots in the road.

He thought this area would be a good locale for what he had in mind. Somewhere along the airway, south of Lake Merwin and north of the road that crossed between La Center and Route 503, should be a spot which would meet his requirements. He would know better after making an on-the-spot assessment.

Thursday morning dawned bright and clear. As Dan climbed into his rented LTD he breathed deeply of the crisp clean air and admired the snow covered slopes of Mt. Hood rising to the east. A short drive brought him to Woodland where he turned east and crossed the river. At the T he went right toward La Center. With I-5 looming off to his right it seemed as if he was doubling back, retracing his steps for the first three miles. Steep, wooded hills rose on his left. But about two miles out of La Center the road swung more to the east, then emerged into a cleared area before entering the small town nestled in a bend of the East Fork of the Lewis River.

In the center of La Center he turned left and took another highway which bore east out of town. There were many roads which were not shown on his map and he had some difficulty but eventually located the object of his search, a small airfield shown on the aeronautical chart as Goshen, a 2500 foot, lighted strip less than a half-mile east of the airway centerline. He hoped for a large cleared area around the airstrip but instead found that it actually cut through a small stretch of woods. And while the area was not thickly populated, there were houses scattered along the road in all directions.

Deciding to look further Cooper continued east through two small towns known as Highland and View and intersected State Route 503 at Fargher Lake. From there he proceeded north-northeast to Amboy, a distance of some ten miles.

As a teenager he had visited Amboy many times, but it had been more than eighteen years since his last visit and the town seemed to have shrunk, dried up like an old woman who was only a misshapen caricature of her former self. Locating the county highway that went back toward Woodland, he headed west.

On the right the land rose rapidly in undulating hills from the 300 foot elevation of the road to the 1723 foot Peak of Green Mountain two miles northeast. These hills were heavily wooded and there were only a few houses along the road, this area not being near as populous as the land around the Goshen airstrip

About eight miles out of Amboy he came to a fork. To the left lay the direct route to Woodland, the main Woodland-Amboy road, but to the right the other branch, marked as the Dam Road, looped back northeast. This was an area Dan wanted to investigate.

He didn't remember exactly where the turnoff was, but within a mile he recognized it, the entrance to a secondary track that disappeared into the woods on his right. It was called Spurrel Road.

Taking the turnoff he passed an abandoned house, crossed a small creek that flowed south, and was immediately swallowed up by the dense forest. Proceeding slowly, for the road was narrow and not in a very good state of repair, he followed it eastward for about a half-mile until he arrived at an abandoned mailbox and an overgrown trail that marked the entrance to what had once been known as the Martin Place.

During high school Dan had become good friends with a boy named Ed Martin who had lived here. Ed, a big, strapping six-footer who was another only child, had often invited Cooper to spend weekends with him at this rustic homestead tucked away in the woods. They had hiked over much of the forest that encircled the place, camped out in the surrounding hills, and fished in a nearby branch of Cedar Creek. Occasionally Dan's best friend, Roy Andrews, had joined them on these weekend forays.

In those years the Martin Place had consisted of a comfortable frame house, a weathered barn, and about sixty acres of cleared land which had once been a farm. Ed's parents, Jack and Sybil Martin, did not farm it, but had kept a cow, some chickens and a large garden. Jack Martin, a hulking, bear of a man employed as a Forest Ranger by the federal government, had been happy to share his knowledge and love of the woods with his son and his high school buddies.

When Dan's family had moved to Seattle in'53 he had lost contact with Ed Martin, but years later he had come across his boyhood friend again. When Cooper returned from Okinawa in 1962 he ran into Ed at Shaw Air Force Base where Martin was a navigator on a B-66D, weather reconnaissance aircraft. They had renewed their friendship and Dan had learned of Jack Martin's death in 1960 from an unexpected heart attack, and that Ed's mother, unwilling to stay at the lonely farm, had moved to Portland to live with an unmarried sister.

At that time the old house was standing empty and Ed talked of going back there to live some day. But any plans he might have made were abruptly terminated one stormy night in late '62 when his plane crashed into a small hill near San Antonio while making an instrument approach to Kelly Air Force Base. There were no survivors.

Now, in 1971, Dan Cooper wondered if anyone was living here. It didn't look like it from the condition of the mailbox and the dirt road that had once led to the Martin residence. Parking his car on the side of the road (the drive into the property appeared so rough he was afraid to drive in for fear of getting stuck and stranded), he hiked up a small incline, passed under the large power line which stretched southward from the Lake Merwin Dam some two miles directly north, and emerged from the woods. Before him lay the ancient fields and off to the left, less than a quarter-mile away stood the abandoned homestead.

He thought it would be an ideal place should he decide to proceed with the hijacking. As best he could tell, the power line, which passed along the west side of the cleared area, was very near the centerline of the airway. He should certainly be able to see the dam, which was always brilliantly lighted, and time his jump to put him in the vicinity. The house was boarded up and abandoned, the old barn falling down, and Dan thought it safe to assume no one had lived here in the past ten years. He could easily leave a jeep or some similar vehicle for a couple of days without it being noticed.

Returning to his car, he cranked up and continued eastward on the Spurrel Road. He passed a few houses, some occupied, some empty, and several small fields before, in about two miles, the Spurrel Road rejoined the Dam Road up near the dam. There he turned back to join the main Woodland Amboy road near the Cedar Creek School. A drive of a final eight miles brought him back to Woodland.

Returning to the Portland Airport he chartered a small Cessna to fly him back over the area he had just covered by car. He told the pilot he was a timber cruiser who wanted to take a look at a tract east of Woodland. From the air he was able to follow the lay of the land. He had the pilot take him over the dam, then follow the power line that ran south across the Martin Property. He spotted the farm and Cedar Creek just south of it. Much of the terrain here was rugged but there were numerous cleared areas. On a moonlit night he should have no difficulty distinguishing between the dark green forest and the lighter reflections of the cleared ground.

It was late afternoon before Dan finished. He had an elaborate dinner at the restaurant adjoining the motel, the Telo Star, and thought about his next step. He was still not committed to doing this thing, but he was fascinated by the planning and preparation for it. He decided against going to Seattle and instead checked out and took a night flight to Washington, D. C. Landing at Washington National just before dawn; he rented another car, crossed the Potomac, and checked into the Howard Johnson's on Virginia Avenue across from the Watergate complex.

About eight-thirty he called Jim Parker, the Eastern pilot who had been best man at his wedding in 1968. It was Jim who had first persuaded Dan to try skydiving back in 1966, and that was the reason he was now in Washington making this call. He hadn't done any jumping since he moved from the nation's capitol and he definitely wanted to get in a little practice if he was going to attempt a night jump into a wooded area. He was lucky and caught Jim at home with the day open. They agreed to meet for lunch at Mr. Henry's, a pub on Wisconsin Avenue in Georgetown.

With that taken care of, Dan decided to use the remainder of the morning to accomplish one more chore. After calling to determine exactly where he should go, he drove out to the office of the U. S. Geological Survey on South Eads Street in Arlington, Virginia, where he was able to purchase detailed survey maps of the area east of Woodland. If he should decide to go through with the hijacking he would need them.

Back in Georgetown by 11:30, he was on time to meet Parker at Mr. Henry's. Over a leisurely lunch they reminisced about old times and Dan skillfully brought up the subject of skydiving.

"Yes, I still jump regularly," Parker asserted in answer to Dan's inquiry. "How about you?"

"I haven't jumped since I moved to Atlanta," Cooper sighed, regretfully. "And I sure miss it. Do you suppose we could go out this afternoon and make a jump?"

"Sure," replied the older man expansively. Parker was a good natured, outgoing person who always took other people at face value. He would never think to question a friend's motives. Instead he was pleased with the idea and suggested he call right then to be sure an aircraft would be available.

That was what Dan had hoped would happen. They finished lunch and, after stopping to change clothes, were on their way. Driving south on I-95 for about fifteen miles, they turned west into the sun baked Virginia countryside and continued to the Woodbridge Airport, a twenty-two hundred foot strip near the Ocbquan River. There Parker introduced Dan to the pilot who flew for the club, a short serious looking man with a severe crew cut and thick glassed named Mews, and a Mr. Hudson, who was the jump instructor. Hudson, a thick-set, powerful-looking man with short, wiry blond hair, worked at the small airport and was available almost all the time.

Because it had been more than four years since he had jumped, Hudson took Dan quickly back over the basics. They made several jumps from a four foot platform to practice the proper touchdown technique and reviewed the need to assume the arch position; legs apart, arms outstretched about shoulder level, spine bowed until he could feel the strain at the small of his back. The arch, Hudson reminded him, puts all the weight in the stomach, forcing the body into a horizontal position facing the ground.

They also discussed how he could steer the chute with the toggles attached to the directional lines, how to tell a bad chute from a good one, and then they carefully went over all of the emergency procedures.

The afternoon was warm and sunny with no clouds, the jump a mind-numbing thrill. Mews took them up in a Cessna 206 to seventy-two hundred feet over the airport where Dan, then Hudson, followed Parker out. He had forgotten the excitement of leaping into mid air and floating down under a canopy of silk; the heady rush that comes with the blast of air as one leaves the aircraft, the detached feeling of being above it all drifting down after the chute has opened. On his left the mountains of western Virginia rose majestically in the distance while nearby the river shimmered, smooth and golden, in the late afternoon sun. The sky above him was like the dome of a great cathedral, vast and silent, and he could hear the steady beating of his own heart.

He brought his mind back to the business at hand in time to prepare for the landing. He remembered how to use the steering toggles to turn himself into the wind and how to shorten the risers on one side to slip sideways and align himself with his target on the ground. Just as he touched down he flexed his knees to absorb the shock of hitting the turf. The wind was light and he was able to make a standup landing.

Dan was exhilarated over the success of the jump and even though he had gotten little sleep the night before, he agreed to join Jim and his wife Barbara for dinner at their home in Alexandria. They wanted to hear about Helen and about his insurance job. He painted a rosy picture for them omitting any mention of the problems that had been building in recent months. He explained that his wife was on a vacation with friends at the beach and made a vague promise to bring her to Washington sometime in the future.

Parker had a flight on Saturday but Dan went back to the airport and got in two more jumps under Hudson's supervision. Both went well, giving him confidence that he could make a successful jump in Washington State should he decide to go ahead with the hijacking. However he still thought of the whole project as a pipe dream, a will-o-the-wisp he had devised as therapy for the mental suffering brought on by his problems with his job and his wife.

After an early dinner he checked out of Howard Johnson's and caught an evening flight back to Atlanta, arriving at 10:28. On his way home he stopped for a drink at the Sans Souci and there found Alan and Rod with two girls, Jennifer and Elaine, drinking it up. This being Saturday the bar closed at midnight and so he suggested they all come to his townhouse for a nightcap. He told them he had been out of town on a short vacation but didn't go into detail. Alan commented on how much better he was looking and asked if he had heard from Helen.

"She was over Tuesday afternoon," Dan replied with confidence. "We had a short talk and I think she'll be coming home next week. She took Louise and the children to the beach but I expect them back tomorrow." He got moderately drunk but it was a happy drunk and when the others left he went to bed and slept soundly until Sunday afternoon.

Sunday evening he took the Cadillac out for a drive and on the chance that they were back, cruised by Louise's house. There were no signs of life so he drove on disappointed. He had harbored the hope he could persuade Helen to come home for the night. All his despair of the previous two weeks was forgotten now in his anxiety over her return.

Monday morning she called. "Hi, how was your trip to Seattle?" she asked cheerfully.

"Oh, I didn't make it out there," he answered nonchalantly. "I just went up to DC and visited one of my old airline buddies there. I got back Saturday night. When did you get in?"

"We haven't. We've had such a good time we've decided to stay another day. That's why I called. I suppose we'll leave tomorrow around noon. If we're not too late I'll call you when we get in."

He was disappointed but there was nothing he could say. He told her he'd be home waiting for her call and hung up. Trying to suppress his impatience he sat around the house all afternoon drinking beer and watching TV. About six o'clock he got another call.

It was a boy named Joe Maxwell. He was Janie's current boy friend and Dan had met him at Louise's house on several occasions. "Mr. Cooper do you know how to get in touch with Mrs. Haddock?" he inquired in a hesitant voice.

"No I don't Joe," Dan replied. "My wife called this morning and said they wouldn't be back until tomorrow that they were staying an extra day, but she didn't say where they were."

"I need to get in touch with them," the boy continued in a worried voice. "Someone broke into the house over the weekend and I don't know whether I should call the police or what?"

"Broke into the house?" Dan exclaimed. "What did they steal?"

"I'm not sure exactly. They got a stereo and a small TV that belonged to me and I'm almost sure there is a vacuum cleaner gone too. But the worst thing is the way they wrecked the house. The dining room table is smashed and there are clothes scattered all over the place."

"That sounds a little like Jim Carpenter might be back on heroin and has been there looking for something. Louise might not want to call the police on him. I guess you'd better wait until she gets home and let her decide. Have you been staying there while they were gone?"

"Yes I was here every night until Saturday night when I stayed with a friend. I came back yesterday evening and found it like this. They were supposed to be home today so I thought I'd wait and see what Mrs. Haddock said before I called the police. I thought it might be Jim too and I didn't know if she'd want to bring the police in or not. But when I didn't hear anything I thought I'd call and see if you knew where they were staying."

"They didn't tell me. Did they give you any indication other than they were going to Panama City?"

"They didn't even tell me that much, just that they were going to the beach and would be back Sunday night or early Monday. What do you think I should do?" the boy asked helplessly.

"I guess since you have waited this long it won't hurt to wait another day," Dan counseled him. "Helen said they would be home late tomorrow."

"Well, gee, Mr. Cooper," Joe pleaded. "I don't know if I can stay in this place another night. They broke eggs all over the kitchen and it is starting to smell. I could clean it up but I don't know if I should. Would you mind coming over and taking a look?"

"No, I'm not doing anything," Dan replied. "I'll come right on over."

He experienced mixed emotions as he headed north on Piedmont in his Impala. He didn't want to get involved in Louise's affairs in any way, now or ever again. But the boy obviously was on the horns of a dilemma and needed some advice; and Dan couldn't see any harm in going over and taking a look. On reflection he decided his curiosity was the real reason he was going rather than a desire to accommodate Joe.

From the outside Louise's house looked like it usually did. Joey Haddock's motorcycle was in the garage half disassembled, and an unusually large accumulation of boxes and wrapping paper were scattered around the garbage cans. Maxwell had been watching for him and opened the front door as Dan turned in the driveway. He was a quiet, colorless young man who had attached himself to Janie Haddock a couple of months back, and had been a regular at the house ever since. Dan knew that he ran errands and did other small favors for Louise and assumed this was the reason his constant presence was tolerated.

"Thanks for coming Mr. Cooper," the boy said respectfully, his face grave. "I just don't know what to do."

"How did they get in Joe?" Dan inquired, stopping and surveying the outside of the house in both directions. He could see no sign of forced entry.

"I don't know," Maxwell replied twisting his face into a frown. "All the doors were locked when I came back yesterday and it doesn't look like any of the windows have been tampered with."

"That makes it look even more like Jim Carpenter, doesn't it? He could still have a house key I suppose."

"I don't know about that," the boy murmured as he stepped aside to allow Dan to enter. In the entrance hall he saw a big pile of clothes that he recognized as belonging to Helen. The hall closet was open and apparently someone had taken them out and thrown them down. There were one or two things still hanging in the closet but the shelf in the top was bare. Turning to the right into the living room he noticed a cot had been set up there in the middle of the room. More clothes were scattered around and a chair was overturned, but there were no other signs of damage here.

"I wonder if someone spent the night here," Joe said as he followed Dan's gaze. "That cot wasn't there when I left Saturday. I'm not sure where it came from. Come look at the dining room."

Dan followed him through the living room to the dining room beyond. When they moved to this house Louise had bought a modernistic dining table that consisted of a large oval piece of glass supported by a cork covered base. The glass top had been broken across the middle and pieces were lying askew. Another chair was overturned. "There was a new vacuum cleaner sitting in that corner there," Joe said, indicating the corner next to the kitchen. "I guess they took it, but as you see they left some of the attachments."

"What about Louise's TV and the kid's stereos?" Dan asked, looking back toward the living room. "Hasn't she just bought new ones?"

"Yes she has, but they took all of them somewhere before they left. Maybe they anticipated something like this. The only TV and stereo that was here was mine and now it's gone," the boy replied dolefully.

Dan looked into the kitchen but didn't go in. A carton of eggs had been broken on the floor and apparently a gallon of milk had been dumped also. The empty container lay on its side on the floor which was sticky and beginning to smell. He returned to the entrance hall via the dining and living rooms where he picked up a few of Helen's clothes and hung them back in the closet absent-mindedly. "I don't think I'd call the police before Louise gets home," he told Maxwell. "It doesn't smell too good but it won't get much worse in another twenty-four hours. Has anybody been here beside you?"

"Lynn and Terry and Joan brought me back over here yesterday. They came in and looked around. I left again then and didn't come back until this afternoon. I don't much want to stay here by myself tonight."

"I don't suppose it would matter whether you did or didn't," Dan mused. "There's not much here to steal and I guess they've done all the damage they are going to do."

"You haven't seen Mrs. Haddock's room yet," Joe said apprehensively. "It's the worst."

They walked back through the living room and down a short hall to Louise's bedroom. It was a shambles. Apparently everything that had been in the drawers and the closet had been taken out and dumped on the floor. Underwear and night clothes were mixed with skirts, dresses and blouses. Some snapshots and bottles, which had been on top of the dresser, had been swept off and lay on top of a pile of bedclothes. Some perfume had obviously been spilled because the room had a strong fragrance of lilacs.

"I haven't been in there except to glance around," said Joe as they stood in the door gazing at the squalor. "I figured this would be the best place if the police want to look for fingerprints."

"Yes, but if it's Jim they might find his fingerprints anyway," Dan said with a sigh. "You know he was living here up until a couple of months ago."

"Of course but if it was somebody else they wouldn't have been in this room," the boy explained. "There have been lots of kids over here and it could have been any of them. But they wouldn't have been in here."

"I see what you mean," Dan said nodding. "Well I won't go in either. It looks awful but I don't believe anything is damaged. It's mostly just a big mess. This does look more like something kids would do than it does like anything else. Did they go in Janie or the boy's rooms?"

"There are a couple of drawers pulled open and a chair overturned, but nothing like this. I was sleeping downstairs in the rec room. They didn't do any damage there, just took my things."

"Well, I'm not getting involved one way or the other," Dan said firmly as he turned and started back toward the front door. "I'd recommend you wait until they get back to call the police but that's up to you."

"That was my thinking. I'm glad you agree," Maxwell said seemingly relieved now that Dan had seen the strange mixture of robbery and vandalism that had been visited on the house and still felt there was no harm in waiting for the Haddock's return. "But if you hear from them again, please tell them about it."

"If I do I think I'll just say that you called and said someone had broken in the house and done a little damage," Dan said, turning at the door and looking the boy in the eye. "I don't want to get involved in any way. I guess you know why."

"Yeah, sure, Mr. Cooper. Thanks for coming over."

Dan left and drove back home puzzled over what might have happened. He hated to see Louise's house in such a mess. She never kept it very neat but it would take a lot of work just to get it clean now. The more he thought about it the more certain he was that Jim was the person responsible. He probably had come over there spaced out on drugs looking for something in Louise's room. When he couldn't find it he had gotten mad and broken the dining room table and made the mess in the kitchen. Finally he had left taking the vacuum cleaner and Joe's TV and stereo. Dan felt sure Louise wouldn't want to call the police. He thought about getting someone to help and clean the place for her but quickly abandoned the idea. He had to remember things had changed. Louise and her problems were not his responsibility anymore. In fact he probably shouldn't even have gone over there.

He didn't hear anymore from Helen or Louise and had put it out of his mind by the time he went to the office Tuesday morning. He worked through his mail and was preparing to leave when he got a call from Bob Gordon, the friend who had lived across the hall at the Landmark before his marriage. Bob had just heard of his troubles the day before from Alan and was calling to offer his sympathy and invite Dan to join him for dinner that evening.

"I'd like that Bob if we could go early," Dan replied without hesitation. "Helen will probably call around nine or ten and I would like to be home by then."

"That's all right with me," Gordon agreed. "Suppose I pick you up at your house about seven and we go to the Bull and Bush?"

"Fine. I'll see you then."

Gordon was late but he found Dan in good spirits. They chatted about the Braves and other inconsequential subjects as they left the winding streets of Ansley Park and turned north on Piedmont. It was a dreary evening with rain building toward the west. Black clouds were moving in, streaked with lightning.

They had a short wait for a table so it was after eight before they sat down to eat. Dan didn't want to drink much because he felt he should be completely sober when Helen called, but he gave in and had a martini before they ordered. The food was good and the drink relaxing. However when Bob insisted they have an after dinner drink, he declined.

"You don't mind if I have one do you?" Gordon asked with a smile as he signaled the waiter.

"No, no, go ahead," Dan replied quickly, not wanting to offend. "I'll just have coffee."

Before they could finish, Dr. Stanley Harris came in alone and took a table between them and the door. Dr. Harris was a balding, broad-shouldered man with tufts of curly gray hair sticking out above his ears and a perennial smile. He and his wife had lived in the Landmark too, back in 1968, and he and Gordon were still close friends. Dan knew him as a loquacious, out-going type who always had a funny story to tell, but had seen little of him in recent months. When the doctor told them his wife was out of town and insisted they join him for a drink, Dan felt it would be churlish to refuse.

He ordered a crème de menthe on the rocks and Gordon opted for a Golden Cadillac. 'What on earth is a Golden Cadillac?" Dan asked jokingly when the waitress brought the drink.

"It's made with white crème de cocoa, Galliano and cream," Bob confided. "It's a great after dinner drink."

"It's certainly a pretty drink," Dan replied eying the frothy yellow liquid in a champagne glass with a glint of interest. "May I have a sip?"

"Sure, try it and maybe you'll want to order one yourself."

"Damn, it is good," he said, licking the froth from his lips. "It's as smooth as a Cadillac all right. I believe I will have one."

They were on their second round when the doctor's food came and he was adamant they have another while he was eating. The cocktails weren't that potent yet they had a mellowing effect on Dan. Gordon and Harris were both good conversationalists and as he got caught up in their animated discussions his anxieties receded. "I'm having a good time," he thought to himself. "There's no need in rushing home. She may not get in until late and then she may not call."

By the time the meal was over Dan and the doctor were slightly inebriated and Gordon was definitely high. When he learned that Harris had never been to Uncle Sam's, he was determined that the three of them should go there for at least one drink and quickly overwhelmed their half-hearted objections. If Dan had been driving his car he would have gone on home, but not wanting to be a party pooper, he went along.

When they came out the rain had begun to fall steadily in slivers of silver against the streetlights as traffic hissed past. Behind the patterned glass of the Steak and Ale across the street the lights twinkled red and green. Leaving the doctor's car, they all got in Gordon's Audi for the short trip to Uncle Sam's.

At the big club it was early but the crowd was beginning to gather. They had two drinks at the long front bar while they watched the throng of mini-skirted women and long-haired men gradually fill the large, high-ceiling room that had formerly been a warehouse.

"Bob, I don't want to be a spoil sport," Dan said as he finished his second bourbon and water, "but I'm expecting Helen to call around ten and it's almost that time now. Why don't you and Dr. Harris come over to my place and have a drink. Then after she calls maybe I can go back out if you want to do that."

"That sounds fine to me," Gordon said amicably. "What about you Doc?"

"Let's go!" he replied.

Emerging from the club they found the thunderstorms had passed on, but the air was close and humid and the streets were still wet, the gutters full. Thunder still rumbled in the distance as they piled into the red Audi and drove back to Westchester Square. It was after ten and while Dan wasn't drunk, he was past the point of refusing drinks. He mixed Bob and the doctor each a scotch and water and had Wild Turkey and water himself. Dr. Harris had never seen Dan's house and was given a quick tour. They were on their second drink when the phone rang. Dan answered it in the kitchen.

"Is that you Dan?" Helen asked petulantly in answer to his slurred hello. "I've been calling since eight o'clock. Where have you been?"

Her voice was stern, demanding, but at first her strident tone did not penetrate his alcohol-dulled senses. "I went out to eat with Bob Gordon and we ran into Dr. Harris," he answered evenly. "They're over here now having a drink."

"Well I want to see you," she shot back rancor in her voice. "Can you come right now?"

He felt a worm of unease in his bowels as he recognized the harshness in her voice. "I think so," he stammered. "Give me a few minutes to get rid of them. Where are you?"

"I'm at the Sans Souci but I'm going to Uncle Sam's," she replied still using that impatient tone. "I'll be at one place or the other."

"I'll come as quickly as I can," he assured her quickly. She hung up without further reply and he returned to his guests. "That was Helen," he explained apologetically, "and I've got to go over to the Sans Souci to meet her."

They made appropriate noises and quickly finished their drinks and departed. Locking the door and getting into his Impala he wondered why he hadn't pinned her down to meeting him at one place or the other, or even suggested she come to the house. He decided it was the way she had talked; it had shaken him up and stunned him for the few moments she was on the phone. Yesterday, when she called, she had sounded so normal and things had gone so well when he had seen her last week. He hadn't been expecting the hostility and wasn't prepared for it. It sobered him considerably as various explanations churned in his mind.

She wasn't at the Sans Souci. He found Rod at a large table near the front visiting with Elaine, the girl he had been with on Saturday night, and several other people Dan knew vaguely. Rod told him that Helen had been there for quite a while, but had left a few minutes before he arrived.

"I guess she went on out to Uncle Sam's," Dan said unenthusiastically. "She said she'd either be here or there."

"If you're going to Uncle Sam's could we catch a ride?" asked one of the unidentified girls at the table.

"Sure, I guess, so," he agreed. "Are you ready?"

"Just let me finish this drink," she cooed, a sly smile on her over-made-up face. It took Dan a moment to place who she was, but then he remembered seeing her when she worked as a Go Go Girl at the Kitten's Korner a couple of years back. She was a big handsome woman wearing a tight black dress that did little to conceal her heavy breasts. She introduced herself as Erica and the smaller, mousey blond girl next to her as Becky.

They both joined him in the front seat of the Chevrolet for the short ride north on Peachtree Street. It was close to midnight when they turned left and descended the steep drive that led to Uncle Sam's. The parking lot, big as a city block, was equipped with the new street lights that cast an orange, shawdowless glow on the rows of shining automobiles and the rain-slick pavement. Cabs, limousines and private cars fought for space in front of the club. He always felt uncomfortable in this brassy haze and memories of the Friday night fight crowded his mind as he circled the near-full lot looking for a parking place.

He turned around at the back of the lot and spotted someone pulling out of a space on the end of a row near the entrance of the club. Just as he drove into this choice spot he saw his wife emerge from the front door, directly across the roadway from where he was parking. Erica thanked him as she and Becky slid out and started for the entrance, switching their hips seductively. He waited a moment hoping Helen wouldn't see him and would go back inside, but that was not to be. She had seen him and as he got out and locked the car she descended the steps with lithe grace and, ignoring the traffic, strolled slowly and deliberately across the busy drive carrying a drink in her hand. As he waited he could sniff the far off metallic smell of thunder.

She looked good, even in the shawdowless glare of the orange lights, dressed in a green skirt and white blouse. Over this she wore a sleeveless jacket that was open in front, a loose fitting garment with artful designs embroidered in green and gold on a white background. Dan recognized it as one of the outfits Louise had bought her the week the check arrived. Her hair was combed out full and it bounced as she walked.

"I don't care much for the company you're keeping these days," she sneered sarcastically, glancing at the two girls who were just going into the bar. "Let's sit in the car and talk."

"All right," he agreed reluctantly, unlocking his door and getting back inside. He reached across and opened the door on the passenger's side, then cranked the car and turned the air conditioning on high. It belched out icy sheets of moisture but he found himself perspiring as she closed her door, then turned to survey him with a cold, malevolent stare, her face earnest and angry and determined in the strident glow of the street lights. Thinking of it later he realized that this was the moment when the night simply exploded as first reason, then reality went whirling away.

"Dan you've done some dirty things but what you did to Louise's house Saturday night was just about the lowest thing I've ever seen you do," she said, slapping him with this unexpected accusation in a calm and deliberate manner. Then, continuing in the same smug, self-righteous tone, she flayed him again. "What in the hell was in your mind?"

He was completely taken aback. Whatever he expected, and he had been apprehensive ever since her call, it had not been this. He would never have imagined anyone suspecting him of being the vandal who had done the damage at the Haddock house. He blinked his eyes rapidly and opened his mouth to reply and was stunned by an instant of vertigo. The world seemed to tilt up at a skewed angle leaving him momentarily speechless.

She didn't give him time to find his voice, but continued berating him in the same reproving tone, flailing away at his already wounded psyche. "Come on now Dan," she sneered mercilessly, "don't deny it. It's got your mark all over it."

That did it! Hurt and rage forced him to finally find his voice and he exploded in her face.

"You're the one who breaks things and throws things all over the house," he thundered. "I don't know where you get the idea that my mark was all over it!"

"Then you admit it's got your mark on it. I thought so!" she replied coldly in the same sarcastic way, ignoring his denial.

"I don't know what in the hell you're talking about—my mark all over it," he screamed back at her, his voice breaking into a nervous falsetto as his reason was smashed on the rock of her ridicule.

"Don't get haughty with me Dan. I can tell your work when I see it. Nothing in that house was hurt except Louise's stuff. The kid's rooms weren't even touched. Her room was the one where all the damage was done. That proves to me it was you."

"What about the mess in the kitchen and the dining room table and Joe's things being stolen?"

"You knew how much she prized that table and I'm sure you just took Joe's things for a blind so she'd blame it on poor Jim Carpenter. You thought you were so smart but I know you too well." She sat back against the door and gave him a knowing, superior smile.

Dan was in a state of shock. Suddenly he knew he was going to lose her for good. Terror and loneliness awoke in him. Her accusations left him angry and hurt, disappointed that his hopes for reconciliation were dashed, but even worse, cut to the quick by the fact that she thought he would stoop to such an irrational act. And the way she was acting, so smug and arrogant about it all, added insult to injury. He felt his life disintegrating all around him, like a cliff giving way to the sea.

"Listen," he raged, "if I wanted to hurt Louise I'd find some better way than tearing up her house and breaking a table. I'd get a Judge to take those poor kids away from her or tell her trustees how she spends her money on heroin-addict boy friends and lives in motels while the kids run wild. I wouldn't have to resort to that!"

"You probably would stoop to something like that," she replied still using that cold, reproachful tone that was so infuriating to him. "You're so jealous of her money. You've been green with envy ever since that check came."

"And why shouldn't I be," he stormed back. "She used it to buy my wife away from me."

Their eyes locked across a ten-inch space. "Damn it Helen, I've told you I didn't go near that house Saturday night," he sputtered.

"You'll have to do better than that. The Manley's next door said they saw you drive by late Saturday evening in my Cadillac and Joe said you rushed over there yesterday afternoon and touched everything so if they found your fingerprints you could explain it."

"So what if I did drive by, that doesn't mean I stopped. And it was Sunday, not Saturday. And Joe asked me to come over there. He was worrying what to do when you didn't come home on time."

"There, you admit you were over there. I've caught you in a lie already. Why don't you just admit it Dan?"

His head ached and his mouth tasted foul. The muscles of his back and belly all felt sprung out of joint, strained and achy. Her smug, know-it-all attitude was getting to him worse than her fury and venom during the Friday night fight. She had convicted him without a hearing and was now administering the punishment, contempt and derision. His world went gray as reality went down a hole. "Stop it Helen," he cried, demanding and pleading in the same breath. "Stop it, stop it, stop it."

"Why should I?" she said, smiling contemptuously now. "You did it and I'm not going to let you forget it, ever."

Her total rejection of him and all his arguments made any other words he might have spoken dry up in his throat. His mind locked with a clang like a jailhouse door. He ceased to think in rational terms. Only one message came through—shut her up, stop her mouth from spewing forth lies and more lies. Didn't he love her more than anything on earth? Hadn't he gone through hell for the last three weeks? In a sudden vicious spasm he lurched forward and grabbed her by the throat and choked her. That shut her up!

He squeezed until he knew she must be dead. That was the first thought to get through. She made no struggle as her eyes bulged and her face went pink, then red, then a congested purple; and it could have been five seconds or five minutes that passed while his fingers tightly grasped her neck in hysteric frenzy. "She must be dead," he thought in a mechanical way, and so he released her and slumped backward in the seat, breathing rapidly in harsh, rasping gasps. It was several seconds before she opened her eyes and several more before she stirred. Struggling to get her breath, her face gradually assumed a look of fright, then of stark terror. In that weird orange light she turned her neck stiffly and stared at him with huge eyes brimming with pain, dread, loathing, intense fear. Like a trapped animal, she tried to hypnotize him with that look while she inched slowly away, groping behind her for the door handle.

But rather than immobilizing him, that look of terror tore through him like a ricocheting bullet, provoking a knee-jerk reaction from his panic ridden body which was now somehow disassociated from his impotent brain. Throwing the car into reverse he hit the accelerator hard and turned the wheel sharply to the left as he spun out of the parking place into the wide driveway. Later, trying to reconstruct what had happened and why, he could never decide why he had done it. Had he meant to drive away with her in the car, kidnap her until she came to her senses; or was he merely trying to get away, to leave that blighted spot as quickly as possible? He never knew.

When the car shot backward she had her door partially open and was trying to step backward onto the ground. As he backed up the door swung open wide with her clinging to it but when he put the car in drive and the Chevrolet leaped forward it slammed her between the door and the side of the car. In his travail he hadn't seen the car approaching from his right, a green Plymouth cruising slowly down the driveway in front of the club, but suddenly it loomed there on his right. He tried to miss it but his car was out of control on the wet pavement. It shot diagonally across the road striking the left front fender of the other automobile solidly with his right front fender, careened off, and continued drunkenly on into the side of the building, a few feet beyond. Helen was half-in, half-out of the Impala during the first part of the short trip. When it hit the other car she lost her tenuous grip on the door and was lifted up and out, flung into the air to come down spread-eagled on the hood of the Plymouth. She must have done a complete summersault before she landed hard on her back. The force of the crash shattered the right hand side of Dan's windshield and the glass in the right door. Tiny pieces flew and cut her face and arms.

The Chevrolet came to rest piled against the building with its front end and right front fender completely demolished. The driver of the Plymouth, a young man with stringy blond hair and thick glasses, had hit his brakes when he had seen the Impala make its sudden exit from its parking place, so his car had been practically motionless when it was struck. Its grill and right front fender were mashed in and Helen was sprawled on the hood on her back, her head toward the front. As he looked back she slid off the right side and crumpled into a bloody heap on the pavement.

When Dan's car hit the building it jerked him back to reality. Without knowing exactly what had happened, he realized immediately that Helen had been hurt. His door wouldn't open so he rolled down the window and crawled out, unaware that he had banged his knees hard on the dashboard when the car had stopped so abruptly. Hobbling around the back of the Chevy he saw Helen, a bloody bundle lying in the roadway. "Oh my God," he wailed. "I've killed her."

A group of people had been coming out of the club just as it all happened and it was only a matter of seconds before a crowd gathered. Dan was screaming for someone to call an ambulance but at first everybody only pressed closer for a look. Helen's eyes were open and she seemed to be conscious, but she made no effort to move. Dan, still in shock himself, wouldn't even touch her, much less move her, for fear of aggravating her injuries. Seeing that no one was doing anything for the injured girl, a tall young man stepped out of the crowd and took charge. He took off his windbreaker, folded it and placed it under her head to make her a little more comfortable, then felt for broken bones.

Seeing that she was alive and in good hands for the moment, Dan left and went inside to be sure an ambulance was on the way. The man at the door said that he had called for an ambulance and for the police so Dan returned to the scene where the crowd was still milling about excitedly in the muggy night air.

Pushing his way through the throng, he knelt beside her. "Is she hurt badly?" he asked the young man who was now sitting on the pavement holding her hand and talking to her softly.

"I can't tell," he replied in a quiet, even voice. "She's going into shock and we need to get her to a hospital quickly. Is there an ambulance coming?"

"The man at the door said he called one. It looks like one would have been here by now," Dan said, shaking his head sadly. It was strange but his mind was perfectly clear now. He didn't know exactly what had happened but all the anger and hurt were gone out of him. His only anxiety now was getting her to the hospital.

After what seemed to be an eternity, the police arrived. There were two cars and apparently one of the cops was a sergeant, a dark, balding man with a Roman nose and a full determined mouth. His movements were quick and jerky, his voice harsh and guttural as he barked out orders to his men. He had two of them clear the crowd back and sent the third to call again about the ambulance. Before he could do more, it arrived, red lights flashing. Helen was quickly and expertly lifted onto a gurney and loaded in by the white clad attendants. "Where do we take her?" one of them said.

"I guess you better go to Grady," the police sergeant replied quickly without hesitation.

"Good God no!" Dan interrupted excitedly. "Piedmont's right up the street. Take her there."

"Who are you?" asked the sergeant turning sharply to fix Dan with a penetrating stare.

"I'm her husband and I want her to go to Piedmont," replied Dan with emphasis.

"In that case take her to Piedmont. Tell them I'll be along shortly," said the cop to the ambulance driver. "Now if you're her husband, how about telling me what happened here," he continued turning back to Dan. A feeling of thick tension seemed to hum in the humid night air.

"We were sitting in my car over there," Dan began hesitantly as he indicated the parking area from which the wild ride had started. "I had the engine running to keep the car cool. We were having an argument and she started to get out. I don't know exactly what happened but I think I must have reached over to stop her and accidentally knocked the car into gear and stepped on the gas. It went straight across the drive, hit the Plymouth there, and hit the wall of the building. When we hit the other car she was thrown out."

"How much have you had to drink?" asked the sergeant in a matter-of-fact voice.

"I had a couple of drinks with dinner and a couple of more about an hour ago. I never got inside the club here."

"Your car over there smells like whiskey. Did you have a bottle in the car?"

"She brought a drink out of the club with her when she met me. I guess there was some of it left and it spilled."

"Okay, you have a seat in the back of that police car there. Let me talk to some of these other people."

Dan had been worrying so much about Helen he hadn't realized he might be arrested. It now dawned on him that there would be an investigation and a lot of questions would be asked. What, up to now, had been a private matter was fixing to go public. Two or three people Dan knew were in the crowd and one couple came over and offered assistance. He thanked them politely but was too dazed and grief-racked to think of anything they could do to help now that Helen was on the way to the hospital. Sitting in the police car he was suddenly frightened to find himself close to tears. In his heart he knew he had really lost her now. If she died it was he who had killed her. If she lived she'd never forgive him. He had lost either way and nothing seemed important anymore.

He sat there for what seemed like hours. Once the sergeant came back and asked him more questions. Then he heard the fleshy young man who had been driving the Plymouth excitedly telling his story.

"I never saw him. I never saw him until he shot across the road right in front of me. I just barely had time to hit my brakes. I was going slow, you know, looking for a parking place, and all of a sudden he pulls out of the end of that row right there and comes straight for me. If I hadn't hit the brakes he'd have hit the driver's door and I'd be dead. He took the right front fender right off my car and from somewhere this chick ends up on top of my hood. I just sat there and watched her slide off—like she was in slow motion. Look, that dude's got to fix my car don't he? I don't know if I can even drive it. It looks like the front end is messed up bad."

Finally a wrecker backed into place, hooked on to Dan's car, and towed it away. Another wrecker took the Plymouth and the sergeant came back over to Dan. He read Dan his rights, then told him he was being arrested for driving under the influence of alcohol. Did he want to have an alcohol blood test? Dan said yes. They loaded him into a paddy wagon, locked the doors and headed south on Peachtree Street. Dan couldn't help but remember that it was only a little over two weeks earlier that he and Helen had traveled this same route listening to B. J. Thomas sing about raindrops falling on his head. There was no music this trip and he felt like the whole world had dumped on him.

The police took him to Grady Hospital for the blood test. It seemed like everything took forever. When that was finally over, they took him across to the Atlanta Police Station and booked him. He sat on a bench and first waited to have his fingerprints taken, then waited again for someone to come and take his picture. He noticed by the clock on the wall that it was only 3 AM but it felt like an eternity had passed since the accident. He was filled with a terrible sorrow of which he could not even find a focus. It seemed like a whirlpool going down into the darkness. The blackest depression he had ever known swept over him in a solid wave and carried him down

They put him in the drunk tank with a lot of other men. There were some bunks with mattresses but they were all taken. He found one without a mattress and lay down on the hard steel. He couldn't sleep. He couldn't even think straight. His mind felt separated from his body.

Laying there, his mental faculties in limbo he stared at the peeling gray walls in the half light from a naked bulb in the corridor. Nuances of feelings came and went like tight puffs of smoke. Flocked images tumbled over and over one another in his brain, making no sense. After a time he must have dozed.

The clang of the door to the tank woke him. He heard the guard telling the new prisoner something about a phone. Dan realized then they had pointed out the pay phone on the wall and had said he could use it. He checked his pockets. They had taken most of his personal possessions but had left him some change. He had one dime, a half-dollar, and eight pennies. He decided he should call someone to come bail him out. He got up and found the phone and dialed Rod's number. It was answered almost immediately.

"Rod, this is Dan," he said, his voice still tight with tension. "Can you come down to the police station and bail me out?"

"Yes Dan. I've been hoping you would call. John and Cecile were at Uncle Sam's and saw them take you away. They said they spoke with you but you didn't seem to know what was going on then. Anyway, they came back to the Sans Souci and told me and we all came over here when the bar closed. I'll come down now. How much is your bond?"

"I don't know. I guess they told me but I'm in such a daze. Do you know how Helen is? Is she hurt bad?"

"We called the hospital but couldn't find out much. They said she was still in the emergency room."

"I don't know what happened Rod. We were sitting in the car talking, and the next thing I knew, it was smashed up against the building and Helen was lying in the street."

"Don't worry about it now Dan. She's in good hands. We'll come on down right now and get you out."

He hung up and wandered around the tank his head throbbing. He wondered if he was losing his mind, if he was having a nervous breakdown. He paced back and forth groping for answers like a blind man in an unfamiliar room. He thought about calling the hospital and checking on Helen but the phone wouldn't take his half-dollar. He checked around and found one of the other prisoners who was awake who swapped him two nickels for the half-dollar, and called Piedmont Hospital.

It took some time to get to talk to anyone who could tell him anything but eventually he got the nursing supervisor on the fourth floor and she answered his questions.

"Mrs. Cooper is asleep now," she said in a cool authoritative voice. "Her condition is listed as serious but I think she is doing as well as could be expected under the circumstances. Did you say you were her husband?"

"That's right," he replied evenly, knowing the nurse was wondering why he was not at the hospital. "Is there anyone there with her?"

"Yes, there is a Mrs. Haddock here. I think your wife asked the doctor to call her. She's in the room. Do you want to speak to her?"

"No, not now. Do you know if she had any broken bones?"

"I don't believe so," she replied, more sympathetic now. "She seemed to be in a good deal of pain and the doctor is going to do some more tests on her later today. He gave her a sedative and she is resting comfortably."

"Can you tell me the name of her doctor?" he asked hesitantly.

"It's Dr. Tom Aderholt. His office is in the Sheffield Building if you want to call him later today. I'm sure he can tell you more then."

Dan thanked her and hung up. He felt a little better, a little less confused. A small spark of hope had returned and with it rational thought. At least she wasn't dead. And maybe she wasn't maimed for life. Dan wished there was something he could do. She had to recover. If she didn't, it was the end for him also.

It was seven in the morning before he was finally free. There was some rule about drunks having to spend at least four hours in the tank before they could be bonded out; and they didn't count the time at the hospital. Rod was waiting for him. "John and Cecile went on home," he told Dan matter-of-factly. "They said to call them if there was anything they could do."

"Thanks for getting me out. I should have called you earlier but I've been in such a daze. I called the hospital after I talked to you and the nurse said Helen was resting all right. She didn't think any bones were broken but said the doctor was going to make more tests today. Louise is over there with her."

They got in the car and drove slowly over to Rod's apartment at the Landmark. The thunderstorms of the night before were gone leaving only a few fat white clouds drifting across the innocent blue sky. Upstairs Rod put on coffee and fixed them some breakfast. Dan wasn't hungry but ate anyway. He was still in a deep state of shock and did things mostly by rote. They didn't talk much and after clearing away the dishes Rod asked Dan if he wanted to go to bed there.

"No. If you don't mind, I'll let you take me home," Dan replied. "I have some downers there and I think I'll take two and try to go to sleep for a few hours. I would like to go over to the hospital and see Helen but Louise is there and I'm afraid of a scene. I couldn't take that on top of all that's happened."

"A little sleep will do you good," Rod counseled helpfully. "I doubt if you could see Helen now anyway."

"Rod, I don't know what to do," Dan pleaded, turning humble frightened eyes on his friend. "I want to do everything I can to help make her well. If it means I can't go near her, then I won't go near her. But on the other hand if she wants me I want to be available. I know she is going through a severe mental shock in addition to her physical injuries and I want to do whatever I can to help her get over that."

"I'm sure you do," Rod answered with sincerity. "Is there anything I can do to help?"

"Maybe you could go over there today and talk to Louise. And if they'll let you, you could see Helen," Dan replied, an idea starting to germinate in his overstressed brain which was slowly beginning to function again. "Find out what her mental attitude is and if she wants to see me. Tell Louise we've got to bury the hatchet and work together to get her well as quickly as possible."

"I'll do that," Rod agreed. "I don't know how much I'll be able to find out, but I'll try."

"If you do that, I'll call her doctor later today and see what he has to say. I got his name from the nurse."

Dan slept until three. He had set the alarm for that time so he could call Dr. Aderholt during his office hours. In a surprisingly short time he had the physician on the line answering his questions.

"Mr. Cooper, your wife is doing as well as can be expected," he confided in a lubricous voice. "We took x-rays last night and made some more tests today. There are no broken bones and there is no evidence of any internal injuries. She is complaining of a great deal of pain on her left side. It is most likely a strained or torn muscle. I'm keeping her under sedation and watching her closely."

"Did she suffer any disfigurement doctor," Dan asked oppressively. "She had a lot of blood on her face last night."

"I don't think she will have anything permanent. Her lower teeth are loose and she got a lot of small cuts from the slivers of glass but I don't believe she will have any scars if that is what you mean."

"Yes, she's such a pretty girl. I was just hoping she wouldn't be scarred."

"I don't think you have to worry about that. If she's still in a lot of pain tomorrow I'm going to call in another doctor. It's possible she may have injured her back in some way I haven't detected."

"Doctor, I guess you know how it happened," Dan continued on a contrite tone. "We were having an argument and I lost control of the car.

I'd like to see her but I am wondering if it would be wise. Do you think it would aggravate her mental condition?"

"She's still in shock and under pretty heavy sedation. It might be best to wait a day or two. I don't believe she has asked for you. If she does I'll be glad to call you."

"Thanks a lot doctor," he replied, signing off. "Please call me if there is anything I can do to help."

He tried Rod's number but got no answer. Still tired, he went back to bed and slept until nearly eight, this time waking without the alarm. He tried Rod again and this time he connected. "I talked to Doctor Aderholt and he was fairly optimistic," Dan related. "Did you find out anything?"

"Yes, I spent a good bit of the afternoon talking to Louise. She said Helen was pretty much out of it with the medicine and all, but that it looked like she was not in any serious danger. They think she may have hurt her back in some way but don't know yet. Aderholt is calling in a back specialist tomorrow to run some more tests."

"He sounded very encouraging to me over the phone."

"Well of course Louise is in horror over the whole affair. She didn't say much about you but she went on about how Helen was cut up and bruised and how she was in so much pain."

"Did you get to see Helen?"

"I just stuck my head in the room. She was asleep. She didn't look all that bad."

"Did you ask Louise about my seeing her?"

"I told her what you said about working together to get her well. I think maybe you've misjudged Louise a little. She said she never wanted to cause trouble between you and Helen and if Helen wanted to see you she wouldn't interfere. I think the two of you ought to get together and see if you can't iron out your differences and work together."

"That's what I've wanted to do all along. Of course part of the problem up to now was that Helen wouldn't let me get near Louise."

"Well I asked her about having lunch with you tomorrow and she said she would. I hope that's all right with you?"

"Yes I think that's an excellent idea. Maybe we'll know a little more about Helen's condition by then and maybe she'll be out from under the sedation. In the meantime I'm going to go ahead and send her some flowers. I don't see how that can do any harm, do you?"

"No, that's a good idea," Rod agreed before he hung up.

Dan fixed a ham and cheese sandwich and opened a coke to quell his hunger pains. Sleep and a little food did wonders in restoring his ability to think rationally. Gone were the wild emotions and unreal thoughts that had begun in the parking lot and continued through the previous night, but he was still left with a heavy load of guilt and a gripping urgency to do something to right matters. He put a Tom Jones album on the stereo and sat up until midnight chewing on the problem, developing dozens of scenarios.

First thing the next morning he called a florist and ordered a dozen red roses sent to Helen's room. The card said simply, "Forgive me, Dan." He wanted to go see her badly but after all that had happened he felt the flowers were as much as he dared do without some encouragement. He looked forward to the lunch with Louise and so was waiting at the Steak and Ale on Piedmont when she and Rod arrived at twelve-thirty.

Getting a table, they ordered drinks. Louise was quiet but not unfriendly. At first Rod did all the talking and they both just nodded. Eventually he sat back and said, "Now I've said my little piece. It's up to you two to take it from here."

Dan wasn't sure how to begin, but he realized that now he had to make his pitch to Louise. She sat controlled and stolid, studying him with large blue-gray eyes under heavy brows, a thin sheen of perspiration on her high forehead. Her thick black hair, somewhat oily, was combed back, falling almost to her shoulders, and she smoothed it with one hand as she eyed him unemotionally. He started out shakily, his voice slow, halting and embarrassed. "Louise, I hope you realize that through this whole thing I have had no ill feelings toward anybody. The initial trouble, the Friday night fights as I've come to think of them, were my fault and the next day I was ready to admit I was wrong and make up with both you and Helen. But events just went too fast and everything seemed to go wrong. I'm sorry I didn't believe you at first about telling Helen I was in Daytona, but when she came tearing up to the motel and screeched the tires I couldn't think of any other explanation. Then it looked like there for a while that Helen might come on back and we would make up, but then you went on the trip and got back and your house had been torn up and she blamed me. I really can't remember what happened Tuesday night except that she got in the car and started giving me a hard time. I didn't mean to hurt her. It was strictly an accident."

"She told me you tried to kill her," Louise said in a flat monotone, not blinking, looking at him directly.

His eyes clouded a little and he shook his head reluctantly. "I don't remember, I think she was trying to get out of the car and I started to drive off and lost control of the car."

"She said you choked her until she passed out and then you tried to ram the car into another one."

"I didn't mean to hurt her," he said in a thin fluty voice. He felt helpless and embarrassed; his cheeks flushed a dull red.

"Well you did, and what's worse, she's scared to death of you now," Louise replied in a kind-yet-regretful voice. She seemed morose and unhappy.

"I was afraid of that," he replied sadly. "She'd been drinking a lot and probably doesn't remember how she provoked me. But no matter, I was wrong to lose my temper and I didn't mean to lose control of the car. It just happened."

"I don't think there is any point in dwelling on what happened," Rod interjected, trying to move the discussion off the subject of the accident. "What you two need to do is decide what you can do together to get her well."

"That's right Louise," said Dan a little more cheerfully. "Do you think it would be a good idea if I came to see her and told her how sorry I am?"

"Not right now Dan. She's still not normal in her mind and like I said, she's scared to death of you. It might bring on an attack of nerves."

"All right then, I won't try. I don't want to upset her in any way. But if she wants me, wants to see me or talk to me, I'm available any time. Did she get the flowers I sent?"

"Yes, they came about eleven this morning. She didn't comment on them."

"I guess that's a bad sign," Dan sighed, shaking his head slowly. "She's always loved having flowers so much. You remember how she bought that big arrangement for me in New Orleans when we had the fight about Harvey?"

"She's still doped up most of the time," Louise commented in a worried tone. "She hasn't said much about anything. They did some more tests this morning but I don't know what they found."

"Well Louise, if there is anything I can do, just let me know. I hope this means that there won't be any more hard feelings between you and me?" he asked expectantly.

"No, no hard feelings on my part," she replied quickly, but there was no kindness in her eyes and she didn't sound convincing.

Nevertheless, Dan felt encouraged when they parted. It had not gone as well as he had hoped nor as bad as he feared it might. Outside the lead-tinged sky hinted of rain as a restless wind pushed dirty gray clouds eastward. He returned home feeling lonely, restless and ill at ease. He called Dr. Aderhold again and got more evasive half-answers to his inquiries about his wife's condition. The doctor said he thought Helen had bruised or twisted her back and that might be the cause of the continuing pain. He was still giving her medication for it but he thought it would go away gradually. He wouldn't predict how much longer she would be in the hospital.

Dan went to his office the next morning but about ten he called Piedmont Hospital and talked to Louise. She told him Helen was feeling better and the doctor had reduced the amount of medicine she was taking for pain. She had received more flowers from Rod and several other friends. Dan asked Louise if she would meet him for lunch again and she agreed. He picked her up in front of the hospital at one and they went to the Steak and Ale again.

Dan did most of the talking but Louise's responses gave him more encouragement than they had the day before. He told her to instruct the hospital and the doctor to send the bills to him and asked if she thought it would be all right if he bought Helen some kind of present.

"I don't know of anything she needs Dan," Louise replied in a quiet, almost apathetic voice.

"There probably isn't," he said doggedly determined to have his way about something. "But I never saw her get a present that her face didn't light up whether she needed it or not. I just thought it might give her a moment of pleasure."

"Well it's up to you but I don't know of anything she needs."

He took Louise back to the hospital, then drove to Phipps Plaza where he bought Helen an expensive robe and nightgown. He didn't normally shop there but he knew she put a lot of stock in where things came from, and a gown from Lord and Taylor should please her. On the card he wrote,

"I hope this little gift will make you smile. That's all I can ask. I love you. Dan." They promised to deliver it on Saturday morning.

By noon Saturday Helen had checked out of the hospital. Dan didn't learn of it until that afternoon when he called to see how she was doing. The fact that she was well enough to leave buoyed his spirits and he thought of calling Louise at home but decided against it. Things had gone well with her the day before and he didn't want to be too pushy. She had said she would keep him informed of how Helen was getting along.

He stayed home all day Sunday hoping she would call. By six o'clock he couldn't stand it any longer. He dialed her number and Louise answered.

"Hi," Dan said nervously. "I was pleasantly surprised when I found you had checked out of the hospital yesterday. How is she doing?"

Louise was apprehensive, shouldering a load of anguish. "I really don't think she should have left," she whined in a nasal tone. "But the doctor said she could and she wanted to leave. She's got to go back to see the doctor tomorrow, the special one about her back. And then she's got to see a dentist about her teeth."

"Is there anything I can do?" he asked.

"No, I'll let you know if there is," she replied, sullen now.

"Do you think I could see her any time soon?" he asked hopefully.

"Dan, she has said she doesn't want to see you. We had a talk about it today. I told her about our meeting and she didn't like that. She blames you for everything that happened and told me to tell you not to come to see her, not to call her, or not to bother her. She said that if you come near her again she is going to take out a peace warrant against you."

Dan rubbed one aching temple with his free hand and closed his eyes. He was hurt but not surprised. "Thanks for talking to her for me Louise," he said, trying not to sound sarcastic. "You can tell her I won't bother her. If she wants to talk to me she knows how to reach me. I won't call your house again because she might answer. But please do me a favor. Call me every day or two and let me know how she is getting along. I worry about her all the time and it would be a big help to me if you would do that."

"I'll do that Dan," she agreed so quickly he knew she was just saying it to get rid of him. "But don't call here. I don't want her upset."

The following week he waited for Louise's call but it never came. After a few days he gave up hoping for it. Apparently her show of cooperation had been just that, a show and nothing more. Rod and Alan went over to see Helen on Tuesday and they reported she was up and about. The dentist had put some kind of cast in her mouth to help her teeth, and she claimed she was still sore all over, but they were amazed at her recovery.

"Did she mention me at all?" Dan asked hoarseness in his voice.

"Yes," Alan confided, looking embarrassed. She said if we saw you to tell you she was getting a lawyer and filing for divorce as well as a big settlement for her injuries. I'm sorry Dan but that was what she said."

"Well I might have expected it," he replied, his face a picture of misery.

The gift he had bought for her had arrived at the hospital after she left. On Wednesday the store called and asked what to do about it. He told them to forget it and send him his money back. There wasn't much point in wasting the sixty dollars now.

He had called his insurance company the day after the accident. On Monday he was forced to spend several hours with an adjustor telling him the circumstances leading up to the accident. The man who owned the Plymouth had to be paid off, and the management of Uncle Sam's was asking for damages to the building. Dan's car had been towed to Mendenhall Chevrolet where they were working on an estimate of repairs.

He was scheduled to go to traffic court to answer the drunken driving charge on Friday, October 1st. Once he had time to think about it, he realized he should hire an attorney to represent him. He inquired among his friends and settled on a lawyer named Claude Franklin who was recommended by John Bennett. On Tuesday, September 28th, he went to see him at his office in the William Oliver Building downtown at Five Points. Franklin was in his early forties, tall and wiry with a narrow head and long gray-brown hair. He wore an expensive brown suit and although he was loud and garrulous, he gave the impression of knowing what he was doing. He obviously handled drunk driving cases every day.

After they discussed the situation he called and checked on the blood test Dan had taken at Grady Hospital the night of the accident. The analysis had disclosed that the concentration of alcohol in his blood was only 0.8, just within the legal limit (a level of .10 was sufficient to prove one was legally intoxicated), so technically Dan was innocent. Nevertheless Franklin advised him to plead nolo contendere, no contest. He said he was certain the judge would accept this plea and only levy a small fine.

Dan's driver's license would not be suspended or revoked. He hinted that the police could have filed other, more serious charges, and he felt it was best to dispose of the case quickly in this manner in order to forestall any such developments. Dan agreed and wrote him a check for his fee, three-hundred-fifty dollars.

On Friday morning he was sitting in Room A of the Atlanta Traffic Court waiting for his case to be called when Helen swept in. Dan watched, almost unbelieving, as she and a long-haired, big-headed man moved quickly down the aisle, her high heels taping out a loud staccato on the terrazzo floor. Her appearance was so changed he hardly recognized her. Her face was paper-white except for dark circles under her eyes, and her beautiful blond hair was out of sight under a nondescript brown scarf. She wore no makeup and she looked terrible, her face set, grim as stone. A shapeless beige dress hid her voluptuous figure.

His heart was knocking harder and more rapidly than it should have been; random thoughts flashed into his head and his emotional control slipped several notches as he was buffeted by conflicting sensations. It alarmed him that she was here, in court, and apparently with a lawyer. What did she plan to do? Was she going to stand up in court and accuse him of trying to kill her? Alarm was followed by despair and disgust, a wave of understanding that it was his actions that had reduced the bubbly effervescent girl he had married to this haggard wretch with a face the color of raw dough. And then a warm feeling engulfed him as his heart went out to her in love. But it was finally with a sense of sorrow that he realized that he was now separated from her not only by Louise and her money, but by this accident, and lawyers, and courts. A dark cloud of depression settled over him.

When the case was called the big-headed man stood up and introduced himself as Joe Walker, and in clear resonant tones told the court that he was the attorney for Mrs. Helen Cooper who was injured in the accident. He explained that she had only consulted him the day before and he wanted time to investigate the situation before the case was disposed of. He requested the judge postpone the case for two weeks. Franklin objected and after some consultation with the attorneys, the judge granted a one week delay, resetting it for the following Friday. Later, after Walker and Helen had made a fast exit, Dan questioned Franklin in the hall.

"What did he want to delay the thing for?" Dan wanted to know.

"Probably just to throw a scare into you," Franklin advised him with a grin. "I've talked with the police officer who was there and he isn't changing the way he wrote it up. I don't think we have anything to worry about."

Nevertheless it did worry Dan. He was suffering from guilt and remorse and while he wasn't familiar enough with the law to know exactly what he was guilty of there, in his mind he was guilty of trying to kill his wife and grievously injuring her. Her ghastly appearance today had exacerbated these feelings and imbued him with an even greater sense of hopelessness and frustration. Memories of happier times flashed through his mind and he was engulfed by a poignant sense of the irreversible, one-way flow of time. He seemed bound and strangled by offhand decisions and slight impulsive mistakes that had somehow swelled and festered until they had brought him to this sorry point in time. He despaired, realizing how such inconsequential events can snowball until they seal a man's fate.

And he pondered what lay ahead. Was her love for him completely dead? In spite of everything he didn't think so. He knew his love for her was stronger than ever. Thinking now of how things had been before the trouble—of the soft silky feel of her long blond hair, the set of her full ripe lips, the small upward tilt of her bright blue eyes—he felt weak and sappy and more than a little desperate.

PART V

"If You Go Away As I Know You Must There'll Be Nothing Left In This World To Trust"

Friday, October 1 - Wednesday, October 6, 1971

MORE THAN A little desperate! That was Dan Cooper's frame of mind as he drove slowly home from court that Friday. It was then that he began to seriously consider the hijacking. It did not come as a blinding revelation, this conviction that by hijacking an airliner, demanding ransom, and bailing out into the malevolent darkness, he could somehow heal his wounded spirit and expiate the dreadful guilt he carried. But slowly, painfully he came to recognize that for his own self-respect he must prove himself capable of courage and action, capable of an act so dramatic and irrevocable that whatever happened afterward, he could never again doubt his identity as a man.

Previously he had considered his thoughts of hijacking as a harmless hobby, something to occupy his mind. But now, for the first time, he was thinking of this adventure as a real possibility and he found the prospect tantalizing. Time was blotted out completely as he opened his mind and explored it.

At home, thinking back over the steps he had already taken and putting together an outline of a plan, he found himself stirred by emotions that had been dormant too long. For the first time in months he felt alive and vital.

Even though he hadn't realized it, Dan sorely missed the thrill of flying and all it entailed. He missed the regular excitement of piloting a multi-ton machine worth millions of dollars; being responsible for thwarting its wayward urges and bringing it down safely through any kind of weather to a smooth landing on a small patch of concrete. Even though much of the work of an airline pilot was dull repetitive routine, particularly when compared to military flying, the responsibility was still there and the knowledge that if you didn't do it right, there might be tragic consequences. The punsters weren't far wrong when they said flying consisted of hours of boredom interrupted by moments of stark terror. The job had demanded a certain discipline and returned a certain satisfaction that were now lacking in his life.

He also missed the exhilaration of the breathtaking view of the world from on high with its mighty cities, majestic mountains, endless plains, shinning seas, literally laid out at one's feet. Up there the flyer inhabited another cleaner, freer world and looked down with disdain and not a little pity at the earthbound, crawling like insects across the map in their frantic race from tedium to apathy. He resented the fact that his wings had been clipped and he had become one with them.

And finally he missed being part of the intoxicating world of the jet set, those lucky few who were accustomed to moving rapidly from place to place, from one environment to another, at the drop of a hat or the ring of a phone. He longed for those halcyon days when he would routinely breakfast in Atlanta, lunch in New York, and dine in Miami.

Now, considering the risks involved and the dangers inherent in the scheme of hijacking an airliner for ransom he was touched by feelings not unlike those he had known as a pilot. A surge of tension brought a sense of déjà vu, a reawakening of passions that touched a chord deep within him. He felt his pulse quicken and the adrenaline began to flow as he was overwhelmed by the realization that he might actually attempt this daring project, involve himself irrevocably in this dangerous adventure.

Cooper's forte had always been careful planning, expert organization, and flawless execution. In everything he did from flying to pursuing insurance sales his obsession with these necessary elements insured that his work, while not often inspired or even exciting, was methodical and complete, professional in every way. And he knew these plodder's skills would be essential to the success of the adventure he was now contemplating. He would have to suppress his volatile emotions, cease nurturing the deep bitterness he felt toward the establishment and his fate, and approach this project as a purely practical problem; bring to bear the pragmatic and logical concentration that was his natural style.

And while this obsession with detail might seem like dull stuff to many, to him it was just the opposite. Even the most complete plan could not cover every possibility, every contingency. And the more variables in the plan, the greater the risk, the more chance something would go wrong. That was where the thrill came in. If he had the nerve, the moxie, the courage to take this chance, this gamble as it were, and he succeeded through a combination of skillful preparation and cool competent execution of a precision plan, then he would know an overpowering exhilaration that would be in a class by itself.

Additionally he was entranced by the charade the project would entail. He was sure that everyone, at one time or another, felt the urge to walk away, just quit their job, desert their family and move to another street, city or country, and become someone else. He had felt this urge often, particularly these last few hectic months, and now he realized this would be an opportunity to do something like that. While he wouldn't be completely leaving his old life behind, in the process of preparing for the hijacking he would have to establish a new identity completely divorced from the old one. He would need a new name and a new personality with new tastes and lifestyle; to become someone entirely different, entirely new. The machinations involved in erecting and maintaining such a façade intrigued him.

But he couldn't or wouldn't do it just for the thrill of planning and carrying out a demanding and dangerous project, or for the excitement of being someone different for a time. He recognized that motives were usually complex, a jumble of drives and incentives, and now he probed deeper and tried to analyze his more closely.

Money! It all came back to M-O-N-E-Y. No matter what happened he needed money and lots of it. The Haddock children's policies had been his only sale in September and he had nothing new working. His savings account was below thirty-five hundred dollars and the Continental note was due again this week. He could probably pay another six hundred dollars and renew it—maybe get by paying only the interest due—but the bank might ask for the title at any time and he couldn't produce it. The idea of borrowing from Louise was out. He was going to have to do something about money and he couldn't put it off much longer.

For days his mind had scurried around this problem like a trained white mouse in a maze trying to reach the cheese in the center. Under other circumstances he might have considered some less desperate method of raising money. He still owned his home in which he had several thousand dollars equity, but he knew that he didn't need a few thousand dollars. All that would buy him was a little time. He needed a large amount of money, fifty or a hundred thousand dollars.

And he felt a deep-seated guilt about the accident. Somewhere, buried in his subconscious, was the feeling that only with money could he ever make it right. It was evident that if Helen came back he was going to need enough money for them to live in at least the style in which they were living when they were first married, before he lost his job with Eastern. He hoped that sooner or later her wild fling with Louise would come to an end and she might come back to him. But he felt she wouldn't return to anything less than she had enjoyed before. If she divorced him he wanted to be able to give her enough money to live comfortably. He owed her that much and he needed it to clear his mind of the guilt festering there.

So in sum it was a complex combination of motives that finally compelled Dan Cooper to commit himself to this idea he had first thought about more than two years earlier and had been actively considering for several months. His need for money and desire to expiate his guilt were the factors that finally tipped the scales in favor of action. But even these would not have been sufficient if it had not been for the erosion of his moral value and the bitterness he felt at the establishment. This bitterness with its subliminal message festering and growing in his subconscious for almost two years, had poisoned his mind and twisted his outlook. Still he was not a sociopath, a person without a conscience, one with no perception of right and wrong. Even now he would never dream of cheating one of his clients or defrauding his employer or anyone who put trust in him. But as a result of his disenchantment with many of the institutions of our society—the law, big business, big government—he found nothing morally wrong in stealing from a big corporation and thumbing his nose at those same institutions. In fact the idea gave him a big thrill.

In his planning he gave little thought to the possibility that innocent people might be killed or injured in the hijacking. He knew the airlines had told their crews to cooperate with hijackers and he was sure there would be no shootout on the airplane. Like most fanatics, Cooper blinded himself to other possibilities with sheer belief. Again it was not that he was devoid of conscience. But believing this with absolute confidence allowed him to put the possibility of violence completely out of his mind.

As for his attempt failing and his being caught, he did not seriously consider this either. In the Air Force he had watched his buddies die in freaky but not uncommon accidents and ignored the possibility that he might be next. The psychology that had protected him then was still operative, the self-assurance that "It couldn't happen to me." In this instance he believed that with proper planning and careful execution he had a ninety-five percent probability of success. But part of the plan would be the definition of alternatives if things went awry. He knew from the start that the alternative to success was his death and his fall-back plan must take this into account.

He didn't kid himself that there was the small chance that he would fail and would die. But who would it hurt if he did? Who would care? The agony he had suffered at the loss of his career and then his wife had hardened him, inured him to the idea that there were things worse than death, and so he was willing to risk it. He kept telling himself he had nothing left to lose.

From this point on he never wavered. Although in his mind he always felt he could quit and call it off at any time, he never seriously considered doing so. That week, waiting to go back to court, he reviewed all his previous thoughts on the hijacking, and then scouring until the small hours each morning, he built up a shrewd and subtle plan for its accomplishment. It took long hours of intense concentration that shut out extraneous thoughts as he tried various scenarios, accepting, rejecting, questioning. He spent much of it lying on his back in bed or on the couch in the study thinking through all the things that must be done and the problems he might encounter. Numerous ideas were considered and rejected before he finally settled on a plan he felt would culminate in success. While he stored most of it in his mind, he made a cryptic outline on paper, both as a guarantee that he had overlooked nothing, and as a checklist of things that must be done. He was neither a slow nor a stupid man, but he spent six days at it, leaving the house only when it was necessary.

His first step was to work out a general plan and timetable. He wanted to do it as soon as possible but there were a number of preparatory projects he must complete before the ultimate act. He had definitely decided to bail out in the woods near Woodland. The weather there was usually mild until Thanksgiving, but after that there was a danger that his plans would have to be aborted because of snow or extreme cold. Then there was the fact that his money would run out within two or three months. Unless he could raise additional capital he couldn't postpone it past December for that reason. After working out a list of the things that must be done and estimating the time they would require, he decided to make his attempt during the week of November 21st.

The decision concerning which flight to hijack was dictated by three things: the location at which he was going to bail out (he wanted the flight from the point where he got the money to the point where he left the plane to be at least twenty minutes but not much over an hour); the day and time it must be done, a weekday during banking hours; and the type of aircraft a Boeing727. It had to be a 727 because it was the only aircraft Dan had flown which had a rear stairway. He wanted to hijack an aircraft type he had flown so he would know enough about its systems, procedures and flying characteristics to be able to tell if the crew was following his instructions. A rear stairway that could be opened in flight without adversely affecting the flying of the airplane was mandatory if he was going to bail out. Fortunately the 727 was a popular aircraft flown by almost all domestic airlines.

Because Northwest had a base in Seattle, only one-hundred-fifty miles from Woodland, and operated 727s, he had already concluded they were the logical carrier. Additionally, because most of their operations were remote from Cuba, they had experienced little trouble with hijackers and would probably have few if any anti-hijacking measures in effect. When he checked a current edition of the Official Airline Guide for Northwest 727 flights inbound to Seattle arriving before 4 pm on a weekday, he immediately saw that Northwest 305 would be the best flight for him. Three-oh-five originated in Washington, D. C., and made stops in Minneapolis, Great Falls, Missoula and Spokane before arriving in Portland. It departed there at 2:45 pm every afternoon and was scheduled to arrive in Settle at 3:10. While it wasn't absolutely necessary that the flight he hit depart from Portland, it was more convenient. If he hijacked this flight the crew would be able to get word to Northwest officials in Seattle before the banks closed. And by the time the money had been gathered and other necessary things done, it should be dark when the plane arrived back over Woodland.

Because less people normally fly during the middle of the week, he reasoned it would be best to make the attempt on a Tuesday or Wednesday. That Monday he called one of the major banks in Seattle and confirmed that they stayed open until 4 pm on those days of the week.

He knew he would need copies of the current approach, departure, and en route aeronautical charts for the Seattle and Portland areas. When he left Eastern his subscription to the Jeppesen service had lapsed, but now he wrote them and ordered a complete set of their airway manuals including a year's revision service.

Cooper was well aware that adequate financing is essential to the success of any project and he devoted a lot of planning time to this area.

He made a complete list of all expenses (those connected with the hijack and his regular cost of living) he expected to incur prior to the first of December, estimated his income, and even worked out a schedule of his cash flow. After making an allowance of fifteen percent for cost overruns, he reached the conclusion that he would have enough money without borrowing if he could renew the Continental note without paying anything on the principal; and if he could collect this year's premiums on the large policies he had sold the Burson brothers in time for his commission on this to be included in his November 15th paycheck. If absolutely necessary some features of his plan, which he designated optional, could be dropped, and he also could run late on his house, car, credit card and charge account payments. However if he saw he could not postpone payment of the principal on the car note or collect from the Bursons, he would try to get a second mortgage loan on his home. Should something prevent him from making the attempt in November as planned and he had to put the hijack off until the following spring, he would be forced to do this.

His first thought about a method of taking over the plane had been to use a gun. But after studiously examining the possibilities, he decided a bomb would be better. It carried more of a threat and if something did go wrong it would be a more certain way of ending his own life.

Bomb threats had been used successfully by a number of hijackers. A few had even exploded, enough to make both pilots and officials wary of challenging one. In an early incident on May 23, 1962, a Boeing 707, Continental Flight 11 en route from Chicago to Los Angeles, had crashed near the Iowa-Missouri border when a bomb exploded in the aft lavatory. The explosion caused the rear portion of the fuselage to disintegrate and the tail assembly to separate from the rest of the plane. Eight passengers plunged to their deaths from the shattered aft section and thirty-six more died on impact. One survivor lived long enough to gasp out the grim, fragmented details.

More recently, in February 1970, two bombs exploding on the same day produced dramatically different results. Forty-seven people died when a Swissair plane was blown from the skies, but all those aboard an Austrian airliner survived when the baggage compartment of their plane was shattered by a bomb.

Arthur Hailey's 1968 novel, *Airport*, and the movie that followed, had done much to stamp the image of the bomb-carrying crazy on the minds of the public, and Dan felt certain this was a role he could develop to perfection. In many ways he was almost as desperate as D. O. Guerrero, the embittered, thwarted former building contractor played by Van Heflin, who had killed himself and maimed a stewardess when he detonated his homemade bomb in the lavatory of the fictional Trans American Flight Two being piloted by Dean Martin. Like Dan Cooper, Guerrero had felt he had nothing left to lose.

Still, Dan had never made a bomb, knew very little about them. Going to the public library he reread the parts of *Airport* that described Guerrero's bomb plus other reference material on bombs and explosives. He learned that making a bomb was simple but did not discover a way to buy the necessary explosive without showing identification. However it did not look like an insurmountable problem either.

He would need two false identities. The second one, the one he would use on the plane, was really only a name and a disguise. But he needed another one with identification he could use when he bought the car he was going to need to drive out of the woods after he jumped, and for all his traveling in that area before and possibly after the hijack. Calling the Alabama Driver's License Bureau in Birmingham, he made some inquires. He learned that with only a birth certificate he could get a Learner's Permit. Then, if he came back with a car and a licensed driver, he could take the driving test and receive a permanent license complete with picture the same day. All he needed to begin with was a false birth certificate.

A copy of Helen's birth certificate was in a file he kept in his study. She had been born in Philadelphia, Pennsylvania, and in 1968, shortly before their marriage, she had written the Clerk of Court there for a certified copy. Dan had kept it filed away and now he got it out and took the original to a quick-copy print shop in Buckhead. This particular shop had a Xerox machine which produced high quality copies and he had them use it to make him three duplicates. Then back home, he put the original away and on one of the duplicate he used white-out, liquid paper, to very carefully cover up all the information that was typed in. Then he went to another print shop downtown and had several copies of this blank certificate run off. Using one of these he now filled in the blanks with the proper information for the false identification he planned to establish in Alabama. The name he selected was Benjamin Alfred Butler, and he gave Butler a birth date two-and-a-half years before his own. Finally he went to Atlanta Blue Print and had them make a Photostat of the forged birth certificate. It looked exactly like what it was supposed to be, a Photostat of a birth certificate, and no one could tell from looking at it that it wasn't genuine.

Then there was the need to make additional practice parachute jumps before he made the one that counted. He didn't want to go back to D. C. or jump locally. If, after the hijacking, someone got suspicious, he didn't want them to have any way to trace him.

He knew there were skydiving clubs in most major cities. So what he had to do was locate one in a city he could reach easily by air that would allow him to use their equipment to make a few more practice jumps including at least two at night. Because of the weather this time of year, a southern city would be preferable and so he decided to try Dallas, Houston and Miami. Using his AOPA Airport Directory, he made a list of fixed base operators at small fields near these cities, and then began calling to ask if they had a club operating from their field. At Hull Field near Sugarland, a small town just southwest of Houston, the party who answered informed him that a club jumped from there nearly every weekend and gave him the name and number of its President, a man named Marty Seymour.

Contacting Seymour, Dan gave his name as Ben Butler and explained that he was an American Airlines pilot based in New York who would be laying over in Houston on weekends for the next couple of months and that he would like to join the Texas skydiving club.

Seymour replied that the club was small and did not own an airplane, but said they were always glad to welcome new members. There was a Cessna 182 at Hull which they normally could rent almost every weekend. He was an approved instructor and would be happy to supervise Dan on a couple of jumps this coming weekend if the weather was good. Cooper explained that he was an experienced jumper and that he wanted to make some jumps from high altitude and possibly a night jump. Seymour said that would be no problem and Dan made an appointment to meet the club president at Hull the following Saturday at one in the afternoon.

Another concern was the amount of money to ask for. At the bank he got a pack of one hundred previously circulated one-dollar bills. Using an accurate postage scale in the Massachusetts General mailroom he weighed the money carefully, then measured its volume in order to calculate the exact weight and volume of fifty and one hundred thousand dollars. He was going to ask for used twenty-dollar bills, and this meant that if he got one hundred thousand dollars he would have fifty packages of one hundred, or one hundred packages of fifty, twenties being packaged both ways. He found this would weigh just ten-and-a half pounds and occupy a space approximately twelve-and-a-quarter inches by fifteen-and-three-quarter inches by two inches. Twice that amount would fit easily into an attaché case and so at that point he decided to ask for two hundred thousand dollars.

Finally he thought about what to do with the money after he had it. They were almost sure to take down the serial numbers of at least some of the bills. But it would take time to circulate the list. He could go directly to Las Vegas or the Bahamas and launder it there. In the gambling capitals no one thought anything about a few thousand dollars in cash. He could make the rounds of the casinos buying chips, playing for a short time, and then cashing them in. If he got the ransom in twenties he could change it into fifties and one-hundreds in a couple of days.

One other major consideration remained that of his appearance. While he didn't think there would be any way they could get a photograph of him during the hijack, he would be exposed to at least one person, a stewardess, for two or three hours, long enough for her to get a good look at him. And several other people would see him for much shorter periods. He needed to alter his appearance as much as possible for his role as the hijacker and he also needed to make some changes when he shifted into his other identity, the one he was going to establish in Birmingham.

During the three years he had been married Dan had gained weight, a total of about thirty pounds. He had talked about dieting several times but had done little about it. Now he decided to go on a crash diet. If he could lose twenty or thirty pounds before the hijack that would change his looks a great deal. Afterward he knew he would have no trouble gaining it back. That Tuesday he went to a diet doctor Louise had used the previous year and got started on a strict routine. He was already a member of the European Health Spa so he went to the club near his office in Buckhead and asked one of the instructors there to work out a new routine to build up his strength in the areas he would need for the jump and the walk out of the woods.

In high school and college Dan had participated in several plays and had been introduced to the art of makeup. He knew he could change his facial appearance considerably by simply changing the color of his hair and the way he combed it, and by wearing glasses. Several months earlier one of Helen's hippy friends had left a pair of pink-tinted, prescription glasses at their house. They were large, horn-rimmed bifocals, and when Dan tried them on he discovered they fit him well and the upper part did not distort his vision. He couldn't read fine print through the lower portion but since he would be wearing them mostly when talking with people, he decided to use them as part of his Ben Butler disguise. He also decided that as Ben Butler he would color his blond hair a distinguished shade of gray. He'd let both his hair and his mustache grow out from now until the hijack, then cut his hair short, color it a third color, and shave his mustache to alter his appearance on the day of the crime.

He didn't want to make the long distance calls to Birmingham, Houston, and Seattle from his home phone, so Monday he checked into the Travel Lodge at Tenth Street and the Expressway and made the calls from there. That evening as he was leaving, he stole the license tag off a Ford LTD from North Carolina. He would need it in Birmingham.

On Monday he also went to his bank where he persuaded the loan officer who usually handled his business to renew the Continental note for another three months without a reduction in the principal. And during this week he worked out a settlement with his insurance company on the wrecked Chevrolet. A man who worked in the body shop at Mendenhall wanted to buy it as it sat. Cooper managed to get sufficient money from him and from the insurance company to pay off the outstanding balance on the note and leave him just over two hundred dollars. He was happy to be rid of it. After the accident he didn't ever want to see the car again, much less drive it. He still had the new Cadillac and since Helen wasn't there, he drove it.

Thursday, October 7, 1971

There is no feeling quite like that of waking up one morning following an illness with the realization that one is truly better, that he has passed through the valley of the shadow of death and has reached the far side. Such was the feeling Dan experienced on Thursday when he emerged from his planning sessions to begin the execution of his well-thought-out plan of action. His first step was to take a plane to Birmingham where he would establish the Ben Butler identity. He flew under an assumed name (not Ben Butler or Dan Cooper) and paid cash for his ticket, a method he continued to use thereafter in his travels.

Arriving early, he purchased a morning paper and checked the classifieds for furnished apartments. There were several listings, but after a few phone calls he decided the most suitable was an apartment house on Highland Avenue in South Birmingham. It rented one-bedroom, furnished apartments by the week or month and the prices were modest. There was a phone already installed in the apartments which went through a switchboard so he would immediately have a legitimate phone, and since the switchboard took messages, an answering service. Over the phone the manager, a Mrs. Janoe, told him they had a unit vacant, he could move in immediately.

At the Avis counter he rented a car, a Ford sedan, to get around town that day. Because a credit card and a driver's license were required to rent a car, he had to use his own name for this. But as soon as he left the airport he pulled into a motel parking lot and changed tags, installing the North Carolina tag he had stolen in Atlanta on Monday night. He arrived at the apartment house with one large suitcase and a briefcase. Mrs. Janoe turned out to be a thin, dark woman of indeterminate age with hair on her upper lip and a voice like a file. He introduced himself as Ben Butler and told her he was a refrigeration equipment salesman whose home was now in Charlotte, North Carolina, and that he had just been reassigned to Alabama by the home office in New York. He said he needed a furnished apartment for a few weeks until he could find a house and move his family down. She showed him the unit that was vacant, two drab, musty rooms with a kitchenette and bath that overlooked an alley in the rear. He asked about the rear entrance to the building, and when she told him it was normally kept locked but could be opened with his apartment key, he decided it would suit his purposes and told her he'd take it. She surprised him then by asking him to fill out a credit application. He had answers ready for this eventuality, but most of them originated in his imagination and so would not stand an actual credit check. However, since she was willing to let him move in immediately, he doubted she was going to even check with the local credit bureau, much less call Charlotte or his fictional employers in New York. The refrigeration equipment company did exist, but if she called there she wouldn't find out much.

She gave him the key and he proceeded to unpack his big suitcase. He had brought some old clothes, linens, toilet articles, and a few personal items to give the apartment a lived-in look just in case Mrs. Janoe or some service man came in. He probably wouldn't ever spend a night here but he wanted to keep up appearances.

His next step was to call one of the local driving schools. With brisk assurance he told the instructor there that he had just moved back to Birmingham after living in New York City for several years, and while he knew how to drive, he had no valid driver's license. He arranged to take an hour's instruction and use the driving school's car to take the test for a driver's license the following Wednesday.

Next he must locate a printer who could prepare him some business cards in a short time. He called four before finding one who would promise to have them by the following Tuesday. He drove there, dropped off the information and a small deposit. These new cards indicated that Benjamin A. Butler was the Southeastern Sales Manager for the refrigeration equipment company and listed his new Birmingham address and telephone number.

Leaving there he drove to the Driver's License Bureau. Parking his car a block away, he walked just in case anybody was watching. Inside he used the forged birth certificate to obtain a Learner's Permit. He had put the gray coloring in his hair that morning and when they asked his height and weight he cut an inch off his actual height and twenty pounds off his weight. He had to take a written test but it was not difficult and he passed with flying colors.

Returning to the apartment he took a nap, then showered and shaved before going out to dinner. In the fine autumn weather he walked down 20th Street to the Parliament House where he enjoyed a prime rib dinner at the Rib Room. Back at the apartment house he exchanged the tags before driving back to the airport, turning in the rented Ford, and taking a late flight home to Atlanta.

Friday, October 8, 1971

When he returned to traffic court the next morning things turned out just as Franklin had predicted. Helen and the bombastic Mr. Walker were there, but other than having a court reporter make a record of the proceedings, they did nothing. The judge accepted his nolo contendere plea and fined him $150.00. Helen looked better in a new white linen suit, but her hair showed signs of neglect and she was still pale.

After paying his fine he came out into the hallway and found her there, standing alone, apparently waiting for her attorney. When she saw him she froze and he heard a distinct, ivory click as her teeth came suddenly and violently together. Her skin was too white, the eyes circled with bruised looking brown rings, the lines etched too deep. She eyed him as if he was a tiger in a poorly built cage

"Hello, how are you feeling?" he asked in a concerned voice, trying to put her at ease.

Without making a reply she turned her back and looked the other way. For just an instant it stopped him cold, but then he mentally shrugged and went on. He remembered his resolution to suppress his emotions and be objective. Besides, he didn't want to press her and he certainly didn't need any more scenes. It wasn't a good time or place to talk anyway.

Saturday, October 9- Sunday, October 10, 1971

The next morning Dan flew to Houston to do parachute jumping. His flight landed at the new Intercontinental Airport a little before ten, and after renting a shiny blue Impala sedan from National, he drove into town and checked into a Ramada just off the Southwest Expressway near Richmond. There was plenty of time to change into his skydiving clothes and drive to Hull Airport to meet Marty Seymour at one.

The jump instructor was a small man, made somehow larger by a veneer of cocky toughness. Skinny as a fencer, he had little blue eyes which sparkled with friendliness and Dan liked him immediately. They spent a short time getting acquainted and Cooper, by now adept at playing a role, deflected the personal questions and put at rest any doubts the jumpmaster might have harbored about his knowledge of skydiving. Seymour had extra chutes and had arranged for the plane for a 2 pm departure.

They chuted up and walked out to the aircraft where Dan was introduced to Page Garfield, the owner and pilot. Garfield, a heavy man in his forties, had bright blue eyes and a serious corn-fed face that lit up when he smiled. Seymour explained that Garfield was a real estate broker who was happy to fly the jumpers in order to help pay for his Cessna, a tired looking Skylane painted a dull red and white.

The first descent was a standard static line jump from three thousand feet and it went off without incident. Satisfied that Dan knew what he was doing, Seymour agreed that the next one could be made from ten thousand feet with a ten second delay.

They chuted up again and Garfield maneuvered the straining Cessna skillfully through the long climb to the selected altitude. In position at last, the cocky Seymour grasped the strut and stepped out into the bright October afternoon. The wind tore the words from his mouth and flung them away, inaudible. Dan plunged out after him.

Assuming the arch, he held a stable position while counting to ten. A short distance below and behind him he could see Marty doing loops and barrel rolls. Suddenly he flattened out and as Dan watched, the Texan's chute opened almost lazily.

He pulled his rip cord and waited for the opening shock, but as he sailed on past Seymour, now suspended in his harness, Dan realized with an unwanted thrill that something was wrong. Looking up, he saw he had a bad chute, a streamer.

For just a moment it seemed his heart stopped there in the silence of the big, cloudless Texas sky. But he recovered quickly and with sweaty hands calmly reached up and unsnapped the cape wells—the two hinged metal plates near each shoulder on the harness—stuck his thumbs in the thick wire rings then revealed, and tugged. The main chute came free and he felt himself accelerating again as he arched forward, flipped over and snatched the D-ring on the reserve chute attached to his chest. It furled out immediately and he got a severe shock as it blossomed above him. But it was a welcome sight and the balance of the long descent was relatively uneventful. Despite the fact he was suspended from the chest rather than from the back, he made a good landing.

Seymour congratulated him on his quick recovery from the streamer and insisted he go up for another jump immediately. This one was made from three thousand feet and he only counted to three before pulling the rip cord. It was routine.

That night he dined at the Kensington Club and enjoyed a couple of drinks at the Steak and Ale on Shepherd before going to bed early. Seymour met him at the airport again on Sunday afternoon and they made two jumps from ten thousand feet with the ten second delay. When these went well, Dan convinced the jumpmaster to set him up for a night jump that evening.

They took off as soon as it was dark. The weather was good and there was no wind on the ground. As the little Cessna made its steady climb to ten thousand feet Dan watched the moon rising, changing slowly from orange to mystic, silent silver. Off to the east, the shimmering glow of Houston's urban sprawl spread across the horizon, but below the lights on the small airfield looked very dim and far away. Although he had done lots of night flying in all kinds of weather, this was something different. His heart was galloping in his chest.

But when it came the jump was little different from those he made that afternoon. He counted to ten, pulled the rip cord, felt the jolt of the chute opening, looked up to be sure the canopy was fully deployed and the lines weren't twisted. Then, using the steering toggles to guide it, he maneuvered himself toward the center of the runway, midway between the ends. Close to the ground he saw his draft die with the wind and was coming straight down, knees flexed, when he hit the asphalt so hard it jarred his teeth. Rolling to one side, he came up quickly to collapse the chute. He had hit the ground harder than he had ever hit during the daytime, but he wasn't injured, just shaken up. He felt pleased, certain that with one or two more practice jumps, he would be good enough to make the jump from the hijacked airliner.

Monday, October 11- Tuesday, October 12, 1971

He spent a second night at the Ramada but was up in time to catch a Delta Early Bird back to Atlanta. There were two major projects to work on during the next two weeks: selling insurance and the bomb.

When he had been working out his plans for the hijacking, his first thought had been to use a gun to take over the plane. But as he reflected more seriously on it, he had concluded that a bomb would be much better. If he made it properly and let the crew see enough to know it was real, it would be a much more effective weapon, one they would be less likely to challenge. The only drawback was that he didn't know how to make one. However a small amount of research had disclosed that all he needed was an electrical source (a battery), a blasting cap, and some explosive. Dynamite was the most common explosive available and he found ten different firms listed under the heading of Explosives in the Yellow Pages. This week, he must decide how to get his hands on some.

He felt he must keep his job as a cover and in order to be sure of doing this, he must sell some insurance. Once each month he was required to sit down with Tom Vaughn and go over his sales plan, review policies in underwriting and list potential customers he was working. Dan was sure that after his long dry spell the manager had given up on him and therefore would not be expecting a lot. Recently their monthly planning sessions had become very perfunctory. However he must make some sales, show some results in the form of new business, or he might be discharged.

Coming up with a list of prospects was not difficult and he could easily make it look like he was doing more than he actually was. But he had to make a few sales or the manager would begin to suspect he was doing something else with his time. So he had concluded he should work extra hard for the next two weeks in an effort to close at least two or three quick sales. As long as he had a couple of policies in underwriting, even small ones, he could satisfy Vaughn and nobody would ask questions.

He called on a number of prospects, old and new, and as a result of this effort wrote two small life policies during the second and third weeks of October. The first was for $20,000 on one of his previous customers, an executive with Eastern named Andrew Robertson. The year before Robertson had agreed that he needed to buy $40,000 in life coverage, but only bought $20,000 at that time. When Cooper saw him on Tuesday night he convinced Robertson it was time to go ahead and purchase the other $20,000, a participating, whole life policy.

The second sale was to a young woman named Nell Brady, a client referred by Rod Kerry. She called Dan on Friday, the fifteenth, and he made an appointment to see her the following Monday evening. Going to her cramped and cluttered apartment on Buford Highway, he found a short girl in her early twenties with heavy breasts, imperfect teeth, and a snarl of long black hair. She was very frank and down-to-earth when she told her story. She was unmarried and pregnant. The baby's father was a married man she had been seeing regularly for several months. He had agreed to support her if she would have the baby rather than go to an abortionist. She was willing to do this but wanted some life insurance in case she died in childbirth and the baby didn't. Dan thought the idea a little strange, but didn't look a gift horse in the mouth. He wrote her a $25,000 term policy and picked up a check for the first year's premium.

The bomb was one of the few items in his plan that required more research. The problem was obtaining the dynamite in some way which couldn't be traced to him. Of course it might be possible to just walk in and buy it, but he was sure they would ask a lot of questions and make him show identification if not a permit to buy it, and he didn't want to call any attention to himself at this point. He could use his new Ben Butler identity and he would do this as a last resort, but he was also considering the possibility of stealing it. He only needed a few sticks and one or two blasting caps.

He knew contractors used dynamite for removing rock at construction sites. About half of the firms listed in the Yellow Pages under Explosives appeared to be people who did this sort of work. On Monday and Tuesday, the 11th and 12th, he visited several construction projects where they might be blasting. In each case he represented himself as a concerned homeowner who lived nearby. He came across two sites where dynamite work was scheduled soon. At an apartment complex off Memorial Drive near I-285 they were planning to blast that Thursday, and at another under construction nearby they said it would be a couple of weeks. His schedule called for solving the dynamite problem before the end of the month so he decided to come back on Thursday and see what he could do.

In the financial section of the Atlanta Constitution there were several firms who advertised for second mortgage loans on homes. That Tuesday morning Dan called one, Southland Acceptance on West Peachtree, and talked with a Mr. Terry, one of the loan officers there, about the possibility of applying for a second mortgage loan on his town home. Terry, who had a powerful telephone voice and an unctuous manner, assured him they would be happy to loan him the difference between his first mortgage and ninety percent of the appraised value of his home. The whole process would take about a month to complete and there would be a few charges for the appraisal, the credit check and so on, but with Dan's job and the appreciation of homes in the Atlanta real estate market, he was sure it would be approved. To start the process it would be necessary for Dan to come in, fill out a credit application, and leave a check for the fees. Dan told him he would think about it.

Wednesday, October 13, 1971

He returned to Birmingham on Wednesday, a bright and cloudless day. Taking an early morning flight, he again rented a nondescript Ford. This time he waited until he was in the parking lot behind his apartment house to change the tag. There was no one around and he backed into a parking place with the rear of the car next to a fence. Opening the trunk to cover his activity at the rear of the sedan, he removed the Alabama tag, stashed it out of sight behind the spare, and installed the North Carolina plate.

Closing the trunk, he crossed the parking lot and climbed two flights of dirty stairs to the apartment where he left his briefcase and coat before using the front stairs to descend to the desk to check for mail and phone calls. There was a message the printers had called on Tuesday afternoon to let him know his business cards were ready, but nothing else. Back upstairs he called the driving school to confirm his appointment. It was for ten o'clock that morning and he arranged for the instructor to pick him up in the alley behind the apartment house.

The driver's license test went off without a hitch although the talkative instructor made him nervous asking personal questions for which he had to invent answers. He was given his new permanent Alabama Driver's License with his picture on it. With gray hair combed straight back and the large, horn-rimmed glasses, he looked like a different man.

As soon as the driving instructor dropped him off at his apartment he used his rental car to make a beeline for the printers to pick up his business cards. From there he went directly to the bank nearest his apartment, a branch of the Security Exchange Bank, and opened a checking account. When they asked for identification he showed his new driver's license and his business card. He deposited $250 in cash and was given a set of temporary checks and told the permanent ones should arrive in the mail in about a week.

His next stop was the post office. At the Branch nearest his apartment there were no boxes available for rent, but downtown at the main post office there was no problem. He had to make an application and was told to return in a couple of days.

On the way back to his apartment he stopped at three different gasoline stations, an Exxon, a Sunoco and a Texaco, and picked up credit card applications. Paul Wallace, a friend who lived at The Landmark, was a credit supervisor at the Gulf Credit Card Center in Atlanta, and he had once told Dan that some major oil companies did not bother running credit checks on credit card applicants if the application looked good. His company, Gulf, did, but he specifically mentioned Sunoco and a couple of others. Having a gasoline card in Ben Butler's name was not necessary, but it would be a good piece of identification if he could get one or more.

Back at his apartment he filled out all three applications. He listed the refrigeration equipment company with their New York address and phone as his employer, showed his salary at $15,500 a year, and claimed he had worked for them for eight years. He gave the address of the apartment house as his home address, but indicated that he owned his home, had lived there for five years, and was making mortgage payments to a savings and loan there in Birmingham. He used his new account at the Exchange Security as a bank reference and for credit references he listed two non-existent gasoline cards, one with Amoco and one with Gulf, an imaginary charge account with Sears, and another with Pizitz a local department store. In the space for account numbers he listed fictional numbers but used his own credit cards with Gulf, Amoco, and Sears as a guide to the proper order and numbers of digits in each of these numbers. Opposite Pizitz he left this space blank. If the oil companies ran a credit check they would draw blanks and would just not issue the cards. If they only looked at his application they would conclude he was a solid citizen with good credit and he would have another piece of identification for Ben Butler.

With all his chores accomplished, he still had time to kill before dark. After mailing the gasoline card applications he took in a movie and ate an early dinner downtown. Returning to the parking lot behind the apartment house, he changed tags, then drove to the airport, turned in the rented car and flew home to Atlanta.

Thursday, October 14-Friday, October 15, 1971

The next morning dawned gray and cool. Cooper put on old clothes, jeans and a blue windbreaker, and drove out to the construction site off Memorial Drive. He was early but the blasting crew was there first. Again he played the role of the concerned neighbor. The construction boss let him watch the blasters setting the charges and told him how much dynamite they were using in each case. He found no opportunity to steal anything, but came away with a lot more knowledge about the use of explosives. As he was leaving he noticed the blasting crew loading their equipment into a light blue Ford panel truck. He noted several boxes that looked like dynamite stacked in the back. He wrote down the tag number of their truck and decided his best bet might be to follow them around from job to job until he found an opportunity to slip into their truck and remove a few sticks. It would take a lot of time and there was some risk, but he thought it worth a try.

As soon as he got home he called the tag bureau and asked for the name of the owner of the panel truck. It was registered to H. L. Thorndike and

Sons. Looking in the telephone book he found them listed at an address on Piedmont Circle. That evening he drove by and checked it out. It was an old house surrounded by a chain link fence. There was no sign, but the blue panel truck was locked up there inside the fence. Dan circled the block and surveyed the area. There was a bowling alley across the street and down a short piece. Parking in their lot he found he had a good view of Thorndike's premises.

He was back there, in position, at daylight the next morning. He didn't have long to wait before the men arrived. The previous day he had carefully scrutinized the four who made up Thorndike's blasting crew and now recognized them as they came in. The man who was definitely the boss and must be Thorndike was a tall, sturdy specimen in his late forties with a leonine head and a commanding voice. He arrived first driving a Buick Skylark. Two ropey young guys in their twenties came next in a green Ford pickup. Dan assumed they were the sons. The fourth man, a heavyset, bald-headed red-neck who looked older than the others, was dropped off by a woman driving a ragged, white Pontiac. Dan watched as they loaded the panel truck and drove away. He thought of following them but it was Friday and he wanted to attend the weekly sales meeting at his office plus he had an appointment later that morning with Thad Burson. Besides, his new blue Cadillac was a little too obvious to use for tailing and the men might remember him from the blasting job the day before. He made plans to come back the following week.

This month was the first anniversary of the $400,000 worth of policies he had sold to the Burson brothers who owned Burson Aviation. When he called on Thad, the one who managed the business, that Friday he was hoping they might be in the market for more coverage. In a very short interview Burson agreed to let Cooper quote on his group health and accident policy which was coming up for renewal the first of December, but declined to talk any further about life insurance. While he was there Dan was able to pick up the check for the renewal premium on the policies they had purchased the previous year. The first renewal commission was fifteen percent of the premium of roughly ten thousand dollars, so it made his month financially and meant he wouldn't have to take out a second mortgage on his house.

Saturday, October 16, 1971

He was hardly out of bed Saturday morning when Helen's old friend Alma Austin called offering to come over and cook for him. Alma was a tall, slender woman with an attractive, angular face and flashing blue eyes. She had a lithe, athletic body with small firm breasts, a good waist, flat hips, and hard thighs. Her luxuriate honey-blond hair fell in waves behind her ears in a style that made her look older than her twenty-four years. She had been on the trip to Hartford with Helen in 1968, and while they had remained friends, Dan couldn't help but remember how Helen had condescendingly treated Alma like poor relations when they had bought the house in 1969.

She had called several times in the last few weeks and had let Dan know in no uncertain terms that he had her sympathy in his current troubles. She wasn't working just now and was living at home with her mother in East Point. She had offered to come over and cook or clean for him before, but up to now he had declined her offers. He had a maid who had worked for him since the Landmark days who came once a week and did the heavy cleaning. But he did miss the wholesome, home-cooked meals that Helen had been so good at fixing, and besides, he was lonely. He decided to have Alma over for the day.

He drove to East Point in the Cadillac and picked her up. She came bouncing out of the house wearing jeans, a pink sweater over a white shirt, and enormous sunglasses. At first her conversation was guarded and reserved, but as she gradually relaxed, she slipped into a garrulous mood that Dan knew as her usual style. They returned to his house and she fixed a light lunch, tomato soup and grilled cheese sandwiches, which they ate outside on the patio in the strong autumn sunlight. As she chatted gaily on about inconsequential things he couldn't help but be delighted by her vivacious, outgoing warmth. She had removed her sweater leaving her arms bare, and he found himself admiring the play of muscle, the texture of her skin as she punctuated her conversation with wide gestures.

After cleaning up the luncheon dishes Alma suggested they go grocery shopping so there would be something to cook for dinner. "Why don't you just take the car and go down to the Kroger at Ansley Mall," he suggested casually. "Here's fifty dollars. Do you think that will be enough?"

"I should think so," she replied in a surprised voice.

"I want to stay here and watch the football game," he continued without pause, ignoring the shock in her voice. "If you've got any left over when you get through at the grocery store, stop at Fred's liquor store and get some booze. I drink Wild Turkey but also get a bottle of whatever you drink."

"I'm not much of a drinker," she said laughing, quickly regaining her composure. "But I might get a pint of vodka."

The football game was in the final quarter before she finally returned, the Cadillac stacked with brown paper bags. "You must have tried to buy them out," Dan said jokingly as he helped her carry the groceries in.

"They were busy this afternoon and then the traffic was bad too. And I drove out to Rich's at Lenox Square to get a cake."

"Well it doesn't matter. I've been engrossed in the game."

"I ran into Helen," Alma said quietly as they were putting the last of her purchases away.

Dan turned to stare at her as if she had just produced a live rabbit from one of the grocery bags. "At the grocery store?" he stammered, surprised at the hoarseness in his own voice.

"No, she was in the park," Alma replied warily, watching to see what affect her story was having on him. "She was driving a new Monte Carlo, a 1972."

Dan felt the tension return almost as if someone had thrown a switch. During the past week he had begun to relax, not thinking about Helen. He had put all the trials and tribulations, all the twisted and guilty feelings in the back of his mind and closed the door. Now with two innocuous remarks Alma had opened it and they all came rushing out. Suddenly all the strength went out of his legs and he had to sit down.

"Was it a rental car or did Louise buy it?" he asked in a weak voice as he slipped into one of the breakfast room chairs.

"She said Louise bought it for her," Alma continued in an acerbic voice. "It's very pretty, brown with a tan top, a sun roof and all the extras."

"Well Louise needed two cars anyway,' he said stonily. "I imagine Janie uses the bus all the time."

"She said they were buying a big home in Martin's Landing out near Roswell," Alma continued like a pot of water that would not stop boiling. "It sounds like those kids are driving Helen up the wall. She said she was staying over at Lynn's this weekend to get away from them."

He couldn't help but smile at that. He didn't know what Helen's situation had been before they were married, but since she had lived with him the house had always been spotless. She had a place for everything and everything usually stayed in its place. He could imagine how frustrated she was becoming with Louise's methods of non-housekeeping and the kid's untidy habits.

"She was a little surprised to see me driving your car," Alma continued, bubbling on.

"Did she ask about me," he asked hesitantly, not really wanting to hear the answer.

"She wanted to know how you were getting along. I told her you were losing weight and writing a lot of insurance."

"Was she by herself?"

"No, she had a cute boy with her," Alma babbled on, oblivious to the trauma her casual revelations were causing him. "I should say a cute man, he looked about twenty-one. She introduced him as Gary and said he was a marine."

Dan felt a stab of bitter jealousy like an unexpected attack of gas. Apparently she was already out with a new boyfriend. It had only been a little over three weeks since the accident. Still maybe he wasn't anything but a friend. Louise's house was always full of stray people who followed Janie or one of the boys home, or he might be someone who was visiting Lynn.

"How did she look?" he asked quickly, anxious to get off the subject of the cute marine.

"Better than she did the last time I saw her. You know she came to see me about ten days ago—I think I told you. She's got that thing off her teeth and all her cuts and bruises are gone. She said she is supposed to wear a back brace all the time but she wasn't wearing it today."

"That's good then," Dan said, encouraged by the news of her recovery. "I'm so thankful she's not suffering anything permanent from the accident."

Alma prepared a magnificent dinner. She had bought a standing rib roast and with it she served baked potatoes, asparagus with hollandaise sauce, a tossed salad and hot rolls. For desert there was vanilla ice cream and devil's food cake with white icing. It was the first decent, home-cooked meal Dan had eaten since Helen left, and he devoured everything she put on his plate, pleased that she was interested enough to come over and cook. Afterward she wanted to go to the drive-in movie and see a horror show double feature. Horror movies weren't Dan's bag, but it would have been churlish to refuse after all she had done for him.

They were no sooner settled at the movie than Alma sent him to the snack bar for hot dogs and cold drinks. Then he had to go back for popcorn and more drinks. After the big dinner they had eaten he wasn't the least bit hungry and it was hard to believe she was. When the lights came on at the end of the first feature he suggested they leave. She didn't want to go but Dan said he was developing a headache and thought he should take her home. She offered to spend the night at this house but he got out of it by telling her he thought Helen had detectives watching it. He compromised by agreeing to take her out for Sunday dinner.

Sunday, October 17, 1971

. . . was one of those gorgeous October days that make that month the envy of the others. There wasn't a cloud in the innocent blue sky as they drove out to the Plantation Restaurant in Stone Mountain. Alma was talkative as usual and brought up the subject of the trip north in sixty-eight.

"We had a rough time of it after Sam left us in Hartford," she said, her expressive face changing constantly as she spun her tale. "We both worked for a few days in the cocktail lounge there at the Hilton and that was where Helen met Harvey. He was friendly and helped us out a lot."

"What did Harvey look like?" Dan asked pointedly. "Helen said she ran into him in New Orleans, but the man I saw her with didn't fit the description she had given of him earlier."

"I'd say he was about forty, medium height, medium build. He was very distinguished looking—a little gray at the temples, smoked a pipe and wore expensive clothes. If it had been me he was interested in I'd probably still be there."

"The guy I saw her with in New Orleans didn't look a day over thirty," he replied smiling humorlessly. "He had blond hair."

"He could have dyed his hair. He had a youngish, handsome face and with blond hair he would look younger."

"Oh well, it doesn't matter now. Nothing much matters about Helen anymore," he sighed, gazing out the window at nothing.

"That's right Dan," Alma said with a rush, her blue eyes flashing. "You might as well forget her. She's not worrying about you. Rosie McGrew called me this morning and said she saw Helen dancing at Uncle Sam's last night with that cute marine. I don't guess her back is bothering her too much if she can do the boogalu."

"It doesn't sound like it does it," he replied miserably.

The restaurant was busy but it didn't take them long to heap their plates with several delectable items from the big buffet. After they sat down and started eating Alma launched into a long discussion of Helen's family. "Her real mother lives in D. C.," she confided breezily between bites. "She went by to see her when we stopped there on the trip."

"Yes, I remember she used to get a letter from her occasionally but if she ever wrote her mother she never mentioned it to me. I think she is ashamed of her family."

"She never let me meet any of them. She talked a lot about the time when she lived on a farm in Virginia. I think she was in a foster home then."

"I didn't realize that," he said puzzled. "She has talked to me a little about that part of her life. I think she was happier then than during other times of her childhood. I just assumed her parents were still together at that time. She said they had a big farm. She was about twelve or thirteen."

"She told me once that she had five mothers. Some of them had to be foster parents."

"No wonder she has such a sense of insecurity," he mused. "Maybe that's why she was always telling me I was going to throw her out. She'd probably been thrown out of foster homes as a kid and had developed a fear of it. When she accused me of wanting to throw her out she was just preparing herself for the worst. You know, I've thought about it a great deal, and I think all of her talk about it acted as a suggestion to my subconscious. Her insecurity was infectious and when I got drunk and lost my temper with her that was exactly what I did. But I don't think I would have done that if she hadn't talked about it so much."

"She deserved to be thrown out the way she treated you," Alma replied with asperity. "She didn't appreciate a good thing when she had it."

"Maybe she just saw a better thing and went after it," he commented grimly. "If I hadn't thrown her out Louise might not have been so sympathetic."

"Well she's getting fed up with Louise now from what she tells me. But she'll probably hang around as long as the money lasts."

"You know Alma, I think Helen is somewhat of a mental masochist. I think she likes to torture herself. Did I ever tell you about the time she took all the downers?"

"No, when was that?" she replied, a keen look brightening her eyes.

"It must have been last spring sometime. It was after the wreck in the Continental. I was working real hard and spending a lot of time with Louise and her troubles with Jim Carpenter. It was before Louise and Helen became such good friends. I had been out very late one night drinking with a prospective insurance client and after all that time he had put me off. I came home in a bad mood and when she started in on me I said something nasty. She went off to the bedroom and after a while she came back and told me dramatically that she had taken twenty downers. I didn't believe her but I called her bluff. I picked up the phone and called an ambulance. When they came I told them what she had said and had them take her off to the suicide clinic at Grady. I didn't even leave the house. She called early the next morning and said they had released her and would I come get her. I was asleep and still a little drunk and I told her to take a cab and I'd pay for it when she got there. She was boiling mad but there wasn't much she could do. When she got home I found out she didn't even have any shoes on. Poor baby, they had carried her off without any."

"Well that's something," said Alma, a little awed. "She never mentioned it to me but then I haven't seen her regularly since the first year you were married."

"I felt real bad about it afterward," he confided, shaking his head sadly. "If I hadn't been so drunk it wouldn't have happened. They pumped her stomach and made her see a psychiatrist before they would release her."

"It sounds like she asked for it," Alma commented laconically.

"One other time she cut her wrists with a razor blade. That upset me a lot more. It was one night last summer. We got into an argument about something and she jumped in her convertible and screeched off. She came back a half-hour later and showed me where she had sliced her wrists a little. Fortunately it wasn't deep, but it was ugly. She had tried to do it with a blade from one of those Trac-II razors and it wouldn't cut deep enough to do any serious harm.

"What was her excuse for doing it?"

"She said I was a beast to talk mean to her and that she had gotten depressed. I think she sensed how depressed I was about that time and it made her insecure. I don't really know though, I'm no psychiatrist."

"If you're smart you'll forget her and get a divorce."

"You'd probably like that," thought Dan. He didn't like Alma saying unkind things about Helen, but he put up with it. The fact that she was interested in him stroked his ego and gave him confidence. Apparently she couldn't see what a mess he was, mentally and emotionally. If he was fooling her he could fool strangers and that was a large part of what he must do to accomplish his goal.

Monday, October 18- Wednesday, October 20, 1971

On Monday he went into the office to turn in the check he had picked up on Friday from Thad Burson, and to get off the request to the group underwriters for a quote on the group health and accident policy for Burson Aviation. Later he rented a brown, 1970 Ford sedan from Enterprise Leasing. He told them his car was in the shop and that he might need it the rest of the week. It was sufficiently nondescript to make a good car for tailing the Thorndike crew. As an extra precaution he put the stolen North Carolina tag on it.

He was parked opposite their place early on Tuesday morning, but he sat around until nearly noon before anyone showed up. Apparently they weren't working. When someone did put in an appearance it was Thorndike himself. A tall skinny woman was with him, probably his wife. They went inside and stayed a couple of hours. When they locked up and left Dan called it a day. It looked like a washout.

On Wednesday morning he tried again with better results. The four men showed up just as they had the previous Friday. Again they loaded boxes and tools into the blue panel truck and then drove away, Thorndike and the older man leading in the panel truck, the two sons following in the green pickup. Cooper fell in behind them as they joined the cars churning out Piedmont and then Roswell Road to Sandy Springs where they turned left onto Johnson Ferry. It was a long trip but the traffic was heavy and he was able to keep them in sight without being obvious. They crossed the Chattahoochee and continued another mile or so before turning into a large building site near the intersection of Johnson Ferry and Lower Roswell Roads. He cruised on past as they pulled up and stopped in front of a house which apparently served as the office for the construction company.

He went on around a curve before stopping to turn around and drive back slowly. There was a large parking area on the north side of the house and he pulled in and parked among the numerous other vehicles already there. The house and the two trucks belonging to the dynamite crew were about fifty feet south, directly in his line of vision.

It wasn't long before Thorndike emerged from the office followed by a short man wearing jeans and a red nylon jacket. The other three men alighted from the trucks and they held a short discussion, then all five crowded into a battered black Buick and drove around the house and back onto the site. They were probably going to look over the job.

Figuring this was his chance, Dan hurriedly left his car and headed for the blue panel truck. But he found it locked. He glanced in the driver's window and saw the boxes of explosives and tools in the back. Keeping a furtive watch, he moved silently around the vehicles checking all the doors without success. Disappointed, he returned to his car.

It wasn't long before they came back. They opened the panel truck and began to unload things they needed. He kept watch all morning but found no chance to go near the truck again. Time slowed to an inchworm's crawl and his feet got cold. Outside the wind moaned. Traffic growled by. It was frustrating but Dan had the patience to wait and watch. He hoped they might go to lunch and give him a chance to go down onto the site and pick up some dynamite, but they sent one of the younger men in the pickup for their noon meal and ate it there.

He stayed until they were finished about three that afternoon. He had not been able to get near any dynamite and he was in a somber but not a depressed mood as he cranked up and drove home. Reviewing his options he thought again about Thorndike's office. Apparently he kept his supplies, including dynamite there, and although he had a phone at that address, it was not manned during the day when they were out doing a job. But it was sure to have a burglar alarm making it very difficult to break in and steal anything. On the other hand they were careful on the job and never left the panel truck unlocked unless one of them was right there. He couldn't see any easy solution but decided to follow them to at least one more job.

Thursday, October 21, 1971

The morning sky was overcast, the weather not so much cold as damp and raw. Dan followed the Thorndike crew again as they left the office and motored south on the expressway. Past the airport they took I-285 westbound and got off at Old National Highway. Turning left, they traveled south again for only a short distance before turning right into a building site where a sign said new condominiums were to be built. He continued on past, then turned around and came back. There were a number of cars parked around the trailer that served as headquarters for the project and he pulled in among them.

As he sat there watching, Thorndike came out of the trailer with a heavyset black man wearing a yellow Cat hat. "Lock the truck and let's go take a look," he shouted at the others, loud enough for Dan to hear. Not waiting for them, he and the man with the yellow hat disappeared around the far corner of the trailer. The others got out slowly, the two younger men from the pickup and the fourth man from the panel truck.

"I ain't got the key to lock the truck," whined the older man suddenly in a fluted voice. "Thorny's got the keys in his pocket."

"It'll be okay," replied one of the younger men. "We'll be right back."

The copper taste of excitement was in his mouth and his heart hammered heavily in his chest. The minute they disappeared around the trailer Dan was out and walking swiftly toward the panel truck. He took one quick look around. Seeing no one, he opened the driver's door, stepped inside, and shut it carefully. He was very nervous now, excitement humming through him like power through a high voltage electrical cable, as he surveyed the clutter in the back of the van. It didn't take long to spot the wooden boxes marked Explosives, but at first he thought they were all nailed shut. Then he saw one that had been opened near the rear doors and moved back quickly to examine it. The top had been removed but the box was nearly full of sticks of dynamite, each about a foot in length. Stooping, he was helping himself when he heard someone coming.

His heart almost stopped. He didn't know what to do. It might just be someone passing or it might be one of the blasting crew returning to the truck. He did the only thing he could do; he sank down to lie flat as possible on the floor of the truck, hiding as best he could among the scattered boxes and equipment.

He heard the door open, then the fluted voice of the old cracker singing to himself in a high falsetto. He didn't dare look up, but lay face down, his head throbbing, his vision blurred and jittered crazily. He wondered what they'd do if they caught him. He quickly made up his mind to run. If the man looked back and saw him, he'd open one of the rear doors and make his escape that way. He had the dynamite and if he was fast enough he could get to his car and away before the old man knew what was going on.

It seemed like an eternity, but it was only a second or two before he heard the door slam and the key turn in the lock. The man had apparently come back to lock the truck but hadn't seen him. Dan licked his dry lips and tried to control the trembling of his hands. There was no question about fear now. It was coiled lazily in his stomach like cold water. His face was pale, shinny with sweat as he glanced hurriedly about, looking for detonators. He finally found a box but it was nailed shut. He thought of taking the whole box but knew they would miss it, almost immediately. Calming himself as best he could, he scrounged among the equipment until he located a hammer to open the box. Taking only two caps, he replaced the lid and tapped it shut again.

He slipped the detonators in his pocket and stuck the dynamite in his belt under his jacket. Listening and not hearing anyone moving about outside, he opened one of the rear doors and stepped out. There was no way to lock it from the outside without the key, but maybe that wouldn't matter. If they noticed it was unlocked, they'd think it was an oversight on their part. He didn't think they'd miss the ten sticks of dynamite and the two caps he had taken. He had worn gloves so even if they did and took finger prints, he was safe once he left the scene.

There was no one in sight as he closed the rear door of the blue van and walked rapidly back to his rented Ford, his heart in his throat. Once inside he went limp and for a moment everything swam away from him into shades of gray. He began to shake all over and it was several minutes before he could pull himself together enough to crank up and drive away. It had been a close call, but he had made it. Driving back to town, he slowly began to unwind and as he did he sensed something else, a warm feeling of secret delight growing inside him. He had the dynamite now and he could go ahead with phase two of his plan on schedule. It would begin the following Sunday, October 24th.

Friday, October 22, 1971

The next day he went to his office long enough to attend the weekly sales meeting and deal with his mail. Leaving about ten, he drove by his bank and made a large cash withdrawal. At home he left the money and his Cadillac, picked up the rented Ford and departed for Birmingham.

The rain that had been threatening all week had finally arrived and as he drove west it fell in monotonous gray sheets. Approximately fifty miles of Interstate 20 was still under construction making it necessary to travel on US 78, a narrow, curvy two-lane deathtrap that wound its way slowly through the numerous small towns of Northwest Georgia and Northeastern Alabama. He still had the stolen North Carolina tag on the car and he drove cautiously being extra careful not to have an accident or get a ticket. He stopped in Heflin long enough to grab a hamburger and a coke, then pressed on. The trip took nearly five hours but he gained an hour in the time zone change and arrived a little after two, Birmingham time.

His first stop was the main post office where his application for a box for Ben Butler had been properly returned enabling him to rent one for six months for twenty dollars. He picked up a Change of Address card and later dropped it in a handy mailbox.

His last stop that cold, rainy Friday was the Security Exchange Bank where he used the first of his new permanent checks to withdraw $25 in cash. In less than two hours he had finished his business in the Magic City and was on the rainy road home.

In all his dealings in Birmingham he had been careful not to leave fingerprints on anything that might survive his hijack attempt. He had to be certain there would be no way anyone would be able to tie him to that name later on. While the Ben Butler identification was not the one he would use on the aircraft when he actually did the hijacking, it would be his covering identity, the one he would drop back into while he was making his way out of the jump area and, if it wasn't blown, out of the general area. If he was stopped and questioned while leaving the jump area he wanted to have an identity other than his real one that was good enough to stand a routine check. If he was stopped and questioned but not detained, and then later the FBI did an extensive background investigation on Benjamin A. Butler they would eventually come back to Birmingham, to the apartment house, to the driver's license bureau and to the bank, so he had been very careful in handling the papers he had filled out. It had been awkward at times but he felt it necessary and he had managed it. In addition he wiped down the apartment thoroughly before leaving even though he expected it to have a new tenant within a week.

He had been forced to rent cars in his own name twice in Birmingham, but it would certainly be a long shot for the FBI to start checking on everybody who rented cars in Birmingham around that time. He didn't think anyone who knew him as Ben Butler had even seen what he was driving but even if they had, he had used the stolen North Carolina tag as another cutout.

The trip home was even slower and more tiring than the one over. Driving was like going into a wet, black tunnel. He stopped for a not-so-quick dinner in Anniston, and didn't get back to Atlanta until after ten. Stripping off his raincoat he briefly thought of going out for a drink but decided against that. Instead he mixed himself a large bourbon and water and called Alma. The liquor got to work on the chill inside him and his spirits rose when she answered and exclaimed, happy he had called.

She had a taste for gossip and he had to listen to a long recital of the week's events before he could get around to inviting her out to dinner on Saturday night.

"Ooh, Dan," she wailed, "I'd so like to go but I've already promised Mother I'd go to Columbus with her this weekend. We're leaving in the morning and not coming back until Sunday evening. It's my Uncle Joe, he's been sick and she wants to go see him and needs me to help with the driving."

"That's all right," he said without any real show of disappointment. "We'll make it another time. Have you heard form Helen this week?"

"No, I called over to Louise's on Tuesday but one of the boys answered and said they were out looking at houses. I asked him to tell Helen to call me but she hasn't."

"I guess they are busy spending Louise' money," he replied, envy in his voice. "Listen, I'm sorry you can't make it tomorrow night but I'll call again. Have a big time in Columbus."

After he finally got her off the phone he tried Alan to see if he was available for dinner on Saturday. But he got no answer and none at Rod's number either. He gave up and went to bed.

Saturday, October 23, L971

On Saturday morning he returned the rented Ford, paying the bill in cash. He was also finished with the stolen North Carolina tag, and so he put it in a brown grocery sack and dropped it in the dumpster behind the Holiday Inn on Piedmont Circle after being sure there were no fingerprints on it. Then he drove out to the airport and purchased a one-way ticket to San

Francisco on the noon flight the following day in the name of Robert Collier, one he had pulled out of thin air. He paid cash and told them he was staying at the Hilton Inn even though he knew if they called there they'd draw a blank.

Back home by lunch time, he dialed Alan's number. This time he got an answer. Rod was there having breakfast and Dan invited them to join him for dinner. They decided to eat at The Abbey, a unique restaurant located in what had formerly been a church on West Peachtree near Third.

Even though they had reservations there was a short wait before they were seated. While a harpist in the choir loft played chamber music they chatted about the weather (turning cold), the Falcons (still losing) and other inconsequential things. When they were seated and had ordered drinks, Dan brought up the subject he most wanted to discuss

"Have either of you talked with Helen or Louise recently?" he asked casually, trying to hide the tremor in his voice.

"I called Helen one day early this week," Alan said half turning to face Dan, his handsome face crinkling into the tiniest of smiles. "She said she saw Alma Austin driving the Cadillac, her car she called it, and wanted to know if I knew what was going on. I had to tell her I didn't."

"She's in the bars nearly every night," Rod contributed with some relish. She bought me a drink one night this week.

"Did she mention me or say how Louise was doing?" Dan asked Rod.

"Not directly," Rod replied evenly. "She was busy telling me about things they were doing. They're still looking at houses and she doesn't care much for the Monte Carlo, wants something bigger."

"I don't think Helen is enjoying herself that much," Alan put in. "If you'll just play it cool a little longer I'll bet you'll be hearing from her and I don't mean from her lawyer."

"That's one encouraging thing," Dan commented wryly with a laugh. "I haven't heard any more from Mr. Joe Walker."

Sunday, October 24, 1971

He had turned down their invitation to go nightclubbing after dinner in order to get to bed early. On Sunday morning he packed carefully and was at the airport well ahead of departure time for his flight to San Francisco. The three-and-a-half hour flight was uneventful and he arrived in the

City by the Bay in the early afternoon. Before he picked up his luggage he called and made a reservation under the name of Ben Butler at a motel on Pacific near Van Ness. Not wanting to have to struggle with all his luggage on the bus, he splurged and took a cab into town.

He purchased a copy of the Sunday paper at the airport and that afternoon and evening he made several calls. What he was searching for was a furnished apartment he could lease or sublease for two or three months. There were lots of possibilities but he narrowed them down to three which he planned to visit the next day.

Monday, October 25, 1971

The first thing Dan Cooper did the next morning was walk up to Van Ness Avenue and visit an automobile dealer who specialized in recreational and camping vehicles. There he was greeted by a big, fleshy, red-faced salesman with a sagging beer belly and hands like hams who introduced himself as Pete Warren. When Cooper explained what he wanted, a four-wheel drive vehicle in serviceable condition for under $1500, Warren frowned and chomped on the cigar sprouting from his rotund face but led Dan to a back lot and showed him a 1967 Ford Bronco, a sad looking little car with chipped paint and bald tires.

"We're asking twelve-fifty for this little jewel," Warren allowed in a low-pitched, husky voice furred by many years of cigarettes and liquor. "But for that price we could probably put a set of recaps on her. Want to take it for a spin?"

They cranked it and Dan gave it a good tryout. He wasn't a mechanic but, except for the tires, the sturdy little car that looked like a jeep with a white camper top on the back seemed to be in good mechanical condition. The odometer showed over 65,000 miles and the chalky, blue-green paint was not appealing but he thought it would serve his purposes admirably. He offered $1,000 for it on the condition they would install the recap tires, and after the obligatory haggling, they settled on a price of $1,100 plus tax. Warren wrote it up and Dan gave him a $100 cash deposit, arranging to come back and pick it up late that afternoon.

From there Cooper took a cab and visited the three apartment possibilities he had called the previous day. At the first the resident manager proved far too nosey, and the second was such a dump he passed it up, at least temporarily. The third had no such drawbacks and he quickly decided to take it. A small, claustrophobic efficiency on the second floor of a dun colored, three-story building on the corner of Buchanan and Haight, it was reasonably clean and conveniently located. Bargaining with the resident manager, a decrepit gaffer named Overturf whose face was a spider web of lines, Dan got him to agree not to charge any rent for the few days remaining in October on the condition he paid the $100 deposit and November's rent in full on the spot. He didn't have to sign a lease and could have immediate possession. Overturf wasn't concerned about references. Cooper's story now was that he had separated from his wife, quit his job with the refrigeration equipment company, and was moving to the bay area to get a fresh start. He told Overturf he had saved some money and was planning to take several camping and sightseeing trips before he looked for another regular job. He hoped this would explain his not spending a lot of time in the apartment and would also be helpful backup information in case the manager was later questioned by the authorities.

Leaving his new apartment he walked to a nearby bank, a branch of Wells-Fargo, and opened a checking account depositing $50 in cash and a $200 check drawn on his account in Birmingham. That and the Alabama Driver's License were all the identification required. While there he purchased a cashier's check to pay the balance due on the Bronco.

Returning to the automobile dealer's showroom he paid for the Bronco and had the papers made out using his new address on Buchanan. They gave him a Bill of Sale and a temporary registration form which he put in the glove box of the car. Leaving there he went back to the motel, checked out, and drove to his new apartment. Again he unpacked his suitcase of old clothes and placed enough personal items around to give it a lived-in look.

Tuesday October 26- Wednesday, October 27, 1971

The next morning he went shopping for camping equipment, a few clothes and other supplies. The first thing he bought was a new, forest green tent with a gray bottom that would blend well with the background in the Washington woods. Erected it would stand forty-five inches high and be large enough for him and lots of supplies. For sleeping he purchased an olive drab sleeping bag made with prime northern goose down, and an air mattress.

His plans called for two packs, a smaller day pack he would carry onto the airplane to hold the money when he jumped, and a larger backpack with frame. He preferred they both be used. At a second-hand store on lower Market he found a faded gold backpack in good condition which would do for the larger of the two. At the same store he also bought a heavy blue parka that showed signs of wear

Unable to find a suitable used day pack, he returned to the camping store where he had purchased the tent and selected a dark green day pack made by Famous Trails of San Diego. It was 17" by 13" by 6" and came equipped with adjustable padded shoulder straps and an adjustable waist belt with fastex buckle. In addition to the main compartment which could be opened fully by unzipping two nylon coil zippers that met at the top in the back when closed, it had a large patch on the same side that also closed with a zipper. It was made of a strong, light-weight synthetic fabric.

In the sporting goods department of a large department store he bought a second parka, this one a light green color. In luggage he found a Hartmann attaché case in black leather similar to the brown one Helen had given him for Christmas in 1968. It was very large for an attaché case, big enough to hold his homemade bomb and several other necessary items.

By early afternoon he had everything he needed. Packing the Bronco carefully, he departed San Francisco headed east, across the Oakland Bay Bridge on I-80. Just past Vacaville he turned off this busy road onto I-505 and drove north through soft gray rain, the wipers thudding back and forth in a slow, steady rhythm.

Traffic was light here and he made good time. It wasn't long before this spur intersected I-5 coming north out of Sacramento. As he joined this highway and continued northward the little car swayed and rattled, rippling rain slanting in streaks along its windows. The air was shivery, wet, and smelled of ash, while the countryside loomed damp and depressing, its fall colors muted by the gray of the day.

He stopped for the night at a small motel just south of Redding, California, and spent the evening watching TV on an ancient black and white set. He would finish the trip to Portland on Wednesday.

By the next morning the rain had ceased and as he pulled onto the interstate the sun broke through the heavy gray clouds like combers being pushed rapidly eastward by the blustery wind. That day on the long, lonely ride north with that cold, westerly wind crying through the cracks, Cooper once more reviewed his entire plan and reflected on his reasons for taking such a drastic step. He tried to be honest with himself and in so doing admitted that his bruised ego was at least partially to blame. Successful completion of this dangerous game, a game that would test his strength and try his nerve, would help restore his self-esteem, so badly battered in the last few months.

And though he knew it was morally wrong to steal, his shriveled conscience did not bother him at the thought of bilking a major airline (or more likely their insurance carrier) out of $200,000. His two years selling insurance had given him more than a glimpse into how big business operated, and he knew that $200,000 wasn't a drop in the bucket to such corporate giants as Northwest-Orient or Massachusetts General. Insurance companies rarely lost money since they could offset losses by raising rates, or denying or fighting claims until the claimants, little people like him mostly, were on the financial ropes and ready to settle for anything. And the law, in its ponderous, pontifical approach to justice only aided these modern-day robber barons who cloaked their avarice behind a façade of righteousness and caring.

For now he planned to continue his job as a life insurance salesman but as soon as the hijack was over and something settled between himself and Helen, he was going to leave the blood-sucking insurance industry and look for a new career. He no longer took pride in his ability to sell since he had become cognizant of the fact that it was based on his capacity to exploit greed and fear. In his bitterness he even rationalized that this was the primary reason for his current sales slump and concluded he would be more successful selling something tangible like cars or real estate.

But he didn't allow his mind to run in this narrow squirrel cage of cause and effect for long. As he made his way slowly northward through the spectacularly beautiful state of Oregon on this lovely fall day he banished negative thoughts and bathed himself in nostalgia, fondly remembering his childhood: the heady excitement of high school football games; hayrides under a harvest moon; dances in the school gym; kisses stolen from nubile girls in the back seat of Roy's '46 Ford; camping in the solitude of the big woods.

He rattled into Portland late Wednesday, stopped at a cheap motel on the south side of town, and went right to bed. Making such a long drive in the little Bronco had proven very tiring, but it had performed splendidly and he concluded he had made a good buy.

Thursday, October 28, 1971

Cooper was out before eight on Thursday morning and after a quick stop to purchase a couple of last minute items, started for his planned camping site at the old Martin Place. Leaving the main highway at Woodland, he crossed the river and turned left onto the Amboy Road. When he came to the split just past the Cedar Creek School, he bore to the left on the Dam Road, and then shortly thereafter turned off to the right onto the Spurrel Road. He had met only one or two cars since leaving Woodland and saw no one as the Bronco crunched its way along this little used thoroughfare, only an occasional glimpse of a bright slice of October sky between the towering trees. Arriving at the entrance to the Martin property, he shifted into four-wheel drive and made his way slowly along the overgrown drive that led to the house and barn. The weather had apparently been dry and he had no trouble even though the going was rough.

Stopping at the house, Cooper looked it over thoroughly. Obviously no one had lived here lately. The shutters were closed with boards nailed solidly across them, and the regular locks on the front and back doors had been supplemented with large Master padlocks to discourage intruders. While it needed a coat of paint, the old Martin house did appear to still be livable. It was possible that Ed's mother or some of his kin still came out here occasionally.

The barn, on the other hand, was falling down. He had thought of parking his Bronco in the barn but after one good look decided against it. Part of the roof was gone and one wall sagged ominously. The next big blow or next winter's first good snow storm might see the structure just collapse.

Leaving the homestead, Dan followed what had once been a jeep trail that led east to Cedar Creek. It skirted the western edge of the cleared area and crossed through a little neck of woods before ending in another small clearing that overlooked a broad bend in the otherwise churning creek. It was here, in this tranquil spot, that he and Ed had so often pitched a tent and spent their weekends fishing, hiking and talking about girls.

And it was here he would camp this trip while he explored the nearby countryside in preparation for his return by parachute on the evening of November 24th.

This clearing was fairly flat and at some time in the distant past, probably when the Martin Farm was being cleared, a small sawmill had operated here. About the same time or possibly when the power line was being erected, someone had taken advantage of the typography and fixed a place for equipment to traverse the fast-flowing stream at its broadest point. Cutting down the banks, they had lined the creek bed with hardwood logs thus creating a ford nearly forty feet wide and a foot deep where the clear water raced over the buried timber.

Dan found the land much as he remembered it. Near the creek big-leaf maple and spruce trees elbowed each other for the sunlight. Brush and saplings had grown up in the cleared areas but walking was not difficult. He made camp on the south edge of the clearing near the creek, erecting his tent and gathering firewood.

This done, he set out to more thoroughly investigate the Martin Place and select the exact spot where he hoped to land on that fateful night.

Getting out the detailed topographic map of the Ariel, Washington Quadrangle, which he had purchased in D. C. back in September, he studied it carefully. The Martin Place was on the northern edge of an area about a mile-and-a-half wide where the land was relatively level and there were numerous cleared areas. This section included Cedar Creek and the main Woodland-Amboy road which crossed west to east just south of and approximately parallel to the creek. There were few houses shown along this road and along another secondary road which branched off of and ran due south, parallel and west of the power line. North of the Spurrel road was a small unnamed mountain which climbed to an elevation of 1014 feet, while a mile-and-a-half south-southwest of the Martin Place was Bald Mountain, a 1552 foot peak. So he must plan to land somewhere in the relatively level area between these peaks. Fortunately there were many clearings.

Obviously the best spot would be on the Martin farm. There were no other houses in the immediate vicinity and the cleared area was large enough that, presuming he could locate it, he would have no trouble landing within it. The only drawback was the power line which crossed from north to south on the western edge of the farm.

Now Cooper walked the perimeter of the large clearing, then stepped off the distance across it in both directions. From north to south it was only about three hundred yards, but from east to west it ran some seven hundred yards, nearly a half-mile. He decided he should aim for a point in the center of the cleared area east of the power line and midway between the trees that outlined the clearing on the north and south. His map showed the centerline of the airway passing directly over the house and while he knew he couldn't count on the airliner being precisely on course, hopefully it would be close enough. Jack Martin had used this land as a pasture for his cow and while it was not perfectly smooth, it was as good a landing spot as he was going to find in this territory.

Locating the exact spot where he hoped to land, he marked it with two boards torn from the rotting barn, then made his way directly back to his camp. It took less than five minutes.

Before going back out Dan took time to open a can of tomato soup for lunch. Building a small fire, he heated it in a canteen cup, then retrieved a beer from a six-pack he had cached in the creek to chill. Sitting cross-legged on the ground in a bar of mote-dusted sunlight he ate slowly, enjoying the pleasant weather and the solitude of the woods. A fat red squirrel picked its way down the side of a mossy deadfall and perched on a rotting stump to watch him with bright black eyes. Dappled light melted through the foliage while birds flew, swooping and cheeping and scolding. The realization came to him that he was enjoying himself immensely doing something he hadn't done in years. Atlanta and his business and marital problems seemed a million miles away and in a way he wished he never had to return.

Later, crossing the creek at the ford, Cooper surveyed the land south towards Bald Mountain. After a steep climb up from the creek bottom, he emerged into another clearing which continued south to the Woodland-Amboy highway. He saw where the power line crossed and continued up a hill amidst the forest, and spotted no houses in either direction. He decided to return and get the Bronco to make a further reconnaissance in this direction.

He did that, driving back west on the Spurrel Road to the Dam Road, then south to the fork where it joined the main Woodland-Amboy road, then back east to where the power line crossed. It took longer to drive it than it had taken to walk. Turning around he cruised slowly westward all the way back to the Cedar Creek School carefully surveying the land on both sides of the road. Turning around there, he drove back and turned right onto the secondary road that branched off to the south almost under the power line. Climbing steeply, it looped westward around a small hill before bearing due south along the flanks of Bald Mountain to an intersection with the Highland-View-Fargher Lake road just east of View. This secondary road paralleled the centerline of the airway and should he jump a little late he might land somewhere along here. There were a few houses and some cleared areas, particularly as he neared View which was nothing but a small clump of houses.

Retracing his route Dan was back at his camp before dark. The temperature dropped rapidly once the sun went down and he was glad he had brought a tent and warm sleeping bag. After supper he set out once more to walk over the Martin Place. The wind had come up and overhead the moon rode the sky like a cold sailor of the night. As he walked away from the warmth of his campfire his mood of euphoria fled and he shivered, wondering what would happen if he broke a leg when he jumped into this deserted field. Or what if he got hung in one of those soaring trees along the creek and couldn't get down. His mind spun with grotesque images and a nagging feeling of inadequacy slipped around him, seeming to tighten and restrict his breathing like an invisible dog collar. He knew that no matter how much planning and preparation he did, he couldn't foresee every problem, cover every contingency. He would have to rely a little on luck. Nevertheless he decided right then to bring along a sufficient quantity of sleeping pills to take his life in the event he should be incapacitated out here in no man's land.

By the time Cooper returned to camp his depression had passed and his mood brightened. The old Martin farm was right on the airway, less than two miles south of the dam—a perfect checkpoint—and as big as the field was, there should be no reason to miss it, even at night in a strong wind. Once on the ground he should have no problem making his way back to camp. Tonight he had no difficulty finding his way over the terrain, even in the dark without a flashlight.

Friday, October 29, 1971

A mild October wind pushed restless clouds from west to east and leaves showered off the trees. Today Dan planned to investigate the terrain west and north of the Martin Place. Taking the Bronco he drove west on the Spurrel Road, intersected the Dam Road, and then took off up a jeep trail that climbed westward. This little-used track followed a draw for a half-mile, then looped back south and east, rejoining the Dam Road a couple of miles south of where it began.

This trail cut through terrain which was wilder, rougher and more overgrown than that east of the Dam Road. At one point Cooper parked the car and hiked off into the forest for a few hundred yards where walking soon became difficult. Towering Douglas firs, sheathed in deeply corrugated bark, rose all around him at first, but these soon gave way to spruce and hemlock. Much of the land in this area belonged to the big timber companies who pursued the practice of thinning out trees, thus allowing the remaining stands to grow faster and taller. But here no one had done any cutting for some time. Giant trees lofted two hundred or more feet into the sky, hiding it from view, imperiously barring both sun and light from their domain. Beneath this canopy were more trees of impressive height and on the ground great carcasses of trees lay felled by storms. Underfoot ferns and moss cushioned his steps. Should he come down in this area he would most certainly land in a tree and even if he got to the ground safely, it would be an arduous journey back to his camp.

Back on the Dam Road he traveled north over Pup Creek, the same small creek which crossed north of the Martin Place and then joined Cedar Creek just north of his campsite. It had its origin somewhere northeast, up on the shoulders of Green Mountain.

Near the dam he turned right onto a dirt road which led to the edge of Lake Merwin and followed the shoreline northeast. There was a sheen on the beautiful mountain lake and overhead the gray sky lightened to mauve as the sun tried to penetrate the scudding clouds. A cold wind buffeted him as he traveled this road along the shore for some three miles before reversing direction.

Returning westward on the Dam Road, he came to another road branching off to the left. His map showed it as the Grinnel Road and it appeared to penetrate to the heart of the Green Mountain area that lay east and south of the lake. He followed it for a short piece before turning around at the Green Mountain School. All of this territory was rugged and looked much the same. If he came down here he would have to find a road, a creek, or a power line and follow it westward until he came to more hospitable terrain.

He was dead tired that night, his legs and shoulders protesting with dull persistent aches, and he slept soundly in spite of the deteriorating weather.

Saturday, October 30, 1971

. . . was chill and the air smelled of snow as Dan set out under racing gray clouds to hike over the terrain north and west of his camp. Leaving the Martin property he headed northwest, climbed a steep hill and then skirted the small unnamed mountain that lay to the north. To the west lay a large cleared area with only small patches of woods breaking it up. The land and trees were very dissimilar from those he had seen yesterday and even at night he knew he would be able to distinguish between them. Here he found a variety of trees, black cottonwoods, maples, fir, cedar, and pine.

Arriving at the Dam Road, he followed it west for a mile or so and then cut due south across two cleared areas and a small patch of woods to reach the picnic grounds on Cedar Creek where an old grist mill had once stood. He stopped and rested here for a long time before continuing, returning to his camp by following the rushing creek eastward.

In most places the banks of the creek were steep with willows and alders growing in profusion near the shoreline and larger trees protecting their flanks. Because he had his map and compass, was familiar with the territory, and could hear the noisy creek even when he couldn't see it, Cooper didn't have to follow every twist and turn and covered the mile-and-a-half in less than thirty minutes.

In his exploration of the countryside he had passed a few cars on the roads, but in the three days he had been here he had not seen anyone on foot or talked with another soul. He was therefore surprised when, arriving back at camp about four, he found a visitor. Approaching he saw it was a short, chunky man wearing a large ten-gallon hat and a bright red nylon jacket. He was sitting on a stump with his hands lying flat on his knees. His dark eyes darted about, filled with curiosity and lively intelligence.

"Hi there," he said without getting up. "You just out here camping?"

"Yes," Cooper replied quickly, feeling a thread of disquiet. "I've just been out hiking through the woods."

"Well, that's all right," he boomed, his voice vibrant, resonant, pleasingly deep. "Folks that own this property don't mind as long as you're careful about fires. I'm just here to be sure you don't shoot anything out of season."

"I just drove up from San Francisco to do a little camping," Dan explained, relaxing now in the jovial presence of this uninvited guest. "I was in this area once a few years ago with some friends and I remembered it as a lovely one."

"Yep, it's God's own country. Gets pretty lonesome this time of year though. You're probably the last one I'll see up here until spring. Well I guess I better be getting along," he said rising and starting toward a battered jeep parked near Dan's Bronco. "Don't guess you've seen any hunters have you?"

"No," Dan replied quickly. "I've been here a couple of days and haven't seen anybody. I'm leaving today and going back south."

"Well, be sure you put out your fire good and leave the place clean. That's all I ask. See ya around."

Puzzled, Dan watched him drive away in the direction of the highway. The man hadn't introduced himself or said who he was although from his conversation it sounded as if he might be a game warden. He hadn't asked Dan's name or for any identification although he might have taken the tag number of the Bronco. But Dan was safe there. Its California tag was registered to Ben Butler and for the moment, that was his name. He ate a cold snack, then started packing.

During his hikes and his evenings here in the woods, Cooper had gone over the operation in his mind again for the umpteenth time. He pictured himself now, ready to depart with his booty, $200,000 in twenty-dollar bills. If he were stopped and questioned he would like to have some hiding place for the money. Before leaving he crawled up under the Bronco and spent some time studying the possibility of a hiding place there.

While there were several areas under the car big enough to hide a small package, there was no place large enough to accommodate the day pack in which he would carry the money when he jumped. He could always remove and redistribute it, but that would take up valuable time. He came to the conclusion that his best bet would be to leave the money in the day pack, cover it with other gear, and hope that, if he were stopped, they would not make a thorough search. The only other alternative would be to bury the money and come back for it later.

After stowing his camping gear neatly in the back of the car, Dan changed into his traveling clothes and drove into Portland. He had time for dinner before his flight back to San Francisco so, after leaving the car in a nearby garage, he enjoyed Chinese Pepper Steak and two Fog Cutters at Trader Vic's at the Hotel Benson on Broadway. Arriving at the airport in time for his eight-thirty flight, he locked the faithful Bronco and left it in the airport parking lot.

Sunday, October 31, 1971

Cooper slept at his apartment in San Francisco that Saturday night, but was up by six-thirty Sunday morning in order to catch an early flight out to Atlanta. The phone was ringing when he walked into his Westchester Square townhouse late that afternoon. It was Alma.

"Hi, where have you been?" she asked in a cheerful voice. "I've been calling for days."

"Oh, I went out of town this weekend to visit friends," he replied, trying to sound casual. "What have you been up to?"

"Nothing. I've been going crazy sitting around my Mother's house. I ought to get out and get a job but I don't have a car."

"Couldn't you get to work on the bus?" Dan inquired laughingly, knowing it was all just talk.

She ignored that and went on. "I've got Mother's car this evening. Would it be all right if I dropped by? I could fix your supper if you haven't eaten."

"Sure, I guess so," he said, now pleased that she had called. He felt lonesome after nearly a week of being alone and knew he would enjoy some company. "Why don't you stop and get some pizza. I've got beer. That way there won't be any mess to clean up. I'll pay you back for the pizza when you get here."

"Okay," she replied without hesitation. "I'll be there in about thirty minutes."

He barely had time to shower and rinse the gray out of his hair before she arrived. They sat on the bed and ate pizza and watched the Sunday night movie on TV. It reminded him that he and Helen had done this often in the first year of their marriage—before he had started spending his nights trying to sell insurance and she had begun spending hers running the streets.

When the movie and the late news were over Alma reluctantly said she had better go. Her Mother would be worried about her car. Dan promised to call during the coming week and suggested they go out on Saturday night. This pleased her immeasurably and she gave him a quick but firm kiss on the mouth when she left.

Monday, November 1, 1971

Leaving home at nine, Cooper stopped at a hardware store where he picked up two dog snaps, then drove downtown to a small tailor shop on Fairlie Street. He had brought the new green day pack purchased in San Francisco to be modified. He needed the two snaps mounted securely on the backside of the pack, the side that would be against his back when he put it on, in the proper position so they could be used to hook the pack to the leg rings of his parachute harness just before he jumped. It would also be necessary to cover the dog snaps with small leather flaps that snapped down so they would not chafe his back when he was wearing the pack. He explained what he wanted and the tailor, a wrinkled black man named Howard, promised to have it ready by noon Wednesday.

From there he went to his office to catch up the paper work that had accumulated in his absence. Nobody seemed to have noticed he hadn't been in the past week, but his box was stuffed with papers. He got busy and by noon had taken care of everything, answering his mail and making a few calls. The quote on the group policy for Burson Aviation was in and he made an appointment to present it to Thad Burson the next morning.

Upon leaving the office he stopped at the C. & S. Bank in Buckhead and rented a large safe-deposit box. Cooper did no other business with the C. & S. and the explanation he was prepared to give if anyone asked, was that he needed a safe place to keep important papers he occasionally was given by customers in the course of his work. He paid a year's rental, gave only his office address, and listed his name as D. Benjamin Cooper.

The purpose of this box of course was a place to keep the proceeds of the hijacking after he had laundered the money in the casinos of Las Vegas. He knew he couldn't let anyone know he was suddenly in the chips and this gave him a convenient place near his office to stash the money where he could get at it easily without exciting any suspicion. If anyone checked at his usual bank, the Trust Company branch near Pershing Point, they wouldn't be able to detect any significant change in the amount of money coming and going out of his account there.

He could periodically remove cash from the box and use it to live on and to pay some irregular bills without running it through his checking account. He had already devised a way to pay off the Continental note in such a way it wouldn't be apparent there was any cash involved in the deal. He would buy a new car and finance the same amount on it he owed on the Continental. With some of the hijack cash he would purchase a cashier's check for this amount at another branch of the Trust Company and give it, along with his personal check for the balance of the purchase price, to the selling dealer. Then he would take the title of the new car to his banker who would have him sign a new note and cancel the old one.

Dan had several other schemes for using the cash without arousing suspicion. Only a few people at the insurance company knew what he was making there and everyone was under the impression he had another source of income: airline retirement or disability, real estate holdings or maybe a big inheritance. He did have a couple of thousand dollars in the airline retirement plan which he could cash in, pretending it was more than it really was.

From the C.& S. he crossed the street to another bank where he picked up a large quantity of the paper bands banks use to hold pack of bills together. He asked for those marked for one-dollar bills—they were all the same. Next he stopped at an office supply store and purchased a paper cutting board and five boxes of legal-size typing paper.

His schedule called for flying back to Houston for more parachute jumping on Thursday. So, that Monday afternoon, he called Marty Seymour from a public booth to tell him he would be in town on Thursday and would like to make a jump that afternoon and another that night, weather permitting. The jumpmaster said he would not be available but would arrange for a couple of chutes for Dan to use and gave him Garfield's number so he could schedule the airplane. Dan didn't tell Seymour, but if the weather should be a problem, he planned to stay over until Friday or Saturday.

He wasn't able to reach Garfield that afternoon but got him at home that evening. The mild-mannered real estate salesman said he'd be glad to take Cooper up on Thursday and they made an appointment for 4 PM.

Tuesday, November 2, 1971

The ninety-day signature note Dan had signed back in August was due this week. On Tuesday morning he was at his bank when they opened at nine and had no difficulty convincing Dave Scott, the obsequious young loan officer who handled his business, to renew it for another ninety days. He paid the interest and told Scott he was expecting a big check around the first of the year which would give him the funds to retire this note.

His appointment with Thad Burson to present the proposal of the group policy for Burson Aviation was for 10:30. He arrived at Thad's office at Fulton County Airport a little early but didn't have to wait. The presentation went smoothly and to Dan's delight, he made the sale. It would mean a good bit of work getting all the employees enrolled, but the first year's commission would run at least a thousand dollars and there would be renewals after that. He made an appointment to come back Thursday, the eleventh, to start the enrollment.

Back home he used the money bands he had picked up at the bank and the paper and paper cutter he had purchased at the office supply store the previous afternoon to put together one hundred packages of one hundred slips of paper, each cut to the size of a twenty-dollar bill. The typing paper he was using, a good quality product with high rag content, seemed about the same thickness as currency. He thought it close enough for his purpose. When he finished he threw away the scrap and packed the simulated money neatly in the new black Hartmann attaché case. It took up about two-thirds of the big case. Filling the balance of the space with clothing, he put it away.

Wednesday, November 3, 1971

Up early, Cooper went by his office, then spent two hours at his health club before going downtown around noon. At a Delta Ticket Office on Luckie Street he made reservations and bought his ticket for the trip to Houston on Thursday. After a light lunch of salad and London broil at Herren's, he walked to the tailor shop on Fairlie to check on the day pack he had left to be modified.

It was ready and he was pleased with the job. For the flaps covering the two dog snaps Howard had found some tan leather very similar to that used for the accessory patches on the sides and bottom of the pack. With these flaps snapped down the dog snaps were out of sight and anyone casually examining the pack would not realize they had been added for a special purpose. The dog snaps were attached securely to the left hand edge of the pack, one five-and-a-half inches and the other eleven-and-a-half inches from the top and inside the pack had been reinforced with another piece of leather, twelve by four inches, so there would be no chance of the pack tearing loose when the chute opened with its powerful jerk.

At home he filled the day pack with his simulated loot, trying it for size. He found the thirteen-by-six inch bottom of the pack would accommodate four stacks of money. The packets of one hundred pieces of paper were about a half inch thick and so he was able to stack the one hundred packets representing $200,000 in a space just under thirteen inches deep. He would use the four inches remaining in the top of the main compartment and the zippered pocket on the front for other necessary items such as emergency rations, extra socks and his maps. Satisfied, he removed the pseudo money from the day pack and repacked it in his brown attaché case along with the two extra shirts and ties.

After eating a quick supper he continued his packing for the next day's trip. The empty money pack was flattened out and placed in the bottom of the black case. On top of it went underwear, socks, toilet articles, his black jump boots, and a pair of dark green coveralls. The high top boots, a pair he had owned since his Air Force days, were worn but serviceable. The coveralls however were almost new, having been among the clothing he had purchased in San Francisco the previous week. They were made of heavy duck and contained numerous pockets.

His jump helmet he packed separately in a bowling-ball bag. The hard hat, a standard motorcycle helmet of dark blue, had been purchased in D. C. in 1965. He had bought the bag, a scotch plaid in dark blue and green, at an airport shop in Miami the same year.

When he finished he mixed a drink and sat down to watch TV. The eleven o'clock news was almost over and he was thinking of going to bed when the phone rang. It was Helen!

"Hello Dan, how are you?" she said in a still, small voice. She sounded strange, not hostile but tense.

"I'm getting along Baby," he replied unsteadily, trying to conceal the emotions suddenly boiling beneath the surface. ""How are you?"

"Not very well," she signed faintly in the same wispy tones. "What are you doing?"

"Just watching the news on TV," he answered, restraining himself with some effort. His face was cheesy, his hands trembling, and he was afraid his excitement would show in his voice. He thought of asking her to come over but, recalling Alan's advice to play it cool, subdued the urge and waited her out.

"I'd like to see you," she continued uncertainly. "Can you meet me?" He wondered if she meant it. She sounded tense and strained; like she was having to do something she didn't want to do.

Getting better control of his voice he answered cautiously. "I can Helen but promise me you won't pick a fight. I couldn't take that."

"All right. I'll be in the park down by the lake—a brown Monte Carlo."

"I'll be there in a few minutes," he said with a sigh, wondering what he was letting himself in for.

He drove into Piedmont Park at the Twelfth Street entrance and started around the south side of the lake. The night was overcast but not rainy, mild for early November. Overhead a quarter moon was struggling to make it through the cloud cover. About halfway around the lake he saw the brown Monte Carlo parked on the left side, crouched under a street light like a forlorn, forgotten pup. He pulled the Cadillac in behind it, got out, walked up and opened the door on the right side.

"Is this seat taken?" he asked with a shy grin, making a try at levity.

"Get in and sit down," she said her voice still tense, brittle. Under the pale light of the streetlamp she looked thin and drawn.

Getting in he had to step over a white Styrofoam cooler sitting in the floor on his side. Ignoring it, he glanced up through the sun roof, now open to the soft night air. "This is a pretty car," he said lamely, trying to break the ice.

"I bought it at Mendenhall," she said, still tense. "I went out to see what was left of your Chevrolet and I saw this one. I took Louise back that afternoon and we got it."

He could see her better now. She was wearing a light colored pair of slacks, a bright blue sweater and a white windbreaker. Her hair was carefully brushed and he could smell it, clean and fragrant. She was sipping on a beer, staring straight ahead.

"These are popular cars. I'm sure you got a good buy," he said evenly, hoping she would relax and look at him.

"Well they wouldn't give me much off on it. I think it was about six thousand dollars."

"That's a lot for a Monte Carlo but I see you've got all the extras," he said, glancing again at the sun roof.

"It's got everything but a tape player. I've been planning to get one installed but I may just trade it. Louise wants something heavier. She still talks about how the Pinto folded up."

"Well she's got the money to buy whatever she wants," he replied quietly. All this small talk made him nervous but he realized they had to talk about something and the accident was too sensitive a subject to jump into without a little warm-up.

"I'm leaving tomorrow and going south for a few weeks," she blurted out suddenly. "That's why I wanted to see you tonight."

"Oh, where are you going?"

"I'm going to Daytona, then driving on to Miami and then taking a cruise to the Bahamas. I've already got my reservations. The ship leaves Port Everglades next Tuesday morning."

"Is Louise going with you?"

"No, I wanted to get away by myself to think."

"That's probably a good idea. I've spent a lot of time alone lately and it has helped."

"That's not the way I hear it," she snapped back accusingly, turning to face him for the first time. "Alma talks like she is your constant companion these days." Her eyes flashed—a condescending look.

"She's been over to the house two or three times. I wouldn't call her a constant companion."

"What was she doing in the park driving my car?"

"She was going to cook supper so I let her take it to get groceries. I didn't expect her to come through the park," he replied without apology. He was beginning to relax and almost enjoy himself. He hadn't even thought of making Helen jealous when he had allowed Alma to come over, but it had happened.

"Well, you ought not to let her run around in the Cadillac. She's a terrible driver Dan. She's wrecked two or three cars."

"She said you had a new boyfriend," Dan said, switching to the offensive without raising his voice.

"If you mean Gary Caldwell, he was just here for a weekend. He's gone back to camp now."

"Alma said he was very good looking," Dan said straight faced, trying to needle her, no longer jealous himself.

"Yes, he's a gorgeous hunk and I may see him again," she replied haughtily, not appreciating his attempt at humor.

"Well I may see Alma again," he said now serious, dropping his effort to lighten the conversation. "But I probably won't."

"She's not the kind of girl for you Dan," Helen said in a concerned tone. "You can do better."

"I'm glad you're interested in the kind of girl I run around with, I'm surprised you care."

"After what you did to me I shouldn't care," she retorted, her eyes blazing now. "Look at me. I'm a nervous wreck. I have to take pills to get started in the morning and pills to go to sleep at night. I have to wear a back brace all the time and I'm always in pain. I've taken to drinking beer. Do you know why? Because it keeps me high without getting me so drunk I can't function. What do you think of that Mr. Cooper?"

These last words came out harsh and stinging. Her face crumpled and squeezed together, her figure shook and trembled, and he was afraid she was going to burst into tears. Conflicting emotions tore at him but he managed to restrain himself and reply calmly with genuine feeling. "I'm sorry Helen," he said, wanting so badly to reach out and touch her but holding back. "I'd do anything in the world to just sponge the last two months off the calendar and try again."

"I would too but I can't. I'll probably be a cripple the rest of my life."

"Surely it's not that bad. I heard you've been dancing."

"I got drunk and tried it once," she said stonily, staring straight ahead again. "Did you hear about me passing out at Uncle Sam's?"

"No!" he said with alarm. "What happened?"

"It was the week after I got out of the hospital. I just couldn't take the house with all those kids. I took a cab to Uncle Sam's and sat around having a few drinks. I guess I had too many or they didn't mix with the medicine I was taking. Anyway I just passed out and fell in the floor. They wanted to send me back to the hospital but I wouldn't go. The bills are high enough without going back there."

"I've never seen any of the bills. I told Louise to have them sent to me. My insurance should pay most of them."

"Louise paid them. My lawyer, Mr. Walker said to save them. He wants to file a million dollar law suit against you."

"Is that what you want?"

"Dan, I'm not sure," she said wanly. Turning to face him she appeared frightened and confused. "That's why I'm going on this trip. I've got to think without all these people around."

"Listen Helen," he said softly with great sincerity, reaching out to place a hand lightly on her shoulder. "If there is any way you can forgive me for what happened, any way at all, I wish you'd forget about a divorce. My insurance will take care of your bills and somehow we'll make a new start. I'm not pressuring you, but I want you to know that."

"I'm glad Dan," she replied. "I really am. I think you better go now. Give me a kiss."

He bent over and kissed her lightly on the lips and a hundred memories shuffled brightly through his mind like a crazy kaleidoscope. "I'm glad we had this talk," he said straightening up. "If you want to see me again don't hesitate to call."

"I'll try to let you know something when I get back. Hand me another beer before you go."

He lifted a beer out of the cooler and pulled the tab to open it. She threw her empty out the open window onto the grass. "I use to never do that," she said dully, indicating the empty beer can. "I just don't care anymore."

"I guess I'll go then," he said, trying to smile. He reached across and kissed her lightly once more, then got out reluctantly. "Call me when you get back."

"Okay, I'll be in touch."

He shut the door firmly, then walked slowly back to the blue Cadillac, got in and cranked up. She was still sitting there sipping beer when he drove away.

Thursday, November 4, 1971

He flew to Houston the next morning. He wanted to think about the jumps he would be making but his mind kept going back to the meeting in the park. It was definitely encouraging. She still loved him. He was sure of that now. She wouldn't have called him to meet her and tell him all those things if she didn't still care. But she was hurt and scared. Poor baby! His heart went out to her and he wished there was something he could do. But he could see now that his best strategy was to play it cool. Last night's meeting could easily have flared into another fight if he had taken offense at any of her provocative remarks. But he hadn't and things had gone well and ended on a good note. No, there was no doubt about it. He must continue to play it cool. And he must go through with the hijacking. It would give him the money he would need to hold her if and when she came back to him.

In Houston he picked up a rental car from Hertz and checked into the Roadway Inn on the Southwest Expressway. In his room he changed into his jump clothes, then repacked the simulated money in the green day pack. He locked it in the trunk of the car and left early so he was waiting at Hull when Garfield showed up a little before four.

The weather was cool with high clouds and light winds and the first jump went off perfectly. He left the place at ten thousand feet, went into a stable free fall, counted to twenty before pulling the ripcord—just as he planned to do the night of the hijack. With the twenty-second delay he was down to six thousand by the time the chute opened and it took another two-and-a-half minutes to float to the ground using a twenty-eight foot canopy. He couldn't be sure what size or type parachute they would give him in Seattle, but the twenty-eight footer was the most common in use and that was what he hoped for. He was also hoping for a sport type chute, something similar to what he was now using, since these were designed with control and safety features other chutes lacked. Today his control was excellent and he landed just where he planned, a smooth, easy, standup touchdown.

They had a little time to kill before dark and the second jump so when Garfield went off to make some telephone calls, Cooper retrieved the money pack from the trunk of his car and placed it in the back seat of the jump plane.

It was dark when the real estate man returned and he found Dan already chuted up, sitting in the back of the Cessna. While they were taxiing out Dan slipped the money pack over into his lap and clipped the dog snaps to the leg rings of his harness. The right front seat and right door of the Skylane had been removed so when they were in position he only had to pull himself up and step out the open door. The pack was large and awkward but he used his left hand to hold it up under the chest chute while he grasped the edge of the door frame with his right. Garfield, busy flying the plane, did not notice the pack in the darkened cabin.

The air at ten thousand feet was cold and Dan wished he had worn his thermal underwear. As he tumbled out into the still darkness he could feel the unaccustomed pull of the twenty-two pounds of pseudo money. As he went into his arch it pressed upward against his thighs. He was perfectly positioned when he pulled the rip cord on the count of twenty and the chute opened normally, slowing his descent with nothing more than the usual jerk. On the way down the money bag floated out from his body, exerting only a slight tug on the harness. He had no problem steering the chute and aimed for a spot of grass to one side of the runway.

But landing with the money pack was different. His touchdown was normal but the bag's weight jerked him off balance and he temporarily lost control of the situation. Luckily the ground was soft and there was no wind to re-inflate his chute and he was able to regain his feet and unbuckle it without injury.

The Skylane landed while he was making his way toward the office. He waved to let Garfield know he was all right, then proceeded to lock the money bag in the trunk of his car before going to turn in the chutes.

Although it could cause problems on landing, he was not unhappy with the money pack. Once attached to the harness it was very unwieldy but there was no danger of losing it. If he reached the ground safely he could discard the parachutes and jump helmet, strap on the pack and look like any other backpacker hiking in the woods.

He paid Garfield and left money for Seymour to pay for repacking the chutes. He didn't expect to return to Houston and he didn't want to leave any loose ends. The success of tonight's jump had convinced him he was as ready as he'd ever be for the hazardous jump near Woodland.

Back at the motel he called and got a seat on a Delta Owly Bird leaving at 10:35. He repacked, dressed and had time to eat a late supper at the airport coffee shop.

Friday, November 5, 1971

It was 2 AM before Cooper got to bed but he was up at seven so he could be present at the Friday morning sales meeting.

He had promised to call Alma during the week but had neglected to do so. Now, on Friday morning, with more pressing matters out of the way, his thoughts returned to the tall, garrulous blond and he dialed her up. She berated him for his forgetfulness but forgave him when he apologized and confirmed their dinner date for Saturday night. He told her he wanted to have a serious talk.

After two hours at the health club, a little grocery shopping, and a stop at Fred's for a fifth of Wild Turkey, he went home for a quiet evening watching TV.

Saturday, November 6, 1971

Cooper spent the greater part of the day rehearsing the hijack. The bomb was not completed but it was far enough along to use for these practice sessions. Using a tape recorder to play back his efforts, he went over the speeches he would make, trying to get just the right inflection in his voice. He also practiced and timed the things he must do after the plane took off from Seattle—changing clothes, transferring the money to his day pack, etcetera—in order to establish the best sequence and keep the time required to a minimum.

Calling for Alma at her mother's at seven in the evening, Dan took her to dinner at the J-D Steak Ranch on Stewart Avenue, a long way from his usual haunts. They had finished eating and were sipping coffee when he put on a sad face and got serious.

"Alma," he began earnestly, looking her straight in the eye, "I don't want to hurt you. You've been very good to me since the accident. But I've got to ask you a favor."

"Yes, Dan," she answered in a subdued tone, knowing the axe was about to fall. "I'll do anything you ask."

"Helen called me the other night and I met her and we had a long talk. She hasn't fully made up her mind to divorce me. I'm still in love with her and I think she feels that way about me also, but she's still scared and upset. What I'm getting to is that things are still up in the air and she's jealous of you and I don't want to aggravate her. If you'll give me a couple of months I think things will work out one way or the other. If she goes ahead with the divorce we can start seeing each other again, but for now I think we'd better cool it."

"Whatever you say, Dan," Alma said in a hurt voice. "I just want to be your friend and help out any way I can."

"I know you do and that's just what I'm asking. I want us to keep on being friends but I think it would be best if we didn't see each other for at least a month. If we do Helen is going to know about it. And if you don't mind, please don't call me. Let me call you. I promise I will, every week or so."

"If you don't want me to call I won't, but she's not going to know the difference," Alma replied defiantly, her eyes flinty, proud, unbelieving.

"Her lawyer may have detectives bugging my phone. She doesn't have many grounds for divorce now but she'd like to catch me in a compromising situation."

"I don't know why you don't go ahead and file against her. Plead mental cruelty. You'd have a case."

"No, I still love her and I'm not pushing it," he said firmly, standing his ground. "Now promise me you won't call, and tell me you're not upset."

"Oh, all right," she said unsmiling. "But I still think you're letting her make a fool of you."

Dan's biggest reason for discouraging Alma was that he expected to be out of town a lot during the next few weeks and he didn't want her calling so often she'd become aware of it. He could make an appearance at the office once or twice a week and keep the people there from noticing any change, but he didn't want her calling every day. In addition it might help things with Helen.

Sunday, November 7, 1971-
Monday, November 8, 1971

On Sunday he once again flew to San Francisco and spent the night in the Buchanan Street apartment. At the airport in Atlanta he bought a bartender's guide and studied it on the flight out. On Monday he went out looking for a part time job as a bartender. What he hoped to do was establish at least one more reference for Ben Butler in San Francisco. If he were stopped leaving the area where he bailed out after the hijack, he wanted to be able to tell them where he lived and where he worked and the names of people they could call to verify these facts. He couldn't afford a full time job and he wasn't sure he could find what he needed, but he went looking.

He spent several hours pounding the pavements before he found it. It was a small neighborhood bar on Church Street, just off Market, and it had a sign in the window. "Weekend Bartender Wanted." Inside, the bar was dark and cool and silent except for the muted rumble of the color TV on the wall. A few regulars were there keeping an eye on *All My Children* while the bartender, a short, portly, prudish-looking man with a round face and a fringe of gray hair, was stacking beer in the cooler. Dan introduced himself as Ben Butler and inquired about the job. It developed that the bartender was Sam Matson and he was also the owner. He explained that he needed someone to work from six until two on Friday and Saturday evenings and from ten in the morning until six on Sundays.

Dan came on relaxed and low-key as he sold himself to the half-skeptical bar owner. His story was that he had recently moved to California from Alabama where he had owned his own bar. When his wife had been killed in an auto accident he had sold out and come west for a change of scenery. He told Matson that he enjoyed hiking and camping and was looking forward to visiting some of the many scenic areas along the west coast. He only wanted to work weekends to keep his hand in, having received enough money from the sale of his bar to support himself for the present. He let Matson know that he wasn't particularly concerned about wages, figuring to do well enough on tips.

The bar owner was very noncommittal at first, but as they chatted he gradually warmed to Dan and eventually offered him the job. Cooper assured him he had made a wise decision and agreed to come in before six the following Friday. Matson explained that he would be there to work with him on Friday and Saturday nights but Dan would have to open by himself on Sunday morning.

Tuesday, November 9, 1971

Taking a morning flight to Portland, Cooper picked up his Bronco and headed north. The day was cool and gray with thick clouds scudding along overheard. Leaving Woodland he took Route 503 northeast through Ariel, the small town on the north side of the Lewis River near the Lake Merwin dam. He wanted to get at least a cursory look at this land north of the river and the lake in case he accidentally came down here.

It was rugged country. In less than three miles the elevation rose from 100 feet at the river to 2955 feet at Davis Peak. In between were steep hills covered with a thick growth of timber. It was not impassable—he had been hiking and camping in this area—but there was certainly no place for a parachutist to land. He would want to be certain he was south of the dam before he left the aircraft.

It was thirteen miles from Ariel to the hamlet of Yale. Dan had traveled this route many times when he was growing up and things had changed little over the last thirty years. Magnificent evergreen trees lined both sides of the lonesome road and below, off to the right, he occasionally caught a glimpse of the tranquil lake, cool and placid like a great salver of beaten silver.

At Yale 503 turned abruptly to the right and crossed the river. Following it south for ten miles he turned right again at Amboy, taking the highway that went back towards Woodland. When he arrived at the Martin Place he found the dirt road leading into the farm muddy. Apparently there had been a lot of rain since his last visit. With a grinding of gears, he shifted to four-wheel drive and splashed along the deserted track.

The woods had the sweet, pungent smell of autumn and as he drove his mind traveled backward to that day in September three years before at Tallulah Gorge when he had proposed to Helen. God, how he missed her! When she left she had taken so much: companionship, laughter, and romance, hope—no, not hope. He still had that. Time didn't heal but it did deaden the pain, and now this project gave him hope for the future. He must succeed. Every fiber of his being demanded it.

At the campsite he spent a few minutes checking the clearing and the creek, just looking things over. Satisfied that everything was the same, he headed back to Portland where he had time for a quick lunch at the Artic Circle Restaurant on NE 82nd on his way to the airport. He was still some thirty minutes early for Northwest 305, but that gave him plenty of time to observe everything that went on in connection with the flight. This might be the only rehearsal flight he would be able to make, and he would have preferred to make it on Wednesday (since he planned to make the actual hijacking on a Wednesday), but doubted the crowd or the routine would be much different on this Tuesday. It was a short flight, only twenty-five minutes, and nothing unusual happened. There were only thirty-one people on board and he hoped there would be no more when he hijacked this flight two weeks hence. He paid careful attention to the routine of the stewardesses and noted exactly where the interphone was located.

There was no metal detection devices being used at Portland and he saw no evidence of any other anti-hijacking measures. In Seattle he used the telephone to check about closing time at all the major banks, looked over the layout of the airport, then caught the first flight out to Chicago. From there he flew to Atlanta.

Wednesday, November 10, 1971

Arriving in the wee hours, Dan went home and slept until noon, then ate breakfast and drove to his office to clean up the paperwork that had accumulated since Friday. That evening he called Alan to ask if he'd heard from Helen.

"I called over to the house last Monday," Alan told him. "Janie said Helen was in Miami and that Louise had flown down there too the day before I called, last Sunday."

Dan thanked him and hung up. He didn't tell Alan about seeing Helen in the park. That meeting had been a very private thing.

Thursday, November 11, 1971

He went to Burdon Aviation to complete the enrollment cards for all their employees. A couple were out for one reason or another, but the office manager said he would catch them in the next few days. Dan agreed to check back the following week.

On his way home he stopped at the 14th Street Post Office, the branch that served his neighborhood, and inquired about renting a box. The clerk said they had boxes available and gave him an application. He filled it out and left it to be verified, planning to return and complete the rental the following week.

Returning home he set out to finish his bomb. He had a small, tidy workshop in his basement where he had been meticulously working on it off and on since obtaining the dynamite and caps. He had begun by building a special plywood box which held the electrical heart of the bomb: two large dry cell batteries (the size used in electric lanterns), two ordinary wall switches, and two blasting caps. Looking at it from the top, it was a rectangle, eight inches wide and ten inches from top to bottom. When it was on its side it looked like a rectangular **C** with the top, ten inches long, being the back of the **C**. The two legs were three inches deep and three inches wide leaving the throat of the **C** approximately two inches deep and four inches in width. The leg that went across the top held the two switches mounted flush on the back of the C with the wiring connections down inside the leg. The piece of wood that formed the back of the C (and which had the switches mounted in it) was the lid of the box. It was hinged at the top, providing easy access to the inside, a catch at the bottom to hold it shut and a small handle he had to pull to open it.

The two short legs of the **C** held the batteries. They were mounted in brackets in such a way that they could be taken in and out easily. Wires ran from this battery bracket to the two electrically fired blasting caps which were mounted in the throat of the **C,** inside the box. The negative wire went direct from the batteries but the positive terminal was connected through the two switches which were wired in series. The switches were mounted horizontally, close enough together that he could touch both at once with one hand, but turned in opposite directions. He had used two and positioned them opposite each other for safety. Both must be switched on (toward the center as he had laid them out) to complete the circuit between the battery and the caps. And since it was necessary to move the left switch to the right and the right switch to the left to turn them on, it was almost impossible to switch them both on accidentally. The insulated wire was all run inside the box and fastened down, the connections firmly soldered.

He completed the box and checked the electrical circuit with a voltmeter before removing the batteries and attaching the wires to the blasting caps. The switches were both off (outboard positions), but removing the batteries eliminated any danger of accidentally firing the caps. He would not reinsert them until he was ready to board the flight. Now he was ready to add the dynamite.

Turning the box upside down, he laid eight sticks of dynamite across and through the throat of the C. He used Play-Dough to fill the space between the sticks, and between the sticks and the box, so that they were all held firmly in place. About two inches of each stick extended on each side of the box. He ran black electrical tap across from one leg to the other to hold the eight sticks firmly in place.

Functionally the bomb was now complete but Cooper decided to add one more touch, just for effect. He drilled two tiny holes, one on either side of the box in the upper leg of the **C**. Through these he passed two continuous strands of telephone wire, clipping the ends so he had two six inch pieces of bright yellow wire sticking out on each side. Then, doubling these ends, he passed them back between the protruding dynamite sticks and stuck them firmly into the Play-Dough. Thus on casual inspection, it would appear that these wires connected the switches in the upper leg of the C to the dynamite.

Finished, he carefully packed the bomb and other necessary items in the black attaché case. They fit comfortably with no problem. There was no danger of the bomb exploding until the batteries were installed and even then there was little likelihood of it going off accidentally. But by flicking two switches that he could reach with one hand, he could detonate it instantly.

Friday, November 12- Sunday, November 14, 1971

He completed work on his lethal bomb Thursday evening. With a good night's sleep he attended the eight o'clock sales meeting at the office, then returned home to pack and color his hair before catching a noon flight to San Francisco. It gave him plenty of time to go by his apartment and change clothes before reporting to work at Matson's at six.

All this flying had almost exhausted his cash reserves, but he had enough to see him through. The pay check he would receive next week would include the big renewal commission on the Burson policies and that should be sufficient to carry him until the end of the month. By that time it would all be settled, one way or the other.

Cooper found tending bar at Matson's to be fun. Friday was a little slow but he was tired well before closing time. He had the day free on Saturday so, after sleeping late, he rode a bus down Market and caught the Powell Street cable car to Fisherman' Wharf where he had a late lunch of clam chowder and crab.

Saturday night was much busier. There were several attractive young women in the crowd, some with men, but many unattached. He thought of trying to make a date with one after the bar closed, but decided against it. His neglected libido could use a sexual stimulant, but it wasn't worth taking some girl to his apartment and having her accidentally discover his real identification or some other facet of his charade.

He had put the idea out of his mind and was concentrating on last call when a petite, dark-haired girl in dirty jeans and a tight sweater approached him at the bar. "Say Ben," she hailed him cheerfully, "what are you doing after closing?"

"Going home to bed I guess," he replied with a tired smile.

"Some of us are going over to this dude's pad and smoke a little when we leave here. Why don't you come along? We'd be glad to have you."

He was tempted to say yes. He was enjoying working around this bunch of young, energetic non-conformists and he thought it would be fun to go to one of their parties. But he was tired and he did have to open the next morning at ten. "How about giving me a rain check on that?" he replied pleasantly. "I'd like to come another time, but not tonight."

"Sure," she answered, giving her head a little toss. She had the palest blue eyes Dan had ever seen, almost as colorless as water. "We're here nearly every Saturday night and we usually go somewhere afterwards to rap and party till daylight."

Sunday was quiet. He opened at ten but Matson didn't show up until late afternoon. It was about two-thirty and there was only one other patron in the bar when two husky looking guys, a blond and a brunette in matching powder blue windbreakers, came in and ordered beers. Taking bottles and glasses, they moved to a table in the rear, shed their jackets, and became engrossed in deep conversation. There was something familiar about the short brunette and Dan surreptitiously studied him in the mirror behind the bar as he idly polished a glass.

It wasn't until the muscular, brown-headed man came striding jauntily back to the bar and ordered two more beers in a slow drawl reminiscent of South Georgia that Dan realized where he had seen him before. It was the young schoolteacher from Tampa, Ross something, that had taken him to the gay bar in Daytona back in 1969. Suddenly he was very apprehensive, wondering if Ross would recognize him.

But it had been two-and-a-half years and fortunately the purposeful young man was concentrating all his attention on his companion, a pale, handsome youngster dressed impeccably in tailored, hand stitched jeans and a tan T-shirt with "Toad Hall" printed on the front. Ross hadn't changed much Dan realized as he continued to watch them from the corner of his eye. His neat, chestnut colored hair was a little longer but he had the same rugged good looks. The tight jeans and white T-shirt he wore displayed his well-developed body to good advantage. Dan would like to have asked him what he was doing in San Francisco but kept the conversation to a minimum.

More customers drifted in and Matson arrived before the two departed. Ross never gave Dan a second glance so apparently he didn't realize they had met before. It buoyed Cooper's confidence.

Off work at six, he went home to his apartment and caught a short nap before taking a cab to the airport to catch the red-eye back to Atlanta.

Monday, November 15, 1971

It got into the airport just before nine Monday morning. Dan went home, washed the gray out of his hair and changed clothes before going to the office.

There he spent thirty minutes with Tom Vaughn completing their monthly planning session. The aggressive manager was pleased to hear about the group sale at Burson's but importuned Dan to call on many more prospects, insisting that if he would do this, the percentages would take care of the sales he needed to get back on track.

He spent another thirty minutes doing a quick revision of last spring's presentation to McKnight. He was thinking of seeing the obtuse real estate man again after the hijack, and on his first night back in town he would come to the office, pick up any paper that had accumulated in his box, and leave this proposal for the secretaries to retype. If his mustache hadn't grown back enough by the Friday following the hijack, he would skip the weekly sales meeting, maybe call in sick. But he couldn't drop out of sight for too long.

Leaving the office, he took his paycheck to the bank. Even after taxes it came to almost fifteen hundred dollars, enough to pay a couple of overdue bills and cover the balance of the expenses he expected to incur.

From the bank he went to the health spa and worked out, then relaxed in the steam room and sauna. His weight loss program and his exercise program had both been very successful, and even though he had lost more than twenty-five pounds, his agility and stamina were much greater than they had been previously. The amphetamines the diet doctor prescribed frequently caused him to feel hyper and uptight, but the workouts at the spa were an opportunity to dissipate much of this excess energy, and he rarely needed the Seconal the doctor had prescribed in order to sleep at night. On his way home that afternoon he stopped by the Fourteenth Street Post Office and completed the rental of a box.

The life policies for Robertson and Nell Brady had been in his box at the office that morning. After an early dinner, roast beef and a tossed salad at Morrison's at Ansley Mall, Dan delivered them both. He spent very little time with either client and was back at Westchester Square before nine. His preparatory projects were all on schedule and now, during the next two days, he would have time for two trips which had been labeled optional in his original plan.

Tuesday, November 16-
Thursday, November 18, 1971

Arising early on Tuesday morning, Cooper used his Cadillac to drive to Birmingham. His only stop there was the downtown post office where he picked up Ben Butler's mail, a bank statement and two gasoline credit cards, one from Exxon and another from Sunoco. Back home at one-thirty, he took a nap until six. Upon awakening he ate a supper of grapefruit and cottage cheese before once again dyeing his hair gray. Dressed as Ben Butler, he packed a small bag and drove leisurely to the airport.

That night he flew to Washington, D. C. on an owly bird flight, then dozed a few hours in the terminal there before catching Northwest 305 to Seattle at 8:30 AM. He didn't expect to learn much he didn't already know about this flight, but it was a safety precaution, making the entire trip on a Wednesday. One thing he did ascertain was that the rear ramp was used for boarding at Great Falls and Missoula. As he expected, there was no change in crew during the journey and the routine between Portland and Seattle was exactly as he had noted Tuesday the previous week. The flight was about two-thirds full out of D. C., but a lot of people got off at the various stops and few got on. Again there were less than fifty people for the leg between Portland and Seattle.

Dan wished he could make his attempt on Tuesday the 23rd with Wednesday the 24th as a fall-back date, but he felt he needed to keep his job at Matson's Bar through one more weekend and there was just too much to do between the weekend and the hijack attempt to make it on Tuesday. But everything looked go for the 24th.

Leaving Seattle he flew to Los Angeles, then took a Delta flight home. It was late and it didn't land at Atlanta until 5 AM Thursday morning. But he slept on the plane and went home and slept again after he arrived. He was up in time to go out to Burson Aviation and collect the remaining enrollment forms for their group policy that afternoon. On Friday morning he'd go to the office for the weekly sales meeting and while there he'd assemble the paperwork for this sale and turn it in.

Dan was in especially high spirits that afternoon when he returned from Burson's. Barring unforeseen complications he would make his hijack attempt next Wednesday, the 24th. That gave him less than a week to complete his preparations and get himself psyched up, but everything was on schedule, under control. He felt so good he wanted to celebrate.

Calling to invite Alma to go to dinner, he caught the loquacious blond at home, eager to see him.

"What have you been doing the last couple of weeks?" she asked solicitously when they sat down for dinner at Yohannans later that evening.

"Working hard and staying out of trouble," Dan replied with a grin.

"I've tried to call you two or three times but never caught you in. You must be bar hopping every night."

"I've been doing a lot of driving and thinking," he replied in a more serious tone. "I sold a group policy and spent a lot of time at the office working on that. Not to change the subject but have you talked to Helen?"

"Yes, I called her one day the first of this week. She had just returned from Miami. She had planned to go on to the Bahamas but said she got to Miami and got so lonesome she decided not to go. Louise flew down and they partied there a few days, then drove back."

"That's interesting to hear. It sounds like she's finding out that money isn't everything."

"Yes, she didn't sound happy to me. I asked her about that marine, you know, the one I saw her with in the park. She said he was fabulous in bed but not too bright. I told her he sounded like he was just her type. Now me, I like men a little older and more intelligent."

Her callous reference to the marine's sexual feats caught Dan unawares. It was like someone had hit him in the stomach and all of the air had left his lungs in a soundless whoosh. He swallowed hard and finally got his breath. "If older men are your type why didn't you make it with Harvey, Alma?" he asked in a strained voice.

"He just wasn't interested in me," she said dejectedly. "Helen had him all tied up, just like it is with you."

"Well, you can't win them all. Don't give up. You'll find the right man yet."

Dan took her home early and came back to the house to go over his final plans and preparations. In another searching review of everything during the forty-eight hours he was traveling, he had decided to add a couple of refinements to his program and now he had to alter his checklist to include these items.

The first of these was concerned with his appearance during and immediately after the hijack. His original plan called for him to be clean shaven during this period, a contrast with the neat mustache he had worn since his Air Force days. Now he was thinking about the possibility of wearing a false beard, either during the hijack, or while making his way out of the area once on the ground.

Wearing it during the hijack had the advantage of disguising his actual appearance more thoroughly than he could possibly do otherwise, but it also had one big drawback. It might call attention to him before he was ready to make his move. Beards were not as common in 1971 as they are today, being worn primarily by hippies and other anti-establishment types, and if he wore one while checking in and waiting for the flight, it might result in his being stopped and questioned or even searched. The airlines were on the lookout for potential hijackers and anyone who looked different or out of place might come under suspicion.

Donning a false beard after he was back on the ground might make more sense. Once there he must change his appearance sufficiently to fool anyone he might meet. He was already planning to carry his jump boots, coveralls, a hunter's hat, and extra socks onto the plane in the attaché case and bowling-bag. It would be easy to add a false beard to his ensemble, carry it in the money bag during the jump, then wear it while hiking and driving out of the woods. It would be less out of place there.

On Thursday night he hadn't fully made up his mind about the false beard but had decided to go by a costume company in San Francisco the following afternoon and see what he could buy. If he was going to use one at all it had to be of professional quality, undetectable under normal circumstances.

The second modification of his plan was simpler. He had decided to purchase one hundred feet of stout nylon rope for use if he got caught in a tree. It could be carried onto the plane in the case with the bomb and put in the top of the money bag during the jump. There it would be easily accessible should he need it.

He had also considered taking along a gun. While he didn't think he would need it on the airplane, it might come in handy if he were stopped later on the ground. However further thought had decided him against carrying one. He didn't think that, face to face, he could gun anyone down. He had built his entire plan on guile and deception, and using violence or even planning for a violent contingency (other than his certain and immediate death in case of failure on the plane) was anathema to him.

Now, after making the necessary alterations in his checklists to accommodate the addition of the rope and the possibility of the beard, Cooper went through a final rehearsal and made one more methodical revue of what he had done and what remained to be accomplished. Then, as part of his plan, he set about destroying everything he no longer needed, and packing the remainder for his trip the following day. He was still in a good mood despite Alma's comment about Helen and the marine, and he had a couple of drinks while he worked.

It was after midnight and he was in the process of going to bed when the phone rang. Even before he picked it up he knew it was Helen.

"Hello," he said cautiously.

"Hello Dan," she hiccupped into the phone. "How are you?"

"I feel pretty good tonight," he replied good naturedly. "It sounds like you are feeling no pain."

"Yes, I've had a few drinks on top of my usual ration of beer," she continued in a slurred voice. "How about meeting me over in the park. Bring the Cadillac. I want to go for a ride in it."

"Helen you've been drinking and I don't want to take any chance on getting in a fight. Why don't we make it another time?"

"What's the matter?" she demanded drunkenly. "Don't you want to see me?"

"Yes, of course I want to see you, but I don't want any fights. I'm in a good mood and I don't want to spoil it. Alma tried to spoil it earlier in the evening by telling me what a good time you had in bed with that marine, Gary."

"Oh she's just jealous. I didn't' tell her I'd been to bed with him. She just made that up to hurt you. Aren't you onto her games by now?"

"If you say so then I believe you. I know Alma would like to see us get a divorce."

"That's right. Now come on over and meet me. The same place as last time. Please honey?" She sounded vulnerable. He could feel it, hear it coming through, in spite of her usual self-confident, know-it-all manner. He decided to risk meeting her.

"Okay, give me ten minutes. You're a mess," he teased. "Making me meet you in the park in the middle of the night."

Pulling on a jacket, he went down, got the Cadillac out, and headed to the park. The night was clear and chilly with no moon. He found the Monte Carlo parked in the same spot as before, a plume of exhaust rising from it like a smoke signal. As he pulled up behind her she got out carrying a beer and walked back to meet him.

"Slide over, I want to drive," she ordered good humouredly.

"You're probably too drunk to drive," he said smiling. "What will I do for a car if you tear this one up?"

"I'll get Louise to buy you a new one," she snapped with mock anger. "Now move over. I'm not that drunk." She prodded him in the ribs and he laughed and jumped away.

"You're certainly in a good mood tonight," he said grinning as he moved over to let her under the wheel. "To what do I owe this good fortune?"

"Nothing. I just wanted to drive my car again and play the tape player. I never got one in that Monte Carlo. We're trading it next week on a Riviera. I wanted one of these, but I try to help Louise watch her money and she really doesn't need this much car."

They pulled away from the curb and cruised slowly out of the park, turning left onto Tenth Street. The car whispered along in near total silence. Low music, a Ferranti and Teicher album, issued from the four speakers of the stereo. When she turned left on Monroe he suspected it, and when she turned left again at Montgomery Ferry he knew she was headed for the Ansley Park Golf Course.

She pulled in and parked in the same spot where they had parked on their first date. "Do you remember the time we parked here and carried on?" she asked clearly, the signs of liquor now gone from her speech.

"Like it was yesterday," he sighed, slumping casually on his side of the car, waiting her out, playing it cool.

She left the motor idling and put the transmission in park. Looking through the tape case that rode the hump between the seats she selected *TCB*, a tape by the Supremes, and substituted it for the one that had been playing. "There's a place for us, somewhere a place for us," Diana Ross crooned softly.

"Here, help me take this back brace off," she said, starting to remove her jacket. "It's driving me crazy."

He reached across and helped her take off her jacket, then pull up her sweater and unstrap some canvas that went around her chest and stomach. The brace itself, a small metal affair, heavily padded, slipped off easily. She rearranged her clothes while he sat holding the brace, staring at it.

"See what I have to wear because of you. I'll have to wear it all my life. All because you lost your temper with your poor Baby."

"Poor Baby gave me plenty of reason to lose my temper. But, of course, you're right. I'm a beast and a woman beater."

"Ha! At last you admit it."

Talk subsided and they sat, each wrapped in their own thoughts listening to the music. She lit a cigarette and gazed out across the deserted fairway, her face pensive. He studied her profile and admired how beautiful she was tonight, more like the old Helen, his Helen, than she had looked in months.

"Dan, I may be ready to come back in another month," she said stonily, tapping the ash off her cigarette. She now sounded completely sober. "That is, if you still want me."

He counted to three before answering. He didn't want to appear too eager; he had to say just the right thing. "Of course I want you back Baby," he finally managed in a somber voice. "Anytime you want to come back." Thinking of his plans for the next two weeks, he went on. "A month from now would be good. I'm going to be gone for a few days around Thanksgiving, but I'll be back in time to get everything set to have you home before Christmas."

"Louise has bought a new house. She signed the papers today. She plans to move on the first of December. I've got to help her do that and then maybe I might be ready to come home."

"Gee, that's wonderful news Baby," he exclaimed, now getting excited in spite of his resolution to play it cool.

"Yes, I think that might work out," she mused. "I haven't told Louise but I miss you and I want to come back and live with you."

She put out her cigarette and turned to face him. He slid over and took her in his arms and kissed her. There was no tenderness in his kiss. It was hard and violent; it bruised her lips and took the breath from her body. She returned it passionately.

"God, I've missed you," she signed as he continued hugging her.

"You'll never regret it Baby, I promise you that," he said in a voice choked with emotion.

They parked there for a long time, embracing and kissing and talking about the times when they were courting. Finally she put the car in gear and drove back to Piedmont Park.

"Would you like to come home and spend the night?" Dan asked guardedly. "It's so late now and you've been drinking. You shouldn't drive out to Louise's."

"No, I better not," she teased shamelessly. "You might get carried away and attack me and hurt my back. What would the doctor and my poor lawyer say? Besides I don't have to drive to Louise's. I've got a suite at the Biltmore."

"What are you doing with a suite at the Biltmore?" he exclaimed.

"I just can't take those kids all the time. I have to get out. Louise lets me go to a motel and stay when it gets too bad. She gives me her credit cards and lets me charge it."

"It sounds like you two have about done in her fifty thousand. How much is left?"

"Oh, it's not all gone. Of course I made her pay all her bills. You know you acted so mad because she wouldn't pay them all right off. Well, I got her to pay those and then buy the house and the cars and a few other things. I guess she's still got about ten thousand in the bank."

"And a lot of bills again too I suspect. You do know that it isn't going to be that way when you come back home don't you?"

"Yes, I understand. That's why I'm having this last fling, helping her get in the house and get it furnished and all. After that I'll be ready to come home and be a good girl."

Returning to the park, they talked intimately for a little longer before she finally left him. He drove home on a cloud. Suddenly everything looked so rosy. He'd pull off his caper next week and be home with the money in less than two. He knew she'd never come back if she faced a life of poverty, but now he'd have the money to do the things that made her happy.

He considered her call a good omen, and when he finally got to bed about three that morning he slept soundly. It never crossed his mind that he might never see her again, that this time next week he might be dead.

PART VI

"Freedom's Just Another Word For Nothing Left To Lose"

Friday, November 19, 1971

11:20 AM

When Dan Cooper boarded the Delta DC-8 flight for San Francisco at Gate 51 he was sobered and solemn. His euphoria of the previous night had faded and now, setting out on the final phase of his adventure, he was all business. It had been a busy morning and he was looking forward to relaxing with a good lunch and a couple of drinks on the three-hour-and forty-minute, non-stop flight.

Leaving his Cadillac locked in the garage; he had taken a cab to the Atlanta airport loaded down with luggage: two matching brown Hartmann cases, the large black attaché case containing the homemade bomb, and the plaid bowling-ball bag with his jump helmet inside. He had checked them all, not wanting to take a chance of being stopped and questioned at the checkpoints now in place at the entrances to all the concourses here. The batteries were not packed in the same case with the bomb, so there was no danger of it exploding accidentally.

Cooper would be doing a lot of changing of clothes and personalities during the next ten days. This morning leaving Atlanta he wore an expensive beige sport coat, brown woolen slacks, and a light-blue, open-collared shirt. In San Francisco he would switch to being Ben Butler who was usually clothed in worn jeans, plaid flannel shirts, and engineer's boots. Most of this wardrobe had been purchased there at discount shops and used-clothing outlets. For his next visit to the woods the following Tuesday, he had thermal underwear and his heavy blue parka.

In Portland on Monday evening he would select an inexpensive suit and accessories off the rack at some department store to wear on the plane Wednesday. Before jumping he would pull on his green coveralls and jump boots; on the ground he would abandon his jump helmet along with the chutes, and don a hunter's hat and his special pack containing the money. In that disguise he hoped to pass as a woodsman during his trip out of the forest.

If things went as planned he would either drive the Bronco or catch a bus out of Portland back to San Francisco on Thursday, Thanksgiving Day. For this he would dress informally but not in the same garb he had worn in the woods. By that time he would be down to carrying the two brown suitcases, one for the money and one for the spare clothes and toilet articles.

Back in San Francisco on Friday, the 25th, he would pick up a new suit that he planned to buy this afternoon to wear when he played the part of a well-heeled businessman when he flew to Las Vegas the next day. He already had reservations at The Sands for three nights beginning on the 27th in the name of Ben Butler. Before he left he would pack up everything in his apartment and leave the keys and an undated note for the resident manager saying he had to leave suddenly. He figured old man Overturf wouldn't come around and find it until the rent was due on the first.

On Friday afternoon he would call Matson and lay some tale on the bar owner about being unexpectedly called back to Alabama on urgent personal business. The old suitcase he had brought out earlier would be packed with the Ben Butler items he would no longer need and left in an airport locker. Finally, when he had laundered the hijack money in the gaming capital, he would fly home to Atlanta under some assumed name wearing the same outfit he wore today, dispose of the Ben Butler ID, stash his cash in the C. & S. safe deposit box, and go back to being just plain Dan Cooper.

He had several options and alternatives to these plans. If he came down in some location completely removed from where he wanted to land, he hoped to pass as a backpacker traveling cross country until he could make it to the closest safe base—the car, the motel in Portland, the apartment in San Francisco, or his home in Atlanta. If he landed in the vicinity of Woodland but was stopped or spotted leaving the woods, he might ditch the Ben Butler identity and return to Atlanta without going to San Francisco or Las Vegas. He could fly from there to the Bahamas to launder the money if necessary.

But that was all still in the future when he landed in California just after one on the afternoon of November 19th. Claiming his luggage, he took the airport bus to the downtown terminal where he left it in a locker while he went shopping for a new suit to wear in Las Vegas. He found what he wanted, a gray pinstripe in a conservative cut, at Brooks Brothers on Post Street. They promised to have the alterations completed so he could pick it up at the "Will-Call" window the following Friday. He also purchased three shirts and three ties to wear with the new suit and took them with him.

From Brooks Brothers he proceeded to the Mission Street outlet of Western Costume Company. There he hoped to buy a false beard that would be good enough to use either during the hijack or on the walk out of the woods. But in this he was disappointed. The crowded showroom appeared to be more of a novelty store than a place to buy a real disguise. All the beards on display were white and went with the Santa Claus suits that were everywhere. When he finally was able to stop a harried saleswoman, a sixty-year-old bantam with frizzy gray hair, he got a short answer.

"Beards? Yes, we've got them," she said shoving a dog-eared catalog at him. "Look through this and see if you can find what you want. I'll be with you as soon as I finish getting this order together."

Scanning the color brochure, a special compilation of costumes, masks, and decorations being offered for the Yule season, Cooper again found only the white beards for Santa's. After waiting another fifteen minutes, he gave up, disgusted. The beard thing was only an option and not a necessary part of his plan.

Outside, he hailed a cab, picked up his luggage, and headed for Buchanan Street. There he put everything away and changed into his bartending clothes before walking over to Market and grabbing a sandwich. He reported to work at six. He believed in being punctual.

06:00 PM

Business was brisk almost from the moment he arrived. By ten, people were clustered two deep at the bar, the room a churn of bodies. Many of the customers from the previous weekend were there and Dan watched for Lynn, the dark-headed girl with the colorless eyes who had asked him to the party. Just before midnight he spotted her standing with a group near the door. In skin-tight jeans and a mauve pullover sweater, she exuded sexuality. Impulsively he decided it was time to expand Ben Butler's lifestyle.

When he caught her looking his way, he called her over. "How about a drink on me?" he offered expansively.

"Sure," she drawled, giving him a dreamy smile. "I'll have a Coors."

"Here you go," he replied, smoothly extracting the can from the cooler, popping the top, and placing it on a napkin in front of her. "How are you doing tonight?"

"Man, I'm floating," she crooned, rolling those glittery eyes upward and grinning broadly. "We got hold of some of that good Columbian weed and I'm really spaced out."

"Who are you with?" he asked casually, leaning on the bar, ignoring other customers waiting for service.

"Oh I came with Harry and Darlene, but I'm not with anybody."

"I just wondered if you were having another party tonight. I don't have to go to work until six tomorrow."

"I'll see if there isn't one somewhere," she said, giving him a wink and another smile. "I'll check back with you in a little while."

It wasn't long before she drifted back to tell him she had talked it up and if he would meet her and some friends at The Station, an all-night eatery nearby on Market after closing, they would go somewhere and party.

Saturday, November 20, 1971

2:30 AM

Her invitation hadn't been exactly what Dan had hoped for, but he had invited himself and so he went. He'd had a few drinks and by the time he got off and walked to The Station he was feeling loose and uninhibited.

At this time of the morning the place was packed with people of all descriptions. He stood in line behind a group of youngsters wearing fatigue coats, strange hats and washed out jeans. Finally he spotted Lynn sitting in a booth with three other freaks, a boy and two girls. She introduced the boy (who really wasn't a boy but a short, husky man of about thirty with a stringy black beard and long greasy black hair) as Harry. The two girls, both blonde and in their early twenties, were Darlene and Sue.

"Hey man, what's your bag?" Harry inquired brashly almost before Dan sat down. "If you got the bread I know where we can score some of that good Columbian."

"I've never been much of a smoker," Dan replied cautiously. "But if you say it's good, I'd like to try it. But where can we go? My place is too small for a party."

"We can party at my pad man if you'll buy the weed," the gregarious Harry roared enthusiastically. All his utterances seemed to smack of the hustle. "I know where I can get some booze too if you want that."

Cooper gave Harry thirty dollars and the hippy rushed off to get the marijuana and whiskey while Dan and the three girls strolled leisurely back to Harry's apartment. It was in a housing project on Height, not far from Dan's place. Darlene and Sue lived there with the bearded hippy and a delicate looking boy with long blond hair named Joe who they found asleep on a worn gray couch in the living room. The cramped apartment consisted of a living room, bedroom, kitchen and bath. The small living room was saved from squalor only by psychedelic curtains—huge flowers in blazing hues of red, yellow, and orange, and the startling color of the walls, a lime green. One wall was decorated with a series of bright posters: Hell's Angels, Baez at Carnegie Hall, The Cast of Hair, and a dangling kitten entitled "Hang in There Baby."

They woke Joe, lit several candles and turned on the stereo, which blared forth a series of hard rock tunes. When Harry burst in with the supplies, the party really took off. Dan had smoked marijuana before, but never as a regular thing. Being a non-smoker, he wasn't used to inhaling, but Harry had a water pipe and Cooper quickly learned he could tolerate a lot more of the acrid smoke when it was cooled passing through the water. They passed it around continuously while talking nonstop about subjects that ranged from the war to politics, to religion, to what they were planning to do for Thanksgiving. Darlene and Sue danced together for a time while everybody else was too busy getting stoned.

At some point, the stereo was turned off and Joe produced a battered guitar. Squatting cross-legged on the floor, the effeminate looking boy captured their attention playing and singing in a pure, vibrant tenor. His repertoire included *Blowing in the Wind, The Sounds of Silence*, and numerous other ballads of the sixties. They all joined in when he began Janis Joplin's recent hit, *Me and Bobby McGee.*

Harry had brought a fifth of cheap bourbon and Dan was drinking that with water and no ice. The booze, the marijuana and the sweet, sad music had a mellowing effect. When Lynn produced a couple of small white tablets and stuck one in his mouth he washed it down with another swallow of the harsh liquor. He didn't know what it was but he felt loose and uninhibited, game for anything. He relaxed on the couch with Lynn and Sue, nodding his head in time with the music and singing along when he knew the words. The girls, equally out of it, cuddled and sang along also.

"In the early morning rain . . . with a dollar in my hand . . ." the boy wailed, his handsome boyish face earnest, his flaxen hair gleaming in the flicker of the candles. Dan was suddenly assaulted by chipped, brightly colored fragments of memory like quick intercuts in a motion picture. The familiar song triggered poignant thoughts of Helen, of Atlanta, of other times; bathed him in a bittersweet nostalgia. But he was too far gone to allow painful remembrances to interfere with his good time. Banishing them from his mind, he laid his weary head on Lynn's ample breast and drifted off to sleep.

12:30 PM

Awakening a little past noon, he looked at his watch and remembered it was Saturday. He was naked on a soiled mattress on the floor in the bedroom of Harry's apartment, and to his consternation he was cuddled up between Lynn and the androgynous Joe who were also unclothed. Sue, wearing only panties, was asleep by herself in the bed. Untangling himself, Dan got up quickly and retrieved his clothes which were scattered about the bedroom. On his way out he noticed Harry and Darlene sleeping nude on the couch in the living room.

He had a headache, a dull persistent throbbing, and his mouth tasted foul. Outside in the sunshine he breathed deeply and felt a little better. A shadow of guilt flicked across his conscience as he walked slowly down Height. This wasn't what he had come to California to do. He was taking a chance getting to know these people, even a little, and he didn't know what he might have said when he was stoned. Still, it had been something different and it had relaxed him, taken his mind off of what was coming up, at least for a few hours.

And he had enjoyed himself—immensely. Despite the hangover he felt content, happy and satisfied with an overlay of a kind of sweet sadness. Perhaps if things didn't work out at home and Helen divorced him he'd come back here to live. Even in his short stay he had discovered that life in San Francisco was more open and relaxed than anywhere in the East. So many here, not just the hippies but almost everyone he met, seemed to be an arrested adolescent going through a long period of introspection, egocentricity and concern with things physical. They found time to enjoy the beauty and cultural attractions of the city, their friends and themselves. Money was necessary but not the most-important-thing it had been in Dan's life for the past three years. Here a man could work a part time job and find happiness in other things.

Lynn came in again that night and visited with him at the bar. She didn't say much about the night before except to indicate she had enjoyed it. Neither did he. When he didn't suggest getting together again, she drifted off and left well before closing. He went home for a good night's sleep.

Sunday, November 21, 1971

10:00 AM

Cooper was there by nine-thirty and had the bar open at ten, but it was almost noon before he had his first customer, a big balding man with a basset hound's face who was one of the regulars. Around two he saw Rod and his blond boyfriend walking past, moving in the direction of Market. Wearing the same blue windbreakers, they promenaded by without even looking in. By four when Matson arrived they had all of six customers, but the crowd gradually gathered and by the time Dan left at six the place was half full.

After stopping for a quick supper, he went home to make preparations for tomorrow's departure. If, after the hijacking, the police stopped him and got the name Ben Butler and this address, he would simply not come back. He had told both Matson and Overturf he was going camping this week and this gave him an excuse for taking most of his belongings. He packed meticulously, but purposely left $200 in emergency funds in the pocket of a dirty shirt thrown on the floor in the closet. Before leaving on Monday he would carefully wipe everything for fingerprints.

Monday, November 22, 1971

06:30 AM

His GE clock radio came on and Dan bounded up to put on water for instant coffee. The radio and the small bright kettle were the only new things in the tacky apartment. Both had been purchased in Birmingham when he realized he might actually sleep in the place there. While he normally didn't oversleep, on this mission he wasn't taking any chances.

The weather was cool and foggy when he departed his apartment a little before eight bound for the California Motor Vehicle Department office on Fell Street. He left early and walked for the exercise. They were already open when he arrived and he quickly turned in his Alabama Driver's License, took the written test, and was issued a temporary California Driving Permit. It showed the same information that had been inscribed on the license issued to Ben Butler in Birmingham except for his new California address. There was no picture.

By eleven he was on his way to the airport in a cab. He carried the same four pieces of luggage he had brought with him from Atlanta on Friday. Dressed casually in faded jeans, a denim shirt, and his green parka, and sporting the Ben Butler glasses, he looked like a native. His hair, tinted a handsome, silver-gray color, was long and shaggy, falling over his ears and collar; his mustache was luxuriant; his sideburns full, bushy.

He picked up a newspaper in the terminal and read it on the direct flight to Portland. There was nothing out of the ordinary in the news, war rumblings in the Middle East, a fight between Nixon and the Democratic Senate over a tax bill, and little else.

Arriving before one, he picked up the blue-green Bronco and drove to the Roadway Inn on NE 82nd where he rented a single room on the ground floor and paid for four nights. He told the desk clerk he might stay through the weekend.

02:00 PM

The sky was overcast and gloomy with occasional rain falling. A cold wind buffeted him as he went about doing some final shopping that afternoon. At a Firestone Auto Store he bought chains and a new battery for the car. He didn't want to take any chances on it not starting when he needed it. At a sporting goods store he picked up two hundred feet of thin nylon line, the kind of light, stout rope used by mountain climbers and boating enthusiasts. He had planned to buy only one hundred feet, but now, thinking about the height of some of the trees out there, he impulsively concluded that if he was going to bother with it at all, he should get two hundred.

He found a motorcycle shop and purchased a face plate for his crash helmet. Parachute jumpers normally did not use them, but he might fall into a tree and wanted all the protection he could get.

Finally he purchased the suit, shirt, tie, belt and shoes he would wear during the hijack on Wednesday. He tried everything on to be sure it fit properly, and then waited while they hemmed the cuffs of the trousers.

On the way back to the motel he stopped and filled the car with gas, then went by a supermarket where he bought several items of food, some to take to the woods, some to keep at the motel for snacks. Picking up an evening paper, he was reminded that today was the eighth anniversary of John Kennedy's assignation in Dallas. Thinking of those tragic days in November of 1963 he reflected solemnly on life's fragility, the sinister randomness of chance, the inevitability of endings. Was he a Lee Harvey Oswald about to unleash unknown forces with tragic consequences? He hoped not. Yet he knew that sometimes you become involved so deeply in a thing you can't see all its dimensions, it becomes too much a part of you. He was so sure, so sure that what he was doing was right, that the end justified the slim chance that something would go amiss. And yet, now, at the eleventh hour he suddenly felt a need for reassurance.

Brooding this way, his brain in a whirl, he drove slowly back to his motel where he put away his purchases, then nibbled a sandwich in his room. When definitive answers continued to elude him he finally came to the realization that it was too late for logic, that it was fanciful and ridiculous to have second thoughts at this point. He had made his choice a long time ago. He couldn't go back on it now.

Tuesday, November 23, 1971

06:15 A.M

Up early, Cooper stepped outside to check the weather. He found the sky still overcast and the temperature in the forties, but there was no rain. Back in the room he dialed the FAA Flight Service Station to get their forecast. It called for low ceilings Tuesday and Wednesday with intermittent light rain and temperatures remaining in the forties. A cold air mass was moving down from the northwest and would probably move into the Portland area early Thursday with more rain and possible snow. It didn't sound good but this time of year he couldn't expect it to be perfect. As long as he could get out of the woods before the cold front hit he should have no insurmountable problems. He decided to go ahead as planned.

The night before he had washed the gray out of his hair and colored it a dark brown. Now he dressed for hiking in his sturdy jump boots and heavy blue parka. He packed the Bronco carefully using one of his innumerable checklists, and was away from the motel by seven.

The streets were almost empty in the calm of the early hour. Along NE Lombard Street the traffic signals flashed eerily in the early morning blackness. A worm of self-doubt still wiggled somewhere in the back of his mind, but he ignored it as he crossed the fog-covered river and drove north in the leaden, half-light of the slowly awakening day.

The dirt road leading into the Martin Place was muddy but he had no trouble making it to his planned campsite by Cedar Creek. Parking the Bronco out of sight amid the trees, he set up camp near the creek. It had to look to anyone who happened upon it as if he had gone off into the woods and might return at any time. Of course anybody who found him camping here this time of year would think him a fool, but his story was that he was a misplaced Alabamian living in San Francisco who didn't realize the weather would be this bad in November.

Walking back to the center of the farm, he removed the boards he had left on the spot where he hoped to land, and remarked it with a very large X done in white toilet paper. If he bailed out at the proper time, and if he had any visibility at all, he thought he would be able to spot this big marker which contrasted so sharply with the surrounding greenery. If so, he could guide his parachute to a safe landing here, out of the trees and the power line and within a short distance of his camp. He weighted the paper down with small rocks and pieces of brush so it would not be blown about. A good rain would dissolve the paper and wash it away, but he hoped to be back here before any significant weather arrived.

Returning to camp he gathered a large stack of firewood, most of which he placed inside his tent in an effort to keep it as dry as possible. The majority of his supplies would be locked inside the car. Cooper had brought all the usual camping equipment plus extra clothes and food in case he was to be marooned up here in a snow storm. He spent better than an hour carefully wiping the inside of the car and all the items he would leave here to remove any fingerprints. He left the Ben Butler glasses and five ten-dollar bills in the pocket of the green parka. Placing the car keys in a Hide-A-Key magnetic key holder, he stuck it out of sight in the right rear wheel well.

01:00 PM

He hadn't eaten any breakfast but had stopped at a café and had his thermos filled with hot coffee. Now he drank a cup and ate two fat ham and cheese sandwiches he had prepared last night and brought along. The excitement of his mission gave him a hearty appetite and he attacked his lunch with vigor. Finished, he was ready for the long walk back to town.

Once out of the woods Cooper wanted to pass as a long distance hitchhiker. To support this image he now carried the worn gold backpack he had purchased in San Francisco. But it contained only his thermos and a few other, lightweight items. He donned a worn looking Stetson hat which would keep the rain off but did nothing for his ears, now tingling in the cold. He had purposely not shaved since Saturday, and with his bushy mustache and grubby clothes, he looked the part.

It took less than forty minutes to cross the Martin property and follow the Spurrel Road west to where it joined the dam road. He wasn't sure what his story would be if he met somebody or was offered a ride, but he didn't see a soul.

Once on the Dam Road he made good time. There were few cars here or on the main Woodland-Amboy highway when he came to it. He didn't even try for a ride until he hit the Interstate at Woodland. But he was there quite a while. It was beginning to get dark when a seedy looking geezer driving a faded Dodge pickup gave him a lift. Luckily the old man was going all the way into downtown Portland. Dan got out there and found a cab to take him to the motel. Now, with everything in place, he experienced a lightness of spirit, an eagerness for the morrow.

07:00 PM

Not wanting to go out for dinner, Cooper made himself a sandwich in his room. After eating he mixed a drink and took out a letter written during the long flight west the previous Wednesday. Sitting down, he now added a heading, and then soberly reread this document he hoped would never be seen by another soul.

Roadway Inn
Portland, Oregon
November 23, 1971

My Dearest Baby,

If you get this letter the chances are good that I will be dead. Tomorrow afternoon, carrying a bomb, I plan to hijack Northwest Flight 305 between here and Seattle and demand a ransom of $200,000. If I get the money I intend to parachute out into the country northeast of Woodland, Washington, where I grew up and where I have a car awaiting me.

You may wonder why I am doing this. I find that a little hard to answer myself. It is partly for the money. I haven't been able to earn enough in the last two years to keep you in the style and manner to which we both have grown accustomed. I think that is the main reason for our troubles and I realize that without some extra money to tide us over while I am looking around for a more profitable business or profession, our marriage is certainly over even if we make another try at it. With the money I think there is a good chance to overcome our past problems and shape a happy future.

But going further than that, I think I am doing it because I feel a great sense of guilt over the accident. Even though I was out of my head, there is no doubt in my mind that I tried to kill you, and that knowledge has been like a malignant cancer eating away at my guild-ridden conscience. I feel I must atone for that despicable act in some way. I am taking a big risk in this attempt. It is my way of atonement.

In addition I feel that because of the accident I owe you a certain indemnity. If I am successful in my attempt and live, we will have the money to help us make a happy life. If you decide to go ahead and divorce me I will have funds to support you for a long time if that is necessary. Should I be killed I have close to two hundred thousand dollars in life insurance on which you are the beneficiary. Because of the circumstances I have left it all directly to you with no strings attached. In that eventuality I hope you will get sound financial advice from an attorney or investment counsel on how to use this money to provide you an income. Don't blow it all in one big spree.

In summary I guess I'm doing this in expiation for my past mistakes and to provide money to make another try at our marriage. At the moment I've lost so much I feel I have nothing left to lose.

It may be possible that you will need this letter as proof of my death. I will be carrying identification in the name of Benjamin A. Butler, but if the bomb explodes there may not be anything left to identify. In that case this letter should serve as proof. Another possibility is that I will bail out and be hurt or lost and die without getting back to civilization. In that case it may be hard to find the body but eventually they will have to declare me dead.

*My plan at the moment is to mail this letter in such a way that should I be successful I can retrieve it without you seeing it. If I am not, I hope it finds its way into your hands at least by early January. If by some fluke you should receive it before December 15*th, *don't take any action until that date. If I land other than where I plan to land, it may take several days to walk out of the woods, and then it might take me a few more to get home.*

Whatever happens Helen, I want you to know I love you more than anything in this world. I've never stopped loving you and never will. Please forgive me all my past mistakes.

Your loving husband,
Dan

When, on Monday the previous week, Dan had gone back to the 14th Street Post Office and rented a box, he had paid the box rent up only until January 1st. His intention was to address this letter to Helen at that box and put his name and home address in the upper left hand corner. If he did not return and claim it, the letter would lay in the box until it was closed for nonpayment of box rent on January 10th. At that time it would be sent to their home. By then he would have been missed and Helen would undoubtedly be living in the Westchester Square house and thus receive it.

But now he found himself experiencing some second thoughts. This afternoon, on the long walk back to town, it had dawned on him how well he was functioning without his wife. She had been gone almost three months and of course the first one had been devastating, but since then, since he had launched this hijacking project, he had gotten along amazingly well. Perhaps it would be better if they got a divorce. If he survived the hijacking (and he felt very confident he would), he could give her the house and the car and a little money and come back out here somewhere and start his life over. He'd have to live simply, he couldn't flash money around, but that would be no problem and with the proceeds of the hijack to see him through, he could take his time in finding a new career.

Tonight, re-reading the letter, he was again visited by the creepy feeling that maybe he was not doing the right thing for the right reasons. But once more, after some reflection, he banished his nagging doubts. His plan was a good one. If he succeeded he would destroy this letter and could then reassess his options. If he failed it would serve its purpose. After addressing the envelope he put it away and went to bed.

Wednesday, November 24, 1971

08:00 AM

The phone rang; a cheerful voice told Dan Cooper it was eight o'clock. Looking out, he saw the same soggy skies. A call to the Flight Service Station confirmed yesterday's prognostication. They were forecasting overcast all day with ceiling not above one thousand feet and visibility not above three miles in light drizzle and fog. The cold air mass was still expected to move into the Portland area early the next morning. This system worried Cooper. It could dump a lot of snow out there where he was planning to jump. However if the forecast was accurate and it didn't arrive until the next morning, he should be down and back here in the motel before it struck. He didn't want to have to postpone the hijack, particularly now that the car was in place. There was no snow on the ground now except on the higher peaks, and if he waited another week there well might be. He would like more ceiling to help him spot his landmarks on the way down, but this wasn't absolutely necessary. Of course the low ceiling could work to his advantage also. If he bailed out in solid cloud they certainly wouldn't be able to see him and pinpoint exactly where he went out. That could give him the extra time he might need to locate himself and get out of the woods. Although he had some reservations, his decision this morning was again a Go.

He ordered a hearty breakfast, two eggs, ham, toast, orange juice and coffee, brought to the room where he ate it leisurely while watching the Today Show. The news was still routine. The lead item concerned the Senate okaying a big appropriation for arms. His mind fastened on unimportant details as he tried to shut out the thought that this might be his last day on earth.

Breakfast finished, he dressed in sport coat and slacks and called a cab to take him to a nearby barber shop. There he had the barber cut his hair a little shorter than he normally wore it and thin his sideburns and mustache. Returning to the room he shaved off the mustache and sideburns completely before showering and applying more color to his hair, turning it a patent leather black. It would take the mustache a couple of weeks to grow back to a reasonable length, but he wouldn't be home for several days and he would stay out of sight for a few more until he looked enough like his old self to go out in public.

Because of his weight loss his face, which had become round and cherubic during his married years, now appeared thin and drawn. To enhance this lean, cadaverous effect, he used tweezers to pluck his normally bushy eyebrows down to a fine line and combed his hair straight back, flat against his head. Next he used a Max Factor Pan Stick to change his complexion to a dark olive hue, a shade that blended well with the jet black hair. Then with perverted cleverness he used a few strokes of carefully applied eye shadow to change the lines around his mouth and under his eyes and the shape of his chin. With these alterations his appearance was totally different. He didn't think his friends in Atlanta or those who had known him as Ben Butler would recognize him now. As a fatal touch he donned a pair of yellow wrap-around sunglasses and surveyed himself in the mirror. Satisfied, he put them aside and began packing.

He would carry the large black attaché case and the bowling-ball bag. First he placed the jump boots in the case, one at either end with their tops overlapping in the center. A hunting knife in a scabbard was sewn to one boot and a small pocket that held a compass to the other. Next the money bag, folded flat, was laid in the center of the bottom and on top of that went a surplus Mae West, an inflatable life jacket, purchased at an Army-Navy store. Then in the center, on top of all this, went the bomb.

Now he coiled the nylon rope neatly around the bomb box in such a way that it served as a buffer on all four sides. It fitted tightly at the top and bottom holding it firmly in place. The ends were bound to the coil with stout twine tied with a slipknot. Thus when he transferred the rope to his pack it would not tangle or uncoil. In the space remaining between the rope and the boots on the ends, he inserted his flashlight, a pair of warm, fleece-lined gloves, a waterproof container of matches, and a couple of packets of dried food rations.

Next came the ticklish part, arming the bomb. First he sat the case firmly on a table with the top open. Then, after being certain both switches were in the OFF position, Cooper raised the cover of the bomb. This would be the first time the batteries had been installed since he had connected the wires to the blasting caps and he held his breath as he slipped first one, then the other gently in place. When it didn't explode he let out the air he had been holding in his lungs in a long, thin sigh, and then closed the top with a snap.

Finally he used four pair of gray woolen socks to fill in any extra space and cover all the items in the case except the bomb. Only then did he lower the top of the attaché case gingerly on this dangerous baggage. A half-inch piece of foam rubber glued to the inside of the top of the case held everything firmly in place

Those items that remained were packed quickly into the bowling-ball bag. In addition to the helmet it held a hunter's hat, fur-lined with flaps that came down over the ears and tied under the chin; the green coveralls, rolled into a tight ball; a small canteen with canteen cup in a canvas cover; a pair of thin leather driving gloves; and his maps.

Now he dressed. First he donned the thermal underwear, then the shirt, pants and tie he had purchased on Monday. The shoes which came next were also new, but he wore a pair of old brown socks he had brought from Atlanta.

Before he finished dressing Cooper called to check the weather one more time. The only change was that the cold air mass was now expected to arrive in Portland around midnight. He didn't like to hear this. Although he should certainly be on the ground before then, he might not be out of the woods. And the fact that they had revised their forecast indicated the movement toward Portland had accelerated. It might continue to accelerate and the bad weather might arrive even before midnight. These thoughts flew rapidly through his mind as the weather man droned on. When he finished Cooper got the winds aloft forecast for the next twelve hours at Portland and Seattle for ten thousand feet and thanked him.

Slipping on the jacket to the suit, he sat down and wrote out the note he would hand to the stewardess once they were airborne, and then put it away carefully in his right outside coat pocket. Using the winds he had just obtained from the weather man, he made the final calculations on his schedule and put it, his hand computer, and his in-flight checklist in the right inside coat pocket.

Now, referring to another checklist, he finished dressing. His Ben Butler wallet containing fifty dollars, two blank checks (one on the account in San Francisco and one on the account in Birmingham), the temporary California Driver's Permit, the two gasoline credit cards, and one of his business cards from Birmingham with Overturf's name and phone number written on the back, went in his left rear trouser pocket. In his right front trouser pocket he carried $277 in a money clip. In the left a small plastic change purse holding the key to his San Francisco apartment, two dimes, two quarters, four hits of speed, and thirty Seconal. He didn't think he would need the speed—he was on such a natural high right now he didn't think he would ever come down—but he might want it if he got tired from a long walk and needed a little extra energy to make a last effort. He certainly hoped he wouldn't need the Seconal.

He put the letter to Helen and a short checklist he would use at the terminal into the other inside coat pocket. Four folded sheets of plain typing paper went in his left outside coat pocket; two plain ballpoint pens and a pocket comb into his shirt pocket. A clean handkerchief in his right rear trouser pocket and he was ready.

Over two hours remained until flight time. With his meticulous preparations almost complete, he sat down and for the last time went through a mental rehearsal of what he thought was going to happen. During sales training the dynamic Herman Clark had taught that the best way to be successful in persuading others to do what you want was to anticipate their reactions. Dan had gone over and over the way things might go, and thought he had anticipated every possibility. And he had a plan to handle each of these possibilities. It was all written out, almost like a script, and now he read through it one final time. He had been over it so often he had it committed to memory, but read it once more, reinforcing his confidence. From here on everything was on automatic.

Almost ready to leave now, he took a towel and wiped everything he might have touched.

He was leaving the gold backpack, his suitcases, a few clothes and some miscellaneous articles, but there was nothing here that could lead the authorities back to Dan Cooper of Atlanta, Georgia. The balance of his money, approximately four hundred dollars, was tucked inside the cover of his Ben Butler checkbook in the inside pocket of his sport coat hanging in the closet. He messed up the freshly-made bed so it would appear he had slept in it and threw the towel on the floor in the bathroom.

Outside a thin fog writhed round the buildings and drifted across the parking lot. The humid air was ripe with a confusion of smells, the pungent aroma of fried foods overlaid with the faint odor of garbage. Leaving the room door unlocked, Cooper moved hastily to the dumpster behind the restaurant and deposited a trash bag containing his notes and all the other miscellaneous items he wanted to discard. On the way back he stopped to hide his room key under a dripping bush. In the room, he held the phone with his handkerchief and called a cab. Then, slipping his sunglasses into the breast pocket of his coat, he gathered up the attaché case and helmet bag and returned to the parking lot to wait.

01:30 PM

The cab took longer than he had anticipated, but he still made it to the terminal with more than an hour left before departure. He paid the cabbie with two singles and told him to keep the change. Dropping the letter to Helen in a mail drop, he put his luggage in a storage locker before going to the Northwest counter to purchase his ticket.

He had made his reservation by phone on Monday night and they had the ticket ready. He knew the fare was twenty-five dollars even and had the money on the outside of his roll, a twenty and a five. The balance of his money was in tens except for one five and five ones. Placing his ticket in the inside coat pocket where the letter had been, he crossed to the terminal restaurant for a quick lunch. He didn't have time for a leisurely meal so he ordered one of their blue plate specials, a Salisbury steak with green beans and corn. He wasn't hungry but didn't know when he would be able to eat again and thought he had better make the meal a hearty one. He finished with a wedge of apple pie and coffee.

Before leaving the table he scanned his terminal checklist for the last time. After paying for his meal he crumpled and trashed this cryptic list on the way to get his luggage. He was anxious to get to the gate early so he could be among the first passengers to board. He didn't know how full the flight might be, and he had a definite seating preference, the rearmost seat on the left side of the aircraft on the aisle. It was also necessary to keep the window and center seats of this group unoccupied. If the flight was full or nearly so, he would postpone his attempt, but during the past six weeks he had called and checked the availability of seats on this flight at every opportunity, and had never found it sold out between Portland and Seattle. Still, tomorrow was Thanksgiving and he couldn't be sure.

02:10 PM

Cooper was the first to check in with the gate agent. There didn't appear to be many boarding here, but he didn't know how many might be continuing. The flight, which originated in D. C., had made stops at Minneapolis, Great Falls, Missoula, and Spokane. As soon as his ticket was pulled he walked over and stood next to the loading gate in order to be first in line when the flight was called.

When it came time to board there were about fifteen people waiting. On board he counted only twelve more who were continuing. He felt pleased. The flight would be less than one-third full. Moving quickly back to the seat he coveted, he placed the case with the bomb on the center seat in that row, then slipped the helmet bag out of sight under the center seat in the row ahead. Now, safely on board, he took out his sunglasses and put them on.

Once the door was closed and the girls started their preflight briefing, he carefully moved the bomb case to the floor in front of him and put his feet on it so it couldn't slide away. No one had taken the seats across the aisle. In fact he had the rear third of the cabin to himself.

While they were taxiing he took the blank paper from his left coat pocket and one of the ballpoint pens from his shirt, and after wiping them with his handkerchief, put both in the pocket on the back of the seat in front of him. He also removed the arm rests between the three seats so he could slide easily from one to the other.

02:55 PM

The 727 had left the gate a couple of minutes late but there was no delay at the end of the runway. The two stewardesses in the rear cabin took their places on the jump seats as the plane taxied into the position for takeoff.

Cooper knew from his previous trips on this flight that as soon as they were airborne one of the stews would go up front to help serve refreshments to the first class passengers. The other would remain back here. This was the one he would approach. He had been studying them both since he boarded.

They were a contrast. The shorter one (he found out later her name was Florence) was a vivacious, outgoing young woman with a keen, infectious smile. Her thick brown hair was cut short to frame a round pleasant face with regular features which included large penetrating blue-gray eyes. Abundant breasts and hips seemed about to burst the seams of her uniform as she bustled about getting the passengers settled. The other girl had a thinner, more aquiline face and that, combined with the mass of dark hair piled on top of her head, made her appear much the taller. Her figure was slim and willowy and she moved with slower, more graceful movements as she fluffed a pillow or passed out magazines. He heard the shorter girl call her Alice.

One of the most critical points of the whole drama would come when he handed his note to the stewardess who remained in the rear of the cabin. If she did something rash it might endanger the whole project. Of course the girls were briefed on how to handle hijackers, but you could never tell how a woman might react. In his planning he had given himself the option to pass, to postpone his try to another day, if the stewardess he had to approach appeared to be highly nervous or unstable. Fortunately that was not the case with either of these women. All systems were still Go.

03:05 PM

His heart was in his throat as the airliner thundered down the runway and rose deliberately into the leaden winter sky. As the girl named Alice sprang up and passed going to the front cabin, Dan realized he was approaching the point of no return. If he chose he could sit quietly and they would be in Seattle in twenty-five minutes. But he had psyched himself up to do it, had almost hypnotized himself into the role he was about to play. His hands sweaty and his heartbeat roaring in his ears, he unbuckled his seat belt, picked up the bomb case, sat it in his lap, and opened it. Finding the switches with his left hand, he used the right to take the pre-written note from his right hand coat pocket. His throat was as dry as sandpaper and he had to swallow twice before he was able to speak.

"Stewardess," he croaked at the shorter girl as she started up the aisle.

"Yes sir," she answered obediently, turning to him. "What is it?"

"Here, this is for you," he said tersely, his throat still dry, his voice rasping.

She took the note and without looking at it, stuffed it in her pocket and started to turn away.

"No, read it now," he almost yelled, upset that things were already going awry.

She stopped, took the note back out, unfolded and read it, a look of puzzlement on her attractive face. Suddenly it was replaced by one of incredulous fear as the meaning became clear. As she blanched and looked up at him with wide, staring eyes, he spoke quickly in a quiet, reassuring voice that surprised even him. "Don't panic," he said.

As soon as he saw she wasn't going to lose her composure, he slid deftly over into the window seat and told her to sit down. She continued to stare at him unbelievingly, but did as he asked. Pointing to the pocket in the seatback in front of her, he said quietly, "There are paper and a pen in the seat pocket. Please take it out. I want you to write a note to the Captain. Place the note I gave you in the pocket."

Again, as if by rote, she did what he told her. Her compliance with his instructions in a calm and efficient manner gave him reassurance, and he went ahead smoothly with his plan. He slowly dictated the message to the Captain giving her time to write it down. When he mentioned the bomb she glanced over at it. Holding it with his right hand, he deliberately raised the top of the case and let her get a good look. He hoped she understood it was the real thing.

When she had finished writing he gave her a grim look, his eyes like hazy steel, and spoke in a voice that was precise and firm. "Now take that note to the Captain. Tell him not to disturb the passengers—make some excuse for the delay at Seattle. When you know something definite you can come back and tell me. In the meantime I'll be waiting here with my hand on the trigger. Now get going!"

The girl got up and headed for the cockpit. He felt a fierce sense of elation. He had done it—passed the point of turning back—and he thought he had done well. He was sure he had impressed her with the fact that he wouldn't hesitate to detonate the bomb if they tried to play tricks on him. He purposefully didn't want any of the pilots to come back to where he waited. Therefore he had been compelled to convey the seriousness of his intentions through the stewardess. To a large extent, the success of the whole scheme depended on how well he had done that. He felt he had done a good job and this fed his optimism.

As soon as Florence started toward the front of the plane Cooper moved back into the aisle seat, retrieved his original note from the seat pocket, and returned it to his right coat pocket. Then he settled down to await developments. He wasn't sure how long it would be before she returned. In his planning he had estimated anywhere from seven to twenty minutes. She would tell the Captain, they would talk it over, and then he would put through the requested calls. It would depend on how fast things moved on the ground.

03:21 PM

Less than ten minutes had passed when he saw her coming back, making her way steadily down the aisle. He gave her a hard stare hoping to read something from her manner. A man on the right side up forward stopped her for a moment, but she said something to him and kept coming.

"The Captain is doing as you asked," she stated tonelessly with only a trace of nervousness dancing in her eyes. "He will call me on the interphone as soon as he knows anything."

"All right," he replied briskly. Please use the cabin speaker to inform the passengers that the rest rooms back here are out of order. If they need to go they must use the one up front in first class."

She did as he requested, then got water and aspirin for the man who had stopped her. "Don't say anything to the passengers," Cooper warned her as she started up the aisle. "I'll be here watching you with my hand on the trigger." He made this last remark in a stern, menacing tone. She must think, and convey to the others, that he was just short of being crazy. But he must display enough calm she would feel reassured and not do anything unexpected. It was a fine distinction and he had spent a lot of time during his planning and rehearsal sessions studying just what he should say and do to convey this impression. So far he thought his act was convincing.

But now he frowned, a little uneasy because she had returned without any definite word about the money and parachutes. He had told her to come back when she knew something definite. Apparently she had misread his meaning. Maybe he had not been specific enough about what he wanted. When she looked his way Cooper signaled her. "Can I help you?" she inquired in her best airline voice as she approached him.

"Yes, I think you misunderstood my instructions earlier. Please get on the interphone with the Captain and find out what is going on. I want some kind of estimate on time."

She did as he asked and for a couple of minutes they carried on a three-way conversation with the cockpit. They had no estimate of time yet but his requests had been relayed to Seattle. They were cleared to Seattle to hold. The Captain promised to call back when he knew anything further.

Dan dismissed the stewardess and she drifted back to the front of the cabin. A worm of unease continued to gnaw at his confidence but he dismissed it as unjustified. It was too early to expect any firm word from the ground. None of the pilots had made an appearance and so far the passengers suspected nothing. There wasn't anything to worry about—yet.

Minutes later he noted the airplane banking. Immediately he timed the turn and surmised they had entered a holding pattern. Just then the Captain came on the cabin speaker and said they had minor mechanical difficulties and would be holding for a while to burn off excess fuel. Cooper smiled for the first time since he had handed the stewardess his note.

04:08 PM

They had been airborne just over an hour when he heard a buzz from the interphone on the wall behind him. The stew answered and warily he listened to her end of the conversation, watching her intently. Holding the phone in her left hand she stepped forward, leaned over toward him and spoke quietly. "The Captain said to tell you they are getting the money and the parachutes and bringing them to the airport. They will call him back as soon as they arrive but he estimates it will take another hour. In the meantime he would like to send the First Officer back here to talk with you."

"No!" Cooper said emphatically, his voice suddenly thick with fury. "I don't want anyone back here but you. You can relay any message the Captain has for me." He was very stern now, his face a studied mask as he continued. "Tell him that if he tries any tricks or does anything other than what I tell him to do, then it is curtains for all of us. Now tell him that!"

Startled, she flinched back at the violent reaction her suggestion had provoked, and then meekly repeated the message to the Captain while staring at the hijacker the way she might stare at a snake she had just realized was poisonous. Dan hoped he hadn't overdone it with that speech. He meant for the Captain to hear it through the interphone. It might get the message across to the cockpit that the hijacker back here meant business. He definitely wouldn't allow anyone back here but the one stewardess. He could watch her and handle her, but anyone else was an unknown. He didn't want any unknowns cropping up now.

She hung up and turned to face him, her face grim. "He won't send anyone back," she said, fright now showing itself in her twisted face. "He'll call again when the money and the parachutes arrive at the airport."

"Very well," he replied briskly.

They continued to circle for more than an hour. The Captain came on the speaker again about delays. The passengers were restless and giving the stews a hard time. The tall brunette had returned from first class cabin and was busy commiserating with the unhappy travelers. She didn't come back to where Dan sat, but he caught her occasionally glancing at him. He was sure she had been briefed on the situation by now. Little by little his body began to ache from the tension. He had to keep one hand on the switches and he used the other to keep a good grip on the case. He must stay on the alert.

05:18 PM

When the interphone finally buzzed again it came as a big relief. The shorter girl answered it and relayed the Captain's message. "They have your money and parachutes ready on the ground," she said, her voice tense. "The Captain is awaiting your instructions."

"Very well," Cooper replied crisply. "Tell him to take us down. When we land I want him to taxi back to the takeoff end of Runway 45 Left and park on the far side, away from the terminal. Have them meet us there and first fuel the plane to maximum capacity. When that is done the other two stewardesses can use the front entrance to bring the money and the chutes on board. If everything is in order, the passengers and then two stewardesses can deplane. As soon as they are off we will depart for Mexico City. Warn him not to pull any tricks or let anyone on the ground pull any. You are to standby here to relay any further instructions.

As she repeated his words slowly to the Captain he felt his pulse quickening. Now would come the big risk. Up to this point he had been ninety percent certain of what would happen—he knew airline policy and procedure well enough to predict that. But now came the encounter with the authorities on the ground. He thought they would cooperate and do what he said. He was basing his plan and thus his life on that—but he couldn't be sure. The FBI was a big unknown. Would they try to spring some trap on him? He hoped not, but he reminded himself that if they did he was going through with setting off the bomb. He had nothing left to lose now.

The descent and landing was uneventful. He kept his stewardess (as he now thought of Florence Schaffner) back by the phone. The Captain came on the speaker as soon as they were on the ground and told the passengers they would be deplaning in a remote area. Glancing out the window, Dan saw buses, fuel trucks and other vehicles waiting as they taxied by.

"Remind the Captain he is to refuel first," he told the girl, wanting to be sure everything was done exactly as he had specified. "When that has been completed he is to have the fuel trucks leave."

As they parked on an unused section of runway on the west side of runway 34 Left he pulled the shade on the window in his row and had the stewardess pull those on all the other windows in the rear of the aircraft. Many of the passengers got up out of their seats, anxious to deplane. Talking in a jabber of excited voices, they crowded forward expecting to get off immediately. They could see people outside and couldn't understand what was causing the delay. The Captain came back on the speaker and told them to keep their seats, that it would only be a few minutes more.

The tension was almost unbearable. Outwardly Cooper remained calm and determined but inside he felt tightness in his chest, a flutter in his stomach. He wished now he had brought along a gun as a backup. He was having second thoughts about detonating the bomb. Determined as he was, he didn't really want to kill anybody, himself included. He found himself silently praying they wouldn't try any tricks.

The unhappy passengers settled back into their seats and Dan decided that now was the time to change his position. "I am moving to the rest room," he told Florence who was standing in the aisle, just forward of his seat. "Please stay by the door so you can relay any messages between me and the Captain."

Before she had time to comprehend what was going on, he scuttled into the rearmost washroom on the left side and slammed the door. In making the move he momentarily closed the top of the bomb case. But as soon as he was inside he sat it down on top of the lavatory and re-opened it.

"Can you hear me all right?" he asked through the door.

"Yes I can," came the hesitant reply.

"Now get this straight," he acerbated, cracking the door so she could hear him better. "I do not want anyone else to come back here. If I even suspect you are trying to trick me I will detonate this bomb and that will be the end of it. Be sure you understand that and that the Captain and those on the ground get the message. And don't tell the Captain I have changed seats.

06:15 PM

Cooper had a dual reason for changing his position. Although he did not expect the FBI to try to come on board while the passengers were there or while they were deplaning, it was a possibility. Now, if they did rush the cabin they would not find him where he had been sitting previously. And, he now had the additional protection of the galley and a couple of bulkheads between himself and the front of the plane. There was a slim possibility that one or two of the passengers were sky marshals. He didn't want to give them a clear shot.

The Captain came on the speaker once more to promise the passengers that their long wait was almost over. "We will unload from the forward door as soon as a portable ramp arrives," he said.

"I have some further instructions for the Captain now," Dan told Florence as she stood by at the intercom. "As soon as the fuel trucks depart the second officer can come out of the cockpit and open the front door. The passengers must remain in their seats. Then the ramp can be moved in place and the airline people outside can bring the chutes and the money to the top of the stairs, just outside the door. The other two stews can bring them back here. The second officer is to stay by the door and be sure the passengers do not leave nor anyone from the outside comes on board. I don't want anyone from outside coming into the cabin. No one! Is that clear?"

He paused and she nodded assent.

"When I have checked the money and the chutes I will tell you and the passengers can begin deplaning. While they are getting off the Captain is to start the engines and prepare for immediate takeoff. Tell him to depart to the north and climb to 10,000 feet. Have you got all that?'

She said yes, and then repeated it all to the Captain who relayed instructions to the ground. Cooper, who stood just inside the rest room with the door partially open, listened carefully to what she said and twice corrected her. She seemed to be in control of herself but he could tell she was extremely nervous.

06:50 PM

It was a relief when the girl said the refueling was finished and everything on the ground was in readiness. The second officer came out of the cockpit and stood by the front door, awaiting the word to open it.

"Ladies and gentlemen I must ask for just a few minutes more of your indulgence," said the Captain in grim tones over the speaker. "We must bring a few items on board and then you will be able to offload. Mr. Anderson, the Flight Officer will supervise this. Please give him your cooperation."

Dan was sick with dread but he managed to keep a cool outward appearance. This was the most critical moment of the entire operation. If the FBI was going to try to shoot him it would have to be in the next few minutes. Determined now, he realized he could not let himself be hedged in by inhibitions. If they stormed the cabin he would detonate the bomb. He strengthened his resolve by telling himself he'd enjoy taking a couple of those gung-ho, self-righteous FBI bastards with him.

He gave Florence the word to proceed and the process began. By popping in and out of the rest room Dan could see that his instructions were being carried out. First the tall stewardess named Alice brought the money bag. He had her set it down in the aisle near the rest room but did not examine it immediately. The blond stewardess from First Class followed with one of the chutes and he told her to place it in a seat across from him.

While they were returning up the aisle he asked Florence to open the laundry sack, and then glanced hastily at the stacks of money inside. It was about the right size for ten thousand bills and the ones on top were used twenties bound in $1,000 packets. Satisfied, he ordered her to put the bag in the window seat in the last row.

He waited until Florence was back in position between him and the front of the cabin before stepping out of the rest room long enough to take a quick look at the first chute. It was a sport-type back pack which appeared to be packed properly and showed no signs of having been tampered with. Just as he retreated to the rest room he saw the stews coming with two more chutes.

When Dan stepped out to examine the chute it was the first time he had been out of reach of the switches on top of the bomb. Back in the rest room he picked it up and eased his head out to tell the girls to put the other chutes in the seats in the row just ahead of his position. That was when he saw the man in the black raincoat. A short, balding man in his forties, the intruder was following the women and carrying the last chute. He was less than ten feet away when Cooper saw him.

It was as if Dan was a raging rodeo bull and the man had just waved a red flag in his face. All his self-control evaporated and his temper exploded. Without thinking about the fact he was exposing himself, he stepped out in the aisle, the bomb still cradled in his left arm, and shouted hysterically. "Get back!" he shrilled at the little man. "Put down that chute and go back immediately or I will set off this bomb. Do you want to die man?"

Tina Mucklow, the blonde stewardess, saw the problem and took immediate and decisive action. "You there," she said to the man in the raincoat. "Put that down and get out of here. This minute!"

"Listen," the man replied, stopping a few paces up the aisle. "I'm just from the FAA. I'm not FBI. And I just want to talk to your man. Ask him if I can come on back for just a second."

"No!" screamed Cooper, almost beside himself with rage that they would disobey his instructions. "Get the hell off this plane this minute or I will blow it to hell and back! Stand there one more second and see if I won't!"

"You had better get out of here right now," the blond stew said as she took the last parachute from the man and began physically pushing him back up the aisle. As he turned and beat a retreat Dan stepped back into the rest room.

"He's leaving," Florence assured him. "Can we begin deplaning the passengers now?"

"Yes, go ahead," he replied in a still tense voice. "But you'd better make it fast. I don't think I can take much more of this tension."

07:34 PM

Alice was up front helping get the passengers out and Cooper was keeping Florence back near the rest room and the interphone as a hostage against any surprise attack. Tina Mucklow came back to tell him they were almost finished and assure him everything was all right.

Just as the last passengers were leaving the coach section Dan spoke up. "You there—the blond stew. Why don't you come go to Mexico with us and let this little girl get off? She's had a pretty hard day."

"You don't mind if I go and she stays?" Florence asked in awe, a look of relief lighting up her pretty face.

"No, that's what I said," he replied evenly, much of the tension now gone from his voice.

"Go ahead then Florence," Tina said. "I'll stay."

"Get on up there then," Cooper ordered. "Tell the Second Officer to close the door just as soon as you and the other girl are out. You Blondie—stay there in the aisle and tell me when it's done."

He could hear the engines running now. As soon as she signaled that the door was closed he stepped out in the aisle, the case still under his left arm, and grabbed the interphone. "Let's get this show on the road Captain," he said, elation and a measure of relief now evident in his voice.

In a matter of seconds they were moving. Dan and the girl both settled into seats as the plane accelerated down the runway. He checked his watch. The time was 7:39. Taking out a pen, he wrote it on his cuff.

The moment they were safely airborne he instructed Mucklow to go forward and lock herself in the cockpit with the crew. He watched closely as she retreated up the aisle, a grim look on her pretty face. When she entered the crew's quarters, he put the bomb down on a nearby seat and picked up the interphone again.

He felt he had it made now and his confidence, which had wavered dangerously during the long minutes on the ground, came flooding back. The worst was over. If they were going to try to trick him they would have done it while the plane was on the ground. Even if the FBI had somehow slipped a gun to the Second Officer he wasn't likely to use it. He could see if anyone came out of the cockpit and he still had his bomb where he could get to it in a couple of seconds. Of course he wasn't where he wanted to go yet, but he had passed the point of greatest risk, the initial approach and the time on the ground. When he spoke to the Captain he had a note of triumph in his voice.

"Good evening Captain, this is the hijacker speaking. I want you to continue your north departure, level off at 10,000 feet, and set up cruise at exactly 200 knots indicated. Please file a flight plan to Mexico City via Victor 23 East to Portland, Victor 23 to Bakersfield and so on. You and your crew are to remain in the cockpit at all times. Please turn out the overhead cabin lights, unlock the rear stairs, and dump the cabin pressure now. If you want to ask me a question, just come on the speaker. Is that clear?"

"Yes, it's clear," replied the Captain evenly in a rich, bass voice. "But at 10,000 feet we can't make it to Mexico City without a refueling stop."

"Well how about stopping in Yuma?"

"At 200 knots we can't even make it that far. Standby just a minute while I check my charts." Dan of course knew the airplane could not fly more than four hours at 10,000 feet and at 200 knots that meant a maximum of about 800 nautical miles. His objective was to keep the crew guessing as to his intentions in hopes they would not have time to trick him, to do anything other than what he instructed them to do.

After a short pause the Captain was back on the interphone. "We can fly down Victor 23 to the Yuba intersection just south of Red Bluff, then cut across the mountains and land at Reno for our first refueling stop.

From there we can probably make it to Yuma, then Mexico City. Is that all right?"

"That will be all right as long as we go via Victor 23 East to Portland and then on down Victor 23. Will you give me a time check now and call me when we are over the Settle Vortac southbound with a Portland estimate?"

"Roger, we show the time to be exactly forty-three minutes past seven. I'm dumping the cabin pressure now."

Dan checked his watch and found it also showed the time as forty-three minutes past seven. The overhead lights went out and his ears popped as the pressure inside the cabin equalized with that on the outside. Now he had to get busy.

Still carrying the bomb case, he moved forward to the very front of the rear cabin where he turned on two reading lights on either side of the aisle. This created a small pool of light through which any crew member would be forced to pass before they could approach him.

Retreating to his original seat, he retrieved the helmet bag and began changing clothes. The light from the galley gave sufficient illumination for the moment.

Removing his tie and street shoes, he pulled the coveralls on over his suit, then sat down and put on two pair of woolen socks and his jump boots.

Now, glancing frequently in the direction of the cockpit, he turned on a reading light, took out a check list, and began filling his pockets. His maps, already divided into two packs and folded carefully to fit, went into the front breast pockets. The fleece-lined gloves went into the lower front pocket on the left and the flashlight slid into the lower front pocket on the right. The packets of dried food were placed in the two back pockets.

Next he lifted the bomb gently from the case and sat it in a seat. Then, taking out the May West, he slipped it on and tied it in front. It was a precaution in case he landed in Lake Merwin or some other large body of water. Unfolding the day pack, he placed his matches and the two extra pair of socks in the large patch pocket on the front and zipped it shut.

Now he had to repack the money, transferring it from the laundry sack to the main compartment of the day pack. He had practiced doing this with his pseudo money and the operation went swiftly—until he encountered an unexpected problem.

His practice money had all been packaged one hundred bills to the bundle, and when he had packed it into this modified back pack, four bundles to the layer, the twenty-five layers had taken up about thirteen of the seventeen-inch deep pack. About four inches of space remained in the top. This space was where he planned to carry his hunter's hat, his rope and his canteen.

But a goodly number of these packs had only fifty bills in them and despite the fact they were rubber-banded into bundles of $3,000 each, they were more bulky than he had anticipated. Now, with the pack almost full, he still had several bundles of bills remaining.

He realized also that the problem was compounded because he had bought two hundred feet of rope rather than the one hundred he had originally decided upon. Now, with all the money, there was barely enough room left in the main compartment for the rope and space for nothing else.

Cooper made a quick decision. He unzipped the patch pocket on the front of the pack and stuffed in the hunter's hat. Breaking several bundles of bills apart, he slipped a couple of packets into each of the deep lower front and back pockets of his coveralls, then crammed the others into the patch pocket with the hat, matches and socks. Finally, shifting the money around, he took the already-coiled rope and made it fit in the space remaining in the main compartment. The last four bundles of money went in on top of the rope before he zipped it shut.

That left the canteen and he was considering what to do with it when the Captain came on the speaker. "We just passed the Seattle Vortac at five-three. Our estimated time over Portland is 23 minutes after the next hour," he said professionally.

Cooper picked up the interphone to reply. "That's fine Captain. Now do a good job of staying on course and maintaining the proper altitude and air speed. And don't deviate from my instructions. I still have this bomb back here. Is that understood?"

"Roger, understood," the Captain's voice boomed back over the speaker.

There was no way Dan could be sure the Captain was doing exactly what he was told. But he had to take some chances. He knew that the 727 would not fly at two hundred knots without the flaps down and looking out now, he noted that they were partially extended. He had also checked the time they had flown north before making a broad turn to come back over the Seattle Vortac which was located on the airport, and now saw that the time to return, seven minutes, was the same. Sitting down for a moment, he took his schedule card from his inside coat pocket and completed it. Having already calculated everything except the estimated time of arrival at the checkpoints, he had only to compute these starting from their time over the Seattle Vortac southbound, seven fifty-three. The complete schedule read as follows:

CHECKPOINT	HEADING	DISTANCE	TIME ENROUTE	ESTIMATED TIME OF ARRIVAL
Take Off	340			07:39 PM
Turn Around Point	340		7 Minutes	07:46
Seattle Vortac	195		7 Minutes	07:53
Lake Merwin Dam	195	79.0 NM	22.7 Minutes	08:15.7
Jump Point	195	1.2 NM	.3 Minutes	08:16
Portland Vortac	195	23.8 NM	7.1 Minutes	08:23.1

These times and estimates were only good if the Captain maintained the correct speed and if the winds were the same as forecast earlier. But the fact that the Captain's estimate for Portland was the same as his meant he was no more than a minute off. They were covering about 3 1/2 miles a minute and if he could land within 3 miles of his target he would be happy. He would jump at 8:16.

Slipping the schedule and his checklist into the right front pocket of his coveralls, Cooper again checked his watch. It was now 7:56. They were past the Seattle Vortac and the next checkpoint was the Lewis River. It was time to get ready to jump.

He flicked on another reading light and examined all the chutes. While the first of the back packs was a sports type, the other was not. It appeared to be a military chute equipped with a device which would cause it to open automatically at a preset altitude. He didn't dare use it. One of the chest packs was equally useless. It had no snaps to attach it to the harness and no D ring. But the fourth chute, the other chest pack, appeared serviceable. Picking up the sport back pack, Dan pulled it on and adjusted the harness.

Before going any further he donned the leather driving gloves and repacked the bomb and the few loose items remaining—the laundry bag, his street shoes, tie, sunglasses and computer—in the black attaché case, and strapped it and the helmet bag down with seatbelts. Then he began lowering the ramp. He didn't expect there to be much suction with the cabin pressure dumped, but he wasn't sure. At first he just cracked it open. It shrieked like a freight train highballing through a narrow tunnel, but there was no noticeable suction toward the hole. He decided to leave it there for a few minutes while he finished getting ready.

Moving swiftly, he used the laundry bag that had contained the money to wipe everything he might have touched. Next he disarmed the bomb by removing the two batteries, and then turned again to the problem of the canteen.

He could just forget it, do without it. But he had a strong desire to take it. If he were to get stranded in the woods below for a day or more he would need it, particularly the canteen cup in which he could heat water to make hot drinks or soup. The day pack was equipped with accessory patches, small leather patches with slits through which a strap could be passed to attach various items that would not fit inside. The canteen cover had a small strap for attaching it to a belt and this could be used to hook it to one of these patches. But it would be flopping around loose when he jumped and might injure him in some way.

It took only seconds for these thoughts to flash through his mind. Making another snap decision, he fastened the canteen to the accessory patch on the top right side of the pack, then, breaking open the useless chest parachute, he used his hunting knife to cut a long strip of fabric from the canopy. Finally he wrapped this twice around the canteen and the pack and tied it, binding the canteen tightly against the side of the pack.

Ready to go now, he attached the money pack to the parachute harness at the leg strap rings, and then snapped the remaining chest chute in place above it. It was now very awkward to move because he was weighted down with the chutes and, when he didn't hold it up, the money bag dropped down and banged his knees.

He started lowering the ramp further, a little at a time. The shriek became a dull roar as the stairway dropped out of sight leaving a yawning black hole through which he could feel the cold, wet night. When the

Captain came on the speaker and asked if there was anything they could do for him, he couldn't answer right away. He finished lowering the ramp, and then picked up the interphone to reply.

"Please give me our DME to the Portland Vortac," he requested in a confident voice.

"Forty-point-two," replied the Captain immediately. "Anything else?"

"No."

Forty miles. He took a quick glance at his schedule. Forty miles from Portland put them only fifteen miles north of the river. He checked his watch. It was 8:10, they were right on schedule. There was no time to lose now.

He pulled on his hard hat and fastened the chin strap. Then, dropping the bomb batteries and the empty laundry sack into the bowling-ball bag, he threw it back and out the opening where the stairs began. Finally he closed the black case, and grasping it firmly in his right hand, struggled back toward the opening, encumbered by the chutes and the money bag. He hadn't realized it would be so awkward to move about with the two chutes and the money, but he was afraid to walk around this close to the open stairway without everything attached to him. The plane was bouncing about in the turbulent air and he had to use his left hand to steady himself as he staggered down the aisle. He could be accidentally thrown or sucked out and he wanted to be sure he had everything important with him if that happened.

Back near the opening he had difficulty keeping his balance. Holding to a seat with his left hand, he flung the case out into the black sky. He checked his watch, then, turning on a reading light, went through his in-flight checklist for a final time. There was nothing he had overlooked or forgotten. Satisfied, he tore this checklist and his schedule into little pieces and let them flutter off into the void behind the aircraft. He had intended to do the same with his ticket and the note he had given the stewardess, but they were in his coat under the coveralls and harness, and he couldn't get to them. He'd just have to wait and destroy them after he reached the ground.

Grim and determined, Cooper checked his watch for the last time. Patiently he watched as it came up on eight-fifteen, one minute to go. Then, counting off the seconds, he started slowly down the ramp, tightly clutching the hand supports on both sides. The plane was bouncing and bucking like a Brahma bull in a rodeo ring, and it was cold as hell, even with all those clothes on. Looking out and down he couldn't see a thing but blackness. They were flying through broken clouds and the lights from the aircraft were diffused and distorted like streetlights in a heavy fog. He felt no fear now, only the slight apprehension that goes with doing any difficult and exacting task. Off to his left he saw a flash of lightning, something rare in the Northwest, and then it was time. Just as the thunder began to roll, he jumped.

08:16 PM

As soon as he stepped off into nothingness Cooper began counting again, this time to twenty. To free fall to six thousand feet would take approximately twenty seconds. Falling through rain mixed with snow he couldn't see a thing, but as he counted he arched properly so he was falling face down. The sensations were surreal; no sense of falling, of time or space; only cold, opaque wetness enveloping him like something from a space fantasy.

On the count of twenty he pulled the rip cord of the backpack with a quick tug and felt the familiar, reassuring jerk as the canopy blossomed in the black void above him. His heart was trip hammering. He felt as if he had just mainlined a double hit of speed.

Now he could feel the pull of gravity but there was still nothing to see. He had calculated it would take another two-minutes-eighteen-seconds to drift to the ground if he landed in the area he had selected. But because he could be off to the east, on the slopes of Green Mountain, he must be prepared to land at any time. Desperately hoping to break out of the clouds in time to see something he could recognize before he hit the ground, Cooper peered anxiously downward, but the snow and rain were too thick.

Counting seconds again, he was up to one hundred thirty-five when abruptly he was crashing down through an enormous tree. Wet boughs slapped; stiff, spiky needles stabbed. Curling into a tight ball, he banged heavily into first one limb, then another as he fell through the thick growth at the top of the tree. Realizing he had to stop his headlong descent, he reached out; grabbing, clutching, grasping—a desperate attempt to slow his plummet toward the hard earth below. He got a grip on a limb; it bent, broke with a sound like a rifle shot. Falling again; out of control he frantically grabbed another branch; swayed crazily in the cold wet darkness;

got a second hand on it; felt it about to give way; kicking, got his feet on a lower limb; hung there breathing hard, fighting vertigo, suspended among the rain-slick boughs as his parachute, its air spilled, slithered past like a long white serpent on its way to the ground.

His panic subsided when the chute stopped below him, still in the tree, exerting only a slight downward pull on the harness. Once he was sure it wasn't going to snatch him off of his precarious perch, he let go of the limb with his right hand, reached up and with almost numb fingers unsnapped the left cap well, then quickly unsnapped the right cap well. He pulled the pins that disconnected the chute from the harness and heard it slip toward the ground. Next he gingerly unhooked the chest chute and dropped it through the branches below. He heard it bouncing downward but the noise of the wind and rain prevented him from hearing it hit the ground far below.

Before doing any more he had to move in, toward the trunk of the tree, and find a more secure perch. The limb he was clutching was about four feet above the one on which he was standing, and neither seemed strong enough to support him. In spite of the rain and the cold night air, sweat began to pour down his face. He could see little but moved automatically in the direction of sturdier limbs. Smaller branches got in his way but slowly and with great care, he worked his way inward until he reached the trunk.

The wind, keening through the trees, was unnerving and his heart was racing, but he realized that the worst danger was now past. Although the limbs were wet and slippery, they were abundant and with the help of his rope he was sure he could work his way safely down. Still standing on one limb and holding to another, he reached over and pulled the money bag up until he could partially unzip it and remove the rope. He was working in the dark and the rain, his vision so restricted he had to do everything by feel. Once he had the rope out and the pack re-zipped, he uncoiled it and tied one end to the upper limb where it joined the trunk of the tree. Then, reaching into the right pants pocket of his coveralls, he extracted his flashlight. Shining it downward he could see a profusion of limbs and foliage but not the ground.

Fear gnawed at his stomach as he considered the problem of getting down from this height, but slowly and deliberately he began his descent using the rope to support his weight when a foot slipped or he had to make a long drop. The muscles of his legs cramped and trembled, but he continued working his way cautiously downward, a limb at a time, shifting his weight carefully from one to the next. The twenty-one pound bag of money was in the way, but he was reluctant to drop it for fear he might lose it. Despite all the obstructions it took only a few minutes to reach the lowest large limb. From there he could see the ground some thirty or forty feet below. Off to one side the white of his parachute reflected the weak light from his flash.

As quickly as possible he looped the long rope around the lowest limb and pulled it taut. Now, grasping it firmly with both hands, Cooper started lowering his body toward the ground, steadying himself with his feet against the trunk. The narrow nylon line cut painfully into his gloved hands, and the muscles of his thighs felt heavy, like weights, as he moved cautiously downward. He had gone approximately two-thirds of the way and was within ten feet of the ground when he sensed the rope starting to give. Either it had broken or the knot at the top had given way, but suddenly he felt it going slack in his hands. Pushing away from the trunk with his feet, he let go and jumped.

Off balance, he hit hard and went sprawling. He was on unleveled ground and as he fell he hugged his chest, tucked his chin and turned his left shoulder down in the direction he was going. The forward momentum took him into a shoulder roll, then back onto his feet, then down again. He rolled and tumbled several feet through the underbrush before he came to a stop, half in, half out of the water on the edge of a creek.

He wasn't hurt, but was severely shaken by his abrupt arrival back on terra firma. It was raining hard and he was soaking wet, dirty from his roll down the creek bank, and chilled to the bone. But he was on the ground in one piece with the money. He still must find out just where he was and get away, but now the knot of fear in his stomach began to dissolve and he couldn't help but feel some elation knowing so much of the danger was past.

Hastily he unbuckled his harness and got out of it. He was having difficulty seeing through the wet and scratched visor, so he removed his helmet and tossed it into the creek. For just an instant it bobbed on the surface before it disappeared on the fast moving current. Satisfied that it would be carried off quickly, he also removed his Mae West and threw it into the boiling waters of the rushing stream. Then, removing the hunter's hat from the front pocket of his pack, he pulled it on and fastened it under his chin.

He had planned to leave the parachutes where he landed, but now decided it would be wise to gather up the one he had deployed. He couldn't be sure how long it would take him to get out, and if the weather cleared, a plane flying over in the morning might spot it. He rolled up the fabric of the opened chute and weighted the bundle down with the harness and the unopened chest chute which he found near the base of the big spruce tree. He covered it all with broken limbs that had come down from the tree and some brush. Then, removing the bundles of money from his pockets, he stuffed them into the top of the main compartment of his pack, where the rope had originally been. The rope he retrieved and recoiled. He might need it again.

08:39 PM

Cooper did all this by rote, almost without thinking, giving his mind a short rest before he tackled the problem of where he was. His plan for locating himself once he was down was to walk in a square using his compass, and hope that in that circuit he would recognize the area and figure out which way he must travel to find his camp. If he didn't spot something recognizable in the first square, then he would enlarge it to cover more territory. But visibility was severely restricted by the storm making this plan impractical, at least until dawn. He could remain here until daylight, utilizing whatever shelter he could find, and then set out, but he was afraid the police would have the area blockaded before then and even if he made it out of the woods, they would catch him.

Obviously he must make at least a try at finding himself tonight. Gunning his mind into action he examined his situation. To begin with he was on the north side of a creek bank. He wasn't sure it was Cedar Creek, but it could be. It was deeper and wider here than the creek at his campsite so he reckoned that if it was his creek, he needed to go east, uphill, to find his camp. He picked up the money pack, adjusted the straps, slipped it on his back, and started following the creek in an easterly direction.

All his senses were sharpened now as he examined the forest around him. The trees here were thick and the rain was so fine it fell against his warm face as a drifting mist needled with cold. Moving slowly, studying the terrain and the trees, he hadn't gone more than fifteen yards before things began to look familiar. And when the creek made an abrupt turn to the north he knew exactly where he was—just south and a little west of his campsite. A few more feet brought him to the clearing. He realized now that the water was much higher than it had been at any time he had seen it, and this made the creek difficult to recognize. At the ford the water was three feet deep.

Now he was excited. It was less than fifty minutes since he had left the airliner and he was back at the campsite. He could be out of here and gone almost before the plane got to Reno.

09:05 PM

The rain had slackened and after depositing the money bag in the cab of the Bronco, Cooper decided to build a fire to get warm and dry out a little. Even the wood he had left in the tent was damp, but a can of charcoal starter helped and in a few minutes he had it burning brightly. Then he got the idea of burning the chutes. If he should be stopped on his way out and was detained, he didn't want anyone coming back to his campsite and finding chutes nearby. He walked back into the woods and located them with no difficulty. Carrying everything back in one trip, he threw it all on the fire. The chest chute was dry inside its pack and when he popped it open and tossed it on, it blazed up immediately. But the chute he had used was soaked and didn't want to burn. The heavy covers and harness only charred.

The fire warmed him, but he realized he needed to get out of his wet clothes and moving toward Portland. He drove the Bronco over near the fire and while the chutes were burning, he went about stowing his gear.

Taking the tent down, he hastily packed it in the back of the Bronco along with his sleeping bag, the deflated air mattress and several smaller items. With the money pack lying on its back across the front seats, he opened it and first transferred the remaining money from the patch pocket to the main compartment. Then he used a shirt and some underwear to cover the cash and fill up any empty corners. He arranged everything so that if anyone started unzipping the main compartment it would appear to be stuffed with dirty clothes. Finally he slipped the pack in amongst the other camping gear in the back.

Now he took off his wet coveralls. Removing the gloves and flashlight but leaving the maps and food packets in the pockets, he rolled them into a tight ball and thrust it under the right seat.

Warming himself again at the fire, he removed his note for the stewardess and his ticket from his pockets and burned them thoroughly. Then, using his shovel, he picked up what was left of the chute harness and carried it to the creek and threw it in just downstream of the ford. The water was rising and he hoped it would be carried far away before becoming lodged in the undergrowth. If he was lucky it might make it all the way to the river or better still be buried under sand and silt at the bottom of the creek.

While he was at the creek he took the pills, the speed and the Seconal, from his pocket and threw them into the swift flowing water. If he was stopped he sure didn't want to be detained for carrying drugs.

009:34 PM

He had used up another thirty minutes burning the chutes and now he became apprehensive about the time. He hadn't intended being this long. He put out the fire by shoveling dirt over it, and then crawled into the car to change clothes. Cranking the engine, he turned the heat on full and moved into the right seat before stripping off the wet clothing. He removed the money and wallet from the pants, rolled the suit, shirt, underwear, socks and jump boots into a soggy bundle, and then pushed it all under the left seat. After toweling off the best he could, he put on dry underwear, jeans, flannel shirt, engineer's boots and his green parka. He slipped the wallet and the money in his pockets, and he was ready to go.

It was nine-fifty by the time he finally got started. If they knew where he jumped they might be looking for him by now. But they wouldn't expect him to be alone and have a camping outfit up here. Still he couldn't be sure. At every step he was dogged by the unpredictable. He had been lucky so far, extremely so, but chance still hung, like a black cloud, ready to rain on his parade at any time. He couldn't relax until he was safely back at the motel in Portland.

It was snowing now. It had started to come down in big wet flakes. That was good. If it snowed for a few hours it would cover any traces of his presence in the woods, maybe for days. By that time he would be long gone. But he wasn't out yet.

The road across the Martin property was almost impassable. It had rained more that day than he had thought. The cold air mass the weather man had talked about had obviously arrived a few hours ahead of schedule bringing those heavy rains and now snow. He slipped and slid along the treacherous track under dark tree branches etched against the gray snow-sky like runes.

It took almost fifteen minutes to get to the Spurrel Road. Approaching it he put out the lights and crawled along. He didn't want to be seen coming out of this drive. When he reached the road there was no traffic and he wheeled out quickly, flicked on his lights, and picked up speed. It wasn't likely they would stop him now, but he wished he was rid of the wet clothes. He didn't know what to do except take them back to the motel and put them in the dumpster.

10:13 PM

Dan got one more scare. Just as he approached the intersection where the dam road merged with the main Woodland-Amboy road he saw a state patrol car. It was headed west on the main road and Cooper slowed to give it time to pass in front of him. But instead of continuing toward Woodland, the police car suddenly braked and made the sharp turn back to its right to head northeast on the dam road. As it turned its headlights splashed across the Bronco, and as they went by the driver glanced over and waved. Cooper was petrified for a moment now knowing whether the man was signaling him to stop or was just being friendly. When he looked in the rearview mirror and saw the patrol car disappearing northeastward, he pulled his heart down out of his throat and hurried on.

Since the patrol hadn't stopped him he didn't have to worry about road blocks. If they knew he had come down where he had, they would be doing that quickly. He reached the Interstate at Woodland without further incident. It was now twenty minutes after ten, over two hours since he jumped, and still no signs of unusual activity. But he didn't go looking for any.

Dan was back at the Roadway Inn before eleven. He felt happy, a sense of relief, and extremely tired. He had been tensed up, operating at peak mental capacity for almost eight hours, and now it was behind him. Several things remained to be done but the danger was past and only a fluke, a piece of the worst kind of luck, could spoil his success. He had made plans as to just what he would do when he got here, but all of a sudden his memory went blank and he just couldn't think. Leaving everything in the Bronco including the money, he found his key under the bush, went to his room and had a drink. It sure tasted good.

He turned on the TV just in time to catch the eleven o'clock news. The hijacking was the lead story. They showed pictures of the plane on the ground in Seattle, then said it had just landed in Reno and the hijacker was not on board. The newscast made it sound like the authorities thought he had jumped out after the plane had landed and that they were searching for him in Nevada. That sounded good but it might be erroneous information the FBI was putting out to throw him off his guard. Still Dan felt no qualms sitting here safe and warm while they searched for him outside in the cold, wet night.

Sitting there sipping his Wild Turkey and water, he gradually began to relax and start thinking again. The state patrol had seen the Bronco. They might not know he had jumped out near there now, but if they didn't they probably would know soon. And they just might connect the two. Perhaps he had better abandon the car—right away.

11:30 PM

When he went back out it was snowing heavily and there was no one about. Removing the money bag and coveralls, he took them back to his room and returned carrying the gold back pack and two large, heavy-duty garbage bags. He rechecked all the pockets before placing the wet clothes into one of the bags. The leftover supplies and the smaller items of camping gear went in the other. Cranking up, he drove cautiously down the road stopping at two different motels. At the first he dropped the two bags and the empty pack in a dumpster. At the second, a large Sheraton Inn, he parked the Bronco and wiped the inside again quickly to remove any possible fingerprints. He had been wearing gloves tonight except when changing clothes, but he wasn't taking any chances. He took the papers from the glove box, then, using a screwdriver he had brought along, removed the tag from the car. Now if it was found they would have no way to trace it back to Ben Butler, much less Dan Cooper. He smiled remembering a story a friend who worked for Beaudry Ford had told about a new Thunderbird which had been stolen from their lot. It was found some eighteen months later at the Air Host Inn with four flat tires. The car had been driven less than fifty miles indicating it probably had been sitting at the motel unnoticed for almost the entire time. Dan hoped it would take that long or longer for anyone to notice the abandoned Bronco, but even if they found it tonight he didn't think they could connect him with it. He left the tent, sleeping bag and air mattress in the back and locked it before walking the half-mile back to the Roadway Inn through the thick snowfall. Around him the silence was intense as the night ticked away toward one in the morning.

Back in his room he tore up the Bronco papers and flushed them down the toilet. The tag and key he put in another garbage bag. Now the next thing was to unpack the money. He emptied the pockets of the coveralls, checking to be sure he had removed all the packets of cash he had carried there. Removing the rubber bands and repacking the loot neatly in the bottom of one of his brown suit cases, he counted it and discovered he was $12,000 short. He took it all out, re-counted it and once more checked the coveralls and the patch pocket of the money pack to be sure he had it all. There still was only $188,000.

He wondered if they had shorted him. That was possible. But it was also possible he had lost the $12,000. He had stuffed bills in four or five different pockets and he didn't think any of them could have worked their way out while he was wearing the parachute harness. But maybe, when he hit the ground, somehow a couple of packets had worked loose. Or perhaps when he opened the pack in the tree to remove the rope some of the money had fallen out without his realizing it. It really didn't matter that much, he still had $188,000, yet it bothered him.

The dirty coveralls joined the now empty day pack and other items he no longer needed in the last trash bag before he tied it shut and took it out to the dumpster. Now that it was all over, everything done, Dan was flooded with a warm peace, an almost drunken exaltation. A wave of exhaustion washed over him leaving in its wake a gentle, pleasurable tiredness. After another drink he took a hit of speed, and then had a long, hot shower. He never did go to bed.

Thursday, November 25, 1971

06:00 AM

The bus for San Francisco departed the Greyhound Station on SW Taylor Street at seven-fifteen. At six Cooper began preparations to leave. He had already washed the black out of his hair and colored it gray, and now he used a few deft touches of makeup to skillfully alter his appearance once more. An eyebrow pencil thickened and extended his brows, lines under and around his eyes aged his face, and small wads of wet toilet paper stuffed in each jaw subtly changed its shape. A little rouge, carefully applied, gave him a ruddy complexion.

Satisfied with his new visage, he dressed in a blue denim shirt, jeans and his engineers boots (the jump boots had been discarded along with the wet clothes), then finished packing. The money took most of the space in one of the suitcases, but he used underwear, socks and a dirty shirt to cover and pad it. Everything else went in the other bag.

After calling a cab, he once more wiped the room for fingerprints, and then put on his green parka, gloves and Stetson hat. He didn't bother to tell anyone at the motel he was leaving, but dropped the key on the dresser before he set the lock and pulled the door shut.

Outside the early morning air was chill, the northwest wind cold and biting, but the precipitation had stopped. The cab arrived in a matter of minutes, its tires crunching on the snow. He humped the bags into the back seat and they were off.

Wearing the big hat and horn-rimmed glasses he always wore as Ben Butler he looked nothing like the sketch that was on the front page of the morning paper. He bought a copy and read the story while eating breakfast at the bus station.

He gulped a second cup of coffee before buying his ticket and checking his bags. In the loading area a mud splattered coach was departing for Seattle with an uneven roar and the stink of diesel smoke. Skirting it, he boarded the San Francisco bus and looked for a seat. It wasn't crowded and he took one near the back on the right side.

A long, dull, sixteen-hour ride lay ahead on this Thanksgiving Day, 1971, but after the relentless pressure, the heart-stopping suspense, the unexcelled excitement of the past twenty-four hours, Cooper was ready for it. On the basis of everything he knew now, he felt it safe enough to return to his Buchanan Street apartment, then go through with his plan to travel on to Las Vegas as Ben Butler. With just a little luck he'd be finished and on his way home to Atlanta and whatever awaited him there. He felt no guilt now, only a sense of joy, accomplishment and new-found freedom. It was a good feeling.

Across the aisle a buxom, teenage girl with golden hair and a fair, unblemished complexion whispered conspiratorially while making cow eyes at her companion, a very tall, very thin drugstore cowboy with scuffed boots and glistening black hair coiffed in artful waves. As Dan watched the homely boy suddenly laughed aloud, his blue eyes dancing mischievously, face lit up with a grin like a lantern. With practiced hands the youthful Casanova hugged the smiling girl affectionately and simultaneously popped a battered portable radio out of the shoulder bag at his feet. He flicked it on and as the nearly empty bus rolled swiftly out of Portland on that cold, blustery, Thanksgiving; the haunting, nasal tones of Janis Joplin filled the early morning air:

> "Freedom's just another word for nothin' left to lose,
> Nothin', I mean nothin' honey if it ain't free, ah ha,
> Yea feeling good was easy Lord when he sang the blues.
> You know feelin' good was good enough for me,
> Good enough for me and my Bobby McGee."

The End

AFTERWORD

THE D. B. Cooper skyjacking was memorable because of the mystery it left behind; it was only one of the many that took place during that period. Three days later, while the lawmen were still searching the woods around Woodland for any trace of Cooper, three murder suspects hijacked a TWA 727 at Albuquerque, New Mexico, and forced it to fly to Cuba. The forty-three passengers were released during a refueling stop in Tampa.

But the apparent success of Cooper's adventure spawned imitators. Less than two months later, on January 20, 1972, Richard Charles LaPoint, a twenty-three year old former Army paratrooper, hijacked a Hughes Air West DC-9 as it was preparing to take the runway at the Las Vegas Airport. LaPoint, who gave his name as John Shane, approached a stewardess and said he had a dynamite bomb in a small black satchel. His demands for $50,000 and two parachutes were promptly met and the sixty-seven passengers and two stewardesses were released before the plane took off about 12:30 PM, bound for Denver. Just after two, after having some difficulty finding a suitable door from which to jump, the hijacker left the aircraft at 12,000 feet and parachuted into a Colorado wheat field. FBI agents apprehended him there some two hours later with a sprained ankle and other minor injuries suffered in the landing. The money was recovered and his bomb was discovered to be a fake consisting of red highway flares.

The downward trend in the number of aircraft hijacking attempts which had begun in 1970 and continued in 1971 was halted in 1972 although the number of successful attempts continued to fall. But, no doubt as a result of the Cooper affair, there was a sharp increase in the number of attempts to exploit the hijacking for personal enrichment by holding the aircraft for ransom. In 1972 thirteen passengers or crew members and twenty-two hijackers were killed and twenty-nine others, including five hijackers, were injured.

On August 8, 1972, a ski-masked hijacker, who extorted $2,000,000 from United Airlines—the highest ransom ever taken from a U. S. airline—was shot and captured by FBI agents at Seattle-Tacoma International Airport, some six hours after he commandeered a plane at Reno, Nevada.

In Houston on October 30th four armed hijackers, including a father and two teenaged sons, shot their way on board an Eastern jet at Intercontinental Airport. After killing a ticket agent and wounding a ground crewman, the men, who were wanted in connection with an Alexandria, Virginia, bank holdup in which a policeman and bank manager were killed, forced the plane with forty persons aboard to fly them to Cuba.

The hijacking craze was finally brought under control in 1973 when the screening of all passengers was made mandatory at the nation's airports. This began on January 4, 1973, at the order of President Nixon, following two hijackings in which one person was killed and one wounded, and $2,000,000 in ransom was collected by the hijackers. Following the institution of the one hundred percent screen, the hijackings came to an abrupt halt. During the first six months of the screening, more than thirteen hundred potential airline passengers were arrested for a variety of crimes including illegal possession of weapons, and over eight hundred guns were confiscated at boarding gates.

Nothing further was heard of the man known as D. B. Cooper until February of 1980. Following are excerpts from several articles which appeared in the nation's newspapers that month. They contain the only new information to surface concerning the mysterious hijacker as of this writing.

Atlanta, Georgia
March, 1983
From THE ATLANTA CONSTITUTION, February 13, 1980
TOTS DIG UP PART OF 'COOPER' MONEY
From Press Releases

PORTLAND, ORE—Twelve weathered stacks of $20 bills—part of the $200,000 ransom taken by the legendary American hijacker "D. B. Cooper" when he parachuted from a commercial jet over the rugged Pacific Northwest in 1971—were unveiled Tuesday by the FBI.

Agents said no trace of Cooper has yet been found though they claimed discovery of the money reinforced their long-held theory that Cooper was killed in the daring plunge that has made the aerial bandit a folk hero in the Pacific Northwest.

Children digging in the sand on a family picnic on a Columbia River beach north of Portland uncovered up to $3,000 of the $200,000 Cooper commandeered.

"I thought it was play money," said Denise Ingram, 5, of Vancouver, Washington. She said she and her cousin, Brian Ingram, 8, "both found it. It was buried in the sand. I gave it to Brian, so he could hand it to my aunt Pat."

The child said she was with her mother, Crystal Ingram, on a Sunday outing for several Ingram relatives and their children at a popular fishing sand bar.

Harold Ingram later "took it to the FBI" Crystal said, "I didn't think it was gonna be no big deal."

William M. Baker, assistant special FBI agent in charge of Oregon, said that the money was found about five miles northwest of the Interstate 5 Bridge connecting Portland and Vancouver, 20 miles downstream from the point where Cooper is believed to have bailed out of the Northwest Airlines 727 in a freezing rainstorm on Thanksgiving Eve 1971.

Held together by a rubber band, the packet of $20 bills was so badly deteriorated the FBI could not make an exact count of the amount, a bureau spokesman said, but was able to identify it as Cooper's cash by checking serial numbers on the bills.

The FBI said it was searching the area for more loot and clues as to the fate of Cooper, the only known hijacker in U. S. history who has not been apprehended.

From THE NEW YORK TIMES, February 14, 1980

F. B. I. REPORTS NEW FINDING OF MONEY FROM HIJACKING

Portland, Ore., Feb 13 (UPI)—Agents of the Federal Bureau of Investigation found wadded $20 bills today in muck dragged from the Columbia River six years ago and said the money was part of the $200,000 ransom collected in 1971 by "D. B. Cooper" before he parachuted from a hijacked jetliner and disappeared.

The first money was found by children on a family outing Sunday on a sandy beach on the north shore of the river 5 miles northwest of Vancouver, Washington. It totaled about $3,000 and the serial numbers checked matched numbers on the ransom bills.

A bureau agent, Ralph Himmelsbach, said that more money was dug up by agents yesterday afternoon and this morning.

"We have the Army Corps of Engineers and geologists out there," Mr. Himmelsbach said. "An agent who was out there said it looks like they'll be able to help us out."

Mr. Himmelsbach said the geologists and corps scientists probably would be able to determine whether the shore material where the money was found came from the middle of the Columbia River, washed downstream from the Washougal River or was carried upstream from the mouth of the Lewis River and dumped at the site.

From THE SHREVEPORT TIMES, February 15, 1980
FBI TO SUSPEND BEACH SEARCH FOR COOPER LOOT

VANCOUVER, Wash (AP)—The search along a Columbia River beach for more money from the D. B. Cooper hijacking eight years ago probably will be suspended Friday morning FBI officials said Thursday night.

Meantime the FBI said a geologist concluded that several thousand dollars found Sunday by an 8 year old boy on a family picnic was deposited on the beach after 1974.

FBI agents continued digging Thursday without finding any more of the $200,000 that Cooper took with him when he bailed out of a plane on Thanksgiving Eve in 1971.

The search began Tuesday along the river's north shore about three miles southwest of downtown Vancouver. Another batch of money was found on Wednesday.

Not a trace was found Thursday as agents completed their search of the sandy riverbank said Jack Pringle, assistant agent in charge of the Seattle office which took over the search operation.

"In all probability we will not be back out there tomorrow," Pringle said Thursday night. "They really have no further places to search."

He said geologist Leonard Palmer of Portland State University concluded that the dredging operation in 1974 did not put the money onto the beach because the bills were found above clay deposits put on the banks by the dredge.

The FBI speculated the bills could have washed into the Columbia from a tributary and were studying flood records.

"However they got there they must have been deposited within a couple of years after the hijacking," said FBI agent Ralph Himmelsbach. "Rubber bands deteriorate rapidly and could not have held the bundles together very long."

Pringle disagreed with Himmelsbach's idea on when the money arrived at the beach.

"I think it got there in the last two years, maybe three, and its highly probable it came up on the bank in high water or with a piece of ice," Pringle said.

From THE NEW YORK TIMES, February 17, 1980
TO TOWN OVER WHICH HE LEAPED, HIJACKER LIVES
By Robert Lindsey
Special to the New York Times

ARIEL, Wash., Feb. 15—"D. B. Cooper can't be dead, insisted Dave Fisher, who runs the Ariel Store and Tavern in this hamlet on the western slope of the Cascade Mountains. "He is a hero to everybody up here," the storekeeper said of the legendary hijacker, speaking with an awe that he might have used in talking about Nathan Hale or Charles Lindbergh.

Agreeing, Richard Purdy, a tavern regular who is being pursued these days by a man from Chicago who wants to record a song Mr. Purday wrote—"The Ballad of D. B. Cooper,"—said, "He's the little man's hero—there's a little bit of outlaw in everybody."

Legends die slowly at the Ariel Store and Tavern, a modest place in this community of 300 or so people that earns its income from logging, summer tourists at nearby Lake Merwin and increasingly, the D. B. Cooper legend.

Regardless of what the Federal Bureau of Investigation says, most of the customers here insist that D. B. Cooper is still alive. Besides, Mr. Fisher acknowledged, keeping the legend alive is good for business.

This week an eight-year-old boy, Brian Ingram, found scraps of money along the Columbia River near Portland, Ore., 25 miles south of here, that, according to Federal agents, had serial numbers matching those of currency given 98 months ago to an airplane hijacker who has become a kind of mythic figure in the Northwest, like Paul Bunyan, or Big Foot, the half-man, half-animal giant some woodsmen say they have seen.

Treasure hunters, trackers, tall-tale tellers, imposters, even two men who searched the lake with a submarine looking for Cooper—the regulars at the tavern have seen them all. Near a pot-bellied stove, over beer and sausages, they retell the story of the hijacking again and again, and as far as they are concerned, they know it better than anybody else.

Thus, they say they have a right to view skeptically the claim made this week that discovery of the money indicated the hijacker had not survived his fall because, if he had, he would surely have taken the money with him.

Carl Steinwachs said he thought the hijacker probably simply had to bury the money to lighten his load while escaping. Another customer theorized that after the hijacker landed he hitched a ride in a car to Portland, became involved in an accident and in a panic, threw the money in the river.

Asked to explain why D. B. Cooper had so captured the imagination of people here, the regulars at the tavern offered various explanations. But perhaps Mr. Steinwachs, a 29-year-old welder, gave the most straightforward answer:

"Everybody is trying to make a buck, but everything is against the ordinary guy. Look at the politicians. They get themselves elected and pretty soon they're stealing money; I don't think there's an honest politician in the country. Look at this bribery thing back east.

"And look at big business; the oil companies take every dime out of my pocket to fill my tank and you can't tell me they're honest. D. B. Cooper was just an ordinary guy who did the same thing, but he did it in the open, blatant and daring, not like the big businessmen and politicians who are sneaky. It took a lot of thought, planning and nerve, and I think he got away with it. I think he's a hero, and I'd hate to find out that he was dead."

"I still keep looking for him every time I cross the dam," said John Berg, an employee of a power company that operates a hydroelectric system in the Merwin Dam.

In a way, D. B. Cooper has become as celebrated a missing person as Judge Crater, and indeed he has provided a profitable mystery for the people who benefit from tourism here.

Each year on the first Saturday after Thanksgiving, a "D. B. Cooper Day" is held at the tavern to commemorate the hijacking. Last year more than 250 people from at least seven states toasted the hijacker.

Author's Notes

I wrote this novel beginning in November of 1973 after being prompted by an article in *The Atlanta Constitution* on the second anniversary of the hijacking. I didn't finish it until 1983 and after trying unsuccessfully to market it in 1983 and 1984 I put it away for twenty-seven years. I now have decided to get it back out and self-publish it.

D. B. Cooper is still missing but there have been some developments in all these years. Just last year Crown Publishers published *Skyjack, The Hunt for D. B. Cooper* by Geoffrey Gray, a non-fiction retelling of the story and an examination of several suspects, all now dead, who might have been Cooper. Gray had access to FBI files that gave much more detail about what actually took place on the airplane that day. I thought of revising my story to more closely reflect this evidence but my story is as believable as any and so I did not change it.

Richard Kavanaugh
Shreveport, LA
January, 2012

CPSIA information can be obtained at www.ICGtesting.com
Printed in the USA
LVOW062317040712

288751LV00003B/5/P